Gunrunner. Empress. Star of Indrana.

I am what the years of this life have made me and now at the end of it, I am faced with a choice—stand and fight or find a way to trick a bigger, stronger enemy into turning tail and running.

The fate of the whole galaxy hangs on my decision.

Praise for

THE FARIAN WAR

"Action- and emotion-packed, folding political tension, personal relationships, and trauma into a vivid space opera that does not pull any punches."

—*Library Journal* (starred review) on
Down Among the Dead

"Twisty and clever and magnificent, full of political maneuvers, space action, and genuine feeling. The end broke my heart in the best sort of way. I cannot wait for the next book."

—Beth Cato on *There Before the Chaos*

"Wagers achieves a rare balance of action...tension, and quiet moments, keeping pages turning while deepening the portraits of Hail and the friends and foes around her. Fans of the original trilogy will welcome Hail's return, and any space opera reader can easily jump in here."

—*Publishers Weekly* on *There Before the Chaos*

"A perfect blend of political intrigue and realistically conveyed action....Kick-butt women, space battles, complex relationships, and fiendish plots abound."

—*Barnes & Noble Sci-Fi & Fantasy Blog* on
There Before the Chaos

OUT PAST THE STARS

By K. B. Wagers

THE INDRANAN WAR

Behind the Throne

After the Crown

Beyond the Empire

THE FARIAN WAR

There Before the Chaos

Down Among the Dead

Out Past the Stars

NEOG

A Pale Light in the Black

OUT PAST THE STARS

THE FARIAN WAR: BOOK 3

K. B. WAGERS

orbit

orbitbooks.net

Cover design by Lauren Panepinto
Cover illustration by Stephan Martiniere
Cover copyright © 2021 by Hachette Book Group, Inc.
Author photograph by Donald S. Branum

Orbit
Hachette Book Group
1290 Avenue of the Americas
New York, NY 10104
orbitbooks.net

First Edition: February 2021
Simultaneously published in Great Britain by Orbit

Orbit is an imprint of Hachette Book Group.
The Orbit name and logo are trademarks of Little, Brown Book Group Limited.

The publisher is not responsible for websites (or their content) that are not owned by the publisher.

The Hachette Speakers Bureau provides a wide range of authors for speaking events. To find out more, go to www.hachettespeakersbureau.com or call (866) 376-6591.

Library of Congress Cataloging-in-Publication Data
Names: Wagers, K. B., author.
Title: Out past the stars / K.B. Wagers.
Description: First Edition. | New York, NY : Orbit, 2021. | Series: The Farian war ; book 3 |
Identifiers: LCCN 2020028507 | ISBN 9780316411271 (trade paperback) | ISBN 9780316411295 (ebook) | ISBN 9780316411288
Subjects: GSAFD: Science fiction.
Classification: LCC PS3623.A35245 O98 2021 | DDC 813/.6—dc23
LC record available at https://lccn.loc.gov/2020028507

ISBNs: 978-0-316-41127-1 (paperback), 978-0-316-41129-5 (ebook)

Printed in the United States of America

LSC-C

Printing 1, 2020

For Sabs

All warfare is based on deception.

Sun Tzu wrote this millennia before I was old enough to read, long before my father pressed a book into my seven-year-old hands in a desperate attempt to distract me from picking on my sister.

Sun Tzu was, by all accounts, a masterful tactician, a great general, and though I know how badly legends twist our stories into something that fits the desires of the listeners—his words on warfare sank into my soul even at that tender age.

I have built my life on them, in one form or another throughout the years. I am not one to shy away from a fight, but I will choose the route of deception time and again if it is available to me. Especially if it keeps my people safe from danger.

Gunrunner. Empress. Star of Indrana. I am what the years of this life have made me and now at the end of it, I am faced with a choice—stand and fight or find a way to trick a bigger, stronger enemy into turning tail and running.

The fate of the whole galaxy hangs on my decision.

1

Welcome, Star of Indrana, we have been waiting for you."

I stared up at the Farian god, lost in her golden eyes.

A moment before she'd appeared as the Dark Mother, as Kali, and folding my hands to bow at the awe-inspiring sight had been instinctive. Now she looked Farian, like Fasé, but taller, so much taller, and commanding in a way none of us could ever hope to match.

I had come to this place with Aiz Cevalla to speak with the Farian gods, or fight them if they would not listen, but I was thrown by their warm greeting, and the implication that they'd expected me was a heavy echo of Kasio's words to me earlier.

The seer of the Council of Eyes had said the gods wanted to speak with me, and standing here now seemed to prove her words true.

"You've been waiting for me?" I asked. "Why?"

"Our people are coming for us. We need your help to stop them."

"Oh Shiva," I murmured as all the scattered pieces finally fell into place in my head. The aliens who'd attacked the Svatir, the *hiervet sveta*, the monsters of light. The prophecy and the magnitude of what I'd done, what I'd called down on this galaxy by my decision not to fight the Farian gods.

The light would swallow us all. For a moment I tensed, considering the violent option I'd worked so hard to avoid, but then Sybil's words echoed in my head. *"I saw a light that is not light spreading. We all fight—we will all die. We surrender—we will die."*

Fighting was the option that would kill us all, I didn't dare let myself forget it. I dragged in a breath; the memories Dailun had shown me were suddenly clear in my head. "You're the deserters they were looking for; you're the Hiervet."

Emmory and Gita moved in concert to my side, their weapons out. How they had crossed the sands so quickly to reach Aiz and me, I had no idea. But I was grateful now for the solid presence of my BodyGuards.

The image of the gods in front of me shifted again. The trio was now smaller, though still a good hand-span above me. They were pale and slender, bipedal, but with limbs longer than a human's that ended not in hands but a split tentacle with a rough gray-blue surface.

The Farians, the Shen, even the Svatir looked and behaved enough like humans that it was comforting. The Hiervet decidedly did not look like us, so much so that it was going to take someone better with words than me to describe them properly.

I tried for a moment to return to the illusion of them as Farians and was surprised when I couldn't. Now the only way to tell them apart was by the mark below their left eyes. On the Hiervet in the center it was a solid horizontal rectangle bisected vertically by a row of five dots. The other two had the same rectangle, but the one on the left had four dots and the one on the right had only three in the same flat black.

"We are as you say, Star of Indrana." The slow baring of all-too-human-looking teeth by the creature in the center who moments ago had presented as a Farian woman was terrifying. "We should take this somewhere more pleasant, yes?"

A blink. A heartbeat. We were no longer in the arena but in a room that looked far more like something one would find on Indrana than in the hideout of an alien pretending to be a god. It was cozy, the windows reflecting a setting sun I suspected wasn't real.

There was a fireplace and a table at one end of the long room. A trio of high-backed wooden chairs at the other looked just throne-like enough to make my eyebrow rise incrementally and my shoulders lock up.

"Majesty."

Emmory's quiet voice was a balm soothing the slight edge in my gut. I had so achingly missed that tone it was a wonder I didn't break apart right there.

"I'm all right," I murmured over our private com link and then aloud. "I think some introductions are in order."

The Hiervet in the center smiled again. "I am Thyra." They gestured to the right. "This is Priam."

The Hiervet with four dots dipped their head briefly with a surprising amount of reverence.

"And Adaran. Welcome to Etrelia, Star of Indrana," Thyra said with a sweep of their limb.

I recognized the name, remembered it from the negotiations and Adora spitting the challenge at Aiz: *"You can have your father's soul when the whole of the Pedalion lies dead and Etrelia is burning."*

"Welcome also, Mia Cevalla and Fasé Terass. The other sides, the ones who help keep the balance." Those wide, black eyes turned to Aiz, and every muscle in their body tensed. "You slayed that which was ours, Aiz Cevalla." Thyra's voice held a wealth of anger, but Aiz was unmoved.

"I did it to save my people from your chains. The Star has convinced me not to fight, Thyra, but I won't apologize for the choices I've made." He dipped his head in acknowledgment. "I thought I killed you."

"You almost did. Your sister saved me."

"Why am I not surprised?" he replied.

"You should die for what you have done." Priam snarled the words, but all three looked as though they were about to pounce.

"Careful," I said, putting a hand across Aiz's chest. "He's my crew."

"Is that so?" Thyra tilted their overlarge head to the side, vertical eyelids sliding shut once and snapping open again.

I met what I thought was a challenge with a smile. "It is."

"You keep deadly company, Star of Indrana."

"Oh, you have no idea." I headed to my right, gesturing for Mia and Fasé to follow, and took the center seat of the row of ornate chairs.

It was going to take me a while to get a read on the Hiervet's facial expressions, but I guessed the narrowing of eyes was a universal signal for annoyance.

Or it was possibly a response to my challenge; I had just sat in their chairs, after all. I crossed one leg over the other and studied the trio in front of me with all the poise of the empress everyone expected me to be.

"Well, you wanted me here. Start talking."

The Hiervet started talking, but not to me. Instead a rapid-fire discussion in a language both lyrical and sharp as broken glass broke out among the trio.

"Sha zhu, *perhaps do not taunt the gods.*"

I glanced at Hao. He stood by Gita's side with a hand on his gun. *"They're not gods,"* I subvocalized over our private com link.

"You know I don't believe in them, but they look a great deal like the Old Gods."

I frowned. *"The Old Gods, really? That's what you see?"* I switched to the main channel. *"Everyone give me a read on what those three creatures look like to you."*

The answers from the others were predictable, split between the Indranan gods I'd seen initially and the Farian gods who'd appeared right after.

Johar, however, had a decidedly different take. *"You know those really big wasps on Pintro XVI? They kinda look like the love child of those and the folks who live underground on Yuzin. All blue-gray pale and spindly, but everything is put together wrong."*

It was the same thing I could see, and I managed somehow not to turn my head to stare at her in awe.

Indula wasn't so controlled, and Iza elbowed him in the side with a muttered curse until he snapped his head back to the Hiervet. Thankfully our hosts didn't seem to notice, though they did wrap up whatever argument they'd been having and turn their attention back to me, leaving me no time to ponder Johar's revelation.

"Star of Indrana—"

I held up a hand. "Let's get this out of the way first. I am Empress Hailimi Bristol, here to broker a peace between the Farians and the Shen on behalf of humanity. You three are a wrinkle in an already complicated situation, but I'm willing to see what I can do for you once the matter at hand is settled. In the meantime, you can address me as 'Your Majesty.'"

Thyra studied me for a long moment. I wished I could somehow return to seeing them with the façade of more humanlike faces, and wondered if it would even give me an accurate sense of what they were thinking to see them that way.

Focus, Hail. You'll want to learn to read their faces as is, and now's as good a time for it as any.

"Why the Farian names?" I asked. "What are your real names?"

"These *are* our real names," Thyra replied. "The names we chose when we arrived and the genders we picked when our images resolved to please the Farians. We had no names before and discarded the designations we were given a long time ago."

"The images that resolved to please *us*? You pretended to be Farians. You landed on my planet and enslaved my people." Fasé had finally recovered from her shock, and the venom in her voice startled me. I reached out and put my hand on her knee.

An identical expression flowed across the faces of all three. Embarrassment? They shifted as if they were in discomfort, tapping the splits of their top limbs together rapidly.

"You don't know how lucky you are. The universe out past your stars is a dangerous place. No one comes to this corner, this desolate little galaxy. No one bothers you. It seemed the perfect place to hide. We wanted nothing to do with our creators and their endless wars. When we lost to the Svatir, my squad and I saw our chance."

"Your chance to what?"

"To disappear. To live a life denied to us."

"You are deserters," I repeated, remembering the scene Dailun had shown us of the captured Hiervet and their desperate pleas that they were hunting criminals. "You ran from your people, set yourselves up as gods, and have been manipulating the Farians for years. All this after your people attempted to invade this galaxy and subjugate the Svatir. Tell me why I should help you with anything? When by all accounts if I kill you it will stop your people from declaring war on us."

Thyra took a step forward and froze when the sound of weapons powering up suddenly filled the air. I didn't tell Emmory to stand down, instead leaning back in the chair and waiting to see what the Hiervet's reaction would be.

"Your Majesty."

Mia gave an almost imperceptible gasp, and I imagined that if I could see the illusion of the Farian it would look as if Thyra were folding her hands together and bowing, but instead her overlong appendages were twisted together.

"None of what you believe is correct, Your Majesty. I need to show you the history of our people. There is too much to tell, too much that would be missed, but I can show you." She extended one limb.

"Bad idea." The warning came from Emmory, Hao, and Aiz at the same time.

They weren't wrong, but this whole thing had been a bad idea from the very beginning. Still, I knew the value of trusting their judgment. We were in an unknown location with unknown adversaries and I wanted to retain the upper hand.

"I think, perhaps, it's best if we return to the Pedalion first," I replied. "You want my protection from your people? It comes with a price. You have to tell the Farians the truth of what you are and what you have done. You will help me broker this peace. You will let the Shen come home. You will let those Farians who wish to live and die do so. I am done with this charade of you as gods, are we understood?"

The noise that came from Thyra could best be described as a sigh. "I know, it does not make it any easier, Your Majesty. But we will do as you require." She held out her limbs. "If you will all put your hands on each other, we will take you back."

I shared a look with Mia as we got up from the chairs. Her face was carefully blank as she reached for Fasé, and I wished I knew what she was thinking.

All three Hiervet crossed their limbs over their narrow torsos and I tightened my grip on Mia when reality blacked out around us, resolving in between one heartbeat and the next as the now familiar white marble of the Pedalion chamber.

"Well, that is a neat trick," I muttered. We were standing on the star in the center of the floor and I didn't protest as Emmory moved us off it with a few quick steps to the side. "You can actually move locations, not just make things look different."

"Short distances, Your Majesty," Thyra replied. "Though if you had fewer people we could have gone farther."

"Price of being in charge," I replied. "You get used to it."

The chamber was empty, silent, but that didn't last for long. Emmory moved at the shouting, stepping in front of me and bringing his gun to bear on the guards who rushed in.

It was unnecessary. They took one look at the Hiervet standing beside me and dropped to their knees.

2

Rotem and Sou followed, the pair skidding to a stop with simultaneous gasps before they, too, went to a knee. They managed it with slightly more decorum than the guards, bowing their heads and holding their hands out, palms up at their gods.

There was a moment of silence. Nobody moved.

I suddenly had little patience for this display of obeisance, especially as unearned as it was for the Hiervet.

"We'll be here all day at this rate," I muttered, then said louder, "Rotem, get up. Where are the others?"

"Your Majesty?"

"Did I stutter?" I waved a hand and crossed to them. "Get these guards out of here, get the rest of the Pedalion. We need to talk."

I folded my arms over my chest, watching his gaze flick to Thyra before he scrambled to his feet and started issuing orders.

"When's the last time they saw you?" I murmured to Thyra.

"Not since the early days, Your Majesty, and for many they have never looked upon us."

"Shit, I ruined a moment there, didn't I?" It was an unrepentant apology and I watched an expression I was willing to bet was disapproval flicker across Priam's face.

I heard Hao unsuccessfully muffle a laugh behind me. Thankfully it was lost to the rush of the guards as they left with Sou following behind. Rotem pressed his hands to his heart as he approached.

"Anemi." He bowed low.

"Rotem." Thyra reached a limb out and put it on the back of his head. "It is so good to see you."

I felt a little pinch of guilt. I was about to change their lives. The Farians would be irreversibly altered by the knowledge that their gods were not gods after all. The fallout would be huge.

However, it was the right thing to do. I knew that without a doubt.

"Your Majesty." Rotem's eyes were shining with unshed tears as he straightened. "I don't know how to thank—"

"You're not going to want to," I said as gently as I could, and he frowned in confusion.

"I don't understand."

A second commotion echoed through the chamber as Sou returned, dragging a protesting and cuffed Adora, Yadira, and Delphine. The Council of Eyes trailed behind, all of them in jet-black veils and spiked silver headpieces.

Of course they knew what was coming.

"That's interesting. I am a bit surprised to see Adora in cuffs; do you think it was her threatening to kill me that finally did it?" I said to Aiz as Thyra and the others moved forward to meet the Pedalion.

Adora had thought she'd bested us and turned Sybil to her cause before we'd all been thrown into the well of souls. It appeared that her behavior just prior to that moment hadn't gone over well with the rest of the Pedalion.

"Maybe," he replied, shaking his head. "You're going to let them make fools of themselves before you tell them the truth?"

"It costs nothing to give them this."

"I hope you are right."

"They're about to lose the foundation of everything they believed in, Aiz. You made your peace with what the gods were a very long time ago; give them this moment."

"It's a curious thing where you find compassion in a world so intent on beating it out of you."

"Practice," I replied, with a slight smile that faded with my next words. "Though the truth is, this is less about compassion and more that I recognize that the Farian leadership will remember how I chose to destroy their faith." I gave him a steady look. "I need their support. You need their willingness for peace. Fasé needs them to listen. And none of that will happen if this moment goes poorly."

"That's incredibly mercenary of you. I don't know why I continue to underestimate you, Hail."

"Me either." This time my smile lasted. "Though to be honest, thinking strategically is a skill set I had long before we met."

"That's the truth," Hao muttered from behind us, and I swallowed back the laugh that threatened.

"I made your life easier, Hao, and you know it." I lifted a shoulder, watching as the members of the Pedalion clustered around their surviving gods.

I had a sudden memory of my sisters and me greeting my father after he'd returned from a tour off-planet. The grief that followed was muted somewhat from the razor-sharp pain that I was used to feeling. Unlike Hao and the others, my family was truly dead and gone, though their ghosts had haunted me on Sparkos along with the others.

But the universe had given me back my brother and my Trackers along with everyone else I'd feared dead from the embassy explosion.

"No!" Adora's cry dragged me back to the present. I felt Aiz stiffen at my side as we looked to the group of Farians and Hiervet.

My BodyGuards formed up around me, hands tight on their still-drawn weapons. Aiz cursed softly and I knew that everyone could now see the Hiervet for what they truly were.

Adora was attempting to scramble backward, her efforts hampered by her bound hands and Sou's grip on her shoulder. The others stared at the Hiervet with expressions on their faces that ranged from confusion to outright horror. Sybil merely looked resigned and met my eyes with a shake of her head.

"What have you done?" Adora demanded. Her head swung wildly between me and the Hiervet. "What have you done to our gods?"

"The Star is the one who can see through the light. The one who calls out the rot from its beautiful façade." Sybil's voice rose above the noise in the room like a chant, echoed by the other seers.

"No!" Adora shouted. "I refuse to believe it. I warned you all this would happen! The Shen have corrupted your precious Star and she in turn has murdered our gods and replaced them with these things!"

Fuck.

Out of all the accusations I'd expected from Adora, that was not one of them. And it was a good one, just the right amount of doubt into an already tense situation. People believed what they wanted to, not necessarily what was true.

I arched an eyebrow, keeping my protest to myself. At this point it wouldn't do me any good if the other Farians decided to believe her accusation.

"I want everyone to be ready to move if this goes sideways." Emmory's order over the com was a wash of cool wind in a heat wave. *"Hao and Gita, you've got Hail. Johar, you're on point. Everyone else will cover the retreat. Make for the ship."*

The ease with which he tasked out me running for my life while they stayed to die was something I hoped I never got used to, but I didn't interfere and instead kept my eyes locked on the drama playing out across the floor from us.

Thyra made a tsking noise, reaching out and tapping a limb to the center of Adora's forehead. The Farian went limp, nearly sliding to the floor before Sou got a better hold on her.

"A crisis of faith is a difficult thing," Thyra said, looking in my direction. "Your Majesty, do you mind if we deal with this?"

"Not at all," I replied. I felt a sudden need to be back on the *Hailimi Bristol*. I'd gotten Rotem to declare my ship as Indranan soil, and it was the only place of guaranteed safety on this entire planet. If this went badly there was nowhere else I wanted to be. "We'll go back to our ship and discuss things while you handle this. Have someone contact me when you're settled."

I shared a look with Emmory and headed for where I thought the door was without waiting for a reply from Thyra, but I could feel the eyes of Farian and Hiervet alike boring into my back.

Emmory and Zin, as well as Aiz and Mia, were walking backward with their gazes locked on the group at the far side of the chamber.

"Star of Indrana."

I stopped just short of the blank white wall at Sybil's call and turned. "Yes?"

She crossed to us, her pale silver eyes unreadable, and folded her hands together as she bowed to me. "I will come see you on your ship later?"

"Yes, I think we need to have a conversation."

She nodded as she straightened, reaching past me and tapping twice on the wall. The door ground open and I didn't look back as I left the Pedalion chamber and the Hiervet behind.

The ready room of the *Hailimi Bristol* was filled with a cacophony of voices in a dizzying mixture of languages. I should have been more relaxed back in the safety of the ship, but it was taking more effort than I wanted to admit not to tell everyone to shut up.

I stood in the wash of it; most of these languages I spoke to some degree or another, but it didn't stop my auto-translation function on my *smati* doing what it could to sort the words out in my head.

Hao and Dailun were having a rapid-fire conversation in Cheng with Alba tossing in a comment here and there. That bit was easy for me to follow; the surprising part was that Alba also appeared to be speaking in Cheng, not in Indranan.

Emmory and Gita were having a quick meeting in the back corner with the other BodyGuards. Mia, Aiz, and Talos were in the opposing corner from them and my ears kept picking bits of their Shen out of the mess.

Fasé was in a discussion with three Farians who'd met us en route to the ship, and I couldn't even begin to make out what was going on there beyond a solid guess that Fasé was telling them what the gods truly were. Their exclamations had been angry enough to make Emmory pause, but Fasé had waved him off before he could cross to her.

The debrief had seemed like a good idea given the quickly shifting landscape, but now I was regretting my decision. I wanted to be in the quiet of my room, not trapped in this too-small space with far more people than was comfortable.

Even if I did trust all of them with my life.

"Majesty." Admiral Hassan leaned against the wall next to me, her arms crossed over her chest and her brown eyes sweeping over the room with the same assessing gaze I knew I'd been using moments before.

"Inana."

"So, not gods."

"Not gods," I replied. "Just aliens with delusions of grandeur. If you can fucking believe it." I blew out a breath as the noise continued to grate on my nerves and shifted. "Sybil basically told me that information and I just let it slide."

I knew that Emmory was watching me out of the corner of his eye. He shared a look with Zin and I found myself wishing the others would follow their example of a silent conversation.

"Hail." Emmory's voice was suddenly in my head over our private com link. *"Hands."*

Bugger me.

I uncurled my fingers from the butts of my guns, very deliberately not looking at my *Ekam*.

"And breathe." That order was more gentle.

I dragged air into my lungs. It wasn't a surprise I was on edge after the last twenty-three hours of one adrenaline-spiking moment after the other. I hadn't truly been expecting the gods to be willing to talk. I'd been expecting a fight. A fight I'd spent months training for. The fact that it had been taken away from me had unsettled me completely.

I really needed to hit something.

"Everyone be quiet."

I didn't raise my voice. I didn't have to. The room fell silent at my order.

"I'll be honest, that whole thing didn't quite play out the way we expected." Laughter filled the room. It eased some of my tension, reminded me that whatever else, I trusted these people just as much as they trusted me. I rubbed my thumb against my lower lip, my mind flipping through the options and possible ways this could all go sideways on us in the blink of an eye. "I expect that the coming days will be equally chaotic; however, peace between the Farians and the Shen is still the priority."

The surprised look on Aiz's face was predictable, but he didn't interrupt.

"I've leveraged at least part of that through the Hiervet Farian gods." I frowned at the cumbersome description. "But you three are going to have to do the real work. Aiz." I turned to the Shen. "Have you updated your people on what happened?"

"We sent a message that we were safe but no details. I'd like to tell them the entirety of it face-to-face."

"Get with Admiral Hassan. I don't want to risk sending you off-planet, but you can speak with the fleet over the coms. Will that work?"

"It will."

"Fasé, you'll spread the word with your people, but I need you to wait until I give you the go-ahead. I don't want Adora's faction to latch onto the fact that the news is coming from you."

"I agree. We will revisit our demands for peace from the meeting on Earth," she replied with a look at Aiz, who nodded.

"Can you give me rough numbers on your people?" I asked.

"Here on Faria?" Fasé glanced at the others and then at the ceiling, pursing her lips in thought. "Half a million? There are probably twice that who support us but can't necessarily be counted on to do so publicly unless they are assured the Pedalion will not retaliate."

"If I give them that assurance, will they stand with us?"

"Yes." She looked at Aiz and Mia, took a deep breath, and crossed the room, her bare hands extended. "We should be allies, Mia and Aiz Cevalla. I want the same for my Shen brethren as for my people. If we present a unified front it will be much harder for the Pedalion to deny us."

I held my breath as the siblings studied Fasé in silence.

"While I admire your optimism, Fasé, peace is not so easy as us just deciding to be allies," Aiz replied.

"The first step of anything requires little more than a willingness to take it. I know the journey will be hard, but it is one that has needed people to step on that path for thousands of years. I acknowledge the wrongs done to you by my people. I would like for us to find a way to keep it from happening in the future."

"A future of peace," Mia whispered. She looked at her brother. "If we can achieve our goals through peace rather than war, isn't that a better option?"

"I have been fighting for so long I thought I'd forgotten what the dream of peace felt like. Then someone reminded me." Aiz glanced my way, then nodded to his sister. "It will start here, with us."

They took Fasé's outstretched hands and the anxious violence in my chest relaxed a little.

"Peace is a noble pursuit, Majesty, but what of after?" Emmory's question wasn't quite the same as an explosion in the room, but I'd have been lying to myself if it didn't make me tense up all over again.

There was something much worse than a few aliens masquerading as gods headed our way.

3

The Hiervet were coming. I knew that all the way to my bones. The same crawling, awful feeling I'd get just before a job went to shit.

This time, however, I was the one in charge. I'd made the call and pressed forward even though I knew that not fighting the Farian gods would result in this new dilemma. There wasn't anything I could do now but deal with the consequences.

And hope that my decision to let these three Hiervet live didn't kill us all.

"I'll deal with it after we've gotten the Farians and the Shen to play nice," I said to Emmory. "But you're right. We have to get a clear picture of what we're up against, including what we're going to be fighting. I'll speak to Thyra again and see if I can't get a handle on their situation. Hao, I want you, Dailun, and Alba to put together a timeline for the Hiervet's invasion of the Svatir. At the moment they're the only reliable source of information we have."

"You don't trust the Hiervet Farian gods?" Judging from the look on Hao's face he liked that term about as much as I did.

"I trust the people in this room."

If I hadn't been looking at Hao when I said it, I'd have missed the way his eyes flicked to Aiz and then back to me. He didn't comment, though, merely tapped Dailun on the arm and headed for the door. Alba left with them and I turned back to Aiz.

"I'm going to leave the negotiations up to the three of you," I said.

"You're not joining us?" Mia asked.

I shook my head. "You've got more than enough people slotted to be in these talks already. I may pop my head in from time to time just to keep the Pedalion in line." I grinned. "But you don't need me. You'll sort it out on your own."

"You're expecting an awful lot from us," Aiz replied.

"I am. Make it work."

Aiz huffed a sigh at my implacable response and raked a hand through his hair. "Hail, you can't believe we will sit down and just agree to peace after all these years."

"Adora has been removed from the equation and I've done everything possible to give you a level field. I'm not an idiot. I know how hard this will be. What I expect is for you to act like the leaders I know you are and not the rabble the Pedalion has been treating you as." I tapped him in the chest. "You win a negotiation by being ahead of the other side. They already underestimate you; use it to your advantage. All of you."

"All right, Hail. We will do this for peace and our people's future," Aiz agreed. "What do I tell our people about the Hiervet?"

I stared at him, realizing too late he wasn't joking. "It's your fleet, Aiz."

"You're in charge, Hail."

"Of you," I replied, pointing a finger at him. I didn't need this dance on top of everything else. "Not of the entire Shen."

"The Shen go where Mia and I tell them to go." Aiz lifted a shoulder, his brown eyes boring into mine. "And for the moment we follow your orders. When peace is decided we will turn our attention to the Hiervet and you will be in charge of all the forces."

"No. That was not the agreement." My brain was scrambling to remember what it had been, and it was coming up woefully short.

"Aiz, stop needling her." Mia held a hand out before her brother could say anything else. "It must be you, Hail. I could not rally the Farians to fight what is coming. Fasé could not rally the Shen. Only you have the ability to command us all."

Panic gripped me. Every time I thought I had a handle on what being the Star of Indrana meant, it seemed like the universe threw a new twist in.

"I can't," I whispered. "This is too much."

Mia stepped forward but Emmory intercepted her. "That's enough," he said. "We're all tired. It's time to step back and reassess the situation. It's time for us all to get some rest."

I sank back against a console and reached down to pull Johar's knife from my boot, flipping it between my fingers as the others were ushered out of the ready room. The need for the kind of clarity only pain seemed to bring was a throbbing echo in my head. I fought against it as Emmory rested a hip on the nearest table.

Zin took up a station out of arm's reach, just far enough away from me that it would have been a stretch to get to him or Emmory before the other one shot me.

I wasn't sure if they did it deliberately or if it was just habit for them. They were so linked, so able to know each other's thoughts and feel each other's emotions. They could move in tandem if they chose.

It made me suddenly, desperately, lonely.

"I miss Portis." The words and the accompanying sadness slipped out before I fully registered them. I dropped the knife and pressed my hands to my eyes as the grief I thought I'd survived came back with a vengeance.

I expected hesitation, or at least a moment as my Trackers tried to figure out if I was faking my sudden tears; but there was neither. Emmory wrapped his arms around me, pulling me into his chest as Zin completed the circle behind. The pair of them were a wall, shutting out the world as I wept.

"I am so tired of being alone. Of being the one everyone expects answers from."

"I know," Emmory said, surprising me again when he didn't deny it.

"I thought I was past this. I said my good-byes on Encubier. This is who I am—empress, Star of Indrana. Why am I losing it now over the thought that everyone is expecting me to be in charge for the coming battle?"

"You know it doesn't work like that." Emmory's voice rumbled against my ear. "Do you want the list of everything you've endured since you came home and our wonder that you're still standing upright despite it all?"

"You need to sleep, Hail," Zin murmured, his arms tightening briefly around me before he stepped away. "I'll go clear a path."

"The grief doesn't go away," Emmory whispered against my hair after the door closed behind Zin. "It ebbs and flows like the tide. Sometimes I miss my brother so much the pain puts me on my knees and it takes everything I have to get back up."

I hugged him close. "I'd thought I lost you both." The words burned in my throat. "I know we've been through it before, but—"

"I'm here now." I felt him shift as he pressed his cheek to the side of my head.

"I love you, you know that, right?"

"I love you, too."

I held on a moment more before I pulled away and scrubbed at my face with a shaky exhale. "Thank you."

"For what?"

"Not lecturing me about my behavior."

Emmory chuckled. "I get it. You were geared up for a battle and it got pulled out from under your feet at the last second. I don't blame you; the rest of us are on edge, too."

"Yeah, the problem with me is that it's all amped up beyond safety levels." I picked up Johar's knife and headed for the door.

"Hail, do you want to go home?"

I stopped and looked back at Emmory. "What?"

"Do you want to go home?" he repeated; his dark eyes were steady, not the least bit of uncertainty in them.

"I can't quit. You know that better than anyone."

"I'm not talking about quitting," he said. "I'm asking you, Hail Bristol, if you want to go back to Pashati."

"What brought this on?"

"I've been thinking more about something Gita said to me. This is more than one person should bear alone, empress or not. You don't have to carry the salvation of everything on your shoulders. It isn't right."

A swell of emotion filled my chest. Crossing back over to him, I reached out and cupped his face with both hands. "Emmory, what did I do to deserve you?"

"You trusted me enough not to run."

"I did, didn't I? It was a good decision, all things considered," I said with a smile. "Could you do it, Emmory?"

"Do what, Majesty?"

"Go home. Knowing what's at stake." I let him go and backed up a step but kept my eyes on his. "Could you just go home and pretend like that choice hadn't doomed everyone?"

"No, Majesty." The answer was grudging, dragged out of him.

"I thought so. Did you know Cire warned me we would butt heads because we were too much alike?"

His mouth twitched into an unwilling smile. "I wasn't aware she had."

"She was right. We are alike. Which is why I know that if death is coming for us, we'd rather meet it head-on than sit around and wait for it to take us."

Emmory was correct about the value of rest, and when I woke several hours later the edginess and the need to punch something were gone.

"We don't have to take all the BodyGuards with us to visit Thyra,

Emmy." I set down my chai and held my hands up at the Look I received in reply. For some reason, my *Ekam* was back to treating me more like an empress and less like someone who could take care of herself.

Could have something to do with you being on an alien planet in the middle of a situation that could turn to war at any moment, Hail; cut him some slack.

"I would bring more if I had them, Majesty."

"Fair enough." It was an unsubtle reminder that we were down to only seven official BodyGuards, the attack on Earth having thinned their ranks considerably. "We are bringing Jo with us, though, and she's an army in her own right."

"Let him do his job, *sha zhu*," Hao said from his seat in the corner of my room.

I looked in his direction. "I always do."

"Liar." Emmory huffed a laugh. "We hadn't even been back on Pashati a full day when someone tried to kill her. Not only did she hit the man before I could get to him, but she shoved Zin into Nal, the woman who was my *Dve* at the time."

"How have I not heard this story?" Hao asked with a grin.

"I was reasonably sure she was going to shoot Emmory in the back. She was working for my cousin," I supplied, picking up my chai and grinning at Hao over the rim of the mug. My humor faded as I remembered. "That seems like such a long time ago." An unwelcome vision, of Nal's face as she died, appeared before my eyes.

"Majesty—"

"It's fine." I waved my free hand before Emmory could apologize. "Anyway, I know this is a show of force and as much as I dislike the necessity of it, I realize it's important to remind the Farians and the Farian Hiervet who I am." I set my mug down and got to my feet, smoothing out the deep green sari I'd settled on with Stasia this morning. "We should get going. You minding the ship while I'm gone?"

23

Hao rose. "I'll be with Dailun and Alba in the ready room working on that timeline for you."

"I'll come see you when I get back."

He put a hand on my arm. "Don't trust them, Hail. Whatever they say."

I nodded in acknowledgment and followed Emmory out the door. The other BodyGuards waited at the bottom of the *Hailimi's* ramp and came to attention as we disembarked from the ship.

I felt the weight settle onto my shoulders. Somehow I could keep it at bay while in the safety of the ship, but setting foot on Farian soil once more meant I was empress, Star of Indrana.

Bugger me.

I straightened my spine and headed across the patterned surface of the white landing pad, making for the group of guards set a polite distance from the ship. Farther away, behind a second row of guards, I could see the throng of Farians who had gathered.

"Emmory, what's that all about?"

"They're hoping to catch a glimpse of the Star of Indrana," Jo murmured with a grin before my *Ekam* could answer. "You're something of a celebrity, Hail."

"*Uff.*" I exhaled with a shake of my head, remembering the statue Hao had mentioned. "I wish they wouldn't." The way the two guards snapped to attention as we reached them told me I wasn't going to get that wish.

"Star of Indrana, we've been sent to escort you to the gods," one of them said, executing a deep bow.

4

I bit back a curse and only just managed to keep the shocked disappointment off my face. It had been almost a full day but the Pedalion apparently hadn't announced the news of the Farian Hiervet to their people. The fury was back in my gut and for a moment I wished I'd decided on my uniform and guns rather than a sari. My arrogance had led me to assume that the Pedalion would do what I ordered—and maybe they had—but there was little chance that everyone on Faria would change their minds overnight.

"Majesty." Emmory put a hand on my back. The guards had started toward the sharply angled building at the end of the pathway and I lengthened my stride to catch up.

We followed the guards through the winding corridors and past the now-familiar entrance to the Pedalion chamber to a smaller entryway at the end of a hall. The guard knocked twice and Priam opened the door.

"Your Majesty," he said with a smile that sat oddly on his alien face. "Thyra said you were coming."

"Yes, where is she?" Anger made my voice sharp and Priam backed up a step. I batted away the guilt as the expression on his face dropped away.

"I'm right here, Your Majesty. Good morning." Thyra unfolded herself from the nearby desk and stood. The room was half the size of the Pedalion chamber so it wasn't terribly cramped with all of us, though I was grateful to Emmory as he sent Gita outside along with Kisah, leaving the five of us alone with the three Farian Hiervet.

"Good morning. You want to tell me why the guards who escorted us are still calling you gods?"

The look on Thyra's face wasn't familiar enough for me to get a handle on, but her next words made me suspect it had been surprise. "I couldn't tell you, Your Majesty. The Pedalion assured us that our people would be told the truth."

"They are not your people."

"Of course, Your Majesty." Thyra dipped her head in acknowledgment. "Habit, you understand, is hard to break. What can I do for you today?"

"You said you needed to show me your history. What did you mean?"

Thyra held out a limb. "I can re-create memories for you to view. It works much like your *smati* recordings, though our ability is part of our genetic structure."

"Majesty, you should not let her touch you." Emmory's protest was soft over the coms.

"I am reasonably sure she won't kill me after going to all the trouble of bringing me here, but if she does, go ahead and lay waste to this place."

"And if she takes you over or something worse?" he asked.

"Fair point. You do this with me, then."

"Are you ready, Your Majesty?"

I looked at Thyra. "My *Ekam* will need to be shown also."

"It will be more difficult, but I understand."

I reached out for Emmory's arm, giving him a moment to pass along instructions to the others before I closed my hand around Thyra's outstretched limb.

We didn't move, but the room around us vanished, replaced by another. One that seemed endless with row upon row of upright tubes that glowed a faint greenish-blue in the dim light. The creatures inside flickered, at first appearing humanoid before they solidified into the familiar form of the Farian Hiervet who was showing me this. I wondered why Thyra was going to such trouble to hide who they were.

"My people started as an experiment, Your Majesty, and ended as outlaws. We were created to be the perfect soldiers, the perfect infiltrators. We are not ourselves. We are a reflection, a mirror of everything around us." She looked down at us. As tall as we were, Thyra stood head and shoulders above both me and Emmory.

"You can see right through that, though, can't you?"

"What gave it away?"

"Nothing you did. The Star of Indrana will see the rot." Thyra gestured at the space around us. "It has been known for a long time, and I have seen your life unfold, thanks to Sybil. You have a knack, Your Majesty, for getting to the heart of things."

"Seems it's necessary."

"We cannot help what we are; the ability that allows us to hide in plain sight is both conscious and not."

"It's a defense mechanism?"

"That is not how it started, but it is what it has become," Thyra said. "We can consciously manipulate our surroundings and our appearance, but when my companions and I landed on Faria so long ago, we mimicked their appearance unconsciously for our own protection. We were traumatized by our fight with the Svatir and expected the Farians to treat us in the same manner."

The room dropped away and was replaced by a sterile white lab with a dizzying array of consoles and technology I couldn't even begin to recognize or guess at their purpose.

A single Hiervet was in the middle of the room, curled up on the floor, surrounded on four sides by a shimmering field. I put a hand out, surprised when it connected with the flickering blue wall. The Hiervet inside didn't react. "Is this real?"

"No, Your Majesty. It is a memory, but it will be solid under your fingers for as long as I can maintain it."

"Who made you?"

"The best word for your understanding would be a business," Thyra replied. "The Infrastructure created us. We were their crowning glory, the pinnacle in bio-soldiers. Created to fight in wars we had no stake in, then decommissioned when the next new thing came about. We had no rights. We were sold as property to the highest bidder. There was a revolt and my ancestors stole the technology used to create them, fleeing to your galaxy where we could hide in the shadows of this deserted corner of the universe."

The room changed again, resolving to military barracks. Hiervet standing at attention, waiting for instruction. The sounds of shouting outside filtered into the room, but none of the soldiers reacted.

"We struggled to survive. We were alone and hurting and wanted nothing more than to be left to live our lives in peace."

"How long ago?" I asked, watching the Hiervet around us as they trained and lived. I wondered how much of this Thyra was manipulating to make sense to me, but I couldn't detect a lie. The answers were being given freely; however, that didn't mean they were the truth.

Couching a lie within the truth was the easiest way to make it believable. The question was, what part of Thyra's easy explanation was she trying to hide from me? My gut said there was something.

"We don't keep track of time the same way you do, Your Majesty. My answer would make no sense. We have been here long before you humans." Thyra gestured around us. "It was enough time to help distance ourselves from our past and let those who created us lose interest in finding us."

"Not much distance from your past. You attacked the Svatir."

The same expression as before, the one I thought was embarrassment, flowed across Thyra's face. "It was a misunderstanding," she said.

"I'm sorry, a what?" I cleared my throat. "You started a war with them by accident?"

"We were searching for a place to live. Your galaxy was thought to be deserted. We stumbled upon the Svatir while exploring; we did not realize how dangerous they were. We were excited at the possibility of other living beings after so long alone. We tried to make contact, and it went badly."

I watched her, still unable to decide if what she said was the truth or a lie. There was precious little I could go on as far as the kind of body-language tells I was used to. And I wasn't about to inform her that Dailun's story—the Svatir's memory of this event—was wildly different from the story she had just spun.

One more puzzle. One more reason to doubt that these Hiervet could be trusted.

But their cooperation was important. Without the blessing of their former gods there was no way to get the Farians to stand down, and the war that would erupt with the Shen would drown all of us in blood.

The world around us morphed into a battlefield. Screams of the dying hold the same terror and pain no matter what race you are, and they filled the air. The explosions shook the ground.

"It had been a long time since we'd had to fight but it is wired into our very souls, and despite our efforts the monster within us surged to the forefront with a vengeance. We'd kept the weapons we'd fled with; the fear of our creators finding us was always in the back of my people's minds, I think. We fought back, and in doing so our people lost themselves again. A small group of my people and I escaped."

There was a flicker, a slight flutter in her right eye as the lid slid almost closed, but Thyra appeared to stop it with a conscious effort. Something about what she'd just said was a lie; I just didn't know which part.

"My squad and I were separated in the retreat; our ship was damaged and we made a last desperate jump." Thyra waved a hand and the battle vanished. "We ended up here."

Faria. I watched as the memory of the Hiervet's arrival on the planet replayed around us. I didn't recognize any of the faces, but I assumed Aiz and his father, even Adora were somewhere in the crowd. Possibly the elder members of the Pedalion as well.

It would have been the same had the Hiervet landed on twenty-first-century Earth. I could see the awe, the fear in their eyes.

"You lied to them. Told them you were gods."

"They assumed and we didn't correct them." Thyra tapped her limbs together, the movement suggesting more embarrassment or agitation. "We were alone and scared. Faria seemed the perfect place to hide, especially once we realized what they could do."

"Do?"

Thyra's smile was so human it was unnerving. "Their ability to control energy."

"You—" I fumbled for the words as I stared at her. The scene around us continued, forgotten. "Mia said healing was not a skill unique to the Farians."

Another look I couldn't identify slipped across Thyra's face at the mention of Mia's name, disappearing before I could get a handle on what it might indicate.

"We have been in your galaxy a very long time, Your Majesty. So have the Farians. So have the Shen. You humans are so young." Thyra shook her head. "A practical impossibility to have not only survived but thrived in this isolated place."

"If you tell me we only survived because of you, I might punch you."

Thyra laughed, a strange throaty exhale that sounded like an airlock cycling. "No, Your Majesty. Humanity is responsible for their own survival, as miraculous as it is. We looked in on you when the future was revealed to us, but otherwise thought it best to leave you alone."

"Okay, so if healing is a skill unique to the Farians, how come I can do it?" I repeated my earlier question, swallowing back the urge to add, *How is Johar able to do it?*

Thyra was silent for a long moment, blinking her vertical eyelids at me in a rhythmic pattern. "You misunderstand, Your Majesty. I am not saying that their ability to heal is a unique skill. It is their energy that is unique and the way that it interacts with us. It has kept us alive far longer than our creators designed."

"Their excess energy," I said.

Thyra tipped her head to the side in a dismissive gesture. "If it makes you feel better to think so. That is what we told them all those years ago. The truth is a bit more complicated. Energy like this is not something that can be separated and contained. It pleased them to think of us as their gods, so we took what was our due."

Anger flooded through me. Thyra's words took what pieces I'd known about the Farians and their gods and slotted them neatly into a horrific picture. These aliens had enslaved them without firing a shot. They'd *fed* off them. Worst of all, they didn't see anything wrong with it.

Thyra seemed unaware of my fury as I unclenched my jaw with a great deal of effort. "So, what now?" I asked.

"I do not know, Your Majesty. Our lives are in your hands. There are only three of us left thanks to the Cevallas." Her attempt at calm was spoiled by the sharp way she said Mia and Aiz's last name. "However, that is a discussion for another time. I have shown you what you needed to see. We should go back before your people worry."

Everything shifted and suddenly we were back in the room.

"Emmory?" Zin's quiet voice broke the silence.

"We're all right," he replied, and the tension dropped from the room.

I blinked dry eyes; my *smati* clock said almost ten minutes had passed even though it hadn't felt like it. I didn't let go of my *Ekam* as I nodded to Thyra. "I appreciate the history lesson. It was helpful."

"I'm glad, Your Majesty." She dipped her head in return. "We'll be here if you need to speak with us again."

The dismissal was fascinating and earned her the ire of my Guards, but I turned for the door without giving her the reaction I knew Thyra wanted.

We were back out in the hallway and headed for the Pedalion chamber before Jo spoke. "Someone want to tell the rest of us what that ten-minute staring contest was about?"

"History lesson," I replied, and then came to a stop. "Emmory, did you get a recording?"

He gave me the Look and I grinned.

"Sorry, that's not what I meant; let me see?" My *smati* pinged and I closed my eyes for a moment to better focus on the image in my head. "Interesting."

"Majesty?"

"They look like Farians." I tapped a finger against my lips as an idea took shape in my head. "Zin, if I give you both these recordings, can you split-screen them with a single audio?"

"Should be able to, ma'am, and if I can't I'm sure Ragini could."

The Indranan tech specialist had come on the *Vajrayana* with Admiral Hassan. Her involvement at the battle of Canafey had tipped the scales in our favor and I was glad to have her expertise at my disposal again. "Good, here's both files, make it happen." I started walking again. "Once it's done, spread that around to our people. I want everyone to have a chance to see what Thyra is claiming happened to them."

I want everyone to see their true faces.

"Claiming?" Jo asked. "You don't believe her."

I laughed. "I don't. There's something off about this." I gestured around. "And the fact that they've been feeding off the Farians for who knows how many years only makes my gut scream louder."

"They're doing what?"

I came to a stop for a second time as we rounded the corner and came face-to-face with Fasé, Mia, and Aiz.

5

I looked around the hallway. It was deserted except for us. "Thyra admitted that she and the others have been feeding off your people."

"Hail—"

"I know." I cut Fasé's exclamation off and reached out to tip her eyes up to meet mine. "I know you're angry. I know it will get worse when you see what I'm about to show the Pedalion, but I need you to let me handle this part without interfering. I promise you: I'll see this through to the end, just trust me."

She stared at me for a long moment, her gold eyes searching my face for something before she finally saw whatever she was looking for. "I trust you, Star of Indrana. Now and always. And I will be there when you need me." The words were an echo of what she'd said to me on Encubier after Hamah's attack, and it loosened the knot of dread in my stomach.

I released her and nodded. "Good. Let's go talk to the Pedalion."

"We just left there," Aiz said. "They're not in the chambers but the room farther down."

"You met with them already?"

"Yes," Mia replied, falling into step at my side as we continued down the hallway. "The formal start to the peace negotiations will be tomorrow. We had just finished the preliminaries when I heard your voice, so we came to see why you were here."

"Thyra showed me where they came from."

She glanced at Fasé. "You're not only worried about what they've done to the Farians."

"There's more," I replied. "But now isn't the time for it."

We hit the door of the room and I didn't slow for my Guards, though it earned me a sharp *"Hail, damn it"* over the coms from Emmory.

The four members of the Pedalion looked up, as did the other Farians still in the room, though at a wave from both Sou and Rotem they filed out past my BodyGuards.

"Good morning, Your Majesty."

"*Itegas* Rotem. I spoke with Thyra this morning and have some information for you, but before we get into that, do you want to tell me why the Pedalion hasn't yet informed its people of the truth?" It was a guess on my part, but at the look the two Farian men shared I knew I was right.

"We were waiting," Rotem replied.

"For Pratimas?"

Aiz choked on a laugh. Rotem's mouth tightened. I ignored both of them and pointed a hand at the door behind me.

"Your people deserve to know the truth and if you won't tell them, I will. The time of veneration for these so-called gods is at an end. They have been using you." I moved to the wall and put my clip of Thyra up for them to see.

"You misunderstand, Your Majesty. I am not saying that their ability to heal is a unique skill. It is their energy that is unique and the way that it interacts with us. It has kept us alive far longer than our creators designed."

"Their excess energy."

"If it makes you feel better to think so. That is what we told them all those years ago. The truth is a bit more complicated. Energy like this is not something that can be separated and contained. It pleased them to think of us as their gods, so we took what was our due."

34

Fasé's indrawn breath was painful but I looked to the Pedalion, who stared at the image in shock. Delphine got to her feet. "Your Majesty—"

"Announce this news to your people or I will. When I come to see you tomorrow to officially request that you make peace with the Shen and with Fasé's people, it had better be done, or I will take them and leave you all to the devastation that is coming. Are we understood?"

"Yes, Your Majesty."

"Good."

"There's got to be a better name for them than gods," I said to Hao as I sipped at my chai from the comfort of the chair in my quarters. He was sprawled in the couch opposite, a cup of tea in his hand. Stasia had refreshed our drinks after dinner and then disappeared out the door with only a nod to my thanks.

I rubbed at the edge of my mug with a fingertip. "Just calling them the Hiervet doesn't work. It's too confusing with the bulk of the Hiervet bearing down on us. I thought Farian Hiervet might be better."

"It fits as well as anything," Hao replied. "You didn't ask me to come see you just to talk over naming conventions, though. What's up?"

"I don't trust them." Putting the words into the air brought a swell of relief, and I relaxed my grip on my mug.

"I'd be disappointed in you if you did." Hao made a little "go on" gesture at me. "Why?"

"Their story was clean. Did you see it?" At Hao's grunt, I continued, shifting in my chair so I could rest my forearms on my knees. "It all made perfect sense. Except for that ridiculous bit about starting a war by accident—which not only doesn't at all match the story we got from the Svatir but is completely unrealistic. How can you possibly start a war by accident?"

"Portis almost did on Mars, remember?"

I laughed. "Knowing what I know now about him I'm almost inclined to believe he did that deliberately to keep me from getting killed."

Hao stared at me for a long moment and then muttered a curse, shaking his head with a laugh of his own. "That son of a bitch. You're not wrong. He probably did."

We lapsed into silence until Hao drained the last of his tea and set his cup aside. "I miss him." His confession was barely a whisper, the echo of my previous words ringing loud in the room. "I missed both of you, Hail." He lifted his head until his eyes met mine. "I was going to com you when I got back from the quiet after Gy's death and beg you two to come with me to Po-Sin's. You were the only thing that made the thought of taking over the operation bearable because I knew with you and Portis watching my back, we'd all be okay."

I put my mug down on the desk and reached my hand out, squeezing his fingers when he took it. "If it makes any difference, I would have said yes and you know he would have, too."

"He would have said yes because you did, but he would have been pissed as hell at both of us the whole way. That's always how it worked." He grinned and winked. "But here we are instead without him."

I blinked away my tears. "We'll muddle along, right? I think he'd be proud of how we've managed to stay alive this far."

"Possibly." Hao smiled. "I confess I'm a little grateful that you're the one who ended up with the responsibilities, little sister. I just get to be along for the ride."

"You're such an ass." I let go of his hand with a glare and reached for my chai again.

"The Farian Hiervet's story is too clean," Hao said once he was finished laughing at me. "You're right to be suspicious. It's practiced, polished. Sort of how you tell a lie so many times even you start to believe it?" He shook his head. "The inconsistencies about the war are almost explainable as two sides of the same story. The Svatir would have interpreted anything as an invasion because that was their mind-set. And the Hiervet could have just been defending themselves from the attack."

"But the Farian Hiervet are also warriors," I replied. "I don't buy that they went from super soldiers to pacifism after a single revolt, and given their behavior with the Svatir and then the Farians it seems more likely they came to this galaxy looking to conquer it. Aiz fought them. Thyra carries herself like a fighter. Even as strange as they look to me, I can still see it."

"A happy coincidence, that's just what I wanted to talk to you about," Aiz said.

I looked away from Hao to the Shen standing in the doorway and raised my eyebrow.

"Emmory said to come on in," he replied.

Out of the corner of my eye I saw Hao tense, and the humor that had been in his golden eyes bled away.

"Hao, you promised."

"Don't blame him, Hail," Aiz said, baring his teeth at my brother. "Would killing me make you feel better, Cheng Hao? I can give you a free shot."

"That's not my name any longer," Hao replied evenly. "Believe me, Aiz, if I were going to take my revenge, it would involve making you watch, unable to save her, as your sister bled out on the floor."

"Hao!" The frozen sharpness of Hao's words drove into my chest with the force of a blade.

The humor slipped from Aiz's face. "You would be dead before you could lay a hand on her, and all the pleading the world would not convince me to resurrect you."

37

6

"Enough." Two pairs of eyes, one whiskey brown and the other gold, swung my way as I stood. "There will be no killing," I said. "Of anyone, is that clear?"

"He almost destroyed you, *sha zhu*." Those golden eyes of his were molten with anger. "That is the only appropriate revenge."

"You saved me, *gege*." The sick feeling in my gut was rolled up with a fury I hadn't ever directed Hao's way and tangled in the love I could see on his face. "If you have any love for me at all you'll never say such a thing in my earshot again." I stepped between the two men. "Aiz, you will not touch my brother, or you will deal with me, am I perfectly clear?"

Aiz watched me for a moment as if trying to decide how serious I was before he nodded once.

"Now. Did you have something to discuss or did you just come in here to pick a fight and ruin my evening?"

"Is everything all right, Majesty?"

"We're fine, Emmory. Though stand there in the door and shoot one or both of these idiots if they decide to start pissing on my things." Wrestling with my own emotions, I pointed at the chair I'd vacated. "Sit down, Aiz."

"I'm assuming you mean stun them, Majesty?"

I shrugged. "Either. Maybe they'll behave better if they don't know which you're going to pick."

"Yes, ma'am."

I turned around and spotted Aiz grinning at me. "What?" I snapped.

"It's a treasure to see the empress make an appearance."

"She's always been like that," Hao murmured. "Even before they put a crown on her head."

"Start talking, Aiz." I ignored the warm glow Hao's praise put in my chest.

"Thyra and the other so-called gods—"

"Farian Hiervet," I corrected absently.

Aiz dipped his head in acknowledgment of the new term. "You're right. Whatever lies they've told about the rest of their people, when my father and I fought them, they knew what they were doing. I expected the same kind of fight, hence your training."

I saw the flinch Hao couldn't quite hide and for a moment contemplated hitting Aiz for the comment. My training at the hands of the Shen had been brutal, designed to push me past the limits of human frailty. Hao was right; the combination of thinking everyone I loved was dead and the training had put me on the brink of madness. Aiz had wanted me to be able to fight gods, and in so many ways he'd succeeded, but the cost had been high. Now I had no gods to fight, just an unknown army bearing down on us, and no amount of training in the universe could make it so I would triumph over that.

"Why bother telling me the truth?" I shoved a hand into my hair and gritted my teeth in frustration. "They had the Farians under their thumb; they could have easily lied about all this."

"They want you cooperative."

That was from Emmory, and I glanced at my *Ekam*. He was staring at Aiz and I realized that he was still as angry as Hao, he was just better at hiding it.

"Why me? What the fuck is it about me that has the Farian Hiervet so convinced I'm the solution to their problems? I cannot fight an army alone, and I swear to Shiva I will shoot the first one of you who laughs at me."

"You're not armed, little sister."

"I could take Emmory's gun and have all three of you dead before you realized it."

"She's not lying," Aiz said, and the smile slid off Hao's face. "She'd shoot me first because though I'm the farthest away, I'm also the biggest threat. While your brain was trying to figure out what's happening, she'd take you and then Emmory because he's the most likely to hesitate over killing her."

"I'd probably shoot Emmory next, to be honest, since he's closer. Hao's fast but the shock value would work to my benefit."

He was also probably more likely to hesitate than my *Ekam*, but I decided to let Aiz have his misconceptions. I'd realized early after my return that Emmory understood the threat I presented. Right now, he was watching me as much to keep me from hurting anyone else as to protect me.

Hao knew I was dangerous; he'd seen me wreak the kind of vengeance that gave even the most hardened gunrunners nightmares. The woman standing here now was even worse, a battle-hardened and blood-drenched killing machine. But Hao also would always think of me as his little sister and assume he was somehow safe from me.

I shrugged a shoulder, suddenly uncomfortable over how my joke had turned into an earnest discussion of my new fighting abilities. I couldn't seem to escape it, no matter how hard I tried.

You're not the same person you were, Hail; better to just acknowledge it and move forward.

"Why me? The Hiervet"—I pointed at Aiz—"and the Shen and the Farians all want something from me. But I don't understand what it is about me specifically."

To my shock Aiz laughed. It wasn't mocking, but a genuine laugh that warmed his whole face. "I used to think this was a game of yours. This humility. You truly don't see it, do you, Hail?" He pointed at Hao and at Emmory. "They do."

I wanted to scream, *See what?* But Aiz wasn't finished.

"You are special, Hail. I'm not talking about the futures they've all seen or this chosen one shit." He waved his hands in the air. "Though Mia and the others would smack me for that irreverence. You are a born leader, and they are rarer than people think. Those who can convince others to follow with little more than the strength of their own actions. You are like a tidal wave.

"Honorable ones. Rogues. Rebels. You charm criminals and princes easily and drag them into your wake. Entire armies have thrown themselves at your feet. This could be dangerous in the wrong hands." He exhaled, his humor fading. "Except you take none of it lightly. I have never once seen you be thoughtless about the people under your care—be they human, Shen, or Farian. The Farian Hiervet want you because they think you can save them from the consequences of their choices and turn aside this army of their people bearing down on us."

"They're right, aren't they?" I didn't even begin to know how to process what Aiz had just said to me, but judging from the looks on Emmory's and Hao's faces he wasn't the only one who felt that way. In so many ways it made me more uncomfortable than the previous conversation about my deadly abilities.

"They want my help because of a desperate need for self-preservation. But we're in the same fucking situation they are if the Hiervet attack us. I hate to say it but I'm starting to wonder if I should have followed through and fought them."

"No." Aiz's easy dismissal was unexpected. "You made the right call. If there is to be peace between my people and the Farians, it must happen without bloodshed."

"I have marveled at this change often enough but it truly never gets any less amazing."

I turned my head to see Mia just beyond Emmory's profile,

and my heart rate kicked up a notch. The barest flicker of a smile appeared, then vanished on my *Ekam's* face.

"Not a word," I subvocalized over our com link.

"I wasn't going to, Majesty."

Still, I watched her cross to Aiz and touch a hand to her brother's chest. "Gentlemen, may I have a moment alone with Hail?"

My heart lurched painfully. I had a fleeting moment where I remembered Fasé talking about how my heart was always so steady.

I doubted she could say the same now.

"Majesty," Emmory murmured as he pushed away from the wall, then followed Hao and Aiz from the room. The door closed behind them.

"You've had a busy day," she said. "Threatening gods and the Pedalion until they bent to your will."

I stayed against the wall, face expressionless and arms crossed over my chest even though I itched with the need to bury my hands in Mia's hair. I hadn't seen or spoken to her since our brief meeting with the Pedalion. "You saw the announcement, then?"

"I stayed with Fasé and her people to watch." Mia lifted a shoulder. "It is strange for us—the Shen—especially those who never had an association with those monsters as anything but what they truly are. My brother, for all his posturing, still sometimes thinks of them as powerful beings, but I don't." Her eyes were filled with sadness. "They have been my enemies for a long time, but I watched the hearts of Faria break with the news that everything they knew was a lie and couldn't help but feel sympathy for them."

I had stayed here on the ship as a precaution in case the situation spiraled out of control. A concession to Emmory, or an apology for my behavior earlier in the day.

"I'm glad you could be there for them."

Mia crossed the room to me, stopping just out of reach. "It is important for our alliance, and I like Fasé. For all our conflict, I understand where she is coming from."

"Good. I like it when my friends get along." I looked down at her, wanting to reach out and brush her curls from her face. "How are you?"

"I am fine."

I spotted the trembling in her hands when she shoved them into her pockets. "Mia, what is it?"

"It's nothing," she whispered, eyes locked on her boots. Then she lifted her head and smiled. It was forced, lacking the warmth I'd come to expect from her, and I pulled her into my arms.

She didn't fight; in fact, she practically crashed into me, wrapping her arms around my waist and burying her face against my shoulder.

"What is it?"

"Nothing. I have seen nothing new for days. I don't know what's going to happen, Hail. All I have are the visions from before and they are—there is nothing but a yawning void in front of me. It is terrifying. How do you live like this?"

The panic laced in her words stopped the gentle tease that I'd been about to say. The realization that it would crush her even further was like a fist in my kidney.

"I could lie to you and tell you that we all live in the present, focused on making every moment count, but you know that's not the truth." I rubbed a hand over her back and pressed my lips to her temple. "We just do it, Mia. We try to live and sometimes try to guess the future. We fail badly at it. It costs us everything, changes us in ways we never even imagine."

"Hail." She pulled back slightly. "If you'd known where this would lead, would you have left your people behind? Would you have come with us?"

"I don't know," I whispered, staring into her gray eyes. "That would have been a difficult choice and I am not certain one that I could have made." I cupped her face. "Would you have asked me to do it? To walk away from my duty and my people? I don't think you would have."

"I did, though." She lowered her eyes. "It was thoughtless and arrogant of me. I am sorry."

I tipped her face back up to mine and kissed her, felt her fingers dig into my back as she sank against me with a sigh I caught on my tongue. "This is what I can tell you, Mia Cevalla," I said in Shen. "We would have ended up here one way or another."

"Is that so?"

"It is," I murmured against her mouth, and I felt her shudder as I pulled her against me. *"Emmory, I'm taking my bios off-line."*

"Yes, Majesty."

I dropped my mouth to Mia's again and let the rest of the world fall away.

7

Aiz was right about my evolution. The woman who walked into the Pedalion chamber the next day was not Cressen Stone, feared gunrunner. She was not Hail Bristol, empress and Star of Indrana. She was not even the broken woman who'd been haunting my steps since Earth.

I was all of these people, the pieces falling into place with the same reassuring sound of an old-fashioned tumbler lock opening.

"Her Imperial Majesty Hailimi Mercedes Jaya Bristol, legendary gunrunner Cressen Stone, Star of Indrana, commander of the Shen forces, and voice of the rebellion," the guard announced as we came through the chamber doors, following my instructions to the letter.

Emmory was on my left, Gita on my right. The rest of my Body-Guards were fanned out behind us. They were all dressed in their uniforms. I was in a deep gray silk sari with a silver crown on my head, my hair done up in an impressive series of braids considering the amount of time Stasia had had to work with. Kisah's help on that front had been invaluable.

The members of the Pedalion were on the dais. Adora's seat was conspicuously occupied by Thyra. Adaran and Priam stood behind her right shoulder, their limbs fluttering, and I wondered if that signified the same nervous worry as a human wringing their hands.

Sybil and the rest of the Council of Eyes stood off to one side, their faces covered by veils of white. The intricate lace crowns they had worn the first time I saw them were gone, replaced by circlets of solid black.

I stopped in the center of the black sixteen-pointed star on the floor and pressed my palms together. "*Itegas* Rotem, I am here to request an audience with the Pedalion to negotiate the terms of peace on behalf of the Shen and those who follow the prophet Fasé Terass."

"Under whose authority?" Rotem asked.

I looked over my shoulder as Johar came through the doorway. She escorted Aiz, Mia, and Talos. Hao followed at Fasé's side, her siblings Veeha and Volen behind them.

"Ours." Fasé's voice mingled with the Cevallas' in the still air.

"This war between the Farians and the Shen has gone on long enough, and this charade by the Farian Hiervet is at its end. Your people deserve peace and freedom," I said.

"And you think you are the one who decides what form that peace and freedom takes, Your Majesty?" Thyra asked, disrupting the formal ceremony, and I saw the Pedalion members flinch.

I shook my head and gestured at Aiz and Fasé. "I have decided nothing. This is what they have asked of me, Thyra. This is the collective voice of millions demanding what is due them."

"And if we say no?"

"Why would you? You face a united front of the Shen and Fasé's people. That means there is a fleet on your doorstep and an army of Farians on this soil. They are ready to fight.

"Then there is me. Adora tried to have me killed on Earth." I spread my hands wide with a smile. I could play the game of going off-script, and the gasps from those assembled as well as Thyra's suddenly expressionless face told me she'd been unprepared for my response.

"I had little patience with you to begin with, Thyra, and I have run out of patience with the Pedalion. I have the whole of humanity at my back. If you wish to test me on this, be my guest. I'd say ask my enemies how that turned out for them, but..."

"Is that meant to be a threat?" Sou asked.

"It is nothing more than a statement of fact." Kasio, the head of the Council of Eyes, lifted her veil as she stepped forward. She swept her bright copper gaze over the remainder of the Pedalion. "We have seen what happens to those who choose to stand against the Star of Indrana. We have seen what happens when the Pedalion attempts it. The Council of Eyes recommends that the Pedalion take the path of peace, not only for the good of Faria but for the good of the galaxy."

"We agree," Yadira said, getting to her feet, and Delphine nodded as she followed.

"The upheaval that was seen is upon us. We will not fight the change; instead we will embrace it and continue forward for the good of our people and all sentient life in this galaxy and beyond." Delphine folded her hands together and shook them toward me. "Star of Indrana, we welcome the end of this long war and wish to be the first to offer our hands in peace to our siblings."

Judging by the shock on Rotem's and Sou's faces, there had not been a discussion of the expected responses from the two younger members of the Pedalion.

Had I said the Farians were fractured? I was wrong; they appeared to be shattered.

"Very well," Rotem said, his mouth tight. "You have your wish, Your Majesty."

"Good." I rubbed my hands together. "I will leave you all to sit down somewhere more pleasant and hash this out." I headed for the doorway.

"Did you seriously just bluff them into agreeing to a peace treaty?" Hao subvocalized over our com.

I dropped one eyelid in a slow wink as I passed him.

The news of the Farian gods' true identity rocked the faith of the Farians right to the core. Riots broke out. New protests that were no doubt urged on by Adora's followers were happening daily even as others celebrated the news of the peace talks.

Adora's followers also demanded her release and, amusingly, my punishment for what they claimed were a multitude of sins. I was privately relieved that a chunk of the population no longer saw me as some prophetic savior.

The unrest didn't interfere with the talks as Delphine and Yadira pressed and bullied the other two members of the Pedalion until they fell into line. I joined them, though I kept off to the side of the spacious room, arms crossed over my chest with Gita and Kisah flanking me.

The room was packed, a security service's worst nightmare, with the members of the Pedalion, Aiz and Mia, Fasé and her contingent, and a host of extras.

"This looks like one of Po-Sin's gatherings," I murmured to Gita. "Right down to the fact that a number of these people want to kill each other."

She huffed a quiet laugh. "How did Po-Sin keep things in order?"

"Healthy dose of fear," I replied. "Gatherings were unarmed, and no one would have dared Po-Sin's wrath by bringing in a weapon. Disputes were to be settled by ship captains only, or in rare cases Po-Sin himself."

"I remember that story Hao told on Canafey, though I haven't been able to get him to tell me the uncensored version."

I smiled. "That doesn't surprise me; maybe one day he will."

"You're becoming as cryptic as one of the future-seers."

The introduction of the people at the table started and I listened for a moment before I continued. "It's not a story he tells often. Surprised me when he did that in front of a bunch of strangers. I think the importance of it was lost on most of them."

"It did the job he intended it to."

"True enough."

We lapsed into silence as the talks began in earnest. I listened with half an ear, preferring to watch the room and the reactions of the various participants rather than focus on the words they were saying.

Aiz was feigning a casual attitude, but I could see the line of tension in his jaw that always happened when he was focused and ready to strike.

Mia, by contrast, was relaxed. Possibly because she was sitting next to Fasé and the budding alliance between their groups had definitely shaken the Pedalion. Fasé was quiet, with a faraway look in her eyes that made me wonder if she was even seeing and hearing what the rest of us were.

The Pedalion was on the other side of the table, various attendants standing behind them. The room wasn't quiet by any means, with people coming and going, and conversations like mine and Gita's filled the air with a low murmur that competed with the voices at the table.

With all the movement, the Farian man pacing by the door shouldn't have attracted my attention, but he did. "Gita, who is that?"

"He's part of the Pedalion's security detail."

"That explains the nerves." I shifted, checked the time on my *smati*, and was surprised by the fact that an hour had already passed. "I'm impressed, no one has shouted yet."

"Give it time, Majesty."

"Is everyone agreed to a short break?" Rotem asked, and the agreements echoed around the table. The noise level rose as people shifted and stood. Aiz leaned down to say something to Mia and then headed for the door when she gestured in my direction. I pushed away from the wall, intent on crossing the room to speak with Mia, and then I spotted the Farian again.

Then I saw the knife.

"Aiz! Knife!"

He and Mia both turned at my shout, and I frantically pointed at the Farian bearing down on her with a grim look on his face. Aiz barked an order in Shen and his people moved.

We were too far away. I knew it even as I shoved the people in front of me to the side and vaulted the table, trying to cross those last impossible meters in a heartbeat.

"Majesty!" Gita's shouted protest was lost in the thudding of my blood in my ears.

Mia turned just as the Farian reached her and all I could do was watch in horror as he drove the knife into her chest. Just above the scar I now knew better than my own. She grabbed for him before he could pull the knife out, locking her hands around his forearm.

There was shouting, chaos, but it all existed on the periphery. All I could see was Mia. I reached her at the same time as Aiz.

"Don't," she said, the word hardly more than a breath of air, but my hand was already on her shoulder and I could feel the pulse of energy.

It was like grabbing onto lightning.

The Farian attacker made an awful sound. I realized Mia was doing the same thing I had done to Hamah during our fight— pumping her pain back into him. Some of it was bleeding into me and I did the only thing I could think of—pushed it away into the Farian. He shuddered as he died.

I caught Mia as she fell, the knife clattering to the floor. Her eyes were rolled back in her head. "No, no. Mia, come on," I begged, pressing down on the wound. I could feel the beat of her heart, a slow, sluggish thump, and somehow I knew that the knife had pierced it, but only barely.

Aiz was there, his hand over mine, his voice low. "Hail, it's all right."

"She's dying."

"And you're all tangled up with her. I don't have time to get you clear, so listen and do exactly what I say. Let me see."

I exhaled a shaky breath and felt his energy slide effortlessly through my hand and into Mia.

"Her heart will stop," he murmured, and mine nearly did with his words. "It's okay. We need it to for just a moment, so don't lose your focus."

I didn't, but the sob still lodged itself in my chest when I felt Aiz's energy stop Mia's heart.

"Just a nick. It's fixed now," Aiz said. "Restart her heart, Hail."

"I don't know how."

"Yes, you do; you think I'd trust my sister's life to just anyone?"

I thought he was a bit insane to be using this for a tutorial, but I didn't say it out loud. Instead I pictured the steady sound of Mia's heart under my ear as we lay in bed together.

"There you go," Aiz said. "Heal the rest of it."

I could feel her heartbeat under my hand again and could almost picture the muscles of her chest knitting themselves back together as the taste of ozone filled my mouth.

Mia dragged in a gasping breath and her sudden convulsion put me on my ass.

"Easy, my sister. You are safe." Aiz whispered the comfort in Shen.

"Majesty?" Gita crouched at my side and put a hand on my back.

"I'm okay." I started to rub at my face, realized there was blood on my hands, and wiped them on my pants instead, swaying into my *Dve* as we rose.

"Hold on to her. She'll be unsteady for a minute or two," Aiz said to Gita without looking away from his sister. Talos took my place at Mia's side, and the grim look on his face was enough to shake me back to the scene around us.

The room had separated. The Shen on our side and the Farians on the other. Everyone was still, the tension in the air enough to choke us.

"Rotem." My call sliced through the air, having the intended effect of dragging everyone's eyes to me. "I would like the Farians to leave the room, right now."

Rotem looked as though he would protest, but Delphine took over. The younger Farian started for the door, ushering the others in front of her.

Fasé caught my eye and nodded once, then gathered her people, and they filed out after. Emmory and Zin slipped through the door as the last Farian left the room.

My knees wobbled and I leaned against Gita with a curse. "I was hoping to avoid this sort of excitement," I whispered as my Trackers reached us.

Emmory didn't ask what happened, which meant Gita had told him when she commed. I offered up a weak smile. "I want the Shen to have an escort when they go to the ship. Please get with Aiz and see what he needs."

My *Ekam* touched my shoulder as he passed. I headed for the door, crossing paths with Iza and Indula as I left the room, and the pair stagger-stepped for a moment at the sight of me before I snapped, "Emmory's in there, go help him."

"Majesty, where are you going?" It wasn't difficult for Gita or Kisah to keep up with my stride, but my strength was returning. Along with my anger.

I didn't answer, shouldering aside the Farian guard in my way and grabbing Rotem by the shirtfront. The blood that remained on my hands smeared over the white fabric. I jerked him onto his toes, ignoring the protests of the Farians around us in the hallway. "Where is Adora?"

"She's in medical, Your Majesty. Under guard. She couldn't have orchestrated this."

"You'd better hope that's not the truth, because my other option is that you are responsible."

His platinum eyes snapped wide in horror. "Your Majesty, we would never—"

"You did it once, Rotem." I cut him off, shoving him away from me before I gave in to the temptation to cause him the same sort of pain I'd just felt in Mia. "You tried to kill her when she was only a child! Where are your medical facilities?"

"I will take you, Your Majesty," Delphine said. "This way." She waved off the guards who tried to join her. "I suspect the empress would prefer no escort. You two go find out if Enix was working alone or if others were involved." Both Farians visibly straightened in response to the snap of command in her voice.

I slowed my pace so that the smaller Farian wasn't running to keep up and also to give my temper a moment to settle. What I wanted to do was kill Adora with my bare hands. Despite Rotem's protest I knew she was behind this attack; my gut wouldn't let me believe anything else.

"Majesty, a moment?" Gita's quiet request came as we reached the door. "Ma'am, I know you are angry."

"I am not sure that word adequately describes my feelings, *Dve*, but continue."

"You had the same look on your face at Canafey, ma'am." Gita was being startlingly formal and at her words I realized why.

Canafey, where I'd dragged a Royal Marine out to the front of the governor's mansion and executed her for betraying us to Wilson.

I took a deep breath. "I am aware that this situation is different on a number of levels, Gita, and will endeavor not to do anything that will result in Emmory shouting at either of us."

Her look was patient but just a shade exasperated. "I am not afraid of Emmory."

"You should be."

"I am worried for you. That Farian in there could kill you if you let her touch you."

The more arrogant part of me wanted to test it and see if that was still the case, but I knew Gita was right to be cautious.

"*Dve* Desai, I promise I will not let anything happen to the Star."

We both looked at Delphine and the Farian pressed her hands together with a small bow. "Obviously it would be better if you didn't touch Adora, Your Majesty. But I understand tempers sometimes get the better of us..." She let the sentence trail off with a shrug of her shoulder and gestured at the door.

I studied the younger Pedalion member for a moment. It was becoming increasingly clear to me that I'd underestimated her, both in her level of power in the Pedalion and in her value as an ally.

"I think Gita is right, Delphine," I said. "I will be on my best behavior."

An answering smile lit her face. "I am not sure that is a wholly good thing, Your Majesty."

"Oh, it's not," Gita muttered.

I took another deep breath, let it out. "Let's go see what Adora knows about this mess."

As we passed into the room, Gita's hissing swear hit me just a second before I saw Priam standing next to Adora's bed.

There is a moment in any interaction where one has a choice— take the offense or roll over and show their belly. I have never been good at the latter, though I've employed it on occasion when necessary.

"Majesty, we should go," Gita murmured over the com link. None of us were armed thanks to the rules of the peace talks, and despite my training with Aiz I wasn't at all sure I was ready to go toe to limb, as it were, with Priam in a space this small.

But for most of my life I'd picked the offensive and I wasn't about to stop now.

"Adora. You seem to have gotten over your belief that Priam and the others are monsters I replaced your gods with," I said.

"Hail. Delphine." Adora dipped her head. She was sitting up in the medical bed, but her hands were covered and bound and her ankles strapped down to the metal braces at the foot of the bed. She didn't make any effort to conceal her disdain, or her glee as she asked, "How's Mia?"

The fury those two words put into my throat was coppery, but

Adora's clumsy poke had the opposite effect of what I'm sure she intended. I'd played this game with some of the best in the universe and she was too used to having the upper hand to know how to handle herself now.

"The assassin missed," I replied softly. "He's dead. Mia killed him even with a knife in her heart. Thanks for the confirmation that you were involved; we'll be sure to put it on your list of offenses."

"Star of Indrana, I have been here with Adora this whole time. She wouldn't—"

I put up a hand, and Priam cut off his protest. "I would never accuse the *Itegas* of directly trying to harm a guest of the Farians," I said. "Though this is your second failure, isn't it, Adora? First Earth, now here."

"What is it you humans say? Third time's a charm." Adora's mouth was tight and she spat the words out with more venom than nonchalance. Priam was watching me, face expressionless. I wondered what was going on in his head.

"Some of us. We also like to say three strikes and you're out." I crossed the room and leaned against the other side of the bed with a grim look. "I'd like a moment alone with Adora, please."

Gita gave me a look but backed to the door only after Priam gave me a nod and disappeared from the room, transporting himself in the same way Thyra had moved us into the Pedalion chamber. Delphine followed my BodyGuard back out of the room and the door slid shut behind her.

"Successful or not, Aiz will not stand for such a thing." Adora smiled. "Your precious peace talks are over before they even got started."

"You'd be surprised how much Aiz has changed," I replied, and her eyes narrowed in response.

"Your meddling won't stop this."

"You brought me here." I spread my hands wide. My own grin was one that had terrified some of the most dangerous criminals in the galaxy, and I watched Adora's vicious expression fade. "You manipulated my people and insinuated yourselves into our empire for the express purpose of getting me here in this moment. I want you to think on that, Adora, when you are feeling more assured than you should be about the outcome. You created this. And you will deal with the consequences of your choices."

I pointed at the door. "Your false gods gave you up as a sacrifice for the greater good. The Farians know the truth of what they are. You are stuck here while I'm out there with Fasé and Aiz and Mia making this peace into something that benefits everyone. There is nothing you can do to stop me."

"I will see you dead for what you have done." The disdain was gone, replaced by an anger that seethed in her platinum eyes. I had no doubt now that if I touched her, Adora would do everything in her power to try to kill me.

I leaned into her space, my face close to hers. "Better people than you have tried and failed. Come at me. I will be the end of you."

8

ack on the *Hailimi* and in the safety of my cabin where I no longer had to pretend to be the stoic empress, I wrapped my arms around Mia and buried my face in her hair, heedless of all the other people in the room.

"I am all right," she whispered. "Thanks to you."

"I didn't do anything." I pressed a kiss to her temple and then forced myself to let her go.

"You warned me and according to Aiz did the bulk of the work in healing me." She reluctantly released my hands as we separated, her fingers brushing over mine. "You should rest, Hail. It is not the first time the Farians have tried to kill me. I doubt it will be the last." She glanced past me at Fasé and offered up a smile. "Present company excepted."

"I would hope it would be the last," Fasé replied. "Rotem sent us a message while Hail was speaking with Adora. He—"

"You went to see Adora?"

I winced and ran my tongue over my teeth at Mia's stunned question. Aiz was watching me with a raised eyebrow and Emmory stood stone-faced by the door of my quarters.

"We had a conversation."

"Is she still with us?" Aiz asked.

"Yes."

"More's the pity. Would be easier if she went to hang out with the souls for a while."

"Possibly." I leaned back against my desk. "It also would have provided her followers with something to rally around. I am only borderline neutral here at the moment. If I'd killed a member of the Pedalion, no matter how justified, that would no longer be the case."

"You're not the least bit neutral here," Mia said.

"Maybe not here." I pressed a hand to my heart and then tapped a finger to my head. "But up here, yes. I would like for the three of you to figure out some way to work through this incident and continue the peace talks." I shot Aiz a look when he snorted. "If it helps, your sister expects you to walk."

Aiz's jaw muscles shifted and he glanced up at the ceiling. The silence stretched to the breaking point, but I didn't take the bait. He wanted this peace now just as much as the rest of us; every choice of his had been to that end. So I waited until Aiz finally allowed his grin to show. "Far be it from me to do what Adora is expecting."

Fasé cleared her throat. "What I was about to say is that Rotem has messaged me with an apology and an offer that the Pedalion will agree to whatever security measures we deem necessary so the talks can continue. I propose we go back to the model on Earth—four participants for each side. Majesty, your presence is not required, but it may help for you to show up occasionally."

"I'm sure I can do that."

The others filtered out of the room, Mia leaving with a last suggestion that I rest, and after pouring myself a glass of whiskey I dropped into a chair with a sigh that was loud in the silence.

"Do you need to yell at me, Emmory?"

"Do you want me to, Majesty?"

I took a drink, hissed at the burn, and leaned forward, resting my forearms on my knees. "Not especially. For the record, Gita objected and I did behave myself. Mostly." I smiled up at him. "Adora threatened me. I told her to bring it. The usual."

Emmory pushed away from the doorjamb, rubbing a hand over

his shaved head as he joined me in the room. I held up my glass, a peace offering, and was surprised when he took it. But he didn't drink right away and the silence settled in the room. I looked up at my *Ekam*, swallowing down the desire to ask him to talk to me, and instead waiting for him to figure out whatever it was he needed to say.

When he finally did speak, it was not what I expected.

"I received a request today from the Raksha," he said after taking a drink and handing the glass back to me. "Or rather, everyone on the Raksha but Admiral Hassan, who I don't think is aware of the request."

"You're saying *request* like it's not, Emmy." I frowned. "What do they want?"

"For me to encourage you to come home once the peace talks are underway. They sent this before the attack on Mia," he said. "Though I doubt the news will change their opinion much."

I muttered a curse into my whiskey. "Apparently neither did my report about what's going on here."

Emmory exhaled. "With respect, Majesty, there's some concern that the threat isn't quite as bad as you think."

This time my curse was loud enough to bring Kisah into the room, though she returned to the corridor when Emmory waved a hand. "Admiral Hassan, my quarters, please," I said over the coms, then slammed back the rest of my drink and returned to the bar.

"You know this thing can get bad fast, Emmory, right? It's not me losing it or not wanting to be empress or whatever the fuck it is they think I'm doing here."

"I do, Majesty. Which is why I'm telling you about it rather than knocking you out and taking you home. I already asked you if you wanted to go and you said no." His dark eyes locked on mine. "I am your *Ekam*, Hail. I go where *you* tell me."

"Majesty?"

I blinked away the sudden moisture in my eyes and gestured at

Admiral Hassan with my glass. "Did you get a message from the Raksha today?"

Inana frowned at me from the doorway. "I did not, Majesty; what's going on?" I watched her face change expression as Emmory sent her the message—shock first and then anger. "Your Majesty, may I—?"

"You have my permission to use any language necessary, Admiral. Perhaps a reminder that I am not sending them detailed reports of what's happening here for my health, and that the only thing accomplished by going behind my back to my *Ekam* is that it pisses both of us off. Let me know if I need to deliver that message in person."

"I will, Majesty. I'm sorry they didn't run this past me first. I'll go handle it now." She snapped a salute and left the room.

"I almost feel sorry for them," I murmured.

"I don't," Emmory replied, taking the glass from my hand. "Go lie down, Majesty."

I nodded and made my way into the bedroom. Sitting on the edge of the bed, I pulled off my boots before crawling under the covers.

I woke to the smell of chai in an empty room. The mug sitting on the nearby desk along with a tray of food was quiet evidence of Stasia's presence. I was going to miss my maid desperately when this was all over.

Rolling out of bed with a groan, I headed for the bathroom. "Emmory, I'm up. Going to turn my bios off and shower," I said over the com.

"Zin's on the door, Majesty, I'll let him know. I'm in the ready room with Admiral Hassan if you'd like to join us when you're done."

"Will do." I checked the time on my *smati*. It was early morning by the Farian clock. The long days on Faria meant our schedules tended to float throughout the day rather than attempting to push our human bodies to the thirty-four-hour span on Faria.

I composed a letter to Alice as I showered, the distraction helping with the panic. Though I'd noticed how it had lessened in the last few days, along with my desire to feel the sting of the edge of Johar's borrowed knife.

Part of me wondered if it would all come rushing back once we were out of danger. If I was ever going to have anything close to a quiet life again, or if I was just stuck in this endless cycle of chaos and despair.

"*Uie maa*, way to be overdramatic, Hail," I muttered, turning off the water and stepping out of the shower to dry off. "Just be happy you're not in a pile on the floor right now."

I flipped my bios back on, dressed and ate with the kind of efficiency that used to impress Portis, and grabbed my half-finished mug as I headed for the door.

"Majesty." Zin greeted me with a smile.

I patted him on the shoulder with my free hand. "How are you?"

"Doing good. Are we headed to the bridge?"

I nodded and we set off down the corridor. The ship was already bustling with people who greeted us as we passed. I waved Commander Nejem back into her seat as we came onto the bridge. "Morning, Sarah, how are you?"

"Holding steady, ma'am. Did you sleep well?"

"I did, thank you."

"*Ekam* Tresk and the admiral are in the ready room." There was no expression on her face as the raised voices floated through the open door. "As you can maybe hear."

"I can." I headed across the bridge as Inana's voice rose again.

"I am well aware of your concerns, Caspel. What I'm saying is they should have been brought to me, or at the very least to Alice. Not to Matriarch Saito and certainly not to Emmory as some sort of directive that I'll remind you is completely illegal."

"Admiral, there was no such directive issued."

I heard Emmory's snort as I leaned against the doorjamb, just out of sight of the people on the screen set into the far wall.

"Don't try that sophistry with me, Caspel. You can frame it as a suggestion, a request." The word was heavy with sarcasm. "None of it detracts from the fact that you fucked this up." Inana faced down the director of GIS. The rest of the Raksha was behind him, while on another screen I could see a very unhappy looking Alice Gohil sitting with Caterina Saito.

Alice had taken over the empire during my time on Sparkos, though my heir had gladly given the position back as soon as we'd decided I was fit to rule again. I was well past the point of wishing I could walk away from all this, though at times like this it was more than a little tempting.

"So, you should all know that I draw the line at one coup per reign," I said, coming all the way into the room to stand between Emmory and Inana. Sharp, indrawn breaths of surprise answered me. Alice pressed her lips together as she tried to hide her smile, but when she met my gaze there was fire in her eyes.

"Your Majesty, that is not funny," Caterina protested.

"Do I look like I'm laughing?" I set my mug down on the table in front of me and leaned both hands on the surface as I stared them all in the face one at a time until they looked down or away. "In the admittedly short time you've all known me, have I ever exaggerated a threat to this empire? Have I ever put my own desires and wishes above that of this empire? Since you put this crown on my head, have I ever given any of you a reason to think that my first thoughts are not of the safety of this empire?"

The collective "No, Your Majesty" wasn't particularly loud but it was delivered without hesitation.

"Then explain to me the rationale behind sending my *Ekam* a message asking him to betray me."

Caspel closed his eyes for a moment. "Your Majesty, you are throwing around a lot of very charged words at the moment."

"Be thankful I am halfway across the galaxy, Caspel. I'd be throwing something other than words." I pushed off the table and crossed my arms. "You have read my reports. We are dancing on the edge of a knife here with a real chance for peace between the Farians and the Shen. I will not leave until that is realized, and I will not leave until I know that the threat coming can be dealt with."

"And that is the problem, Your Majesty," General Aganey Triskan, the head of Indrana's army, said. "This threat is nebulous at best."

"And the product of delusions at worst."

I whipped my gaze to Caterina, but this time the matriarch impressively didn't back down. "You are basing this all on *visions*, Your Majesty. You can't deny how that sounds. Especially coming on the heels of what happened to you."

"Caterina!"

I put up a hand before Alice could continue to tear into the woman sitting next to her, and my heir closed her mouth with a snap.

"Is the Matriarch Council rescinding their faith that I am fit to sit on the throne, Caterina?"

She recoiled as the formal phrase hit her like an actual slap. Part of the procedure for reinstating me as empress would have been for both councils to vote on my competence. It had been largely a formality at the time, even with the trauma of my rescue from Sparkos, but governments loved their rules and I wasn't above using it to my own advantage.

"Your Majesty, that was not—"

"Answer the question."

"No, ma'am. The Matriarch Council has not even discussed the matter." She took a breath. "Your Majesty, you have been gone for more than a year. You should come home."

"Alice, have I missed something in the last forty-eight hours?"

"No, Hail. My last report is still relatively current as to the state of the empire. While Indrana, of course, always needs her empress and we would like to have you home"—she shot Caterina a sideways glance—"we have things well under control. Your mission to facilitate peace between the Farians and the Shen is still a priority and it is my opinion that is not something you can do from Pashati."

"Caspel, has anything changed from your last report?"

The intelligence director shook his head with a resigned smile. "It has not, Your Majesty."

"Very well." I glanced around one more time at the assembled faces. Everyone but Alice looked sufficiently chastised and I knew my heir would take care of any other problems that cropped up. "I think we're done here. Don't pull this cowshit again, or I will come home, but only to knock sense into all of you." I leaned forward and disconnected the com.

"That went better than I thought it would," Inana said.

"Sorry to stomp into the middle of that." I turned around and leaned against the table. "I take it last night's conversation did no good."

"I only sent a message last night. The time difference had made it impossible to speak until now." Inana paused for a moment and then exhaled. "Majesty, no one there is disloyal."

"I know that." I waved a hand. "They're just anxious. I don't blame them for that, but I do blame them for not coming directly to me. Especially Caspel. He knows better. Ironically, he trusts my gut, but he should have taken into account that Caterina doesn't before he talked to her." I rubbed my hands together. "I'd started a letter to Alice before this; I'm going to finish it and send it along because I think the reminder should be in the official record. The next time someone goes around me to you or Emmory to try to get me to do something, I will remove them from their post."

"Yes, ma'am."

I blew out a breath. "Okay, what's next?"

9

In the days that followed, an uneasy peace settled around us. The Pedalion surprisingly agreed to the security proposal and I stopped by a few times to make sure everything was proceeding without further incident.

When I wasn't there, I locked myself away with Dailun, Alba, and Hao and we went through every permissible memory the Svatir had of the Hiervet attack.

It was exhausting work. I am no stranger to violence, but the heights the Svatir and Hiervet reached in their battles was like nothing I'd ever seen.

"Damn." Hao rubbed a hand over his face, breaking the silence of the room.

I stood, hooking my hands behind my neck and stretching the kink out of my back. The blinking notification in the corner of my vision told me I had four messages waiting and that it was well past time when Aiz and Mia would return for the day. "I thought *we* were bad," I replied.

"You mean we humans or you and I?" Hao grinned; it was tinged with shadows and I touched his shoulder as I passed, my rolling gut settling somewhat when he reached up and gripped my hand briefly.

"Both? We've done some shit; so has humanity." I shrugged. "But this is a whole other level."

"It doesn't make any sense." Alba also got to her feet. It was strange, even after all this time, to see her in the same matte-black uniform the rest of us were dressed in instead of her customary skirt and jacket.

"What doesn't?" I wandered to the bar in my room, shooting Emmory a message that we were done for the day. The strict laws of the Svatir on the subject of violence meant only the four of us could see the memories directly, though I was allowed to brief the others on the things we viewed in as much detail as I wanted. "Who needs a drink?"

A chorus of yeses came back at me.

"Thyra said her people were created to be soldiers and that they rebelled and ran away because they didn't want to fight any longer." Alba took the drink I passed her, handing it off to Hao with a murmured "honored brother" in Cheng. He took it with a nod of thanks and I held the sudden bloom of warmth in my chest close. The loss of my family still sometimes hurt, but reminders like this—that I'd gained a whole new family—eased the pain.

The peace negotiations were going well. Adora's people seemed to have quieted under the overwhelming pressure of the majority of Farians clamoring for answers from their former gods. Things were, for all appearances, finally going our way.

"Hail?"

"Sorry." I shook my head. "Mind wandered." I passed over two more drinks and then finished pouring mine. "Right, then they accidentally start a war with the Svatir. We know she's lying about that bit—we've seen the evidence with these recordings. They landed on Svatir, pulled the same image trick they did to Faria." I swore under my breath. "I wish I could pick Thyra out of the bunch." We'd watched the initial meeting with the Hiervet through the Svatir's eyes, a small group much like the story Sybil had told me of their landing on Faria.

"Why tell a lie that's so easily verified?" Dailun asked.

I rolled the whiskey around in my mouth for a moment before

swallowing it and answering. "That's not really the issue here, though."

"What is?" Hao asked.

I leaned over and hit the panel next to the door when it chimed, smiling at Emmory and Zin as they came into the room. "Evening, gentlemen, everything quiet?"

"For the most part," Emmory replied. "It makes me nervous."

I laughed and patted him on the arm. "I know that feeling. The Farian Hiervet claim their brethren still want war, but that they do not. That somehow they alone escaped the bloodlust that reverted the Hiervet back to their programming after the incident with the Svatir."

"I wondered when we were going to get around to that," Zin said, leaning against the door frame.

"There is no way you can watch the Svatir memories and not know the truth of it. The attack was deliberate, orchestrated in such a way to try to keep the Svatir from being able to fight back until it was too late. Thyra and her friends might be dangerous, but that's not what bothers me."

"What does?" Dailun asked.

"The Hiervet *are* dangerous. They are coming for Thyra and the others. And they will roll over the top of the rest of us in the process." I took a drink and shook my head. "All lies break down eventually, and my gut says Thyra and the others may still be involved despite their protests to the contrary. After all, we have Aiz's account of fighting the gods, which happened after Thyra and the others had landed on Faria."

"What about my fight?"

I turned to look at Aiz in the doorway, smiling as Mia slipped past Zin with a hand on his arm. My BodyGuard didn't flinch at the contact, and a second rush of warmth filled me. I handed over my glass without question and she drank the remains of it.

"Rough day?"

"A little." Mia squeezed my arm and continued to the bar. I

watched her, listening with half an ear as Emmory caught Aiz up on our conversation.

Something I couldn't put my finger on had shifted with Mia in the last week. She was quiet, more withdrawn than normal. It could have been the combination of the attack and the pressures of the peace talks, but I didn't think that was all of it.

Of course, we'd barely had any time to ourselves, and what little time we'd managed to find alone had seen us both collapsing into exhausted sleep in my quarters.

"I'm inclined to agree with you," Aiz said before I could follow Mia and check on her. "The fight with Thyra and the others was almost too much for us, and we'd had the element of surprise on our side."

"Have we ever considered that maybe the Hiervet don't want to attack?" Zin's question drew several frowns. "It's just a thought. If we think the Farian Hiervet are lying, maybe them being afraid of the Hiervet is not a bad thing for us."

"Mia's vision showed the Hiervet attacking this galaxy if we didn't kill the gods, there's no reason to doubt it." Aiz shook his head.

And there was the problem. I didn't have a reason for my doubt. All I had was my gut and it was telling me that something didn't add up with all this. However, I didn't agree with Zin's idea that the Hiervet were harmless, not after what I'd seen over the last few days. "Was Thyra at the peace talks today?" I asked.

"None of the Farian Hiervet have been at the talks." Aiz shook his head. "Which is for the best, really. Why?"

"Just curious." I shrugged. "I want to talk to her."

Aiz raised an eyebrow at me. "Now?"

"If she'll see me." I looked at Emmory. "Can we make that happen?"

To my surprise, he didn't protest. "Let me go ask, Majesty."

We'd set up a liaison of sorts with Sybil to help keep us up to date on what was going on within the Pedalion chambers in addition to being able to pass messages along at need. After the arm-twisting I'd done to get the Pedalion to the negotiating table I'd thought it best to back off a bit.

Thyra probably wouldn't tell me the truth, but I wanted to talk to her all the same. Sometimes you could learn just as much from people lying to you as you could from the actual information they were throwing out.

"You want some company?" Hao asked as the others broke into various conversations.

"I'd like that. I was going to ask you anyway. I'm curious which version of them you'll see now. Where's Jo?"

Hao tipped his head to the side as he used his *smati* to contact Johar. "She's in the cargo bay, just got back from a meeting with Fasé's people. Said she's fine to head back out, though."

"I'll meet you down there."

Hao headed out with Dailun and Alba, leaving me almost alone in my room once more. Aiz was speaking with Zin by the door; Mia still stood by the bar, nursing the drink in her hand and staring off into space.

"Are you okay?"

She jumped when I touched her elbow, whiskey sloshing up and over the sides of the glass. "I'm fine."

"I've given that answer enough times to know what it means. Mia, what is it?"

"I don't know," she whispered, looking up at me. There were tears in her gray eyes. "I have a horrible feeling in the pit of my stomach and a yawning blackness of uncertainty where the future used to be. I don't know what to do about any of it."

I heard the fear hidden in her voice, and should have taken the same care as our previous conversation about her lack of new visions, but this time several hours of watching atrocities and the puzzle of the Hiervet dulled my brain and made my reply thoughtless and callous.

"Welcome to being human," I replied. "The rest of us manage our whole lives without knowing what's coming."

It was the wrong thing to say, I knew it as soon as the words left my mouth. Mia recoiled as if I'd slapped her.

"I am not human. I am Shen."

The words were a gut punch that had me breathless. Mia set the glass down with such force I was surprised it didn't crack. She brushed past her brother and Zin while I closed my eyes with a muttered curse.

When I opened them again, both men watched me with nearly identical sympathetic expressions.

"I—" Pinching my fingers to the bridge of my nose with a sigh, I struggled to find the words but gave up. "Bugger me."

"Hail," Aiz said, putting a hand out to me. "It's not you. Mia is—"

"Majesty?" Emmory's voice came over the main com.

"Go ahead," I replied out loud, holding my hand up and shaking my head at Aiz. He nodded once and left me alone with Zin.

"Sybil says Thyra is free to see you whenever is convenient. Should I tell her we're headed their way?"

"Please do." I gestured at Zin and he followed me from the room. "We're on our way to you." My fuckup with Mia was going to have to wait until I got back.

Hopefully by that point I'd have come up with a suitable apology beyond *Sorry for opening my mouth.*

"Star of Indrana."

It didn't matter how many times I saw it, the Farian Hiervet's version of a smile was unnerving. Part of me wondered if it would be less unnerving if I trusted Thyra more, or if it was the fact that I expected her to go for my throat like a sand cat from the Khar desert when she bared her teeth that made me so uneasy.

Either way, I shook off the clinging emotions from my fight with Mia and took the seat Thyra gestured toward with one of her limbs.

"Your Majesty," I corrected.

"Ah, yes. Forgive me."

Hao and Johar settled into place next to me and I leaned back in my chair, resisting the urge to curse when my elbow found one of the sharp edges.

"Did you know that Priam has been speaking with Adora?" I asked.

"Yes, he mentioned that you came to see her after the unfortunate attack on Mia."

"Is that wise, to let him see her?" The interaction with Adora in medical had been rolling around in my brain for the past week and I couldn't get over the fact that neither of them had looked angry at each other when we'd come into the room. My gut said they were up to something. The big question was if Thyra knew about it or if Priam was going behind her back.

Thyra stilled, though I wasn't yet sure if it was the stillness of prey trying to hide or of a predator about to attack. "He is closer to her than any of us. If she will listen, it will be to him. But you didn't come here to ask me about Adora, did you?"

I hadn't, but there was something about Thyra's reaction that made me extremely curious. I'd been rewatching as much of my footage of the gods as I could get my hands on in an effort to get a better handle on their facial expressions, but I was still a long way off from being able to accurately guess at their behaviors.

Which meant I needed to choose my words carefully, and my recent failure in that department didn't bode well for this particular encounter. But I had Hao and Johar with me and I'd picked the pair for very specific reasons.

According to Thyra, it took a great deal of effort for them to appear as themselves, but Johar could see them the same way I did. Hao still saw them as the Old Gods, but he could spot a lie better than anyone I knew, myself included. He also had little use for gods and much like Johar wouldn't be in awe no matter what he was seeing.

"I'm curious about something." I leaned forward, resting my forearms on the table. "Why are you afraid of your people?"

A look I was reasonably sure was shock flickered over her face before it was hidden behind a mask of impassive curiosity I found extremely impressive.

"What do you mean?"

"All this." I gestured around me. "A Farian told me the architecture was because it pleased the gods, but let's be realistic here. This doesn't please anyone." I slapped a hand on the sharp-edged chair arm and tilted my head at her. "So, why the right angles?"

"You are observant." The way her eyes narrowed suggested it wasn't a compliment. "The architecture keeps us safe."

"From?"

"Many things. To answer your question, it keeps us safe from our people. It keeps us hidden."

The honesty was surprising, but unlike Thyra I'd practiced my blank expression in some of the most dangerous bars in the galaxy and I stared at her for a long moment. "So, tell me something. What have you done?"

"I don't understand?"

"People usually only need to be kept safe from other people for two reasons. First is if they've done something. Second is if the people in question are dangerous. You've already told me that your people are not dangerous." I leaned forward with a smile. "So what did you do, Thyra?"

"We did nothing, Your Majesty." Thyra tapped her limbs together several times before she seemed to catch herself and stop. "I told you. Our people are dangerous. You've seen the prophecy yourself."

"You said they revolted from their creators. That they wanted no more of war. You told me the war with the Svatir was an accident."

"All those things are true, but the war with the Svatir destroyed all the progress we had made. Blood will out, Star of Indrana. You know this as well as I do. We cannot change our nature."

I felt Hao stiffen next to me and swallowed back my curse. Thyra, thankfully, was so wrapped up in her desperate lie she didn't notice.

"It has been a very long time since the attack on the Svatir. The things I told you happened when we were still filled with the hope that we could lay down our weapons. But it did not happen. I told you how the war with the Svatir propelled my people back to their vicious and dangerous selves. You are the only one who can stop them."

I wondered, briefly, what her reaction would be if I told her that Mia's vision had called for their deaths to stop the Hiervet from coming to our galaxy.

"You say blood will out, but here you are." I waved a hand in the air. "You've overcome it, why can't they?"

"My squad and I were only able to because of our concentrated effort and the love of the Farians. My people have chosen not to." There was a bite to her voice. It was annoyance, but also... fear?

"Hmm."

The easiest way to let someone trap themselves in a lie was to stay quiet. Apparently it worked just as well on Hiervet as it did with humans.

"Your Majesty, I have not lied to you. Our people ran from our creators because we didn't want to fight. But the war with the Svatir wasn't an accident. My people could not overcome their nature. They wanted that fight but were not prepared for the fury the Svatir brought on our heads." She blinked rapidly and continued.

"Even after the mistake my people made, I knew they would not change. My squad and I ran because we wanted no more of war. But you cannot leave our people. You stay or you die in the fight. Those are your only options. If word spreads of who we are, they will come looking for us. You've already set this in motion; you are the only one who can stop it."

10

've seen some bad liars in my day. But that," Johar shook her head with a whistle. "Wow."

"That's a tangled mess," I agreed. "She was lying like I used to when I got busted by my father. Scrambling to say something, anything to distract us from the real issue. She flip-flopped on the story about how the war with the Svatir started and the irony of it is that it doesn't even matter."

We were back on the *Hailimi*, sitting in the mess hall finishing up dinner. Hao sat across from me, silently picking at his food while Johar and I deconstructed the meeting with Thyra.

"She's spent her whole life not being questioned," Hao said finally. "It's bound to make anyone sloppy."

"The focus isn't really what she's lying about." Johar tapped her fork on her lips. "Or like you said, how the war actually started. The end result was the same—the Hiervet back to their original design as super soldiers."

"It's the truth she let slip in the middle of all that." I nodded. "The Hiervet are after them—either because they are criminals or because they want Thyra and the others returned to the fold, so to speak. I'm inclined to believe the former. We've seen that footage." I shuddered a little at the memory of the Istrevitel torturing the Hiervet they'd captured and their desperate pleas that they were hunting criminals.

"Do we need to know if they did something more to mark them down as dangerous than just being super soldiers?" Jo asked. "Where does it fall on the threat list?"

I sighed. "I don't know. We know the Hiervet are dangerous, we've seen it. Are Thyra and the others worse? Or are they criminals because they did something to piss off the bulk of their people?"

"Now you're making my head hurt." Hao's look was grim. "Maybe we could handle three, but I don't want to fight the whole lot, Hail. We're going to get shredded—even with the Farians and Shen helping."

"This is the Cor job all over again." The images from the fights we'd seen haunted us both and despite my mistrust of Thyra, I knew she was right about one thing.

We didn't want the Hiervet anywhere near this galaxy.

"That fucking job," Hao muttered.

I rubbed a hand over the back of my neck. "Thyra and her squad did something to get the Hiervet to chase them all these years. Nobody holds a grudge for several millennia over something inconsequential."

"You would if you could, *sha zhu*."

I waved off Hao with a grin. "You know what I mean. She wants us to believe that an entire race is coming for them simply because they ran off? I don't buy it."

"On the one hand, if their culture is only focused on war, that could be a major offense," Jo said. "On the other, if you did believe her I'd be talking to you about this great mining opportunity on the outer edge of the Perseus arm of the galaxy." She grinned at me and dodged my halfhearted swing.

"While I dislike agreeing with anything the Shen propose on principle," Hao said, sobering, "I'm starting to question if killing the Farian Hiervet may not be our best solution here. Though I see little point in engaging in a formal fight; let's just put a gun to the back of their heads and pull the trigger."

I wasn't surprised by Hao's suggestion. My brother had done his share of brutal things in his life—as had I—and I couldn't discount the logic of his suggestion if we were still following the path of Mia's prophecy.

"There's two problems with that." I glanced toward the door of the mess hall where Gita and Kisah were on duty. "One, we don't want to risk losing the goodwill of the Farians at this point. Further upheaval will cause more chaos than I'm comfortable with."

"And two?"

I picked up my chai and took a sip. "I don't know that it would do any good to kill them now. I don't know if the future Mia has seen is still valid."

Both Johar and Hao raised their eyebrows. As I said the words I felt a surge of unease. Despite my offensive dismissal of Mia's concern, I apparently wasn't entirely comfortable with the idea of not knowing what was coming.

"First I've heard of this," Johar said finally, leaning back in her seat to study me.

"Mia told me a week or more ago. She apparently hasn't had a vision since we left Sparkos. I haven't had a chance to talk to Fasé or Sybil about it, so I don't know if their visions of the future are intact or not."

"Interesting. How's Mia handling that?"

"Not great." My words were followed by a spike of guilt. I still hadn't apologized for my thoughtlessness. I exhaled, ignoring the look Hao was giving me. "The point is I don't think that killing Thyra and the others will accomplish anything now. We're going to have to come up with a new way to convince the Hiervet they want nothing to do with this galaxy."

"Oh, well, is that all?" Hao grinned and dodged my kick. "Should be easy for the Star of Indrana."

"I'm going to turn you in to Po-Sin for the reward money."

Gita snorted with laughter from across the room and Johar joined her.

"If you do, I won't tell you my idea."

"About damn time someone besides me came up with a plan," I said to him. "Hit me."

"We should attack the Hiervet before they have a chance to even find us. Just end the fight before it begins."

"You want to start a war."

I hadn't heard that level of exasperation from Emmory for a good while, and I bit back the grin that threatened. I'd waited until the next morning to discuss Hao's plan with the others even though I was sure that Gita had filled Emmory in the first moment she could.

Gita stood by the doorway with Zin, her arms crossed over her chest. Hao was in a chair as far away from Aiz as he could get in the small space, and Admiral Hassan leaned against the wall next to him. Fasé was perched on the couch, a poorly hidden smile on her face.

I stood in the middle of the room, facing off with my *Ekam* over Hao's plan to find the Hiervet and hit them before they ever got into the Milky Way.

"Technically I want to finish one before it starts. But if we're being picky—yes. It's a solid plan. We take a group out, find the Hiervet, hit them hard enough to make them think twice about starting a fight, and then vanish." I dusted my hands off. "The Farians and Shen will be at peace, the galaxy will be safe, and we can all go home."

He pinched the bridge of his nose and took a deep breath. "Majesty, I will follow you anywhere. But I feel like I am required to point out, as your *Ekam*, that you want to leave the galaxy and start a war."

"With a bunch of genetically engineered super soldiers," Zin added. "This is not a solid plan."

"It's not even part of a solid plan." Aiz met my glare with a shrug. "What?"

"I'd have thought out of everyone you'd jump at the chance to do this." I also found it interesting that everyone assumed I'd be going even though I knew that hadn't really been part of Hao's plan. Judging from the look Hao was giving me, he'd just figured it out himself.

"I have not survived the Farians this long, Hail, by being unreasonably reckless."

"I would like to point out that this is actually me being reasonable," I replied, waving a finger at him. "If I were being reckless I'd have taken a Farian ship and left."

Aiz grinned at me. "Be that as it may, it's not a great plan."

"Neither is letting them get any sort of foothold in this galaxy." I spread my hands wide. "I'm open to suggestions, but honestly this is the best we've got at the moment. Nobody can tell me how much time we have until the Hiervet show up, so we kind of need to move on it."

"As much as I hate to say it, I sort of agree with Her Majesty," Inana said, holding up a hand. "Yes, *Ekam*, it's dangerous, but striking first very well may put them in a mood to leave us alone."

"Or it could push them to hit us back," Fasé replied.

"Are you just disagreeing because it was Hao's idea?" I asked, and her grin widened.

"Surprisingly, no, Majesty. If I'm being honest I'm not sure I object to the plan in general. I'm just pointing out an alternative to Admiral Hassan's logic."

I shoved my hands into my pockets and rocked back on my heels as I rolled over my next words in my head. "The truth of the matter is no one's got a better idea and since I'm in charge here, I'm telling you all what we're planning to do."

Aiz shared a look with Emmory and sighed. "How many ships do you want?"

"A dozen would be lovely."

"I'll get with Admiral Amo and see which ones she thinks would be best." He nodded once, his mouth still set in a grim line, before turning on his heel and leaving my quarters.

I waited a beat before gesturing at Hao. "All right, out with it."

"You're not going with me, little sister," he said. "This plan did not include you."

Interesting that the last bit was directed at Emmory, and even more interesting was my *Ekam*'s reply. "I know you well enough to know that you'd never willingly put her in danger."

"Not anymore, anyway," I admitted with a shrug. Emmory's smile was fleeting. "Hao, you're supposed to be going to talk to the Svatir, you can't go. What good am I doing sitting here?"

"Here is safe, at least for the moment." Gita's voice was soft and there was concern in her brown eyes that she didn't try to hide.

My *Dve* and I had been at odds on Sparkos because of my decision to help Mia and Aiz. Apologies had been given and accepted, but I knew she'd always be hesitant to put my life on the line.

"I acknowledge how you all feel. However, it will be safer if we do something about it," I replied.

Zin shook his head. "Going head-to-head with an unknown enemy who's likely light-years more advanced than us in every way that matters is not safer."

"I haven't been safe since my boots left Pashati when I was eighteen and we all know it." I rubbed at the back of my neck and sighed. "Is this a token argument so we can tell Caterina with straight faces that I ignored everyone and just did what I wanted? Or are we actually having a fight about this?" I realized as I said it that I didn't want to send Hao or anyone else off to deal with this on their own.

This was my job. My duty. My responsibility. I wasn't going to run from it no matter how terrifying the prospect might be.

"It's genuine concern, Majesty. You have always put others in front of yourself, no matter what arguments you make to claim otherwise. We are, all of us, committed to keeping you from this danger." Emmory's quiet declaration stilled the bark of laughter before it could escape my throat as he nailed my thoughts to the wall behind me. "We were not there when you faced Wilson, and none of us have forgotten that failure." He shook his head as my stomach twisted. "I meant what I told you before; you don't have to put yourself between whatever is coming and the rest of the universe."

"I won't ask anyone to do what I won't do myself. I hate this prophetic cowshit, Emmory, but I am the Star of Indrana. We can fool ourselves into thinking otherwise, but we all know the truth. I am here because I am supposed to be here. I am here to stop this. By any means necessary."

"Then we all go." I stared at Emmory in surprise. "We take the *Hailimi* along with two dozen Farian and Shen ships."

"You—"

Admiral Hassan didn't even attempt to hide her laughter in a fake cough, and I saw Fasé throw a wink in Hao's direction.

Looking around the room, I closed my eyes for a second as I realized just how neatly they had trapped me in my own logic and blew out a breath as I opened them again. "Betrayers," I said, but I smiled. "All right, fine. First we need to figure out where they are."

"Already on it," Hao replied. "When we go to meet the Svatir, Dailun will ask his people to see if there's anything we can use to look for the Hiervet, unless you want to ask Thyra if she knows how to find them?"

I didn't, but we didn't have many options. "I guess I can also talk to her. I'll also speak with the Pedalion about borrowing a dozen ships." I glanced at the time in the corner of my vision and sighed. "First I have this call with Alice, so why don't you all go smirk somewhere else?"

The men chuckled and headed for the door. I reached a hand out to Gita before she could move. "Wait a moment? Fasé, Inana, if you could also stay, please?"

"Majesty?"

Emmory glanced back, then tapped the panel and closed the door.

"I would like your advice on something," I said. "All three of you. Shit." I rubbed my face with both hands.

"Your Majesty." Inana tugged my hands down. Fasé was at her side and the three women studied me for a moment. "Are you okay?"

"I'm—Dark Mother—I'm not. I'm not okay. I fucked something up with Mia and I don't know what to do." The words spilled out in a rush and I watched the reactions that raced across their faces.

Gita's face was nothing but worry, while Inana's held a much softer look I wasn't sure I could decipher. It reminded me of the look on my mother's face when she had come to kiss us good night.

Fasé was smiling and she reached a hand out, laying it over mine; a soothing energy accompanied it and I sank into the chair at my desk and dropped my head back into my hands. "I am a fool."

"You are not." Gita went to a knee at my side.

I lifted my head. "Have you read Portis's reports?"

She didn't even pause at my random question. "I have. They paint a picture of you that's not entirely true." She laughed at my surprised look. "Portis was so obviously in love with you from the beginning. He went to great lengths to hide it, but it's there for those of us who are good at seeing that sort of thing."

"He hid it from himself for a long time," I said, and then laughed. "Until Hao slapped him upside the head."

"Did he now?"

"He has always been a matchmaker." I laughed. "I should make him tell you that story sometime, it would be amusing. Anyway, I was never good at relationships. Portis tolerated me because he loved me and I loved him, too. But this—what am I doing?"

That earned me a surprised look from my *Dve*. "You're asking me for advice about Mia, Hail?"

"I am sure as Naraka not going to ask Emmory about this, or my brother." I shook my head. "Hao hates the Shen."

"He does not," Gita protested, holding up her hands at the look I shot her. "He hates Aiz, maybe Mia also, but not all the Shen."

"That's not better," I said.

She rubbed at the bridge of her nose in frustration. "No, but it's the truth."

"What about you?" It wasn't a fair question to ask; I knew it the moment I let it into the air and Gita flinched.

"Majesty."

"I'm sorry, just forget I said anything."

"No." Gita put a hand on my knee and smiled. It was strained but genuine. "I'll answer it, just give me a moment to get the words straight."

I waited, holding my breath for what seemed like an eternity until Gita looked me in the eye.

"Those people hurt you. Maybe you agreed to it, but you did so under duress. I hate them for it. I hate that I couldn't keep you safe from it. I hate myself even more than I hate them."

"Gita—"

"We've been through this, but the feelings are still there. I don't know that they will ever go away. I have learned to tolerate them for your sake, but will I ever trust them fully? I don't know. Their priority is not you, but their people."

"I wish we could have done that differently." I put my hand over hers and squeezed.

"I know, but it's past, right? We're focused on this and the future." Gita exhaled. "Here is what really worries me, Hail. Mia is going to be the death of you."

11

Her words crashed into me and I tightened my grip on her as I struggled to find a response.

Gita held up her other hand before I could say anything. "I don't mean that as a condemnation, Hail, but it is the truth. Either you will die bashing yourself upon this prophecy trying to save us all. Or we win and you go home. You grow old and you die, while Mia?" There were tears in her eyes. "She will not. She will stay with the Shen and live forever."

I am not human. I am Shen.

It was hard to breathe. I knew Gita was right. Had known this all along even as I let myself feel something for Mia and fooled myself into the fantasy of a happy ending.

"I wish it were otherwise. I said she is starstruck with you and in so many ways she is, but she is also a leader who knows her duty to her people." Gita smiled. "Just like you. I don't hate her, but I mourn all the same for what this love means. You know I have been there, smeared with the grief of losing it all."

"You came back from it." I knew there was desperation in my voice, and Gita shook her head.

"I did, but you've grieved like that once. I wouldn't see you go through it again." She got to her feet. "I am sorry, Majesty. I wish I had better words for you."

I caught her hand before she could move away. "It's all right. I appreciate them."

"With all due respect to you, Gita," Inana said quietly. "She is wrong, Hail." The admiral shook her dark head. "Not about the fact that this may kill you but about if that means you should grieve now for the inevitable rather than just loving.

"I have given the years of my life to this empire and nothing else. Despite opportunities that happened, I always put the empire first." Her smile was brief, ripped away like a leaf caught in a breeze. "I don't regret that choice, but at times I do wonder why I couldn't find a way to love someone and love my empire at the same time. Your mother found that balance and there is no reason why you shouldn't have it either."

Fasé leaned in as the other two women moved to the door and the Farian cupped my face in her hands. "You burn so brightly it hurts to look at you sometimes." She kissed my forehead. "Just apologize, Hail. She will forgive you."

"I will. Do me a favor, will you?"

"Anything."

"Tell Gita to message Alice and let her know I'll be a few minutes late with my com."

Fasé nodded and left me alone, the door sliding shut behind her after she slipped through.

I rested my forehead on the edge of the desk and fought off the tears. Despite Inana's and Fasé's words, I knew Gita was right, had known it even before she'd spoken.

Mia and I were two different worlds. Two separate sets of duties and responsibilities. I'd fought too long and hard to keep my throne and I couldn't walk away from it. Mia had done the same and now we were on the precipice of a final peace for the Shen and she would go on to rule with Aiz—forever.

Face it, Hail. Targets of prophecies don't get happy endings.

The voice in my head was cold, ruthless, and entirely right.

I sat up, wiped the tears from my face, straightened my shoulders, and buried everything into the darkest corner of my heart I could find. Then I pasted a smile onto my face and commed Alice.

"Hail!" Her cheerful expression slid away and she brushed a black curl out of her face. "Are you okay?"

"I'm fine. How are things at home?"

"They're going well." The frown crossed briefly over her face, but Alice was ever the consummate politician and she let me have my distraction. "Everyone is behaving themselves."

I laughed softly. "Good."

"Prime Minister Tesla had a few choice things to say about you not returning home, but Caterina and the other matriarchs pulled her into a meeting yesterday and Shiva, did they chew her ass." Alice whistled, then grinned. "She's lost a lot of her support this term, mostly because she keeps opening her mouth. I doubt her reelection campaign will go well."

"It was a good plan on Caterina's part." The head of the Matriarch Council had been certain that letting Shivali Tesla have just enough rope to hang herself with was the best option, and so far it looked as though she was correct.

"As much as I hate to admit it, it was." Alice shook her head, her rueful smile making the dimple on her cheek wink into existence for a moment. "Taz says it's better for my blood pressure anyway."

"How is he? How's Ravalina?"

"They're both fine. Are you sure you're okay?"

I lifted a shoulder in a non-answer. "I'm sure you've got a list of things to discuss and I'd like to let you get back to your family."

"All right, I won't pry. So, up first is the newest issue with the budget on the repairs to the Canafey shipyards."

I settled back in my chair as Alice dove into the reconstruction work for the *Vajrayana* ships in the Canafey system. The dockyard had been damaged in the Saxon attack on our system, and then I hadn't done us any favors taking Darshan Station by force.

Blowing things up was a lot easier when you didn't have to figure out a way to rebuild them on the back end.

Two hours later I rubbed at my face after closing out the com and stood, stretching with a groan.

The conversation between Emmory and Zin stopped when the door slid open.

"Zin, I have a project for you, if you're interested." The thought had been rolling around in my head since I'd taken Hao and Johar to see Thyra, and it was time to do something about it.

"What's that, Majesty?"

"What do the Farian Hiervet look like to you? Still like our gods?"

"Not anymore, Majesty. We saw her and the others briefly in the Pedalion chambers when they revealed themselves to the Farians, but most of the time?" Zin shook his head. "She looks like a Farian, only slightly—more?—if that makes sense?"

"It does. Hao's the same way. Even though he saw his people's Old Gods at the beginning, now it's just Farians. Jo and I seem to be the only ones who can see them for what they really are. I'm curious how they do it. But moreover, I want to figure out what the expressions on their faces mean." I frowned. "I had an idea that someone could take the images I see and cross-reference them with images from others at the same time."

"Like we did with what she showed you and Emmory?" Zin nodded. "It would give you a baseline on the human expressions and it shouldn't be difficult, ma'am. Assuming we have the material for it."

"Oh, I do." I reached out and shared what I'd pieced together from my visit to Thyra with Hao.

The split picture appeared in the upper corner of my vision, and Zin hummed at the sight of Thyra in her true form. "I wish I could figure out how they do that. It's a neat trick."

"It makes them dangerous," Emmory murmured.

"I should have thought of this sooner," Zin said. "You want this same split format, Majesty?"

"Yes, please. It's a lot of busy work, but I trust you—"

Zin waved me off with a smile. "It's good work, Majesty. And it'll take me less time than if you had anyone else do it. Send me whatever video you have and I'll pull from the BodyGuard files where one of us is in the room with them at the same time. I can compile them into a primer of sorts for you with shots of the more human expressions and the Hiervet ones side by side for comparison."

"Tap Alba if she has time; she's been busy with Dailun but she's got a good eye for detail." I smiled. "Thank you."

"Anytime, Majesty."

"Emmory, let's go talk to the Pedalion." I'd timed the call with Alice close enough that I would catch the negotiations at the edge of the morning break.

We heard the shouting well before we reached the chambers in the Pedalion compound where the negotiations were being held, and I shared a look with Emmory. "Should have known things were going too smoothly," I muttered.

"Majesty, we should probably go back to the ship."

"I know," I said. "You know I'm not going to, right?"

He sighed and gave the guard on the door an impassive look when the woman stepped in front of us.

"Star of Indrana, it is probably for the best if you—"

"See if I can't help?" I slipped around her into the room.

Mia spotted me first, through the frame of her brother and Rotem shouting at each other in Farian, their words flying so fast my *smati* almost had trouble keeping up.

Men, she mouthed with a roll of her eyes. The humor was as surprising as the soft smile that followed it, and I felt a burst of hope that maybe I could salvage something out of the wreckage of my foolishness.

I leaned against the wall, waving Fasé and the others of the

Pedalion back into their seats. Interestingly enough, Thyra was also there, but the Farian Hiervet had remained in her seat when I came in and I wished for the hundredth time that I had a match for the expression that crossed her face.

"We will not yield on this, Aiz!"

"If you will not, then what is the point of all this?" Aiz snapped his fingers. "My people deserve to live here on Faria as much as yours do."

"Our people won't just accept Shen in their midst because you say so."

"No, it will be because *you* say so," I said, and both men snapped their mouths shut. "I stopped by to see how things were going. I see that the answer is 'not great.' What's the issue here?"

"The usual Farian bullshit."

"Aiz." The quiet warning came from Mia and I wondered how much I'd missed out on by not attending the negotiations. I'd thought things were going well, but the atmosphere in the room was like a live wire.

"Rotem objects to allowing us a place to live on Faria."

"It is not me objecting, Your Majesty," Rotem said. "The people will not stand for it."

"What would you know of the people's desires?" Fasé's reply was sharp. "When was the last time you left this tower, Rotem, and actually talked to them?"

"How dare you?" he snarled, turning his fury on Fasé. "You have so little room to speak on this, Fasé Terass, and yet you'd dare chastise me? Where have you been these last few years? Not here."

"I was here for a time, or have you forgotten you all locked me up?" Fasé's laugh was sharp but filled with humor. "I have been doing your work out there, *Itegas* Rotem, caring for my people. I have been laying the foundations of a better world for them while you bowed down to these false gods."

Rotem swung his arm back to strike, but Talos surged to his feet, taking the blow intended for Fasé. I pulled my gun as Talos grabbed Rotem by the wrist.

"Enough," I said. No one moved. "Talos, let him go."

"Would that I could, Star of Indrana," he gritted out, and I realized they were locked in a battle of wills. Worse, it was a fight Talos appeared to be losing.

"Rotem, you have to the count of three to let him go before I paint the wall behind you with your brains." I saw the hatred flash in his platinum eyes but he didn't move. I hit the charge on my Glock. "One."

Talos was going gray. Emmory and the others hadn't moved, but I knew their hands were on their guns and this was about to get bloody.

"Two." I took a step closer, my eyes locked on the pair.

"Rotem, that is quite enough." Thyra's voice broke through the standoff, and Rotem released Talos as if he'd suddenly been burned. Fasé caught him when he sagged forward and only then did Aiz move, slipping his arm around Talos's waist and helping the Shen away from Rotem as he whispered in his ear.

"Would you like to try that with me?" Fasé's voice was a frozen knife cutting through the air.

"Don't think about it," I warned when Rotem opened his mouth. "I'm still hot and I really will put the Pedalion down by another member if you so much as touch anyone else in this room."

"Star of Indrana." Thyra raised a limb, an obvious placating gesture.

I shoved my Glock back into the holster with a snarl. "Damn it, Rotem, your people are tired! Can't you see it? Fasé is right. Do you not speak with them? They want to live their lives without worrying about dying in a fight with the Shen.

"And some are tired of living this lie of eternity you were all tricked into. They want freedom."

"And that we can give," Rotem said with a glance toward Fasé. "To those who seek it. But the land is not within our power, Your Majesty. If we uproot people to settle Shen in their place it will not end well."

"You all realize there is something much worse coming, right?" I saw Thyra flinch at my words. "And if you aren't able to put down your grievances and fight with us, then none of us will survive!"

"Rotem," Fasé said, folding her hands on the table in front of him. "What if some Farians agree to move?"

"Where would they go?" Delphine asked with a frown.

Fasé looked my way. "I believe her Majesty has a suggestion."

"Caterina is going to kill me," I subvocalized at her over the com link without breaking my expression. "The Empire of Indrana would gladly welcome any Farians who wanted to settle permanently with us. Or temporarily," I added when Sou glared at me. "We are allies, after all, aren't we?"

"It will not work." Aiz shook his head. "There are too many of us. It's not that we don't appreciate the generosity of Fasé's offer, Hail. It is a simple matter of population."

"What are the requirements for the Shen to have the same chance at rebirth as the Farians?" I held my hand up before Aiz could answer me. "Thyra?"

The Farian Hiervet blinked at me, eyelids snapping shut and then open again in what I assumed was surprise. "Your Majesty?"

I repeated the question and Thyra shook her head. "It is not about the land, Your Majesty. The dirt of this planet is no more special than your own."

"What?" It wasn't only Aiz and Mia who shouted the challenge; Rotem and the others of the Pedalion reacted with shock. I kept my own shock at bay as the realization that the one thing we'd been trying to achieve had ended up useless.

Crossing my arms over my chest, I waited for the stunned outrage to settle. I knew the Farian Hiervet wouldn't give us the information unless I kept pushing. "You didn't answer my question, Thyra. I won't ask a third time."

"The unique abilities of the Farians were not something we created, they were merely something we encouraged. Our assistance—"

"Your interference," Fasé declared.

I was now sure an annoyed look flashed across Thyra's face.

"Yes, our interference allowed for the random nature of their reincarnations to be more consistent and orderly."

"The genetic markers in your blood."

"Yes." Thyra inclined her head.

"Are those markers what the Shen require?"

Thyra dipped her head again with only the slightest hesitation.

"I'm going to assume you have the ability to access those in a manner less violent than how Aiz got his hands on the rest of it?"

"There is a lab in Etrelia."

"Good. I expect a plan for how to make this happen from you before the next meeting." I turned back to the list of items scrolling across the table in front of me.

"Your Majesty, what do you intend to give us?"

"Give you?" I raised an eyebrow at her.

"In exchange."

I snorted a little laugh as I glanced back at the table for a moment and then sobered. "Thyra, you get the two things I have already decided to give you—your lives and my help with the Hiervet when they arrive."

"But—"

"I realize you are used to being treated as gods. I do not see you as such. Do not test my generosity or my patience." I pushed to my feet with a sigh. "I think that is enough for today; we'll revisit the question of where people are going to live once I have more information from Thyra."

"Your Majesty, if we might?" Aiz put a hand out. "There is one more pressing issue. My father. The others whose souls are being held. Will they be released?"

"I don't see why not," Yadira replied. "Aiz, are you willing to consider a prisoner exchange?"

"Yes," he said.

I watched Rotem, who was frowning. The Farian Hiervet were doing that embarrassed limb-tapping thing and I raised an eyebrow as a horrific idea settled itself into the pit of my chest.

"Emmory, this is about to go badly again," I subvocalized over our private com.

"There can be no exchange." Rotem refused to meet my eyes. "All those judged as traitors faced the gods and their souls were consumed."

Fuck. I only just managed not to utter the word out loud.

"No." Mia exhaled, a painful gasp of air.

Thyra touched her limbs together. "There was no reason to keep them."

"Bugger me," I muttered, stepping into Aiz's path and putting my hands on his chest. "No." He tried to move around me and I pushed back. "Aiz, look at me."

A surge of energy ripping through me was his only response.

12

I could feel the press of Aiz's will against mine. Not even pressing, but sinking in until it was hard to tell us apart. There weren't any words for it, this strange feeling of the very heart of someone being tangled with my own.

I did what could best be described as the energetic equivalent of digging my heels into the dirt. "Aiz, look at me."

He complied, but slowly, and I could feel him fighting my command. We were locked just like Rotem and Talos had been, much like the first time Aiz had done it to me on Rai's ship, only now I was the one who'd frozen him. I almost lost my grip in my shock.

"I get it, believe me, but now is not the time." I hated myself for the words. There were too many ways this could go wrong if a fight broke out.

"Let me go, Hail." His jaw flexed and somewhere in the back of my head a voice was babbling in surprise that I could hold him at all.

"Promise me you won't try to kill them."

I could feel him pushing, feel my grip slipping. And then, nothing.

"Enough, both of you," Mia said, putting her hands on us. "Aiz, *mi corazón eas eínai ragisméni.*" There were tears in her eyes. "Hail—"

I touched her face. "Go. I'll deal with this."

I met Johar's eyes as they headed for the door and tipped my chin upward. She nodded and followed them out. Silence filled the room.

They would have killed Fasé. They would have killed Aiz.

I took a deep breath and counted to ten, then turned around.

The younger two members of the Pedalion wore identical looks of horror, while Rotem and Sou looked grim but unsurprised.

"You knew. You fucking knew. Adora knew. All that time in the negotiations—"

"Your Majesty—"

"No." I sliced a hand through the air, cutting off Rotem's protest. "I should kill the lot of you. Burn this place to the ground and let Fasé start over on your ashes."

"Your Majesty, we did not know." Delphine stood and I held a hand out behind me, knowing that my BodyGuards had moved when she did. "I understand how little difference that makes. We were still complicit for not asking. We will agree to whatever demands the Shen require to put this right."

"You don't have the authority to do that!" Sou protested.

"You've lost whatever authority you had with these lies!" Yadira joined Delphine. "This Pedalion is broken and done. As it was foretold. We were warned and you decided to ignore that warning. We will have to find a better way forward." She held her hand out. "Fasé, what would you have us do?"

"Me?"

"Yadira, you cannot—"

"I can and I will," she snapped at Rotem. "You had your chance to save us from disaster. The Council of Eyes warned us and you did nothing because it didn't serve your ego to bend to change. Therefore we will decide. You can either join us or get out of the way." She turned, held her hand out again. "Fasé, help us save our people."

Fasé glanced my way, suddenly looking very young and uncertain, and I offered up a smile. She gave a jerky nod and rose, taking

Yadira's hand. "I will have to think on this, but I agree we must move forward not only for Faria but for our siblings. The Shen are the ones who have been wounded in this. I will speak with them, if they will hear me."

"Well, I think that's quite enough excitement for the moment." I pushed away from the table. "We can reconvene this evening to discuss things in detail. Fasé, do you want to stay here or come back to the ship with me?"

"I'll go with you," she said, squeezing Yadira's hand before heading out of the room, her cousins trailing behind her.

I let the others go ahead of me, meeting Emmory, Gita, and Hao at the doorway.

"Little sister, you just engineered the coup of the century without firing a shot," Hao murmured.

"I didn't do it. They did." I looked back at the Farians one last time before I walked away. "And the cost of it may have been too high. Let's just hope it doesn't turn into a shit-show."

I wanted to go straight to Aiz and Mia's quarters on board the ship, but instead found myself in the captain's ready room trying to debrief Admiral Hassan and Alice.

Johar's reply to my ping was that things were as well as could be expected.

Sybil spoke with Fasé quietly in the corner. The seers hadn't joined in the deliberations, but Sybil had met us on the way to the *Hailimi* and didn't seem the least bit surprised by the quick run-down Fasé had shared with her.

"Hail?"

I looked back at the screen, smiling as Alice handed off her daughter—the new official heir to the throne—to someone out of the camera frame. "Sorry, what?"

"I said it seemed to go as well as it could?"

"Well, no one killed anyone else so, yeah." I shrugged. "I wasn't expecting the kind of defection that Yadira and Delphine pulled off, and I'm not convinced that either the Farian Hiervet or Rotem and Sou will take this lying down. I don't trust them, Alice." The last bit was soft enough that it wouldn't carry across the room.

"Do what you think is necessary. Bring home Farians and Shen and whoever needs a place." She pressed her palms together and touched them to her heart, lips, and eyes. "Indrana has the room and the resources. We are happy to share."

I knew it wasn't quite that easy, but I trusted her to figure out a way to make it happen if we needed it. "I doubt it will come to that, but I appreciate your backing on the matter."

"Is there any further news about the Hiervet?"

"No." I shook my head. "It's the next thing on the list, though. I don't know how the rest of the negotiations will go. We'll have to wait and see what happens. Gods willing it won't end in bloodshed."

"Don't tempt them."

"Too late for that," I replied with a snort of bitter laughter. "I'll talk to you later, Alice."

"Take care of yourself, Hail."

The screen on the wall went black and I shared a look with Inana.

"You know Caterina is going to scream if you bring several million aliens back to Indrana."

"Caterina would probably be okay with it, surprisingly," I replied, rubbing at the back of my neck. "Prime Minister Tesla? She'll scream. But let her. If it's what needs to happen. If the Shen truly don't have to be on Faria to come back, then what would be the point of them staying here, surrounded by eons of bad blood?" I shook my head and glanced at Fasé. "While the Farians struggle to rebuild themselves into something new? That's a recipe for disaster."

"That seems to be the road we're on at the moment," Hao said as he joined us. "What's the plan?"

"I'm supposed to have a plan for this, too?"

Hao laughed. "You always have a plan. It might be shifting and changing faster than the asteroids around Santa Pirata, but somewhere in that brain of yours is a plan." He tipped his head to the corner of the room.

"I thought you and Dailun were leaving?"

"Not quite yet. Things are chaotic enough around here I figured we should stick around. You might want to go have a word with Fasé before she has a complete meltdown."

I stared at him and Hao lifted a shoulder. "Yeah, I know. She and I get along like matter and antimatter. However, that expression is what someone on the verge of losing it looks like. There's a big difference between leading a rebellion and suddenly being asked to run the whole government."

"Tell me about it," I muttered.

Hao flashed me a grin. "I may not like Fasé, but she wasn't expecting this, and weird fucking reincarnations aside, she still acts like a twenty-three-year-old at times. This will break her if you don't help, and losing her right now could destabilize everything."

Of all the things I'd learned in my time out in the black, the major one was that when Hao dispensed advice, it was best to listen to him. I crossed the room to where Sybil and Fasé sat.

"You never came to see me," I said by way of greeting to Sybil.

"I did not, my apologies, Your Majesty."

"There's a lot you're not telling me, isn't there?"

She smiled. "There is a lot you haven't asked."

"Yadira said the council saw the fracturing of the Pedalion. That you warned them of it."

"We did."

"Are you going to tell me what the warning was?"

"I don't need to," Sybil replied with a shrug. "You just saw it. The Pedalion thought themselves invincible and acted as such. It was their downfall."

I had what felt like a million more questions for the future-seer, but the miserable look on Fasé's face pushed me to put them aside. "I'd like to talk to Fasé alone, if you don't mind."

"Of course, Your Majesty. I will meet you where they are holding Adora when you are finished."

I watched her walk away, my stomach rolling. It was stupid of me to even wonder how she knew I'd planned to speak with Adora next, but my brain insisted on doing it anyway. I took the seat Sybil vacated. Fasé immediately threw herself into my arms, her sob shaking us both.

"It's all right." I wrapped my arms around her.

"I am not prepared for this," she whispered. "Majesty, what have I done?"

"Set your people on a better path, one that leads to peace."

"At what cost?"

"I can't answer that. You know as well as I do, Fasé, our choices lead us in unexpected directions. The better question is what are you going to do with this opportunity?"

She lifted her head. "What do you mean?"

I wiped the tears from her face. "Are you going to continue to think of your people and make the best choices you can for them? Are you going to rise up to this challenge and continue to be the leader I've seen you be? Or will you wallow around because things didn't turn out exactly how you imagined they would?"

Fasé stared at me for a long moment of stunned silence and then laughed. The sound rang through the room, stopping the conversations around us as everyone turned to look.

"Oh, Hail." Fasé shook her head, still laughing. "You've come so far from when we first met."

"So have you." I hugged her back, then pulled away to look at her face. "I am so proud of you, Fasé Terass. You are going to do great things for your people. I don't have to see the future to be able to tell you that."

13

"Majesty, where are we going?" To Emmory's credit he didn't ask the question until we were headed back down the ramp into the night air.

"You and I are going to have a conversation with Adora."

"Hail." My name was barely a breath of air. The wind snatched it and carried it away.

"It'll be all right. Sybil's meeting us there."

"I am, somewhat ironically, more worried about what you might do than for your safety." Emmory didn't slow as he voiced the concern, but kept his steps measured with mine.

I'd been surprised that he hadn't even fussed when I'd tapped his arm and tipped my head toward the door earlier, or that he'd simply passed instructions over to Gita that we were leaving the ship.

It seemed such a far cry from the Tracker I'd first met, the one who'd threatened me over his brother's memory, who'd chastised me about punching an assassin. Then I remembered this was also the same man who'd turned around and given me a gun.

"We've come a long way, haven't we, Emmy?"

He glanced at me and smiled. "We have, Majesty."

"I promise I'll behave myself. I want to see if Adora already knows what happened today."

"You think someone's feeding her information?"

"I'd bet the empire on it."

"I don't think you're allowed to do that, empress or not."

Our humor bled off as we met the guards on the path. They murmured a greeting at my regal nod and moved to the side without questioning where we were headed.

"That's an interesting turn of events," I murmured.

"Do you know where you're going?"

"Sybil sent me directions," I replied. No one stopped us as we strode into the building, through the sharp corridors, and down into the basement. My anger grew in the silence and I had an irrational urge to burn all of this to the ground. The Farians, the Hiervet, all they'd done was cause misery and suffering.

Not all of them, Hail. The normally acerbic voice in my head was gentle this time. I knew it was right—about the Farians at least. They weren't to blame for the folly of their leadership, and hurting them wouldn't punish the people truly at fault.

"Star of Indrana." Sybil bowed formally, the nervous guard on her left following a half second behind. I blinked and lifted an eyebrow upward. I was glad that Sybil's eyes were on the floor, because I realized I'd seen the young Farian at the meeting of Fasé's rebels.

That was the moment when it sank in that no matter what the Pedalion wanted, Fasé had managed to wrest control of the people away from them. She had done it right under their noses. Her rebellion had spread from every corner of Faria and even into my empire. The news of the true identity of the gods had solidified her position, but the foundation was already in place and there was nothing that could shake that now.

They would follow wherever she chose to lead.

And she'll follow you, Hail. The whole of Faria at your beck and call. That's power.

I shook off the slightly menacing voice in my head as the guard unlocked what I assumed was a cell door and then backed away with a second bow. They'd apparently moved Adora from medical to someplace a little more secure.

"You are safe within," Sybil said. "Adora cannot use her energy inside the cell."

I wondered briefly if I could and shared a look with Emmory as we passed over the threshold. Adora didn't seem any worse for wear since I'd seen her last despite the change in accommodations. Her hair was bound back from her face and she was dressed in a dark gray outfit that reminded me of the clothes Fasé had worn in the days after saving Emmory.

The juxtaposition of these two women hit me like a throat punch. Fasé had risked everything to save Emmory—not for me, but for Zin, for the love she could feel stretching and breaking between them as Emmory had died on the floor of Hao's ship.

Adora had sacrificed her family in pursuit of power, and though I tried to remind myself that she'd been as fooled as the other Farians about the nature of the Farian Hiervet, it still wasn't enough to excuse everything else she'd done.

Like paying Jamison to attack us on Earth. I fisted my hands at the reminder, earning a quick, sideways glance from Emmory.

"If it isn't the great traitor and the great failure," Adora said. "To what do I owe this dubious visit?"

"Good morning, Adora." Sybil seemed unbothered by the greeting and I saw the spark of angry fire in Adora's platinum eyes. "I have betrayed no one. I have merely shared the knowledge I have."

Adora snorted in reply and flicked her eyes toward me. "Come to gloat over your supposed victory, Star of Indrana? Or has someone else died?"

"Your anger is misplaced. The Farian Hiervet are the ones who have lied to you and used your people for all these years." I didn't know where my calm response came from but it only served to infuriate Adora further.

"You are a reckless child," Adora said, the hatred plain on her face. "Meddling in things you don't understand. Our gods showed me their true faces a very long time ago. I was chosen to see them because of my faith."

Bugger me. I froze, and fought to keep the expression on my face neutral.

"They told you?"

"Of course they did. I alone was chosen because they knew I could bear the knowledge. You think that just because you can see the future you understand it?" Adora's smile at Sybil's question was cruel. "You don't understand anything about what we're building."

"Then why the performance in the Pedalion chamber—oh." I bit back the curse that wanted to follow my realization into the air. "The others didn't know what Thyra and the others truly looked like."

"Doubt is good for the soul," Adora chirped.

"It didn't work," I replied. "Your followers aren't louder than those who want out from under the Farian Hiervet's reign. There will be peace between the Farians and the Shen no matter what you do."

"I very much doubt that, given my brother's reaction to today's news."

One of the problems with thinking you had control of a situation was overconfidence, and I kept from smiling as Adora gave me more information than she'd probably intended.

"Someone is feeding her information, isn't that interesting?" I subvocalized to Emmory without looking in his direction.

"You were right, Majesty. We know none of our people would have told her."

"Which means it was one of the Pedalion, or Thyra."

"Priam seems more likely, given how cozy you said they were before."

"It doesn't surprise me that you knew of that, too," I said aloud to Adora. "You sent your own family to their deaths."

"My family did not understand the power they were walking away from, and worse, they were trying to oppose our evolution. They deserve everything they've gotten and more."

"We're done here." I turned on my heel and left the cell, the sound of Adora's mocking laughter trailing behind me.

As soon as the door closed and we were far enough away from it, I muttered a stream of curses bad enough to blister the air around me. Emmory stayed quiet. Sybil, thankfully, probably didn't recognize them and any translations would have been gibberish.

The Svatir were nonviolent, but they had some incredible curse words.

"Better, Majesty?"

"Not really." I chose my next words with a great deal of precision. "Sybil, can you take us to see the Farian Hiervet?"

"I cannot, Majesty," she replied even as Emmory glared at me. "We don't have access to Etrelia, but I could call for them."

"Do it. We'll met them in the Pedalion chamber." I glanced at my stone-faced *Ekam*. "It'll give Emmory a chance to get some more BodyGuards over here."

If anything it was far more likely the Farian Hiervet were going to need protection from me than the other way around.

I was leaning against the solid white surface of the Pedalion table when Thyra and the others appeared in the center of the room. My BodyGuards stiffened but didn't move between us, and I straightened slowly to look down at Thyra.

Being on the dais gave me the height I wanted, even if it was a mostly superficial advantage.

"Your Majesty, Sybil said you wanted to speak."

"Yes, I want to know how you are going to make this right."

"Make what right?" Thyra moved toward me, Priam and Adaran following, and I got the sudden sense of a pack of predators homing in on a kill.

I wasn't the only one who'd noticed. All six of my BodyGuards put their hands on their weapons and in a heartbeat I was faced with a choice—back down, or potentially make this situation even worse than it was.

I jumped from the dais with as much casualness as I could feign, the move putting me closer to Emmory than Thyra, and I closed the distance even more by turning my back on her and strolling toward him.

Hao was probably the only other person alive I trusted enough to put my back to a killer and know that I wouldn't end up dead.

"I don't have a lot of time to bounce words back and forth with you, Thyra. You murdered people. Shen and Farian alike. Now that this information has come to light, surely you don't think the Shen will just walk away without some justice."

"Funny that you would speak of justice, Your Majesty," she replied as I turned back to face her. Priam was watching me again, those wide black eyes fixed on me, and something that looked very much like hatred lurked under the surface of his gaze.

"I don't see anyone laughing."

"We dispensed justice as the Farians asked us to do. We protected our children from those who would do them harm. You have done the same, yet I don't see anyone calling you a murderer."

"You'd be surprised," I murmured. "However, you dispensed justice under the pretext of a lie, Thyra. A lie the Shen were trying to expose. It is different."

"It is no different!" The exclamation from Priam startled everyone in the room, and the self-control of my Guards was likely the only reason he didn't get shot. "Why are you defending those monsters when you should be helping us?"

"Priam!" Thyra said something else in their sharp language and after a last look at me, he vanished.

Thyra turned back to me, folding her limbs together and bowing. "I am sorry for his outburst, Your Majesty. This has been difficult for him."

"For him?"

"To see what they have done to you. The Shen are unpredictable things." She waved a limb in the air. "We know your time with them was painful and carried with it a great amount of grief. I wish you would let us help you."

"I'm fine." This time I couldn't back away, couldn't reach back for Emmory to anchor myself against the sudden sick heat in my throat as the memory of Sparkos came roaring back.

"You don't need to lie to me, Your Majesty. I know you are not well. You are not the Star who should have come to us." Her voice was soothing. "I wish only to help."

I suddenly, desperately, wanted to let her.

"Hail."

I froze at Emmory's voice over our private com; my muscles tensed as I prepared to take a step toward Thyra. "I am fine," I repeated, though my voice was too soft to be a proper declaration. "I do not want your help."

Thyra's black eyes flicked briefly to Emmory before they returned to me and she smiled. It was a patient, awful expression that made my skin crawl. "I see. Thank you, Your Majesty, this has been most informative."

She and Adaran both disappeared.

"What the fuck was that?" I asked, and rubbed my shaking hands over my face with a second muttered curse.

It was late evening by the time I made it to Aiz and Mia's quarters on board my ship. Emmory hadn't said a word as I'd gone straight to my quarters and drunk two shots of whiskey, probably because I'd spilled at least half of it in the process, before heading back out again and through the *Hailimi*'s corridors.

The interaction with Adora and then with Thyra kept replaying in my head. It bounced around with such force that it made my head ache. The venom in Adora's voice wasn't anything new, but the hypnotic rhythm of Thyra's that had almost convinced me to walk toward her shook me to my core.

Every instinct I had was now screaming at me to run.

Talos answered the door and the echoes of grief on his face made my own chest hurt in response as I shoved aside everything else. The front room was packed with people, all of them standing with heads bowed and crossed hands pressed over their mouths.

"How are you, my friend?" I offered my hand, relieved when he took it and let me pull him into a hug. The harsh words I'd thrown at him on Sparkos when raging in my own grief came back to haunt me. I'd accused him of having a family to save, only to find out now that wasn't true.

I could imagine the pain all too vividly.

"Torn between grief and rage." He released me and pressed his forehead to mine for just a moment. "I grieved for my family a long time ago, Hail, but the wound feels—"

"New?"

"We have lost hope. That last flicker that our loved ones would return to us is gone. The last possibility that there would be peace with the Farians and we could stop this endless war is shattered like our hearts. It's all gone."

Fear joined the hurt. "Talos, the Pedalion—"

He stopped me with a shake of his head. "You will need to speak with the *Thínos* about this, Hail, not me. But if you have any care for them at all, I will ask you to wait. Now is the time for grief."

"May I speak to them?"

"I will ask."

"Majesty," Emmory murmured from behind me in the hallway. "If the Shen go back to war over this, we are going to be caught right in the middle."

"Tell me about it," I replied. "Wait here."

Emmory didn't protest out loud, but I felt his sudden tension and reached out to touch his arm. "I'll be all right, Emmy, I promise."

"It's not you I'm worried about, Hail."

"I know, but you can't come with me." I left him in the hall, the door sliding shut between us.

There was a solemn stillness in the air. The Shen reached their hands out, murmuring *"Astéri"* as I passed. Their grief coated my tongue like ash, so thick I could taste it with the heat of anger just beyond. Poorly banked coals that would flare to life if I wasn't very careful. I didn't blame them; I couldn't. I was feeling that same anger myself and if it had been my family sent to die like this, I would— I had already waged a war over that very same thing.

Here on the edge of peace, the slightest misstep would cause a war like no one had ever seen.

Mia met me at the door of her room, eyes reddened from tears. "Hail."

"I am so sorry," I whispered, everything else between us falling away in that moment. I wrapped my arms around her and pressed my lips to her temple as she clung to me. "Mia, if I had known—"

"There is nothing you could have done to save him. He was dead the moment the assassin sent his soul back to those butchers." The fury in her words was a snarling thing even as she leaned into me, seeking comfort and support. "In all the things I have seen, never was there a single hint of this."

When I opened my mouth to reassure her, the iron tang of blood hit me like a slap.

"Where is Aiz?"

She turned her head toward the bathroom. "He will not stop. I tried, Hail. His grief and rage will eat him alive."

"Can I?" The open-ended question hung in the air, whispered against Mia's hair, and she nodded once.

"He may kill you."

"You'll bring me back." I slipped out of Mia's arms, ignoring the sudden ache her absence brought, and approached the bathroom, my stomach twisting into knots.

14

Aiz sat on the floor of the open shower with his back to the door, some strange concession to keep the blood contained into a space easily cleaned.

"Go away, Hail."

I will never, for the rest of my life, forget the way his voice sounded. I knew that soul-rending grief. Had felt it too many times breaking my heart to pieces. The depth of his pain was as sharp as the knife he drove relentlessly into his forearm. The wound fountained blood, then closed, and then he did it all over again.

"We are friends, are we not, Aiz Cevalla?"

"What kind of question is that?" He hesitated for just a second before driving the knife into his skin again.

"An honest one. Answer it."

"When I lie to myself it looks like the possibility of a friendship with you."

I couldn't stop the smile. "Only the possibility?"

"I learned too long ago that you humans live such brief lives. The grief of having your friendship and losing it in the blink of an eye can rip a heart apart. I stopped caring about mortals a long time ago."

"Liar. You were there for me on Sparkos when I lost myself. Even though the circumstances had spiraled out of your control, you thought of me." I knelt behind him, reached a hand out, and pressed it flat on his back, feeling the muscles stiffen at the contact. "I overheard you and Mia talking after I killed myself. I wasn't coherent enough at the time to realize how much my descent into madness bothered you or why, but something shifted that day and looking back I can see it. You chose to be my friend when I needed you, risk of grief and all."

I rested my forehead just above my hand. "You did not have to be gentle with me, Aiz, but you were. Even through all these long years, the cruelty of the universe has not snuffed out the spark of kindness in you I can see so clearly."

Another hesitation. Another wound, but with this one he wrenched the knife out and stabbed it back through his arm immediately.

"Hurting yourself won't bring them back," I whispered. "You didn't say the words to me, but they were hanging in the air between us."

"I could offer you solace because I knew your grief was false."

"Cowshit. It was real enough to me, and you would have said the same regardless."

There was a moment of silence and then Aiz let out a shuddering breath.

"Bad enough when they murdered him," he whispered. "When we realized they had somehow stolen his soul from Jibun it was like a knife in the chest. But there was always a hope we would rescue him someday."

"I'm sorry."

"I failed him." The heartbreak in his voice made my vision blur with tears.

"You did no such thing," I murmured, shifting closer, sliding my other hand over his bloody forearm before he could bring the knife down again. I steeled myself for the pain of the blade but it didn't come. "You have led your people to the peace he wanted."

"I haven't," he whispered. "We have no choice but to resume the fight for this horror."

"Aiz." My breath caught and I blinked back the tears, Adora's words ringing too loud in my ears. The pain seethed under his skin and rather than say the words I took what I could from him, clenching my teeth against the burning onslaught.

"Stop." Aiz turned his arm over, linking his fingers with mine. "This is not your pain to carry, Hail."

"You are my friend, Aiz, my crew." I grappled for the right words. All of them felt so weighty in my mouth. "I will carry all that pain and more if it means you don't have to. Let your rage go, Aiz, and let the grief take its place. Your sister and your people are also hurting. Be there for them."

"And then?"

I lifted my head from his back. I knew I couldn't tell him the Shen couldn't fight; even if I believed it the words would fall to the floor without being heard. I knew that rage all too well. So I said the only thing I could. "I will not force you to peace, but I also cannot fight this fight with you if that is where you choose to go."

Aiz sighed, but didn't speak.

"Just promise me that in the morning we can speak of it before you decide?" I whispered. "That is all I will ask of you."

"There is nothing you can say to me that will make this better."

"Not to make it better. To give you a way forward past this endless cycle of pain and death. I know you want vengeance. All I can say is I've been down that road and the victory tastes like ashes in your mouth. Trust me, Aiz, as your friend and for the sake of your people, please, don't commit to war when we are so close to peace."

His exhale was quiet, just a breath of air almost drowned out by the clattering of the knife to the floor. "After everything I have done to you. I owe you that much, don't I?"

He did, but it felt shitty to admit it out loud so I gave him an awkward hug and then got to my feet, stepping out of the way so Mia could rush forward and wrap her arms around Aiz after he stood.

I pulled my boots off on a clean patch of floor before I headed back through the Shen. Talos met me at the door and opened it. I met Emmory's worried gaze and offered up a soft smile.

"Hail?" Aiz's call floated on the air.

I turned to look at him. The Shen had lifted their heads and watched us with their hands still pressed to their mouths, their mourning ritual halted in favor of this moment.

"Yes?"

"Thank you, Star of Indrana." Aiz folded his hands together, touching them to his heart, lips, and forehead before he bowed to me. "It has been an unexpected honor to call you a friend."

I set my boots down at Emmory's feet so I could echo the gesture. "It has and I hope it continues, Aiz Cevalla. I will see you in the morning." I stepped through the doorway and it closed behind me.

"Are you all right, Hail?"

"It's not my blood." I swallowed down the pain and headed down the corridor. "I need a shower."

I caught myself twice mumbling the words to the Aparadha Stotram as I washed Aiz's blood from my hands and hair. Now that the moment was over, the adrenaline dump had left me shaky and nauseated.

Stasia handed me clean clothes and shook her head at my whispered "I'm sorry."

"It's fine, Majesty. It'll clean."

I choked down the smartass comment about the benefits of black clothing and instead dressed in the soft dark pants and tank top.

Hao was in the main room, leaning against my desk and talking to Gita. Their fingers were intertwined and there was a look in Hao's eyes I hadn't seen in a very long time.

I closed my eyes against the sudden well of emotion, my heart feeling like it was going to burst. The thought that my brother— my stubborn, ridiculous brother—might have found love again after the loss of Gy filled me with comfort. He'd lost so much, some of it because of me, and I wanted to see him happy again.

I had the power to do it, at least in some manner. To build a future of peace and safety for those I loved and those who depended on me. I couldn't fail that fragile, budding promise trying to find the sunlight.

They lapsed into silence when I emerged from the bathroom.

"You're sitting on a drive about to go critical, little sister," Hao said by way of greeting.

"Tell me something I don't know." I whispered a silent prayer of thanks for the fact that someone had stocked the liquor cabinet in my quarters before Admiral Hassan had left Indrana. At this rate I wasn't going to have any left when we headed home. *"Hai Ram,"* I muttered, and poured myself another glass of Calasian whiskey. I knocked half of it back without turning around.

"What's the plan?"

"If this blows up in our faces?" I stared at the whiskey swirling in my glass. "We'll have to cut and run." I hated the words coming out of my mouth. Hated even more that there was no way around them. I had one ship and no way to stop the Shen if they renewed hostilities with the Farians.

Renewed hostilities, Hail? Really? Don't you sound like a noble now. Is that what you can call a conflict that's going to destroy two civilizations and potentially ruin humanity in the process?

The sharp-tongued voice burst back into my head with a vengeance and I leaned on the counter, squeezing my eyes shut at the wave of terror that accompanied the words. It mixed with the terrifying lure of Thyra's voice from earlier and sat like acid in my throat.

"I talked to Rai a little bit ago." Hao didn't seem to notice my moment of panic. Or maybe he did and figured the change of subject would help. That was actually a very Hao thing to do.

I paused in the act of pouring a second drink and stared at him over my shoulder. "Go on."

Hao smiled. "There's some understandable hesitation about

preparing for an unknown threat, especially since Rai can't tell anyone the information is coming from you."

"Like it would make any difference," I replied with a laugh, and finished my pour.

"It would, Hail. Your word has weight and not in the 'I'm Empress of Indrana' fashion. Ow."

I turned to see him rubbing the back of his head. Gita was giving him a flat look, and I had to hide my smile behind my glass. Their behavior settled me, as strange as it was. This interaction was comforting.

This was what I was saving.

"Let's hope we don't have to use them," I said, sinking into the chair at the desk. "If we can't run them off with this plan of yours and the fighting reaches that far, we are in the deepest kind of shit."

"Works for me," Hao replied. "Your mysterious army of Hiervet isn't the pressing issue right now anyway, is it? The fact that the Shen are going to go to war with the Farians as soon as Aiz finishes"—he waved a hand—"whatever it was that was going on in his rooms."

"He was putting a knife through his arm. Repeatedly."

Hao sucked air in from between his teeth. "The more I learn about immortality the less I think it's a good idea."

"Hao." Gita's warning was quiet and I looked between my *Dve* and my brother. There was something more there I was missing, but neither seemed inclined to share.

"He's right." I took a sip of my drink and scratched at my scalp. "Shiva, I'm tired. Aiz promised to listen to me in the morning before he did anything. I've got one chance to convince him not to go to war."

"You don't think the fact that Yadira and Delphine promised anything they wanted in exchange will be enough?" Gita asked.

"I don't know. I didn't tell him," I admitted. "It wasn't the right time. Do you think if Aiz asks for his sister's head, or Thyra's, that they'll still say yes?"

"Would you back him if he did?"

I took another drink as I considered Hao's question. "Adora doesn't have it in her to lead a rebellion. She's spent her whole life with everything handed to her. Without the power of the Pedalion behind her she's not much of a threat, plus she's locked up. But Thyra?" I shook my head, thinking again of her hypnotic voice. "Right now I'd take her head in a moment without Aiz even asking for it."

"Wise decision, *sha zhu*."

"I should have just killed them," I muttered, knowing it would get a reaction from Gita. "No more gods. No more Hiervet bearing down on us."

"You should have, but it doesn't do you any good to second-guess yourself now." She surprised me with her agreement and I realized that the scene in the Pedalion chamber had shaken my BodyGuards as much as it had me. "We didn't have an assurance that killing them would have prevented the Hiervet's impending arrival. You did what you thought was right at the time."

"Besides," Hao replied. "You'd have the entire Farian race pissed at you, which I know maybe doesn't scare you—"

I stuck my tongue out at him and he grinned.

"Gita's right. It's too late to second-guess your choices. You've never been one to do that, don't start now."

"Yes, sir, Captain, sir."

Hao's hand twitched like he was about to smack me, but he glanced Gita's way and sighed.

I offered up the remainder of my whiskey as an apology and got to my feet when he took it. "I think that's all the damage we can do today. I am going to bed to try to get some sleep before tomorrow."

"If it works out, Dailun and I will be heading to speak with the Svatir as soon as possible afterward." Hao pressed a kiss to my cheek. "All joking aside, little sister, you did good today. I'm proud of you."

I told myself the tears were from my exhaustion, but thankfully Gita and Hao left me alone without another word.

"Your Majesty? The Pedalion, what remains of it anyway, are here to speak with you."

I glanced up at Kisah as I continued picking over the remains of my breakfast the next morning. "Delphine and Yadira?"

"Yes, ma'am, just them."

"Well, I did enough damage here. You can report back to Emmory that I ate my breakfast."

A blush appeared high on her cheeks. "We don't report on your eating habits, ma'am."

"My ass you don't. Emmory's probably got a log."

"Not an official one," he said from the doorway, a hint of a smile on his mouth. "But we do appreciate it when you make our jobs easier."

I grabbed the last idli and shoved it into my mouth without breaking eye contact with my *Ekam*. I chewed and swallowed as I stood. "Let it never be said I don't put in the effort to make your life easier, Emmy."

That got a full smile out of him.

We headed down to the cargo bay. Gita and Johar waited by the door with Zin and Hao.

"Hail, wait." Hao reached out and brushed a crumb of idli off my face. "Okay, now you're presentable."

The moment was enough to break the heavy band around my chest, and I squeezed Hao's hand in silent thanks and continued through the door.

Sybil was waiting with Yadira and Delphine; all three were dressed in white, gloves covering their hands. "Star of Indrana, Your Majesty." They bowed as a unit, but then Yadira stepped forward. "We come to ask for your protection."

"From whom?"

"Us, I suspect."

I glanced behind me. Neither Emmory nor Gita had jolted at the sound of Aiz's voice. He stood just inside the doorway of the cargo bay—Mia on one side of him and Fasé on the other.

That was an interesting twist. I studied the trio for a moment. They were dressed in black, the cut of the clothing leaning more toward Indranan than Farian or Shen make, and I wondered if Stasia had had a hand in this sudden change of uniform.

"I hope not, Aiz Cevalla." Yadira shook her head. "My sister and I did not know of your father's fate. That horrific secret was kept from us. We speak of the Hiervet. The Star is the only one who can see them for what they really are."

Not the only one, I thought, remembering Johar's description when we'd first met the Farian Hiervet.

"They are coming for us and they must be stopped," Sybil said.

"It would seem," I said carefully, "that the more pressing matter right this second is if we are going to end up back in the middle of a war between the Farians and the Shen." I gestured at Aiz and the trio crossed the room to us. "That is nothing I can help you with, Yadira. The choice belongs to them."

Fasé folded her hands at her waist. Her hands were ungloved. "My alliance with the Shen stands, sisters. If they go to war with you, so do we."

"We do not want war." Delphine shook her head. "Name your price, Aiz. Tell us what it will cost to end this conflict and we will pay it."

"Even if I asked for the heads of your gods and the Pedalion?"

My gut twisted at his quiet response, but I kept my face impassive. This was not my fight, not yet, and I knew that the value of silence sometimes could mean the difference between a negotiation succeeding and one ending in fire.

"Even then," Yadira agreed. "Our lives are a small price to pay for the peace and safety of billions."

"I doubt Rotem would agree." Mia's quiet voice carried a cutting edge, but Yadira didn't flinch.

"He has lost the right to make that choice. He will do as he is told. The Pedalion is broken. It was avoidable, but he and the others chose to participate in this horror. They chose to ignore the words of warning from the Eyes. So now we stand here in the Pedalion's place. If you need lives for this peace—his and ours—they are yours."

Aiz was quiet for a long moment. The silence filled the room. No one moved.

"No," he said, shaking his head, and my heart sank until he continued. "No more deaths. It won't bring my father back. It won't ease the pain of all the Shen who are grieving right now for the loss of their loved ones. More death won't change anything, Yadira. We both know this." He took a step forward and held out his hand. "Remove your glove, take my hand, and let us lay this whole mess to rest."

"You will let it go? Just like that?"

Aiz smiled, but the grief clung to his brown eyes as he glanced at Fasé. "A wise woman once said to me: The first step of anything requires little more than a willingness to take it. One person, willing to lay down their grudges and hatred. Willing to be the better person for the sake of those under their care." He bowed his head to Yadira and Delphine. "We have been at odds, but now is the time for peace. It is no small irony that a Farian and a gunrunner both taught me that."

"Former gunrunner," I murmured.

Yadira peeled off her glove and took Aiz's hand. "Peace starts here. It starts with us."

Aiz looked to the others. "Mia? Fasé?"

Fasé joined them, clasping Yadira's hand and then Delphine's. Mia hung back for just a moment but finally she also stepped forward and took the Farians' hands.

She did not look at me and my heart ached. The tentative truce we'd had over the death of her father was apparently over.

"Majesty?" Emmory's hand was on my elbow.

"I'm all right," I lied. Mia had moved to Aiz's side and was speaking quietly to Sybil. "Well, that went better than expected."

"Tell me about it." He was looking at me and I prayed he wouldn't press me on my lie.

"Makes you nervous, doesn't it?"

"Extremely," he replied.

I grinned and reached around to pat his arm. "Tell everyone to stand down. I think we're okay here for the moment."

"Yes, Majesty."

Aiz approached us, a smile peeking through his beard. "You've got your peace. Happy?"

"It's your peace. You were supposed to talk to me first," I replied.

"I would have," he said. "However, Fasé came to see us and told me what happened after we left the room yesterday. Besides, you'd already said what I needed to hear."

"I did?"

"You've been telling me all this time," he said. "I was just too caught up in myself to hear it."

"We humans call that having your head stuck up your ass." I winked. "It happens to the best of us."

Aiz chuckled, but then he sobered. "Who knows what the coming days will bring, Hail. Saying we're committing to peace may seem to be the hardest step, but the reality is there are so many pitfalls."

"I have faith in you." I pressed a hand to his chest. "Besides, what would I do if you weren't all on my side to face this bigger threat?"

"So we make peace just to go back to war?" He laughed.

"Apparently."

"You lead a strange life, Hail."

"I want a nap when this is all done, Aiz Cevalla. Someone else can save the galaxy next time."

"Let me know how that works for you."

to do about it, but this whole thing is making me want to crawl out of my fucking skin. As dramatic as it sounds, if we leave now we risk dooming the whole galaxy."

"And that's what Caterina doesn't understand. That we are talking about the survival of not just the empire but the whole galaxy. Caspel does, but you and I know he can't put the safety of the empire aside. You can—at least in appearance. We can focus on this problem." He pointed at the floor between us.

I felt my lips twitch and fought to hold in the smile. "Are you suggesting I mutiny against the council's desire?"

"You've technically already done that, Majesty. I'm suggesting that you stick it out and stop second-guessing your decisions. You know something is coming. We don't need proof to trust you, and no one will get through us."

I smiled now. "I don't know what I would do without you, Emmory, truly."

"Am I interrupting?"

I looked away from him to Mia, trying to ignore the sudden jerk of my heart. "Not at all, please come in."

"Majesty," Emmory murmured, and gave Mia a nod as he headed for the door.

"I am sorry I snapped at you. You did not deserve it."

I held my hands out without hesitation as relief flooded through me. "I am sorry. It was a thoughtless thing to say. I forget, sometimes, that you are Shen."

"I am also human." Mia crossed to me, though she stopped in front of me and dropped her hands, the tips of her fingers just brushing mine. "I should not forget that. I have been wallowing and I'm sorry for this also."

"For what?" I leaned back against the wall and forced the words out. All the while lying to myself that I could survive on the memory of her.

"For being useless."

121

I felt my mouth drop open.

"I am sorry I can't provide you with the information you need. I should have known about what Thyra and the others did to my father. I should have looked harder and—"

"I am starting to think that Aiz hit me a little too hard at some point and this is all one long strange dream," I said, pushing away from the wall. "It's the only thing that could account for you thinking that your value lies solely in your ability to see the future."

"I won't fight and now I can't see. What good am I?"

"Mia." I cupped her face, stunned by the pain I could feel rolling just under the surface, and I had to step down hard on the urge to take it from her. "Will you listen to me when I tell you that you are one of the smartest women I have ever met? One of the bravest and most cunning? I could spend a lifetime telling you all the ways I have watched you take care of your people and still run out of time before I ran out of words." I leaned down and saw her gray eyes fill with tears before I pressed my lips to hers.

"It's not about the future or anything else. You matter to me. I know we don't get forever, I just want you for as long as you're willing to stay."

I felt her breath catch on the half sob, half laugh before she threw her arms around my neck and kissed me back.

"It's all right," I murmured against her ear after we separated. "I don't need to know the future to make the right choices."

"You would say that," Mia said with a laugh. "Hail, I—"

I'd never seen her have a vision, but I somehow knew immediately it was happening when she stiffened in my arms. Her fingers locked on my shirt, giving me just enough time to catch her before she went limp and slid to the floor.

"Emmory!" I was dimly aware of the sound of feet as I lowered Mia, cradling the back of her head with one hand. Images flashed in front of my eyes, of a Farian Hiervet and Adora. I saw their escape and heard my own voice issue the order to fire. I saw the chaos that followed. The accusations from the shattered Pedalion. The war with the Farians both here and in Indrana because of the murder of their gods.

Someone pulled me away and I fought against their hold before Emmory's voice cut through the panic.

"Hail, talk to me." Emmory was on a knee at my side. Aiz was opposite, cradling his sister's face in his hands.

"A vision. Aiz, is she all right?"

"She'll be fine." Aiz helped Mia sit up.

I reached a hand out, fingers linking with hers, and the world whited out again.

Mia lay alone in a circle of light upon an operating table. There was blood on her face, her sightless eyes clouded over with the haze of death.

My stomach twisted at the carnage of what looked like an autopsy and the Hiervet who stood behind the table, limbs folded behind its back.

"Failure." The tsking sound was entirely too human and they turned their head to look at me.

A searing pain cut through my chest and Thyra smiled at me as she ripped her limb free. My heart beat a painful tattoo against the inside of my ribs and I coughed, blood flying into the air, spattering over her grinning face.

There was a second pain as she impaled me again and the last thing I heard was the sharp tone of my own smati *flatlining in my head.*

"Hail?"

"I'm fine." I reached up and patted Emmory's shoulder awkwardly, the images and words bouncing around in my head like a wicked hangover. "Help me up." I glanced Mia's way but she was leaning against Aiz as she got to her feet. "I need to talk to Yadira."

"Majesty!" Gita skidded to a halt just inside the doorway. "Yadira and Thyra are here to see you."

"Give me a moment," I murmured to Emmory when the room spun, and felt his grip on me tighten in response. "Escort them to the bridge, Gita. Have Fasé go with you."

"Majesty, why are they here?" Emmory asked.

"Because Adora escaped and took one of the Farian Hiervet, I think it was Priam, with her." I said the words at the same time as Mia and watched as Aiz whipped his gaze to me in shock. "I happened to be touching her when the vision came, I'm assuming that's why I could see it."

"I'm relieved to hear that," he said. "I'm not sure the universe would survive you being able to see the future."

I straightened, sharing a nod with Emmory as he released me, and smoothed both hands down the front of my black uniform shirt before heading for the door. "Take Mia back to your rooms, Aiz. I'll call if I need you."

Despite my bravado, my mind was spinning. I'd seen the choices open to me—let Adora escape with Priam or fire on their ships and kill them. Both events had played themselves out in front of my eyes, the consequences of my decision.

Which one leads to Mia's death instead of mine?

I shook the thought away and felt the brief brush of Emmory's hand on my back, a silent question I answered with a forced smile. I suddenly understood with painful clarity the warning Fasé had given me. The risk of making choices because I knew what was coming rather than based on the information in front of me was all too real.

Untangling the images of me and Mia from the ones I'd seen of Adora, I rolled over the problem as we headed for the bridge. The more mercenary part of me wanted to go with the kill. Get the enemies out of the way as fast and efficiently as possible, as I'd been taught.

Don't leave live enemies behind you, Cressen.

I rubbed at my leg in reflex, the memory of Po-Sin's words accompanied by the phantom pain of my leg breaking.

But Priam was on board, and while I suspected that the Farian Hiervet had willingly gone with Adora there was no way to know for sure. Killing her meant killing him, and that was what brought things into sharp relief.

His death would fracture what was left of the Farian Hiervet even further. It would wipe out the support I already had from the remains of the Pedalion. It would destroy this tentative peace between the Shen and the Farians. It would remove any chance of an alliance that was necessary to face the oncoming storm.

I paused outside the door to the bridge.

"Majesty?"

"Emmory, I'm about to do something that may seem reckless. Do you trust me?"

"With my life, Majesty."

I squeezed his hand once, sent a quick prayer winging out toward any gods willing to listen to me, and opened the door.

"Your Majesty." Thyra turned as we entered the bridge. "*Itegas* Adora has kidnapped my brother. You must stop her."

"Your Majesty, I have a message from Admiral Amo on board the *Infinite Sun*. She's reporting a small force of Farian ships headed their way out of the system. Requesting orders."

The head of the Shen fleet was a gruff, no-nonsense woman I'd met only once during our preparations on Encubier, but I respected her. Marcela Amo would fire on the Farian ship if I ordered it. I only hoped she would also hold her fire with the same fervor.

I held up a hand in Inana's direction with a quick nod. "Get me a time to intercept. Yadira, what happened?"

"Adora was being held in the Pedalion cells," the Farian replied. "About a half an hour ago she overpowered the guards with the help of some of her supporters. Priam was on his way to talk some sense into her. He was apparently taken prisoner and is now on board Adora's ship." She cleared her throat and glanced sideways at Thyra.

"Thyra, would you like to explain how that's possible?" I asked.

"I don't quite understand your meaning, Your Majesty."

"On the display, Majesty, Admiral Amo is relaying eight minutes until intercept," Inana said before I called Thyra out for the liar she was. The very idea that Adora could overpower one of the Farian Hiervet was ludicrous, no matter how many people she'd had with her. I headed for the front of the bridge, Emmory at my side. As we passed Sybil, the seer reached out and touched a hand to my arm.

Priam went with Adora willingly. The gods are fractured.

It wasn't words in my head so much as an impression, a series of stills, but it confirmed my own suspicions.

"Inana, put Marcela up on the screen." I slipped into parade rest, hands behind my back, as I looked at the display. Adora's force was close to two dozen ships, at least three of which were the killer ships.

I wondered how close we were to figuring out how the weapons worked on them or if someone had passed that information on to Warrant Officer Ragini Triskan and her team.

"If I let her run with those, I'm going to have another problem on my hands." I blew out a breath. "It's just going to have to get in line."

"Majesty, I've got Admiral Amo on the com." A window appeared on the display with the admiral. She was older than me, with a streak of gray cutting into her slick-backed black hair. I liked the Shen admiral, though I suspected that would shock her if I said it to her face.

"Marcela, exciting morning."

"Yes, ma'am." She didn't ask where Aiz was, and the weight of his earlier words that I was in charge of the Shen fleet settled firmly onto my shoulders.

"Admiral Hassan, ping Adora's ship, if you would."

There was a beat and then another window appeared on the display. I was somewhat shocked Adora had answered the com at all, but I smiled slowly at her. "*Itegas* Notaras."

Adora sneered at the formality. "Star of Indrana." She made

the title sound like an insult and I heard Yadira's choked-off gasp behind us.

"Where do you think you're going?"

She was unprepared for the question. I could tell by the sudden silence that blanketed our com link. Then Adora shook herself. "We are taking the faithful away from this place before you kill us all."

"You think I'm going to kill you?" I couldn't stop the laugh that bubbled into the air. "If I recall, the last time we spoke the threat was the other way around. You're making a mistake here by running, Adora. Why don't you turn your ships around and we'll have a chat?"

"You betrayed us! You were defiled by the Shen, twisted from your purpose. I have seen the truth of what you've done, Hail. Our lone surviving god has shown it to me."

Priam stepped into the frame and I heard an angry chitter from Thyra behind me. He didn't respond to whatever she'd said, instead focusing his wide, dark eyes on me. "My Farians, your Star has betrayed us. She has slaughtered my brother and sister and replaced them with these false idols."

"Are they broadcasting to the planet?" I murmured, and saw Emmory nod. "Inana, mute us. Can we shut them down?"

"I can, Your Majesty," Marcela said.

"Without killing them?"

There was an awkward pause as Marcela tried to find an appropriate answer, and I felt my amusement build despite the seriousness of the situation.

"I need them alive, Admiral. Don't engage the rest of the fleet. Send in a few fighters for a targeted strike. Shut down their coms and encourage them to get the hell out of here."

"Yes, ma'am. Understood."

"Your Majesty, you're not seriously going to let the Shen fire upon a member of the Pedalion and—"

"I'm ordering the Shen to fire, Thyra. The Pedalion is gone.

Priam has betrayed you. They are trying to undermine your authority, and at the moment they're doing a pretty good job of it," I snapped. The memory of Thyra stabbing me in the chest made my voice sharp, and everyone around me stiffened. "Yadira, you need to get back to the chambers and get a countermessage out now unless you want the whole of Faria revolting right under your nose. We'll discuss how this could have happened later." I waved a hand. "Gita, escort our visitors off my ship."

There was no further protest from Thyra, though I could feel her eyes boring into my back before Gita herded them through the bridge door.

Priam was still talking, but I watched as the transmission fuzzed once and then cut out entirely.

"Marcela?"

"It's done, Majesty, we took out their coms array. No answering fire from the Farian ships and they're continuing out of the system. Do you want us to come closer to the planet?"

"No," I replied. "Hold your position once you're out of Adora's range. Let's not spook the Farians any more than they've already been."

Marcela's eyes flicked past me, and then she nodded. "Yes, ma'am."

"Aiz," I said after the com clicked off.

"Some excitement here, I see." He stepped up to my side. "You let my sister go instead of blowing her out of the black?"

I watched Adora's ships speeding away on the radar. "Dead, she's a martyr and a complication we don't need. She's more use to us alive." I glanced at him. "What?" I demanded. The half smile on his face seemed to be an ever-present fixture these days.

"You are fascinating. Sometimes I can't keep up with how your mind works."

"How's Mia?" I asked instead of responding. I knew full well what he meant, but I didn't want to investigate it too closely. There was a good chance it would all fall apart if I did.

"Resting. The visions are not usually so difficult on her."

"It had been a while," I murmured, and watched him frown. The realization that Mia hadn't told her brother hit me just before a second flash of the future I'd seen from her filled my head.

"You are an abomination, Mia Cevalla, and I will figure out why you Shen survived when all the others would not."

Mia lifted her chin. "We both know how this will end, Thyra. We found the Star and saved her from you. You will not be able to wield her against the galaxy the way you had planned."

The strike put Mia on her knees, opening up a gash on her cheek.

"Hail?" Aiz had a hold of my arm and the frown on his face was deeper than before. "What is it?"

"Still dizzy from before, apparently." I waved him off. "What were you saying?"

"What did you mean that it had been a while?"

"That vision Mia just had was the first since we left Sparkos," I said.

"No one saw fit to tell me about this?"

I met his furious gaze with a surprising amount of calm. "How was I supposed to know she didn't tell you?"

The fury drained away. "I'm sorry. What happened here? I saw Yadira and Thyra leaving looking like they'd seen ghosts."

I couldn't stop the flinch at his phrasing. "Priam left with Adora. Emmory, get the BodyGuards together; we're going to have to head for the Pedalion chamber." I tapped Aiz on the shoulder and gestured toward the door. "Get Mia on her feet in an hour. I'll catch you up as we walk."

16

It was a hectic few hours of damage control while Yadira and the others scrambled to keep Adora's claim that the Farian Hiervet were impostors from tipping Faria completely into chaos.

Once that had died down, long days followed. They were filled with numerous meetings where the Farians and Shen hammered out the final details of the peace accord. My presence was rarely needed so I split my time between refining a plan to hit an unknown enemy and long stretches on the com talking with Alice and the others back home where I tried to convince them said enemy was real.

I could count on one hand the number of times I'd been in the same room as Mia, and until now none of them had been private.

"I missed you." I murmured the words against her temple in the quiet of my room. "I know that's a silly thing, but—"

"It's not." She slid her hands into my hair and leaned in to press her lips to mine. "I missed you, too."

"When this is over I'm taking you somewhere quiet for at least a week," I said, somewhat breathlessly, when we separated.

Mia smiled. "I love that you're optimistic enough to think that will be doable."

"It'll take Emmory a week to find us. I'm good at hiding." The door chimed and I sighed. "Come in."

"Majesty," Emmory said. "Aiz wanted a word."

I let Mia slip away from me, her fingers tangling with mine before we separated completely.

"The Farians lost three more ships last night," Aiz said by way of greeting as he came into the room.

"Presumably joining Adora's force?"

"Yes." He pressed a kiss to Mia's cheek as he passed. "That puts her at almost three dozen ships, though it's still not enough to overcome our combined forces. If she starts firing at us with those *thirions*, we may have some issues."

The name for the brutal ships, roughly translated from Farian as *killers of the faithless*, hadn't surprised me. What had was that Delphine willingly passed over the weapons system schematics without the slightest hesitation. I hadn't mentioned to the Farians that Ragini and Mia's people had been less than fourteen hours from figuring the whole thing out when they gave us the information.

Though Ragini had told me, at great length, how close they'd been until Admiral Hassan silenced her with a look.

I rubbed a hand over the back of my neck with a sigh. "Home Fleet knows about Adora, so if they show up in my empire they'll be in for a fight. Though Shiva knows they'll probably still cut their way through us."

"We could send the mercenaries."

Mia had made the suggestion earlier and I'd turned it down for the second time. Caterina should be proud of me for relying solely on our own forces instead of criminals.

Never mind that I was reasonably sure I should use whatever was at my disposal to keep Indrana safe.

"I already told Mia no," I said with a half smile. "Adora will fuck something up. She doesn't have the patience to plan long term, plus I think she'll stay around here. Faria is what she really wants, not Indrana."

"You're still on edge." It was a statement from Aiz, not a question, and I rolled the words over in my mouth before I let them go into the air.

"I need to hit something. I don't know if it will make this feeling go away or not, but..." I shrugged.

"I'll spar with you." The offer from Zin was unexpected and fear lodged in my throat.

"No."

"You want to fight, I'm offering. We used to spar all the time, Majesty." He looked at Aiz. "Will you supervise?"

Will you bring him back when I kill him?

"Zin, no." I turned to Emmory, but my *Ekam* was terrifyingly silent and I realized the decision had been made without me. "No. I won't spar with you." I shook my head.

Zin held his hands out. "Hail, are you going to spend the rest of your life controlled by the power you now have? Or are you going to learn to control it?"

"Please don't make me do this." I pressed a hand to my mouth.

"The fact that you don't want to tells me everything I need to know," Zin said softly. "You are not a monster, Hail, you are merely someone who knows how to kill. It's time for you to learn how not to."

Zin still had his hands outstretched and the same kindness on his face that had been there from the very first moment I'd looked in his eyes. The trust and love were also evident, and it smoothed over my sick terror at the possibility of killing him. I reached out trembling fingers and put my hands in his.

"It will be okay," he said.

He was right. I knew it. I couldn't spend the rest of my life unable to spar, unable to fight with those closest to me for fear that I would hurt them. I needed to find a middle ground between who I had been and who I was now.

I let go of Zin, crossed the room, and grabbed Aiz by the shirt-front. "Promise me you can bring him back?"

There was no snark, no smile from the Shen as he leaned in and pressed his forehead to mine. "I won't have to, but I promise."

The collection of people sitting off to one side of the *Hailimi*'s gym while Zin and I squared off wasn't a distraction. I'd long since learned to put such things out of my head and focus solely on the fight.

I had never quite gotten the hang of fighting Zin, though to be fair we hadn't been together all that long. He was faster than me, his style well suited to avoiding my head-on attacks. And now, facing off with him, the stark difference between our abilities was staring me in the face.

But I was holding back and we both knew it. I didn't ever want to kill Zin, but I especially didn't want to do it with Emmory watching. So the match had taken on the feeling of a formal bout, with both Mia and Aiz stopping us at unexpected moments to critique or suggest new moves.

"Hey, focus." Aiz snapped his fingers in front of my face, dragging my attention away from where Mia was showing Zin a move that I was sure was going to leave a bruise in the shape of his hand on my back.

"He's always been a gods-damned ghost but it feels like he's kicked things up a notch. How do I defend against this?" I was soaked with sweat and aching. I was also reasonably sure that I'd somehow been tricked into this and that Mia had been training Zin for the last few weeks right under my nose.

"You start actually fighting." He was unmoved by my glare. "I'm serious, Hail. Stop holding back. Fight like you mean it." Aiz put a hand on my back. "You get out of your head and listen to that gut of yours. If you're on the defensive you've already lost. Use some of that skill we both know you have and be where Zin is going to be before he gets there. You have the control not to hurt him, but if something happens and you do we're here."

"Okay." I took a deep breath and straightened, moving to the center of the mat. Zin joined me after a final word with Mia and bowed with a smile.

"Are you ready to stop messing around and fight me, Your Majesty?"

I closed my eyes, swallowed down the tears. "I have managed not to kill any of you with my foolishness lately. I would prefer it stay that way."

"You have not killed any of us," he replied. "Look at me."

I opened my eyes.

"We give our lives for you because that is our choice. Stop treating it so thoughtlessly. Yes, it hurts. Love is knotted up into pain; we don't get to have one without the other."

"I can choose not to hurt you, though," I whispered.

"Hail, that is exactly what I am saying," he continued with a smile. "You know I am your friend, not the enemy. You can control what you have learned. You are smart enough to stop letting this rule you. Have some faith in yourself."

He did not wait for my reply and instead reached out and tapped his fist to mine, then stepped back with a bow.

I responded automatically, bowing in return even as my brain scrambled to make sense of everything he'd just said.

Hadn't I had a conversation like this already? I couldn't pull the memory free, but it seemed familiar—choices and lives and how I should just accept that there were people who loved me enough to sacrifice themselves for me.

I just didn't know if they all realized I would do it for them if the situation presented itself.

You know they do, Hail, that's the whole point.

The voice in my head was as sharp as always, but the words seemed comforting somehow, and a piece of me that had been off-kilter slid into place.

Zin always started bouts with a testing strike. It was designed to set his opponent moving in the direction he wanted, driving them like a sacred cow toward the river.

I suddenly saw, as clear as sunlight through trees, the motion of the fight and moved with his punch rather than as a reaction to it. Time slowed; I saw the surprise cross his face and then the pain as I landed a punch to his back.

I danced out of the way, narrowly avoiding the kick I knew was coming, and dropped to the mat, swinging my own leg out.

It connected with Zin's and he hit the mat hard.

Move in! the voice in my head screamed at me, but I knew better. The last thing I wanted was to get into a ground fight with Zin. I'd seen him at practice with the other BodyGuards, seen how he could even get Emmory wrapped up into a hold before you could finish an inhale.

"Get up," I said.

He grinned at me and scrambled to his feet. "Neat trick, think you can do it again?"

"Probably," I replied. "But you're looking for it, so that's no fun. Have you been training with Mia?"

Zin narrowly avoided the punch I threw on the heels of the question and hit me in the ribs with a strike of his own. I folded in on his hand, using the pain rolling through my body as a weapon, and heard his laughter cut off with a gasp.

I kept moving, slipping under his guard, using the momentum to slide behind him. I grabbed his chin and felt him tense as he braced for the inevitable death from a broken neck.

But I was here. I wasn't lost to some battle madness. I was in control. Instead of breaking Zin's neck, I kissed his cheek and let him go.

The applause echoed through the room and Zin smiled at me. I rubbed my palms against my thighs with a small smile.

"She was watching me practice one day shortly after we landed on Encubier," he said in a low voice before I could walk away. "Said that I could help you if I let her teach me."

"Did she?" I glanced across the gym where Mia and Aiz had their heads together.

"Seems like she was right." Zin took the towels Emmory held out and passed one to me, then rubbed his face with the other. "You've always been in control, Hail, it's important to you. For a little while you weren't and it scared you. It scared us." He smiled. "You're back. How'd you do that?"

I wasn't sure how to respond; I still didn't quite understand what I'd done or how, only that it came to me when I most needed it.

Zin lifted a shoulder, his smile creasing his face. Emmory was silent, watching both of us, and I desperately wanted to ask what was going on in his head.

But Aiz and Mia joined us and I lost my chance.

"It was good," Aiz said. "I would have followed through, but—" He broke off when Mia jammed her elbow into his side and grinned.

"She is not you." Mia smiled at me and touched my side. "You left yourself open, Hail."

"When?"

I saw the frown that flickered over Aiz's face before he could hide it, but he didn't say anything, just nodded to me and headed for the door. My heart had been slowing from the fight; now it sped up again.

"Majesty, I'm going to go clean up," Zin said. Emmory simply smiled at us and followed his husband from the room.

"When you were here." Mia moved closer to demonstrate. "He missed it. I would not have."

I pretended that her hand pressing into my rib cage didn't feel like it was burning straight through me. "Well, I guess that means we'll have to spar so you can show me."

"You know I will not," Mia replied, but she was smiling at me.

I put my hand over hers before she could step away. "That's fine, I didn't necessarily mean here in public."

"You don't understand the power you're holding, do you?" Her quiet question stopped my advance.

I shook my head. There wasn't any reason to lie about it. I didn't understand it and sometimes that scared me more than anything.

"This is life, Hail." Mia took my hand and held it up, linking her fingers through mine. I felt the familiar tingle of her energy across my skin. "It heals, it kills. It powers everything and can end everything. You saw and felt what I did to that assassin. You've done it yourself—to Hamah, and just now to Zin."

I nodded.

"I wish that we had more time, so that I could show you all this with your mind clearer." She smiled softly. "But all I can tell you is that this—" The power surged again and I gasped. "This can save your life, don't hesitate to use it. Especially where the Farian Hiervet are involved. It may be the only thing you have left to fight with when the time comes."

There was an urgency in Mia's voice I couldn't deny, and I tugged her closer. "When this is over, will you teach me more?"

"I could be convinced." I heard the lie even as I felt the shift, the way her energy warmed and my own surged up to meet it as I dipped my head to kiss her.

"I'm sorry to interrupt, Your Majesty."

I stopped before my lips touched Mia's and muttered a curse. "This had better be important, Indula."

When I turned to look, he was grinning at me. "Sybil is here. She's asking to speak with you."

"You're enjoying this," I murmured to Mia, and saw the laughter in her eyes.

"Go talk to Sybil, Hail. I'll see you later." She leaned in and kissed me. I let her go with a great deal of reluctance and headed across the gym with the lingering feel of her rolling under my skin.

"I need to shower first. You say a word and I'll kneecap you," I warned Indula as I joined him at the door.

His grin was quick. "Emmory would beat you to it, ma'am. I will say, if it's allowed, that it's good to see you happy."

I slipped my arm through his and smiled. "It's allowed. You're not concerned?"

"About what?" He blinked. "Oh. No, Majesty. Love is love. In this world, we should grab onto it whenever we can."

I was surprised by the sudden lump in my throat that his words caused and changed the subject. "Did I ever apologize for biting you?"

Indula laughed. "You've been a little occupied. It's not necessary, Your Majesty."

"I'm sorry anyway, I was...I didn't—" The words failed me. I frowned at the corridor in front of us.

"You thought we were all dead," Indula finished softly.

"Yes."

"I'll be honest with you. I'm glad we're not."

It was my turn to laugh and I leaned into him, giggling like a schoolgirl as we made our way back to my quarters. My fear of accidentally hurting one of my people had been shaken loose and the relief was so strong it was a bit like being drunk.

I could handle this power and everything that came with it. I had to.

17

I showered, changed, and met Sybil in the captain's ready room. I didn't argue with Indula or Iza when they settled just inside the door.

"Mia was having trouble seeing any glimpse of the future until a few days ago. Did you? Are we in uncharted territory now?" I asked by way of greeting and sat in the empty chair next to Fasé.

"I did not, Hail. Mia's issue was her fixation on the death of the gods. It was logical for her not to have seen anything past that point until she fully accepted they were not going to die," Sybil replied with a small smile. "What I have seen encompasses far more. You heard Yadira say the breaking of the Pedalion was foretold."

"Why didn't the Pedalion listen?"

Sybil wiggled her head to the side with a sigh. "There was little agreement on it. The older members believed it was only one path—and they weren't wrong about that—but they were unwilling to let go of the things that led them to this point."

"So you told them this would happen and they did it anyway."

"I have been responsible for the major prophecy, but all of us on the council have seen different pieces of possible futures. Over the years we have tried to put them together in a manner that makes sense. You know as well as I do we can't make people believe."

"Or make them make rational choices," I murmured. "Do you know what Adora is going to do? Mia had a vision just before that happened—I could have killed Adora or let her go." I didn't mention that I'd seen my own death or Mia's. Putting them into words felt too much like making them real.

Dark Mother, if I'm going to die, at least let me keep everyone safe with my death.

"I saw disaster when I blew up Adora's ship, so I let her go. But I'm not going to be so generous next time."

Sybil studied me for a moment. "You still made the best choice you could have with the information available to you, Your Majesty. As you always do. I know I have not shared much of the future with you and for good reason; but there are things you now need to know that will help you make the choices to see us through this. You understand, of course, that the number of options open to Adora is limitless." She leaned forward and held out her hands. "However, there are three paths that are more likely than the others based on her history and her current state of mind."

"Priam is feeding her paranoia, isn't he?"

"It needs little feeding, but yes. He's afraid of you, Hail. All our former gods are."

It was the first time I'd noticed Sybil referring to the Farian Hiervet that way. Though my raised eyebrow had as much to do with the sheer ridiculousness that these beings would be scared of me.

"They wanted me here," I protested. "The whole prophecy, everything they set in motion seemed to be designed to bring me to this place, this point in time. Why the fuck would they do that if they were scared of me?"

"They wanted a different version of you than they got. I saw you," Sybil replied. "I told them of you and that your arrival was necessary to keep them safe. So Faria was set on a path to make that happen. We became friends with Indrana to ensure the outcome the gods wanted."

That still gave me the fucking chills. The thought that a whole race of people had slid right into my empire with a purpose they'd shared with no one until now and all because of the Farian Hiervet.

What else are they hiding from me?

"They were afraid even then, not of you but of what they saw coming for them. Thyra questioned me relentlessly about the appearance of what we now know is the Hiervet. She would only say it was a great and terrible force of destruction and that you were the only one who could prevent it."

Sybil shook her head. "The future shifts and changes, Hail. Adora tried to push you to the Farian side with such force that it backfired."

I rubbed a hand over my face. "She thought killing my people and blaming the Shen would convince me to side with them?"

"Yes. Instead you ended up with the Cevallas, who also used the loss of your people against you."

The realization hit me with all the force of a Karsikov railgun. It was a cold truth. The only difference between Adora, Aiz, and Mia was that the Cevallas had known my people were alive the whole time. "They didn't try to kill me."

"You're correct. Neither side genuinely wanted you dead, Hail, but without a doubt the Shen have cared far more for you as a person than the Pedalion ever did, and that made all the difference."

"Are you still angry that I haven't turned out as you expected?" I asked Fasé, and she seemed surprised by the question.

"No, Your Majesty. I was fixated on my own outcome also, and it blinded me. I don't think the revelation of what our gods truly were would have happened if you had been more inclined to trust the Pedalion rather than the Shen. I had unwittingly helped them because of our relationship. The break was necessary, as painful as it was."

I tried to imagine a me who still believed the Farians had our best interests at heart, one who distrusted Aiz—and Mia—but I couldn't do it.

"Not all choices are earth-shattering, and yet they change our lives," Sybil said. "We all have other lives that run parallel to the ones we are living where the ending will be something similar no matter what we do."

"How is this all going to turn out, Sybil?"

"That I can't answer for you. Not yet." Sybil wiggled her fingers at me. "I can show you the three options Adora may choose as I have seen them. You will still have to figure out on your own how to react."

I dragged in a breath and took her hands.

The world spun around me.

I walked alone through the streets of Krishan. The destruction that greeted me was so much worse than what Wilson and his supporters had wreaked upon my capital. The flames that shot from the rubble of buildings should have burned me, but they didn't. There was utter desolation as far as the eye could see and a terrifying silence I knew too well.

My home was lost. Shattered. If the rest of the empire had suffered the same fate, I had no way of knowing, but the destruction in front of me was bad enough.

"The dead walk here."

I stiffened at the sound of Sybil's voice at my side. She surveyed the wreckage with a grim expression.

"She will come for your empire, Hail, even though it will destroy her. The ships she took can level your capital. They will do great damage to your fleet, but they will fall. Adora will die on a pyre of her own making."

"Alice and Ravalina? Taz?"

"They, too, will die if you do not take precautions. You cannot save everyone if you push Adora toward this path, but you could save some." Sybil caught my arm as I turned around, stopping me before I could stride away. "This is not an immediate concern, Star of Indrana."

"You want to let me go."

"You will want to see the other choices before you break from me." Sybil's pale silver eyes glowed and the world spun again.

I was on the bridge of the *Hailimi*. The familiar cacophony of battle swirled around us, but no one seemed to notice Sybil and me as we leaned against the wall on the far side.

"Adora will run with the forces she has, but her path will take her straight to the greater threat," she said, and pointed at the screen. I studied it for a moment, realizing that we were pursuing Adora's tiny fleet toward a more massive force.

"Is that the Hiervet?" A heavy weight settled in my stomach at Sybil's nod.

The blips of Adora's fleet started to disappear, one by one.

"Your Majesty, I have an incoming com from Adora's ship," Captain Saito said.

"Put it through." I hadn't answered her, but it was my voice and I looked over my shoulder.

The future me stood at the railing, Emmory on one side and Thyra on the other, watching the battle take place on the screen.

"You have to help us!" The bridge of Adora's ship was filled with smoke, and blood streaked down the side of her face. "They'll kill us all."

"They'll kill you, maybe." I heard myself reply. "Probably something you should have thought of, Adora, I gave you the choice to surrender."

"Please, you don't—"

The image cut off, as did the blip of Adora's ship.

"Captain Saito, I'm getting multiple weapon locks. They're firing on us."

The ship shook.

"Isabelle, tell them we don't want to fight them." The words left my mouth at the same time they came from future me.

"Working on it, Your Majesty. Ensign Kohli, evasive maneuvers!"

"Aye, Captain."

More orders flew back and forth through the air. I lunged for Sybil as the world around us exploded.

"Hail! Hey, it's me." It was Aiz who I grabbed by the shoulders, not Sybil, and I flailed for a moment before I settled.

The dim light of twilight blurred everything around us, but I could see the smudge of blood on his cheek, and the exhaustion around his eyes wasn't like anything I'd ever seen. There was a gun slung over his back and one on the ground between us. I had a Hessian 45 in my hand that hadn't been there a moment ago.

"You can see me?"

"Of course I can see you, what are you talking about?"

"What is—" I looked around. "Where's Sybil?"

"She's been dead for three days." He frowned at me and touched a hand to my throat. "I know it's been a rough week but keep it together for me."

"What is going on?" I pressed both hands to my eyes. "It's weird, bear with me, can you give me a quick refresher?"

Aiz took a breath, but then complied. "Adora's forces took the capital yesterday, what was left of it after the initial attack anyway. She was far more fucking cunning than I gave her credit for and had her people on the ground spreading the rumor that you'd killed the other gods at the same time she took to the sky with Priam. With the Pedalion broken there wasn't any unified voice to counter that."

"What about Fasé? Her rebellion?"

Aiz's frown deepened. "Did you hit your head? Fasé took off right after the peace talks fell apart. No one knows where she is."

"I am not supposed to be here." I reached out and grabbed him by the shirt front. "This isn't real. I was back on the *Hailimi*, you and Mia already agreed to peace with the Farians. Fasé didn't go anywhere. Sybil was showing me the choices Adora could make and we—"

144

"Hail." Aiz's voice was deceptively soft and he covered my hand with both of his. "This has been hard for you . . . for all of us. Right now I need you to focus so we can get back to base. Then we can talk, okay?"

I swallowed my next words. He was being strangely gentle and I refused to fall apart again. Aiz got to his feet, pulling me up with him, and together we made our way through the ruined streets.

I didn't recognize the Shen who emerged from the shadows and hurried us into the dark tunnel with only a quick greeting. Aiz slipped an arm around my waist with a murmured "It's safer than the surface. Just breathe through it."

I did and somehow made it down and through the heavy doors. I blinked in the harsh light of the single overhead fixture. Aiz didn't say a word, just ushered me down the corridor and into the room at the end.

Gita and Hao looked up from the map on the table in the middle of the room as we came through the doorway and my *Dve* held out her hands. There was a look in her eyes I didn't like at all. She embraced me wordlessly.

"The fighting has moved south," Aiz said, laying his guns on a nearby chair and rubbing at the back of his neck. "Our forces are holding here, but if Adora makes another push we may not be able to—"

Hao, to my shock, put a hand on the Shen's arm. "We'll hold, have a little faith."

"Where's Mia?" I murmured, and everyone froze. "Emmory? Zin? The others?"

Aiz shook his head and shared a strange look with Hao, who came over and pushed me gently into a chair. "Little sister."

Oh, I knew that tone of voice.

I squeezed my eyes shut, suddenly certain his next words were going to hurt, and I didn't want to hear them. Not even knowing this wasn't real.

145

"No, I'm not doing this again." I shook my head. "This isn't real. It's just a future. Sybil was showing me the future."

Hao grabbed me when I tried to slide out of the chair. "Hail, you were there when it happened. You know it's real."

"No!" I slapped his hands away and stood, knocking the chair over so it clattered to the floor. "I am not fucking doing this again. Sybil, where are you?" I screamed the words at the ceiling, heard Hao curse as he grabbed me. The world spun around me again.

18

H ail. It's me. You're all right." Hao still had me by the shoulders, but now I was in the ready room of the *Hailimi*. Fasé was on the floor, cradling Sybil in her arms and crooning softly in Farian to the unconscious seer. I wrapped my arms around Hao's neck and held on.

"Hao." His name was little more than a sob. "Oh Shiva."

"It's all right, little sister," he whispered, tightening his arms around me. "I'm right here."

I didn't know when he'd gotten back, but I was really glad to see him.

"What happened?" I heard Gita's voice just before her hand touched my back.

"I—where's Emmory?" The question slipped out before I could stop it even as I pulled up their vitals on my *smati*, the need for reassurance right this moment overruling everything else.

"He and Zin are on their way."

I exhaled against Hao's neck as everyone's vitals registered. "Help me up." They did and I awkwardly clung to him for a moment longer, blinking away the tears that threatened. "I am so sick of this future shit."

"Finally," he muttered, and touched my face. "Are you okay?"

"Yes." I nodded and crossed to Fasé, kneeling at her side. "Is she all right?"

Sybil's eyes fluttered open before Fasé could respond and the seer reached a hand out to me that I took with only the slightest of hesitations. "I'll be fine," she whispered. "I'm sorry, Hail. I don't know what happened."

Emmory and Zin came into the room; the extra footsteps behind them belonged—I realized—to Aiz and Mia. I squeezed Sybil's hand, then released her. "I don't either. You were with me for the first two futures, but that last future you were missing and it was entirely too real."

Sybil winced as she sat up. "I could only see flashes of it. I've never had that happen before."

I helped her the rest of the way to her feet and then turned to face my *Ekam*. I tried to hide the shaking of my hands as I reached for him, but I knew he saw it. He pulled me into his arms and I buried my face against his shoulder.

"What happened?" His voice rumbled in my ear and I felt the quick squeeze of his arms before he let me go.

I cleared my throat of the tears. "Hao, where's Dailun and Johar? Alba and Admiral Hassan also. I only want to go through this once."

A stunned silence greeted us after Sybil and I detailed out the possible futures we'd seen. At least half of those assembled wore uncertain frowns, and I didn't blame them. If I hadn't seen it with my own eyes I'd be questioning it, too.

The thought of trying to explain this to Caterina and the others made my jaw ache.

"I'm just going to say it. All those options are shit." Hao dragged a hand through his hair.

"What he said." Johar pointed and shook her head. "Don't we have an Adora-gets-hers-and-we-all-live-happily-ever-after option?"

I laughed; it was sharp-edged and hard and I felt Mia's fingers tighten against mine. "It's not a fairy tale, Jo. Besides, this is just one piece of the whole mess and we do need to decide what to do about Adora. Preferably before the Hiervet show up." I glanced in Dailun's direction. "I'm hoping someone has good news for me, but it's going to have to wait until we get this sorted."

"Your Majesty. I recommend we send a message to Caspel right now about getting the royal family out of the capital, possibly even off the planet," Admiral Hassan said.

"You know they'll balk," I replied.

Her smile was tight. "I'll be vague about the 'credible threat' to the royal family. That should handle any objections."

"Thank you." I hated myself more than a little even as I agreed with her that the priority was getting Alice and her daughter away from danger. Sybil had been right—I couldn't save everyone, but I could save some if Adora decided to attack Pashati. "Do it."

Inana gave me a sharp nod and left the room.

"I actually agree with you, believe it or not," I said to Hao, and tapped a finger against my lip in thought. "About these options being shit."

"Good news is that some of what you saw isn't going to come to pass," Aiz said.

I frowned at him. "How do you figure?"

He lifted a shoulder with a smile. "Peace talks happened, Hail. The Shen and the Farians will be at peace. Fasé is still here. If Adora comes at Faria, the playing field will be decidedly different than what you described in the future you saw."

He had a point and I was surprised I hadn't realized it. The memory of Hao telling me to talk to Fasé surfaced, and everything after that fell into line. I'd convinced her to stay. She'd convinced Aiz to make peace.

There is no true shelter for sides that will collapse without each other to lean on.

The words from Sybil's future were loud in my head.

Adora wouldn't be able to get a foothold in Faria because I'd taken five minutes to talk to Fasé and reassure her that she could, in fact, do more than she'd dreamed.

"Why can't I get Adora to surrender?"

Aiz snorted at my question, but I ignored him and kept looking at Sybil. The Farian shook her head.

"I don't know. It's always a choice, but not one I've seen specifically. Will Adora go that direction? I can't think of anything, especially coming from you, that would encourage her to do such a thing."

"She won't ever surrender."

Now I did look his way. "How do you know that?"

"I wouldn't."

"What if Mia's life were at stake?" I saw her flinch when I asked the question.

"That's a shit question." Aiz shook his head. "You know I couldn't, Hail. The safety of my people takes priority over my sister's life, even if I would sooner cut my own heart out of my chest."

"Everyone has a breaking point," I replied. "Everyone is willing to sacrifice themselves for something—or someone—else. I think you're lying about Mia, but I know you'd do it for your people."

Aiz shot me a flat look and Mia watched us with haunted eyes.

"Look, I don't particularly want to kill Adora. You and I both know that will just make her people fight all the harder. But I can't let her run around out there—if she decides to attack us or Pashati or Earth?" I shook my head. "Way too many people are going to end up dead. I'd like to prevent that by taking Adora back into custody as fast and as quietly as possible."

"What's your plan for that?"

"I haven't gotten that far." I tapped a finger on the tabletop. A plan was forming, though, hazy and imperfect in the back of my head. "Dailun, what was the verdict from your people?"

"Not good, *jiejie*," he replied, shaking his head. "As you can imagine, they were not particularly interested in helping us attack the Hiervet. But they claimed to have no way of finding the Hiervet even were they willing to help."

"It was worth a shot, I guess." I sighed at the ceiling. "All right, people. I am open to other suggestions as to how we find the Hiervet before they come crashing into this galaxy."

"Hail, he's not done." Hao pointed a finger at Dailun.

My pilot smiled and folded his hands together. "We thought it best not to waste the trip, so I asked if I could pass a message on to the Istrevitel and approval was given."

"You think they'll help?"

"They did say they would be in touch, honored sister. I felt a representative of yours could request contact and that sending them a message first was necessary given the circumstances. They will hopefully welcome it, even though it was from me."

We will speak with the Star if the time comes. Pray it does not.

Despite everyone's hopes, the time was coming. Even though the Hiervet still seemed as intangible as smoke on the air and I knew we had to deal with Adora first, I could feel the certainty twisting in my gut.

"You did good." I patted Dailun on the shoulder. "We'll wait and see what happens. In the meantime let's focus on our next move."

"Which is what?" Johar asked.

"Finding Adora."

"I was hoping you'd say that," she replied. "Alba and I have an idea."

Johar's idea was brilliant, and oddly in line with the one that had been forming in my head. It also set off a firestorm of protests, not from Emmory but from Hao. "We're seriously considering heading into an unknown situation, and worse, letting her lead us into it?"

"That hurts, Hao." I didn't bother pointing out we'd already decided to do the same thing where the Hiervet were concerned.

"You know what I mean." He glared at me.

"I won't send anyone else," I replied. "Jo's right, if we can have Thyra just take us wherever Adora is and we take over the ship. We'll end this rebellion of hers before it even starts."

"By fucking letting one of those treacherous bastards take you onto Adora's ship," Aiz said. His mouth was set in a tight line and it was fascinating to see both him and Hao on the same side of things. "Anything could happen and an unhealthy amount of the scenarios end with you dead."

"I can't just wait around here until the Hiervet show up, can I?" I set my jaw and crossed my arms over my chest to keep my hands away from my guns. "You're busy. I can go take care of the Adora problem before the tension gets so high around here that someone accidentally starts a war."

"How much worse will the tension get if you go and get yourself killed?"

I gave Aiz a look that could have put a hole in the side of a battlecruiser. "I did a reasonably good job of staying alive before I met you, you know. I don't need a babysitter."

Hao opened his mouth to reply, and I pointed a finger at him with a warning shake of my head.

"Enough, all of you." That came from Mia and Fasé, the pair stepping to my side in a surprising display of solidarity. "Hail's right," Mia said. "What must happen here and now is peace between the Farians and the Shen. Which is our responsibility. It is Hail's responsibility to find Adora before she does more damage."

I bit the inside of my cheek to keep from smiling at the identical looks of frustration Hao and Aiz were wearing and instead glanced in Emmory's direction. *"Ekam?"*

"We go where you go, Majesty."

"Well, that's settled, then." I rubbed my hands together. "I will have to convince Thyra, of course, and see if it can even be done. From there we will figure out who's going."

The crowd broke and Fasé put a hand on my arm before she left, her voice so soft I almost missed the whispered warning. "This will not go the way you plan, Hail, and you cannot hide. Your voice is necessary. Only the Star can turn the hearts of those who are uncertain. Choose your words with care."

"Don't I always?"

A smile flickered over her face. "No, and even worse this time you will not want to, but if you value peace above war, you must."

Fasé's words were still lodged in my brain a day later when I strode into the Pedalion chamber, Emmory and Gita on my heels. Thyra looked up as we entered. The Farian Hiervet sat on the dais and tapped her front limbs together as she stood.

"Star of Indrana, what can I do for you?"

"I'm surprised you were not in the negotiations."

She sighed, and an expression that was either resignation or annoyance twisted her face. "I would have, but Yadira and Delphine felt things would go smoother were I not."

"They weren't wrong. It is good of you to recognize that peace is beneficial to the Farians. It shows you care." I watched the range of emotions skitter across Thyra's face as I spoke and bit back a smile of my own.

It was probably not quite what Fasé had meant about me watching my words, but it was helpful. My continued effort to get a better read on the Hiervet's expressions hadn't abated, and I'd spent what spare time I had watching the compilations from Zin over and over, looking for the patterns.

Some of which may have included deliberately poking at them to get a specific emotion I wanted to see. Zin's catalog of expressions was very helpful, but not quite complete.

"I do care," Thyra said finally. "You see it differently, because of the Shen, but the Farians have been in my care for a very long time. I love them as if they were my children."

There was something about the way she said *children* that made my skin crawl.

"Of course." I offered up my best soothing smile. "I came to talk to you for exactly that reason." That earned me a confused expression and I nearly grinned in triumph.

"I'm sorry, Star of Indrana, I am not following you."

"It's dangerous to the Farians for Adora and Priam to be out there spreading dissent. It's also dangerous for my people and the whole of humanity, since if this peace fails and the Farians and Shen go back to fighting it's only a matter of time before they spill back into our part of the galaxy."

I left the *and the Hiervet are coming* unsaid, but it hung in the air anyway.

"Please continue."

"I've come to request your help."

Surprise, plain as day, on Thyra's face, and also satisfaction. "You are the Star of Indrana."

"And yet I can't teleport myself long distances. Any distance, really." I pointed at her. "You can."

"You need me to take you somewhere?" There was the confusion again.

"I would like you to take me, and a small strike force, to wherever Adora's ship is."

19

ave I mentioned this is a bad idea?"

"Repeatedly and at great length." I shoved my Glocks into my thigh holsters. "Reminds me of that job in the Siberian wasteland when you invited all that bad luck on us by repeatedly bitching about what a bad idea it was." I winked at Gita behind Hao's back.

"You mean the job where I got shot?"

"One of them, yeah." I shrugged, grinning at his look. "What? That one wasn't my fault. You fumbled the code words at the door."

"Sha zhu," Hao said, and then stopped. It was the exhale that caught my attention, and it washed away my amusement. I stepped around Gita, waving off Emmory as I slipped my arm through Hao's and walked him down the ramp of the ship into the cool night air.

"What is it?"

Hao didn't answer, but he rubbed at his left shoulder as he slipped out of my grasp and headed to the edge of the platform the *Hailimi* rested on. He was silent as he stared out at the sharp-edged buildings jutting up in the distance.

I followed, swallowing down the urge to press. I'd shot him in that shoulder on Sparkos and I knew all too well the look on his face, the number of times I'd been on the receiving end of it while on his crew. It was a strange mixture of frustration and love with just a touch of pleading; it was very similar to the Look Emmory often shot my way.

I'd pushed Hao too far, missed the concern in his questions during the briefing as we'd planned out the best way to assault Adora's ship. Call it arrogance, or nerves, or whatever. I should have paid better attention.

"I know that calling what happened to you difficult is a bit like calling a black hole an inconvenience." He shoved his hands into his pockets. "I want to ask you something and you're welcome to get angry with me, but I'd appreciate an honest answer."

"All right, shoot."

"Do you have a death wish?" The question wasn't heated; it was, in fact, barely a whisper. It dragged the vision of Thyra killing me to the front of my mind, and my breath caught in my lungs.

"Excuse me?"

"You heard me." He was still staring out over the city.

"I thought we covered this."

"So did I, but this plan feels an awful lot like you sacrificing yourself to get the rest of us clear. This isn't about me not getting to go," he said before I got the words out. "This is about you and whatever you're planning."

Thyra could take three people to Adora's ship. I'd picked Emmory and Gita because of all my people, they were the only ones who'd died and been brought back, making them at least safe from the touch of Farians. Thyra seemed assured that no Farian would break the taboo against killing with their power, but I wasn't about to hinge the lives of my people on it.

I would have taken Hao, but we'd already had the discussion about bringing him back from the dead and I knew he wouldn't agree to it just for the sake of extra protection.

The reality was any of Adora's people could just shoot us and that would be that. I didn't know if I'd be able to bring anyone back from the dead, my crash course with Mia notwithstanding.

"This isn't about Gita, either. I love her and I hate the thought of sending her into danger. However, she's an adult and can take care of herself. Close your mouth."

I obeyed, though I was unable to keep the smile hidden and Hao sighed.

"I haven't told her yet, little sister, so maybe keep that under wraps for now."

"Of course. I don't have a death wish, *gege*." I turned, my shoulder brushing his, and looked out at the city as I tried to collect my thoughts. "My father spent the first eighteen years of my life teaching me how to live in this world. When I lost him, I was devastated, and then there you were." I felt a tear escape and brushed it impatiently away. "You taught me so much. I will never be able to repay you. You asked the question, let me give you an answer," I said, lifting a hand when he opened his mouth.

"My apologies, Your Imperial Majesty."

I rolled my eyes with a smile at his teasing bow.

"My father may have laid the foundation for who I am, but you taught me how to be a leader. I have done what I can to make sure the empire is safe if something does happen to me, but believe me when I say I don't have a death wish. I would like to go home and give Ravalina the chance to grow up before she has to take the throne. I would like the opportunity to lead Indrana in a time of peace, not just see them through a war. I don't know if I will be any good at it, but I want to try."

I just didn't know if I was going to get the chance. Those words stuck in my throat, refusing to spill out into the open air.

"You will be. You've always been good at this. I didn't teach you how to be a leader, little sister. I only showed you what I saw in you. What you were already capable of doing."

His quiet words wrapped around my heart.

"I also know you would never send someone else in to do a job in your stead and neither will I." I faced him and folded my hands together as I bowed, keeping my eyes on the ground between us. "So forgive me, brother, but I will go into danger—not only to keep you all as safe as I can, but because I am the only one who can do this."

The words I didn't say, that I was all too aware that this could result in a choice between my death or Mia's and that even if I didn't love her I'd die to save her, hovered on the back of my tongue.

I felt his hand slide into my hair, fingers flexing against my scalp for just a moment before he withdrew. Hao took me by the shoulders, urging me upright until I faced him, his gold eyes boring into mine.

"Do not die. That's an order."

"Yes, sir."

Hao nodded once, released me, and turned back to look over the city. I recognized the dismissal, so I left him alone and went back to the ship.

"Everything okay?" Gita asked.

"Yes." I patted her shoulder. "Maybe go talk to him, though?"

She nodded in much the same way Hao had and headed down the ramp toward him. Zin took her place.

"You'd think they're the unlikeliest pair, and yet..."

"They are so similar," I murmured. "It's a wonder they don't murder each other."

"There was a risk early on." Zin laughed. "Still is, if we're being honest."

"She's good for him." I smiled as Hao wrapped his arms around Gita and she returned the embrace. "Gy's death hit him hard, and then to lose the rest of his crew so soon after." I felt the guilt swell that I hadn't been there to help and to say good-bye during Gy's illness. The loss of his crew except for Henna during our desperate race to Ashva had been a shock for us all, but for my brother it had been the loss of everything he'd built.

There was nothing you could have done there, Hail. I let the guilt slip through my fingers without trying to hold on to it.

I leaned into Zin. "I'll keep Emmory safe, I promise."

He studied me for a moment, a half smile playing on his round face. "You know the best way to do that? Keep yourself safe."

"You, too, huh?"

"No, I know you don't have a death wish. You just have an over-developed sense of honor and often feel like you're the only one who should get to sacrifice herself for the good of others. I married a man who's nearly your identical twin."

"Ouch." I laughed and mock-rubbed at my chest. "You wound me. I'm much prettier than your husband."

Zin chuckled. "You are such a shit, Hail Bristol." He reached a hand out, pressing it over mine for just a moment. "That reminds me. I have a present for you. I updated the compilation from your meeting with Thyra."

My *smati* pinged with the file receipt.

"Me being a shit reminds you of the Farian Hiervet's expressions?"

"In a roundabout fashion." Zin squeezed my hand. "I would deeply appreciate it if you would bring my husband back to me, Your Majesty."

I put my other hand over his. "I will. I promise."

He slipped his hand free. "Here comes Thyra. Hail, keep your eyes open. If I learned anything from watching all that footage it's that they're up to something and she's in charge. Observational bias, maybe, but it's hard not to be suspicious."

"If it keeps us safe, I'll take it. I'll also keep my eyes open, I promise," I murmured, and let the polished smile fall into place as Thyra came up the ramp.

"Star of Indrana."

I dipped my head. "Good evening, Thyra. Are we ready?"

"If you and your people are," she replied. "I know where Priam is and we can assume Adora is nearby."

I looked over my shoulder as Emmory approached from behind. I took the Koros 101 from him and slung it over my shoulder. The pulse rifles were presents from Aiz, delivered by Talos a few hours ago along with a report that the negotiations were going well.

*   *   *

"Should be wrapped up by the time you get back."

"Let's hope so." I patted him on the shoulder. "Tell them I'll see them in a bit."

"Stay safe, Astéri.*"*

"You know me."

Talos caught me by the arm. "I do, Hail, which is why I say it. Please come back. My Thínos *already grieve for the loss of their father. I do not want your death to add to that and it would."*

"I promise," I replied; the emotions welling up in my throat were too complex to find words for, but the Shen seemed to understand. He leaned in and touched his forehead to mine, then left.

"Majesty?"

I blinked myself back to the present, shaking my head at Emmory with a small smile. The others stepped back. I nodded to Thyra and took her limb. "I'm fine. Let's do this."

20

This trip wasn't like the first one we'd done. That short hop had us blinking into and out of existence faster than any of us could draw breath. Going to Adora's ship felt like being wrapped in a blanket and dragged down a flight of stairs.

I went to a knee when we rematerialized, bracing myself on a wall as the world came back into focus. Gita was bent over, both hands on her thighs. Emmory was still upright but only through some force of will the rest of us lacked.

"Are you well, Star of Indrana?" Thyra, of course, was unaffected by the jump, and her eyelids opened and closed in a strange rhythmic pattern as she watched us.

"We'll be fine. Do you have a location?"

"I do."

"Go back and tell the others."

"I am shielding us; when I leave, Adora will know you are on her ship."

"It's fine." I waved a hand. "We've got it covered."

I recognized the frown, but Thyra didn't argue and vanished. I counted seconds, waiting for the sound of an alarm that didn't come, and then exhaled a long breath.

"Did you not think Johar's masking programs would work, ma'am?" Gita asked as she straightened.

"I'd trust Jo with my life," I replied, as Emmory reached down and helped me to my feet. "But expecting things to go wrong always seems to work better for me."

When we'd laid down this plan, I knew the only way to make it work was to keep Thyra as much out of the loop as possible. In theory we were here to make sure Adora couldn't run by sabotaging her engines. Thyra was supposed to return to Faria and let Hao and the others know our coordinates so that Admiral Hassan and a joint force of Farian and Shen ships could meet us.

The reality was we were moving to a different location where Gita could hack into the shipboard computer and figure out where we were, then send that information on to Admiral Hassan. We'd hit the engines after and escape on a shuttle in the chaos.

The door of the small room Thyra had dropped us into slid open at a touch. Emmory gave me the Look when I stepped forward and I put my hands up with a smile. "After you, *Ekam*."

"Thank you, Majesty."

I grinned at Gita as we slipped out the door into the corridor on Emmory's signal. The interior was reminiscent of the ship we'd been on after my rescue from Sparkos with the same curved gray walls and bright lights.

But this ship was larger. We had the schematics and Emmory headed aft as I counted doorways in my head.

Emmory and Gita were in sync with each other, their training on display in a way I didn't usually get to see, while I was painfully aware just how off I was in comparison to them. I wondered idly what kind of fast talking I'd have to do once we got home to get Emmory to let me train with my BodyGuards.

Maybe not much, I realized as he stopped us with a raised fist and then waved me forward to the edge of the T junction. He peeked around the corner and gestured. "We're clear. Gita, go."

Gita moved past me, weapon out, and I followed, Emmory bringing up the rear.

"Here." I pointed to the right; the door for the secondary command center was marked on the overlay my *smati* had provided for my vision. Gita guarded the hallway, weapon up and watching the corridor with her dark eyes.

We knew the ship didn't have a full complement of crew. Adora had scraped together whoever she could in her flight off Faria. I didn't want to think about what they would have done with any crew members who were on board who didn't agree with Adora and Priam. Especially with the knowledge that Priam could kill any of the Farians for good.

However, full crew or not didn't seem to matter much for our luck as the sounds of voices came around the corner. "In here." Emmory slapped the panel behind me, opening the door and slipping inside with his gun raised. "Empty," he said.

"You two have to hide," I whispered. The meaning of Fasé's words to me were suddenly very clear. "I have to go to Adora. I need you to get into the coms and broadcast the bridge feed to the rest of her fleet. Then, when you take the bridge back, try not to not shoot anyone."

Emmory's mouth tightened. "Hail, that was not the plan."

"It'll be fine."

"She said she was going to kill you."

"She won't." I shook my head. "Trust me on this, Emmory. She'll kill the two of you in a heartbeat, but she wants me alive or that assassination attempt on Mia would have been directed at me."

I didn't have the words to explain how I knew this, only that as mad as Adora was at me, she hadn't killed me yet. I guessed that had less to do with my ability to stay alive and more with the fact that there was some reason Adora still needed me.

I gave Emmory a little shove as the voices grew louder. "You can save my ass in a little bit and feel super smug about it, okay? But I need to talk to Adora face-to-face."

Emmory discarded whatever he'd been about to say, and exhaled. He tipped his head toward the door with a wordless order and I passed him my guns before I closed the door.

It slid shut between us. I turned and headed down the corridor toward the voices.

"Gentlemen," I said, slipping my hands into my pockets and smiling at the three Farians who came to a startled halt a few meters away from me. "I'm here to speak with Adora."

The Farians didn't quite know what to do with my sudden appearance, so it took longer than it should have for them to cuff me and haul me to the bridge. They didn't search me, but I didn't mention the lapse.

Adora didn't get up from the captain's chair, her platinum eyes flicking over me as if expecting some surprise. When she couldn't find any visible evidence of trickery she looked me in the eye.

"How did you get on board?"

"Long story," I replied with a shrug. "Not really the point of my visit."

"What is the point of your visit?"

Every eye on the bridge was focused on us and I let the silence linger for a few heartbeats before I smiled. "I've come to offer you terms of surrender." I noticed that several of the Farians flinched, and I hoped Gita had figured out how to get into the bridge coms.

Adora laughed, the sound brittle and breaking against the walls. "You've let all this go to your head." She gestured at my cuffed hands. "I have you in custody, what do you think is stopping me from killing you here and now?"

"I am the only one who can offer your people a pardon if they walk away from this terrible path. They were so close to peace after all these years and you dragged them from it. There is nothing to save you from your crimes, Adora, but there is still time for them."

"My crimes? I have done nothing but help my people become better than we were!"

Better? That was the second time she'd said something about

it. I hid my frown at her words and reminded myself that my reply needed to be for the Farians around her, not for Adora. "You tied them to an alien race who use your energy for their own purposes. You sold out your people for your own personal power. You kept them isolated and in chains and waged a war against those who wanted to be free. Listen to me, the Farian Hiervet are not here for the good of Faria. They are here for their own good."

I spotted the looks the Farians around us shared and so did Adora. Her mouth tightened and she pushed out of her chair.

"What do you know of it? You're merely a human, short-lived and useless. The gods wanted nothing to do with you and were it not for this prophecy we would have been content to let you wallow in the mud."

"You had nothing to do with our survival. Humanity found our way out of the mud and into the stars without help from any of you." I kept my voice even and the smile on my face just barely curving the corner of my mouth. "And we can show the Farians how to do it themselves."

I'd learned a lot of things from Hao when I'd joined his crew. One of which was how to bait someone into losing their temper. A person on the verge of losing it gave away more information than they meant to every single time.

Challenge the leader for control.

"Quiet." The blow to my back wasn't as enthusiastic as it should have been and I could imagine the silent conversations going on behind me.

Sow confusion, doubt, and fear.

"The loss of everything you thought you knew is scary, but don't let your fear drive you away from the one thing that can save you."

"You understand nothing." Adora's cold smile cut like a knife. "But I think you will when you watch me destroy your home."

That was the moment I'd been waiting for. The one I'd known was coming for us and why I couldn't just let Adora wander free.

We'd subverted her plans to attack Faria by presenting a united front; now I would talk her out of attacking Pashati.

Get your opponent to make your choice rather than their own.

"You can," I replied. "I'm not saying it wouldn't hurt us, but you're a fool if you think this catches me by surprise. My heir is safe, as is the leadership of Indrana. You will do no more damage to my empire than a child knocking over blocks in a fit of temper."

The difference between Hao and me was that while he liked to manipulate his opponent into making the choice through subtlety, I was more often inclined to do it with a hammer.

Adora grabbed me by the throat and dragged me down until I was at her eye level. I could feel her will sliding against mine, seeking a hold and finding nothing.

"They ruined everything! Twisted you and warped you into an abomination. Thyra warned me it could happen, but I didn't believe you would ever turn your back on us—not with so much at stake."

"I know what's at stake," I replied, carefully sinking the hooks of my own will into hers. "It's why I made the choice that I did."

Adora was too distracted to notice until it was too late. Though even with my advantage, I wouldn't be able to hold her for long. She was far older and stronger than me and all it would take was one of her people to realize that she didn't have control of the battle unfolding in front of them.

"I've seen it, Adora. I can help your people, I can help you. Surrender to me and we'll sort it out. Your only other choice leads to your death."

"I serve my gods to the end." She gritted the words out and I felt her will twist as she tried to escape my grip.

"Your gods will gleefully sacrifice you to the fire for their own selfishness."

I heard the door slide open behind us, the startled shouts of the Farians at Emmory's order to surrender, and then silence.

"Majesty?"

"Little busy." I took hold of Adora's wrist with my cuffed hands, pulling her away from me and then straightening. "Good timing," I said to Emmory. "Are we still on?"

He nodded once, then trained his gun on Adora. I smiled and held out my cuffed wrists. "If you'd be so kind?"

Adora pressed her thumb to the middle and they opened with a click. I gestured for her to drop to the floor and cuffed her wrists behind her as Emmory turned his attention back to the handful of Farians clustered at the far side of the bridge. I smiled up at the main screen.

"Farians, I know you are scared, but soon you will have the choice to fight or surrender. I recommend the latter. Be better than the sum of your fears."

"Broadcast off, Majesty," Gita said.

"Gita, how are we doing there?"

"Locking out systems, Majesty. Five more minutes. Not going to lie, I wish Ragini were here, she's better at this than me."

It was sheer luck on my part that I was looking in the right direction when Priam appeared on the bridge.

"Emmory!" I launched myself at him, feeling the hot sting along my back as I spun us both out of the way of Priam's strike. Adora dove to the side. Gita brought her Koros 101 up and shot the Farian Hiervet in his spindly chest.

The sound Priam made was awful, but when he didn't collapse and no wound appeared, I immediately filed it under laughter rather than pain. "Gita, door!" I pushed Emmory ahead of me as the three of us scrambled for the corridor.

Gita slammed the panel to open the door as Priam started toward us—all spindly limbs and fury. We slipped through and the door shook as the Farian Hiervet crashed into it just after it closed. Emmory fired his Hessian into the panel, turning and shielding me so that the sparks flew into his back rather than my face.

"Bugger me, that was closer than I wanted. Gita, did we get a message off to Admiral Hassan?" I slipped out of Emmory's grasp, brushing away the sparks from his back before they could catch fire.

"Yes, Majesty."

Something in Gita's voice made me turn and I couldn't stop the choked laughter at the poor Farian who was standing with his hands up and Gita's gun shoved against his nose.

"Secondary communication center, now."

The Farian pointed a shaking finger. I saw the muscle in Gita's hand start to shift and reached out. "Let's bring him with us. I want to have a chat."

Gold eyes that were reminiscent of Fasé's flicked to me for just a second and then went blank as Gita knocked him out with the butt of her gun. He folded over, dropping to the ground at my feet with a dull thud.

"We need to move," Emmory said as another bang echoed on the door behind us. He passed me his gun.

I took it with a raised eyebrow. "Emmory, why do you have a 201?"

The Koros 201 was definitely not a shipboard weapon, but that hadn't stopped my *Ekam*. It was, in essence, a mini railgun that fired tiny pellets at a higher velocity than the old-school powder guns of Earth.

"I thought it might come in handy at some point and it looks like I was right. Those Farian Hiervet don't seem to be bothered by energy weapons." He grabbed the unconscious Farian, throwing him over his shoulder. I followed Emmory down the hallway.

"This is it," Gita said. "First door on your left, Emmory." He hit the panel and, judging by the way he slipped inside, the room was empty, so I followed. Gita came in behind me and the door slid shut.

"Excuse me, Majesty." She moved past, heading for a console. "I want to get that door locked before they recover enough to come looking for us."

A klaxon started. The piercing wail filled the air around us and then the ship shook violently.

21

I winced when Emmory dropped the Farian and his head thudded off the floor. I handed my *Ekam* back his gun with a stern look and joined Gita at the bank of computers on the far side of the room.

Yadira and Delphine's breaking of the Pedalion had resulted in a number of surprising side benefits—among them, the downloading of the entire Farian language to our database. The writing on the screens resolved itself as I leaned over Gita's shoulder.

"Now I really wish Ragini were here. The alarm isn't because of us," she murmured, her fingers flying over the keys. "There's other ships out there. I don't—"

"It's the Hiervet." I rubbed a hand over my face, swallowing back the curse I wanted to spit into the air. "Of all the times to show their faces."

Our entire plan to signal Admiral Hassan and take control of the ship had just been blown to pieces with the arrival of what looked to be a small fleet of Hiervet ships.

"Send a message to Inana, Gita," I ordered. "We need to find a way off this ship. With any luck we can escape during the fighting with no one the wiser and they can pick us up."

"Shuttle bay is four floors down, but that's the largest concentration of Farians on the ship because our route will take us right past the bridge." Emmory gestured at the Farian on the floor when he groaned. "This one's waking up."

"Let's have a chat, maybe he knows a faster way down." I grabbed the platinum-haired Farian by the shirtfront and hauled him into a sitting position. He looked past me to Emmory and then snapped back to me as the realization dawned.

"Star of Indrana."

"That's me." I smiled. "What's your name?"

"What are those alarms for?"

I grabbed him by the chin when he tried to look around, feeling his jolt as skin met skin and I wrapped my will around him. Something in the back of my head cautioned about the dangers of doing this and I knew it wasn't wrong. There was a rush of power when the person I'd grabbed had no hope of fighting my hold. It was an entirely different feeling than it had been when I'd stopped Aiz in the negotiations or fought against Adora.

This was power. Too much of it and tainted with something that made me dislike myself.

"Name," I repeated, watching his eyes widen as the realization of what I'd done hit first. The fear followed.

"Orrin, Star of Indrana." His eyes flicked from me to Emmory and back again.

"Good. Orrin, we'd very much like to be off this ship. What's the easiest way to the shuttle bay?"

"Four floors down, but you'd have to go past the bridge."

I couldn't stop myself from tightening my grip on his face and he winced. "Not going to work for us, Orrin. Even though your people come back from it, I'd rather not shoot my way through them."

It was really more about the fact that if someone shot Emmory or Gita, I was the only one who could bring them back, and I didn't want to leave something that important to chance.

"There's another way through, but it's dangerous."

The ship shook and Gita cursed.

"More or less dangerous than where we are now?" I asked.

"Because the Hiervet are knocking on the door and I don't think they came for a chat."

Two bright spots of color appeared high on Orrin's pale cheeks and he pointed just past Gita's shoulder. "There's a service access tube that goes straight down to the shuttle bay."

"Why's it dangerous?" Emmory asked.

"It runs right through the fuel storage for the weapon." Orrin swallowed when I raised an eyebrow. "We're being shot at, ma'am. One of those shots gets through the shield and the whole thing will explode."

"That seems a very poor design choice." I let Orrin go and got to my feet. "Gita, did you get that message out?"

"Yes, ma'am, and a confirmation. I've got a map of the area downloaded to my *smati* and told them where we'd be." She was frowning at the console. "Orrin's telling the truth about the service tube."

My gut cramped in terror, but I ignored it. "That's what we're going to have to use, then. Come on."

"Star of Indrana, please!" The Farian had his hands up and was staring at the barrel of Emmory's Hessian.

"Emmory."

"Easier to just send him back to Faria," he replied.

I saw the panic flicker across Orrin's face and felt an odd well of sympathy for him. "That's rather mercenary of you, *Ekam*. Though you're not wrong."

"Please don't kill me. I heard your speech. It was broadcast to the whole fleet. I don't want to fight."

"Give me a reason not to kill you, Orrin." I crouched at his side again.

"I can fly the shuttle?"

I smiled. "*I* can fly a shuttle. So can these two. That's not good enough to bring along a traitor in our midst."

"I'm not a traitor!"

"You joined up with Adora and Priam and in doing so put all of Faria back on the brink of war with the Shen. Did you think for a second about how that put all your people at risk?"

"Adora said the Shen had driven you mad. That you murdered the other gods, but then you said there could be peace. And I heard…" He trailed off, shaking his head.

I almost responded that it was Adora who was driving me mad, but I kept the thought in my head. "Heard what, Orrin? You're not giving me a reason not to kill you and time is rapidly running out. What did you hear?" I punctuated the words with a poke to his chest.

"I can tell you what they're planning."

"I am already aware of what Adora's planning, she's not going to be able to accomplish it."

"Not Adora, the gods. I heard Priam talking to Thyra, Star of Indrana, they are—"

The ship rocked, and I fell over into Emmory as more alarms screamed through the air and Gita pushed away from the console.

"Move, Majesty. Now."

I muttered a curse at the confirmation of all my gut's screaming. There wasn't time, but now I was going to have to keep this Farian alive on top of everything else until I could get him to tell me just what Thyra was up to.

I grabbed Orrin by the shirt and hauled him to his feet, but I didn't release him. "You're going to stay with Emmory. You so much as blink in a manner that makes me think you're going to hurt him and I won't *ever* kill you, do you understand me? I will keep you alive and in pain forever." My voice was colder than the space outside and Orrin nodded, his head jerking up and down with the movement.

"Good." I shoved him at Emmory.

"Is this a wise idea, Majesty?" he subvocalized over the coms as he caught the Farian.

"It kind of hasn't been from the start," I admitted under my breath, heading for the hatch Orrin had pointed out. *"But what he overheard could be important and I think we're in the middle of that future Sybil showed me. I do not want to be on this ship when those Hiervet get through the shields. We need to get out of here and get word to the others to stay away."*

I was still trying to figure out how I was going to keep them from blowing the *Hailimi* out of the black, but with any luck the Hiervet would be long gone by the time my people showed.

I popped the hatch, looked at Gita.

"Gita, send Hao a message. Tell him—" My brain froze as I tried to think of something to encompass everything I needed him to know in only a few words. "The painting job, Xiao Bai Tolph, he'll know what I mean."

"Done." She finished sending the message, slung her gun over her back, and climbed into the hatch, disappearing down the ladder with a graceful jump.

I did the same, pulling on my gloves and looking over my shoulder at Emmory. He gave me a nod while he herded Orrin forward. I tamped down on the screaming in my brain and scooted, legs first, into the service tunnel.

"Just slide down, Majesty," Gita called up from the first landing.

I obeyed, gloved hands on the outside of the rails as I jumped and slid down the ladder, landing with a jolt. Gita pulled me back and I watched as first Orrin and then Emmory slid down to join us.

I wasn't going to think about the fact that I was in a metal tube. That if the Hiervet scored a direct hit on this very spot we'd be incinerated, trapped, or sucked out into space. The rush of water in a metal coffin filled my head. Something of my determined not-thinking must have shown on my face because my *Dve* put her hand on my back.

"Three more, ma'am," Gita murmured. "You can do this."

I nodded, not trusting my voice. She waited a beat and then jumped. I squeezed my eyes closed and followed.

We repeated the pattern twice more and each time the sound of running water in my ears grew louder. I backed myself into a corner as Gita pulled Orrin in close and grilled him on where the access hatch came out into the shuttle bay.

"Breathe, Majesty." Emmory was standing in front of me, blocking me from Orrin's vision.

"Talk about your fucking liability," I muttered, the laugh that escaped sounding hysterical to my ears.

"You're fine, Hail. You've got this." He leaned in, pressing his forehead to mine. "Breathe."

I dragged in a breath and then another, until my heart calmed down to a pace that wasn't thundering in my head. Emmory waited patiently until I looked into his eyes. "Good?"

"I'm good."

The smile was quick. He straightened. "Gita, we ready?"

"As we'll ever be. I've got no idea on how many enemies. The numbers keep shifting."

"We'll handle it." Emmory turned back to me. "You stay back with Orrin, Majesty. If something goes sideways, you get to a shuttle."

A chill ripped down my spine at the echo of words Portis had said to me not so long ago, but I didn't protest. I wanted to, but I didn't. I just knew that, like with Portis, I didn't want to go.

But this time you will, Hail. The voice was loud in my head. *Now you know what's at stake.* I watched as Emmory and Gita nodded to each other, pulled their guns free, and went to work. This was their job and I knew that as much as I hated letting them clear the bay, it was better to let them do it. They had trained together; they moved with a fluidity I could fake in a pinch but not duplicate. I really should be training with them more.

It wasn't quite as seamless as Emmory and Zin, missing that undeniable sync of a Tracker pair, but it was a thing of beauty to watch. I pulled Orrin out of the hatch and hid us behind a pile of shuttle parts so I could see my BodyGuards after they'd slipped out and moved into the bay.

My speech hadn't touched all the Farians on board and there were plenty who spilled into the bay howling for our blood. Emmory and Gita didn't bother with anything other than head or torso shots, taking out the Farians scrambling around with a calm economy of motion that reminded me a second time of doing jobs with Portis.

It was beautiful. It was brutal. And it was all over in a matter of minutes. The Farians were not prepared for that level of skill. Their centuries-long fight with the Shen had been mostly between space-ships, not people, and it showed.

"Gita, drop."

I appreciated that Emmory kept me in the coms loop. Gita fell to the floor, catching herself with both hands, her gun between her arms. His shot hit the charging Farian right in the chest, the Koros 201 pellet slamming into the man and knocking him back a meter.

He didn't get up.

Gita rolled to her side and then up on one knee in a smooth movement, taking down two Farians on the far side by the door with a pair of head shots.

"Get down and don't move." I pushed Orrin to the floor, bringing my own Koros up and sprinting for the nearest shuttle. The back end was open, obviously torn apart for a replacement or a repair, so I climbed the ladder and flattened myself onto the roof.

The Koros 101 pulse rifle wasn't designed for a sniper, but the bay wasn't all that large and from my vantage point I could pick off people that Emmory and Gita couldn't see.

I shot a Farian who was bringing his weapon to bear on Emmory and watched my *Ekam* spin, eyes narrowing in suspicion.

"Majesty? Was that you?"

"You're welcome."

"I thought I told you—"

"I am technically back with Orrin. Though he's on the ground."

I grinned and shot a pair of Farians as they came through the door. "I feel like Adora knows we're down here. Should we do something about that?"

"I'm voting for getting on a shuttle and getting off this ship before it gets blown to pieces," Gita said when the ship shook again.

"I like her plan. Unfortunately, the one you're on isn't flying anywhere, Majesty," Emmory replied.

"Yeah." I scanned the bay and spotted a shuttle closest to the bay doors that led out to the black. "Emmory, what about that one toward the back?"

"Still predictable with your exit plans, but it'll do."

I laughed. "Shut up and go check it out. I'll cover you."

He sprinted toward the shuttle and I found myself revising my estimate about being able to outrun him as I shot down any Farians in his way. Emmory disappeared into the shuttle and a moment later a Farian went soaring out the door.

I waited as they got up, but they ran in the opposite direction so I let them live.

At least for a little while longer.

"Shuttle's good, Majesty. Get over here."

"Gita, you're next."

"No, ma'am. You come down and get Orrin, we'll go together."

"It's safer this way." I shot yet another Farian in the doorway.

"For me, maybe."

"Understand this isn't the only reason, but you know Hao will never talk to me again if I let you die."

"Hail," Gita sighed, but I could hear the laughter she was trying to suppress.

I grinned and took another shot. "Grab Orrin, Gita, and get to the shuttle. I promise I'll follow."

So maybe I still wasn't all that great at letting them be in front.

My amusement vanished as a blast slammed into the rooftop next to me. I rolled to my feet, bringing my rifle up and returning fire. I didn't hit the Farian who'd nearly shot me, but I made them duck and it bought me enough time to come up with a plan.

It was a shit plan, but it was all I had. I took a deep breath and sprinted across the roof, leaping through the open air and landing on the next shuttle. I caught myself and kept going.

"Emmory, they've got people on the landing above us. Are you going to be able to get those doors open?"

"Gita will have better luck."

"They're almost there." I took another shot at the sniper above me just in case they were suddenly interested in Gita and Orrin as they broke cover.

"Where are you?"

"Coming your way." I ejected the charge pack and slammed another one in, grateful that Adora hadn't bothered to search my pockets.

The last shuttle between me and Emmory was a shorter jump, but something hit me in the back as I leapt and I hit the ground hard.

It hadn't been the sniper, the angle had been wrong, and besides there were no warnings blaring over my *smati*. I rolled, not fast enough, and the next impact felt like a meteor landing in my gut.

22

retched, gasping for air as my body protested the abuse.

"Majesty, we need to go. Where are you?"

I pushed myself upright, gritting my teeth and dragging in a painful breath. "Almost there, give me a minute. We've got a slight complication." I blinked the tears from my eyes as I scanned for the unseen threat.

"Your readings are all over the place. What's going on?"

"Not quite sure." I switched to my *smati*, searching the space in front of me, searching for anything to explain the sudden assault. But there was nothing; even the sniper was gone when they could have lined up a perfect shot on my head and blown my brains out.

"I'm coming out."

"No—" My protest was interrupted by a strike that snapped my head back and sent me flying into the wall. I landed in a heap, curses sliding out of my mouth along with the blood I spat on the floor.

My ears were ringing. I shook my head twice as Priam resolved out of thin air in front of me. Even in my dizzy state I knew he hadn't just dropped in like Thyra had when she moved locations. He'd been there the whole time and I couldn't see him, not even with my *smati*.

"You were supposed to save us! You have ruined everything," he snarled. "Spoiled thousands of years of work with your stumbling."

"You haven't been paying attention, that's kind of my specialty."

I blocked his strike, the impact ringing through my arm as I shrugged off the pain and twisted to grab the limb. Aiz's lesson and the hundreds of hours I'd spent fighting were screaming in my head.

But Priam disappeared again, or at least he seemed to. I realized I still had a hold of him and took a swing, muttering a prayer as I did.

My fist connected with something solid. I tightened my grip on the Farian Hiervet, hitting him again until he flickered back into view.

"What did I ruin, Priam? What were you planning?" I hoped the questions would catch him off guard but he pulled out of my grasp and vanished in the same instant.

Bugger me. How the fuck am I supposed to fight this?

I'd expected to be fighting someone I knew after Aiz's warning about how they'd play with my mind, but Priam just seemed to be content to trick my eyes by not being there at all.

"Majesty!"

"Stay there!" I shouted at Emmory before he could bolt from the shuttle. I couldn't risk Priam killing him.

Dark Mother, think, Hail! How can you fight something you can't see?

I closed my eyes.

The strange shuffling gait of the Farian Hiervet grew louder as Priam rushed me. I waited, counting on my patience and my luck to save me and when I thought he was close I dodged to the side, picking the direction on nothing more than instinct. Pain burst through my left shoulder and I looked down in horrified fascination as the blood welled from the spot where Priam's limb had driven through the muscle.

That wasn't the only cause of the pain that slammed into me; the rolling shock felt like someone had reached inside and was ripping the best parts of me away.

"I am going to eat your soul, Star of Indrana. Humans are weak, watery things, but maybe the stories are true and you will be different." Priam shifted back to visible and I stared up into his black eyes.

I was thankful that just this once I didn't have a quick retort, because it meant my mouth was closed when his head exploded.

Everything snapped back into place with the force of a punch and I couldn't stop the scream that was ripped out of my throat. The bulkhead behind me was destroyed, but it thankfully had led to another compartment and the safety force field on the far side of that room had sprung into place the moment the outside was breached.

"Majesty!" Emmory caught me as I slid to the side, Priam's limb still sticking out of my shoulder. "Deep breath." He barely gave me any time to obey before he yanked the offending thing free.

"Emmory, we have to go now!" Gita's voice was too loud over the com, or it might have been just in my head, which suddenly felt lighter than air.

Emmory scooped me up and sprinted back to the shuttle. "We're in, Gita, go." He lowered me to the deck and turned, slamming his palm into the panel by the door.

"Did you shoot him?"

"I thought the 201 might have better luck, Majesty. I was right." He knelt at my side as the shuttle lifted off. "Let me see."

"Be my guest. I'd heal it myself but I feel a bit funny." I groaned and leaned my head back as he pulled down a medical kit and went to work. "Good job, Emmy. Remind me to give you a raise."

Orrin was staring at us in awe. "You killed a god."

"Technically he did. Come over here and give me a hand."

"No."

Orrin froze at the wealth of violence in Emmory's voice.

"He doesn't get to touch you, Majesty."

I decided arguing was probably bad form and nodded instead. It was better to let my *Ekam* finish his work anyway. I sat up with his help as he wrapped the bandage around my shoulder and felt a sting, followed by a rush of relief as the pain abated. "Get me up, *Ekam*, so I can see." I stood, wincing at the spike of pain that fought through the drugs and ignored Emmory's protest as I slid into the seat next to my *Dve*. "Gita, power everything down as soon as we're clear."

"Yes, ma'am."

From our vantage point we could see Adora's ship and the force of Hiervet that was pouring fire into both her vessel and the others of her tiny fleet. At least four smaller ships were shattered, hulls broken open to the vacuum of space.

"Shit," I muttered as the explosion flashed at the heart of Adora's ship and I turned my head to the side, hoping that Gita had us far enough away from the fight. The shock wave hit a moment later, shaking the shuttle and sending alarms blaring, but a few seconds later silence descended.

"Majesty, the Hiervet ships are gone."

"What?"

"The Hiervet ships warped out."

"Fuck," I muttered, leaning on the console. "What are they playing at? There's at least ten of Adora's other ships intact. Why stop now?"

"I don't know," Gita replied. "Do you want me to tell Admiral Hassan to bring in the fleet?"

"Do it."

It was a thing of beauty to watch the combined forces of the Farians and the Shen warp in and demand the surrender of the other ships. Leaderless and in no position to engage in another fight, they complied, and I slumped in my seat with a relieved exhale.

"Majesty, let's get you to the med bay."

I blinked up at Emmory. "We don't have a med bay."

"We just landed in the *Hailimi*," he said with a patient smile, bending down and slipping an arm around my waist on the right

181

side. I looped my arm around his neck, determined to walk under my own power even though my legs felt like I'd run the Hagran Jahali again.

"It could have gone worse, right?" I asked as we made our way to the back of the shuttle. "Hao's still going to fuss, but I'm alive. Gita's alive. You're alive. I want to talk with Orrin. Also, we should talk about training together; I felt a bit out of step there."

"After we get you fixed up, Majesty."

I hummed and could have sworn Emmory chuckled in response.

Mia and Aiz were waiting at the base of the ramp along with Hao. My brother looked first at Gita and then to me, his golden eyes darkening even as I attempted a smile.

"Hail." Mia moved forward first and I tried to wave her off, but my left arm still wasn't working and my right was busy holding on to Emmory. Her hand was cold against my skin and something about her touch made my stomach roll unpleasantly. Mia hesitated, frowned, and waved at her brother. "Aiz, come here."

"What are you covered with?" Aiz asked.

"Priam, mostly." That reply earned me an impressed look, but I shook my head. "Sorry, not even close. Emmory gets credit for that one."

"Thanks for the guns," Emmory said, patting Aiz on the shoulder with his free hand. "The pulse rifles don't work on them but the 201s work just fine."

"Good to know." Aiz reached out and touched my face. His hand was also cold and I couldn't stop the flinch. "What happened?"

"I was fighting Priam. He impaled me with his limb." I tipped my head toward my bandaged shoulder. "Said he was going to eat my soul, and I'm pretty sure he started the process before Emmory blew his head off."

Mia put a hand over her mouth and I heard Hao curse. Even Aiz's smile faded to a grim expression.

"It didn't feel great, like someone was pulling out bits of me.

Then Emmory shot him in the head and it all came rushing back." The room did a slow spin as the words rushed out of me. "I really should probably sit down."

"Let's get her to medical." Aiz took his hand away with a shake of his head. "I want to consult with Sybil before we try to heal her. I don't know what will happen."

I sighed and leaned more fully against Emmory as we started forward. "Tell Sybil that Adora is dead. Her ship went poof. They should expect her and the other Farians wherever it is they show up when they come back."

"We'll tell her, Hail," Mia said. "Don't worry about it."

"Good. Where's Hao?"

"Right here."

I blinked, but the world refused to focus. "Sorry, *gege*. You were right about that mess."

I heard his choked laugh and then the darkness slammed down on me.

I woke several minutes later to a heated discussion between Aiz and Sybil just out of my field of vision.

"Nope, stay down, Your Majesty." The command was accompanied by a hand on my good shoulder and I sank back against the bed. "Dr. Maalai Vohra, Your Majesty. We haven't met yet."

"I suppose that's a good thing, isn't it?" I hissed in pain, earning a mild look from the older woman as she went back to cleaning out the wound in my shoulder. "Is that necessary?"

This time the stern look she gave me could have put a second hole through my shoulder, so I offered up a placating smile and looked back at Sybil and Aiz.

"They've been going for a solid five minutes."

I jumped at the sound of Hao's voice, and Dr. Vohra's pointed *"Dhatt!"* snapped through the air.

"What are they talking about?"

"What happened to you. Concerns that they're not going to be able to heal you. You're going to have to start being a little more cautious if that's the case, little sister." Hao leaned on the side of the table, still watching the arguing pair. His warning was clear enough, though, and I reached for his hand.

"Priam said I spoiled something thousands of years in the making. And Orrin said—" I broke off, glancing at Dr. Vohra as I realized that this wasn't news I wanted spread around.

Hao gave me a curious glance and I mouthed, *Later*.

"Thyra wanted to come with us when we went to get you," he said instead.

"Really? Why didn't she?"

"Mia." He glanced down at me. "I don't know what she saw, but she wasn't about to let Thyra anywhere near your ship. Which was fine with the rest of us." He cracked his neck. "I don't like them, Hail. The longer we spend around them the more I can't shake the feeling that they're wrong."

"Adora said she was helping the Farians evolve. The implications of that when I think about genetically engineered super soldiers is not good, Hao."

"No, it's not," he agreed.

"Do you think they're a vanguard for the Hiervet?" I murmured the question as low as I could, and though Dr. Vohra didn't change the determined pace with which she was cleaning my wound I knew she heard me.

"It's too easy an answer," Hao replied. "I'd like to believe it, but it doesn't add up right."

"It doesn't, and that is the really worrisome part." I squeezed his hand and then cleared my throat. "Have you two sorted things out yet? I'd like to be able to get up off this bed."

Sybil and Aiz turned to me and then seemed to come to some silent agreement. "I wish it were as simple as that," Sybil said, folding her hands together and approaching the bed. "Your soul was disrupted, and you were terribly injured on top of that. I cannot say for sure what using our talents to heal you would set in motion. We feel it may be best to let it heal more naturally."

I raised an eyebrow. "How long is that going to take?"

"A few days, Your Majesty," Dr. Vohra said. "A standard week at the most. It's a bad wound, but you heal quickly according to your *Ekam*."

"I feel fine now, you know." I let go of Hao's hand to gesture at my shoulder. "Except for this, which one of you could take care of for me."

"Your *Ekam* agrees it is best to be cautious," Sybil said.

"Emmory's not the boss of me. Don't you dare say a word." I pointed at Hao.

"What?" He grinned.

I sighed. "Dark Mother, I'm not getting around this, am I? Fine, if you all won't cooperate, then get your asses out of here and let Dr. Vohra do her work."

It was more surprising than it should have been that they obeyed, and, judging from Dr. Vohra's snort of amusement, all too obvious on my face.

"I had thought perhaps the rumors were just that, but I see now they were true. You are a different sort of empress than your mother was, Your Majesty."

"Did you know her?"

"No, ma'am. May Shiva bring her back to a more peaceful life." Maalai lifted a hand to her heart, lips, and forehead before she returned to her work. "I only knew the empire she grew from her mother's ashes and the sacrifices she made to keep us safe. She seemed a proper lady."

"Yeah, I am not."

"It is not a bad thing, Your Majesty." There was laughter in Maalai's voice. "I grew up in an orphanage on New Delhi and yet here I sit, tending to the hurts of the empress herself."

"I suppose you have heard the story I told Hao about growing up in an orphanage," I said with a laugh of my own.

"It's been in the news some. I know we are not the same, Your Majesty, but you treat people like me as though we are. That, if you'll understand I mean no offense, is not something I think your mother could have ever done."

"You are Indranan," I replied. "How could I treat you any different because of an accident of birth?"

"The fact that it is that simple to you is more important to me than you will ever be able to understand." Maalai patted my shoulder and stood. "Let me get one of the newer skin bandages we're testing for this and then I'll help you roll over so we can look at that scratch on your back."

I'd forgotten all about the early strike from Priam, not much of a surprise given what had happened in the following chaos. Thankfully it wasn't all that deep and with Maalai's help I was able to strip off my shirt and lie back down on the bed.

"Knife, Your Majesty?"

"Same limb that impaled me, if you can believe it. I don't know if they're sharp to begin with or if they can make it sharper at will."

"It's a pity he was blown up with the ship," Maalai replied. "I would have liked to do an autopsy."

I laughed, then swore at the sudden pain. "I doubt Thyra would have approved that, Doctor."

"True, we have no idea of their funeral practices, do we?"

"We know far too little about them all the way around."

"Well," Maalai said, smoothing a second micro-thing bandage over the cut on my back. "If you behave yourself, Your Majesty, you'll heal faster and be able to get out of here sooner."

"I'll see what I can do."

"Hmph. I've heard the news stories about that, too, you know."

23

behaved for a total of fourteen hours before I overruled Dr. Vohra and ordered my *Ekam* to bring Orrin into the med bay to see me.

"If he won't talk to anyone but me and you all won't let me out of this bed, then we'll do it the other way around. Don't argue with me, it's important."

"Yes, Majesty." His jaw was tight with frustration as he turned to go.

"Emmory," I called. "If it bothers you to have him in the room with me, see if Fasé or Mia can join us; either of them can handle any trouble."

He didn't answer as he walked out of the room.

"It's not just that," Zin said, crossing to help me when I tried and failed to push myself upright.

"He's mad I got hurt. We've done this dance before—ow." I blinked at my BodyGuard and rubbed the back of my head where he'd hit me.

"Sorry, Your Majesty."

"Are you really?"

"No. Not unless you're sorry for being so flippant about your own well-being."

I glared up at him, but it didn't have any heat and I sighed. "I was actually just going for practical. Believe me when I say I wasn't trying to get myself killed, Zin." Images of Mia's vision of me and the feeling of Priam's limb piercing my chest collided in my brain, making it hard to breathe. For a moment I almost told him every-thing, but I blinked and the urge passed.

"I would have run if I could have, but it all happened so fast."

"I'm sorry, Hail."

I reached for Zin's hand. "I still have to be empress, hurt or not, and if what Orrin overheard is as important as I think it might be, we don't have the time to wait for me to recover."

"Johar offered to get it out of him."

"Oh, ouch." I laughed. "I want Orrin on our side willingly. I will steal Adora's supporters from her one at a time if I have to. I would rather do that than kill them all. Even if we know they come back, especially since we know they come back. We don't want to have this same conversation a decade from now, do we?"

Zin's lips curved into an unwilling smile.

"What?"

"How is it that Aiz trying to turn you into more of a fighter had the opposite effect?"

"You know the answer to that better than anyone, Starzin. War's a terrible, vicious business. Peace is better." I squeezed his hand and released it as Emmory came back into the med bay with Orrin in tow and Fasé following behind. He released the Farian and the man went to his knees, pressing his head to the floor as Zin shifted to the side.

It didn't escape my notice that he was still between me and the Farian.

"Orrin, get up."

Orrin scrambled to his feet, folding his hands together and bow-ing a second time. "Star of Indrana."

I didn't correct him. Sometimes awe was a very helpful thing. "How are you?"

"Fine, Your Majesty. Your people are treating me very well."

"Good." I waved him to the chair Emmory pulled from the cor-ner. "Let's talk about what you know."

Orrin swallowed. "I saved the recording. I can show you."

Fasé stepped up before Emmory could protest. "You can give me the recording, Orrin, and I will give it to the Star."

He swallowed again and then nodded. Fasé took his hand and silence fell on the room for a several heartbeats. Then she blinked and her golden eyes went wide.

"Hail."

"Let me see." I leaned forward, ignoring the pain in my shoulder, and clasped her hand when she crossed to me.

"None of this was foreseen, Thyra. I do not understand."

We were seeing through Orrin's eyes. I could feel his fear as he shrank back into the alcove he was hidden in as Priam's voice echoed in the air.

"It is fine. The future as seen by Sybil can still be achieved," Thyra replied. "We are in the final stages. Don't despair, my darling."

"But the batch isn't ready and the last didn't come out right."

"The previous group is good enough to follow orders and fight. That's all we need to rid ourselves of Fasé's troublesome rebellion."

"That aberration." Priam spat the word with venom in his tone. "You should have let me kill her."

"It is of no matter. Like the human-Shen just an unexpected result of the experiment. I will handle this, Priam. You do your part. I will not waste our children. Don't worry about the Star, I will bring her back to our side. I have an offer for her that will give us everything we want. She will not turn from it."

More voices sounded out in the hallway and the recording cut off.

Fasé and I shared a look as we separated. "They have an army," I whispered. "An army of Farians. That's what Adora meant by evolution. The Farian Hiervet have been changing you all."

"She said *batch*, Hail. She must be talking about the new Farians who are waiting for souls, but how—" She broke off and grabbed Orrin by the collar, shaking him. "You, what else did you hear?"

Orrin started and would have fallen out of his chair if she hadn't had a grip on him. "That was all of it, *Mardis*, I swear."

"Fasé—"

"Majesty, Thyra is here requesting an audience," Emmory said.

"Where's Aiz?" I sent him a message even as I asked the question. "Fasé, take Orrin back to his cell. Com Johar and have her meet you there. Orrin, I'd suggest you remember anything of even the remotest significance for Fasé here. Johar takes it personally when people refuse to answer questions, understood?"

"Of course, Star of Indrana."

I waited until he'd followed Fasé out of the room before I slid from the bed, ignoring Emmory's glare. "Not going to let Thyra on this ship, Emmory, even if I hadn't just watched her confess with my own eyes."

"You could tell her to go away."

"I could," I admitted, wincing as I braced myself on the edge of the bed. "But I want to see her face when she gets a look at what Priam did to me."

"Majesty, we cannot protect you from her."

"Of course you can." I took Zin's offered arm. "You've kept me safe all this time, Emmory, this is no different. Besides, Aiz just messaged me back that he'll meet us at the ramp. Thyra won't try anything with him around."

That muscle in Emmory's jaw twitched again and I hoped I wasn't going to have to overrule my *Ekam* again for a while. I was pretty sure I'd used up my stock for the next year. I had another reason for wanting to see Thyra, one I hadn't yet shared with my Guards. Sybil had sent me a recording of Thyra hearing the news about Priam, and her response had been interesting to say the least.

"Fine." He was out the door before I could say another word, and

I could hear him on the com calling for the BodyGuards and the Marines to assemble in the cargo bay.

We made our way from the med bay in silence. I'd realized several steps down the corridor that this wasn't my greatest idea. I was far more exhausted by what Priam had done to me than I'd realized.

"Wait a moment, Zin," I murmured as we hit the cargo bay. "Let me catch my breath."

"Hail, what are you doing?" Aiz demanded.

"Speaking with Thyra. You're here just in case things go south." I smiled at his raised eyebrows.

"It's not a good idea for you to be up."

"Sometimes we have to do things that aren't necessarily good for us when the future of our people is on the line, don't we?" That shut him up just like I knew it would. "Okay, Zin, I think I can make it down the ramp without falling over."

My focus was entirely on staying upright and not leaning too heavily on Zin. I wanted Thyra to know that Priam had been responsible for injuring me, but I didn't want to give her the impression I was helpless.

"Keep an eye on her, Zin," I murmured. "If I don't watch my feet I might fall over."

"Your Majesty, I could have come to you," Thyra said as we came to a stop.

"It's all right, Thyra. My doctor says the walk is good for me." That wasn't what Dr. Vohra was going to say when she realized I was out of bed, but the lie was easy on my tongue.

"I have medical training, Your Majesty, I could—" Thyra took a step forward but stopped at Emmory's cleared throat.

"What did you want?" I asked with a smile.

"Well, to see how you were." Thyra tapped her limbs together nervously, unable to hide the fact that she was watching the others around me. "And to speak with you, but this doesn't seem the best timing."

"This is probably the only chance you're going to get for a while," I replied. "And I admit you should probably get to the point; it won't be long before I should sit down again."

"Your Majesty, there is no easy way to say this but I was told you were responsible for Priam's death."

"Priam chose to go with Adora. He was not forced. I confirmed this with my own eyes. However, your information isn't entirely correct, Thyra. Emmory killed him because Priam was trying to kill me."

Her eyes opened wide. "He never would have—"

"What do you think made this hole in my shoulder?" I asked. I could feel the tension of my BodyGuards rising. "Believe me when I say if I could have talked him down I would have, but Priam made his choice."

"I understand, Your Majesty, but—"

"If you're about to ask if we really had to, Thyra, I'll just head you off and say yes. Emmory's job is to keep me safe. Priam was trying to kill me. No one gets a pass on that."

Thyra whipped her gaze to Aiz. "The Cevallas have."

I pushed myself fully upright with a snarl, pleased when Thyra took a startled step backward. "The circumstances were vastly different and if you'd like to stay on my good side you'll never say that again. What passed between me and Aiz on Sparkos was with my consent, is that understood?"

"Perfectly, Your Majesty." She dipped her head. "I will take my leave and go mourn for Priam."

"You do that." I watched her go, waiting until she was out of sight before I turned and went back into the *Vajrayana*. I made it up the ramp and halfway back to medical before my knees gave out on me and I grabbed awkwardly for Zin as I fell.

"Damn it, Hail." Emmory caught me on the other side.

"I'm all right." I couldn't hold on with my left arm, and my right was tangled in Zin's uniform jacket. "Just give me a minute."

"You're going back to medical."

"I am. I'd like to do it under my own power if it's all the same to you." I glowered at Aiz, who'd followed us but hadn't spoken. "Not a word from you."

He lifted his hands. "I don't think you need me so I'm going back to quarters."

"Aiz," I called as he started to walk away. "Thank you."

He smiled and shook his head. "Go lie down, Hail."

"Working on it."

I did what I could to stay upright as Emmory and Zin escorted me. Through some miracle we made it to my bed before Dr. Vohra, and I leaned back, closing my eyes with a sigh.

When I opened them again, Emmory was gone. Zin was by the door, his arms crossed over his wide chest and a soft smile on his face.

"I'm going to have to listen to him rant this evening. I hope it was worth it, Majesty."

"Maybe?" I sighed again. "I never know until everything is over with and sometimes not even then. Sybil sent me a recording of Thyra's reaction to the news of Priam's death. She wasn't surprised he was dead."

"I wouldn't have expected her to be," Zin replied. "If she could pinpoint his location she would have felt it when he died."

"I hadn't thought of that, but you're probably right." I paused, scanning back over the video Sybil had sent me with a frown. "There's something more there, though. She's pissed about Priam. She wasn't expecting this to go down the way it did, and this—"

"Your Majesty, were you out of your bed?" Dr. Vohra demanded as she came into the room.

"I had something important to attend to, Maalai."

"Nothing is more important than your recovery."

I looked at Zin for support, but he lifted his hands with a grin and a shake of his head. I sighed. "You'd think I wasn't actually the empress around here."

24

The rest of the week saw me under Dr. Vohra's steely gaze and Emmory backing her order that under no circumstances was I allowed out of med bay. Which left me little to do but worry over the problem of Thyra's phantom army.

I'd told the others. Aiz had taken it better than I'd expected, though he didn't have any additional ideas about what that army could entail. The Farian Hiervet couldn't manufacture souls out of thin air.

Or could they? Had Thyra figured out some way to grow Farian souls in the same way she'd figured out how to harvest them?

I rubbed at the back of my neck, wincing at the soreness that still lingered in my left shoulder. "This normal-healing thing is cowshit."

Zin chuckled and patted my hand. "The downtime is good for you."

"Why does everyone keep saying that?" I grinned. "I'm teasing, mostly. Between you and me I'm getting restless." I sighed and rubbed at my face. "There's so much to do."

"Let me go talk to Dr. Vohra and see if we can't get you out of here a little early. I think she's forgiven you for your earlier escape."

"Have I mentioned lately that you're my favorite?"

Zin laughed, and I spotted the way he brushed his fingers over Emmory's as my *Ekam* joined us.

"Still mad at me?" I asked.

"I wasn't mad. A little grumpy about it, maybe," he admitted.

"It had to be done, but you were right. Happy?"

"You're not dead. That makes me happy."

It was a simple enough response, delivered in Emmory's solid manner without a trace of flippancy, and it brought tears to my eyes.

"Are you feeling better, Majesty?" he asked.

"Immensely." I smiled at him and held out my hands. "Do I get to leave this Shiva-damned bed?"

"That's Dr. Vohra's call." But he took my hands and helped me slide out of the bed. "Your vitals are good. I am curious what Aiz will say."

"We can go ask him, if you're needing his approval."

Emmory gave me the Look. I grinned.

"Something to say, Majesty?"

"No. It's just nice to have everyone getting along."

"We had a conversation." Emmory's face didn't give anything away and before I could ask just what that meant or when the conversation had occurred, Zin returned with Dr. Vohra.

"An hour," she said. "Not a second more. Am I understood?"

"Yes, ma'am."

I left medical, Emmory and Zin on either side of me. We walked in silence for a few minutes before I laughed. "Honestly, you two, I'm fine. As brushes with death go that wasn't even a three."

"We're scaling them now?" Zin asked.

"I'll admit my metric is a little skewed, but it's just automatic at this point. I'd rather talk about how we're going to handle Thyra and Adaran."

"Two more shots from the 201 would do it," Emmory muttered.

I was still laughing when we got to Aiz's quarters and he looked up from the desk, waving me in with a raised eyebrow.

"You appear to be in better spirits," he said, standing and pointing to the chair. "Sit."

"Bossy." But I sat, privately grateful for the chance to rest. I'd been up and out of my bed in medical a number of times, but it was more than a little shocking how exhausted the walk from there to Aiz's quarters had made me.

Aiz held his hands out and I put mine in them. For a moment there was nothing. Then the familiar electric sensation of his energy skimmed over me.

"How do you feel?"

"Fine." I smiled at his snort. "I really do. A little tired and the shoulder aches, but otherwise I'm okay."

"Tell me again what happened?"

I recounted the incident with Priam, shuddering a little as I remembered the feeling of what had apparently been my soul being pulled out of me. Aiz tightened his fingers around mine and his energy soothed away the discomfort.

"Do you feel strange? Hearing voices?"

"No new ones." I ignored his frown, countering with a bright smile. "Am I cleared?"

"You're yourself, that's for sure." He let me go, leaning down and pressing a kiss to the top of my head. "As obnoxious as a little sister should be," he murmured in Shen so low I nearly didn't catch it.

"You're sure?" Emmory asked.

"Was there a question?" I glanced between them with a frown.

Aiz shook his head. "A concern. Your *Ekam* interrupted Priam when he was trying to eat your soul. Sybil said she's not aware of that ever happening, and the only time I've seen it neither the Shen nor the Farian Hiervet survived the encounter." His smile was tight and I held back the question that wanted to leap to my mouth.

"I am reasonably sure I'm me. Does this mean you can fix this the rest of the way?" I tipped my head at my shoulder but Aiz shook his head.

"Dr. Vohra has done good work on you; it's best to let her continue."

"You're scared of her."

"Terrified." Aiz grinned. "And rightfully so. You should have heard the tongue lashing she gave your *Ekam* while you were unconscious."

"You'd think she'd know by now that nobody has control over me." I pushed to my feet. "Aiz, I don't know what game Thyra is playing, but I don't trust her."

"I am glad to hear it. Things will only get more dangerous from here on out. Speaking of which, I had Admiral Amo split the fleet and send a large part of our ships back to a safe planet."

"Is that wise? You just said things were more dangerous."

"Yes and no," Aiz said. "I don't think the Farians will attack, especially without Adora to fan the flames. Her rebellion will falter and die with her gone. I will feel better if the entire fleet isn't sitting here out in the open."

"I don't blame you for that," I murmured in agreement.

"I sent Marcela with the fleet. I'm technically in charge of what's left." He dodged my halfhearted swing. "Let's keep an eye on Thyra; with Priam dead, she's backed into a corner."

"*Hai Ram.*" I exhaled. "I don't think it matters if they're human or Hiervet, backing someone into a corner always has the same result."

We made it back to the med bay with two minutes to spare, and forty-eight hours later I'd wheedled Dr. Vohra into releasing me fully into Emmory's care.

"She'd never have let me go if she knew how rarely I listen to your orders." I rolled my shoulder and blew out a breath. "Amazing how easy it was to get dependent on the Farian healing ability. What will it do to us if we have to untangle ourselves from that, Emmy?"

"I suspect we'll manage, Majesty."

I hummed, frowning down at my bare feet. Even some of the latest medical tech had come from the Farians; I wasn't sure we'd ever be able to completely separate our societies. The pressure to make sure this didn't all fall apart grew with every moment that passed.

"That's a serious face." Hao stood in the corridor outside my rooms; Alba and Dailun were with him.

"Weight of the galaxy," I replied with a roll of my eyes. "But hey, I've been cleared for duty and it appears the three of you are here to talk to me so that's nice timing." I gestured at the door of my quarters, patting Kisah on the shoulder as I passed.

"*Jiejie.*" Dailun followed me into the quarters. "The Istrevitel wish to speak with you."

"Do they now?" I murmured.

He held out a hand to me. I took it and the message passed from his *smati* to mine.

I closed my eyes, letting the image play out in my head. The Istrevitel who appeared looked startlingly like Dailun, though with darker skin and wider eyes that were black as the night sky. Their hair was a gorgeous teal, swept back from a round face, and a trio of lines in the same color ran vertically down their left cheek.

They reminded me of the Farian Hiervet's markings and I was immediately curious about the significance.

"Star of Indrana, I am Captain Dirah Zov, she/her, of First Company with a message of greeting for you. We would speak with you of the destruction that is bearing down on this galaxy but understand that the appearance of a force such as ours could create"—a smile fought for prominence on her full lips—"unwanted chaos. We are not welcome at home. However, the leaders of the Svatir would also like to meet you and so a spot has been chosen on one of our outermost worlds.

"We have sent this invitation along with coordinates to our little brother and look forward to seeing you at the appointed time."

"Is it wrong that I like her?" I asked Dailun, and he smiled. Though I could see the hesitation on his face and the tension in his shoulders.

"I would caution against trusting the Istrevitel, Your Majesty. I cannot vouch for them or their motives. They are, by all accounts, here for the glory of war and nothing else. If your mission is peace you should be very careful."

"My mission is to keep us all safe, little brother." I leaned in and touched my forehead to his with a smile. "If that is peace, so much the better, but much as we may wish it, less violence is not always the option." I saw the disappointment flash in his eyes. "I promise I will do my best."

"Your Majesty, let me see."

I passed the file on to Emmory and the others and waited for them to watch, rolling over the possibilities in my head. "I guess that's our next step. We'll have to figure out who's coming with me."

"Where do you think you're going?"

I turned and grinned at the trio in the doorway. "Taking a trip to meet the Istrevitel, want to come?"

Fasé hid her smile behind a hand while Aiz had a carefully neutral expression pasted on his face. Mia did not smile back. "You're just out of med bay, Hail," she said.

"Yes, cleared by my doctor and everything. Even Aiz said I was okay."

"Don't drag me into this fight." He held his hands up.

"Are we fighting?" Despite our apologies, Mia had continued to withdraw from me, and I didn't know what to do about it.

"We are not." Mia folded her hands together and shook them at me in a surprisingly deferential gesture that only made me more curious what was going on with her. "I am curious as to where you are going, though."

"I'm up for a bit of a fight," Hao interjected. "Why do we think it's a good idea for you to run off to meet with the Istrevitel? The last time you left here you came back bloody and no offense, Dailun, but we have no way of knowing what their motives are. They may not have Hail's best interests in mind."

"None taken," Dailun replied with a shrug. "You are not wrong, honored cousin."

"You heard them," I said. "We can't have a military force suddenly show up here, and they would hardly invite me to meet with them and a representative from the Svatir government if they were going to hurt me. Think of the intragalactic incident that would come from letting me get injured."

"It won't mean a lot if we're all dead."

I made a face at Hao. "They want to help. I'm supposed to assume they're the enemy?"

Aiz glanced at Dailun. "He just told you they can't be trusted."

"I believe he was speaking in general terms, not in the 'risk to my life' portion of things. Dailun, how upset will they be if we show up for this meeting in force?"

He wiggled his hands and looked to Alba for help. My chamberlain smiled and shrugged. "The Svatir would be upset, Majesty. The Istrevitel would likely be impressed."

"Interesting. So we either impress the ones we need help from or upset the pacifists. No offense, Dailun, but I think I know which way we're going here."

"None taken, *jiejie*. Though you sound like him." He grinned at me and pointed at Hao. "I do not disagree with your decision."

Fasé nodded. "If Hail can secure more allies in the fight against the Hiervet, that is the best course of action for us."

"Good." I exhaled, trying to pretend that things going smoothly for once didn't make my skin want to crawl right off me and out the door. "The next question is will Faria be safe if we take a combined force with us?"

"Adora is in limbo, waiting for rebirth, as are a number of her followers. Even more of them are in custody. Her rebellion lost traction before it ever really got started," Aiz replied. "Faria is as safe as we can make it at the moment."

"That's good news. Dailun, send a message back that we will

be happy to meet Captain Zov on the date suggested—" I stopped and looked at Fasé. "Are we going to be able to travel that far in this ship?" We still hadn't tested the new engines in the *Hailimi*, and getting stuck even farther away from home wasn't a great plan.

"You should, Majesty," she said. "If you bring a larger Farian ship with you, it will be able to tow the *Hailimi* back should there be an issue."

"Duly noted." I smiled. "Obviously you and Mia and Aiz will stay here. Do you want me to leave people with you?" I knew Hao would protest, but it seemed like a good idea to leave at least a few of my people to remind everyone of my presence.

Silenced rebellion or not, I knew all too well how quickly things could flare back up the minute people relaxed.

"I think we're good," Aiz replied.

"I will go with you," Mia said, her words tumbling over the top of her brother's.

25

There was a moment of stunned silence in the room at her announcement. Then Aiz said something in Shen too fast for me to catch. Mia's reply was sharp, equally too fast for the translator in my *smati* as we all stood frozen, watching them.

"I will go with you," she repeated.

I decided it was not in my best interests to ask if she was sure and instead looked around the room and rubbed my hands together. "All right, we'll make our preparations and be under way. Thank you."

People started filtering out. Aiz and Mia left, the stirrings of an argument in their voices and on their faces.

"Fasé?" She crossed over to me when I waved at her. "How are things?"

"Do you mean present or future?" Fasé asked with a tiny smile.

"Both, I guess." I leaned against my desk and studied her. "You doing all right?"

"One would think that should be my line, given that of the two of us you are the more recently impaled." Fasé tilted her head to the side and studied me. "You are bothered?"

"I have a whole list," I admitted. "Which one do you want?"

"Start at the top, we'll work our way down."

I laughed and pushed myself upright to hug her. "We have come a long way from the floor of my ship, haven't we, Fasé?"

"You still keep ending up covered in blood, so I'm not sure," she teased, hugging me back and then letting me go. "But mostly, yes. Also, thank you for the other day. After I saw the future that Sybil showed you, I had to admit to myself how very close I was to running. If you hadn't come to speak with me—" She shook her head.

"You really should thank Hao."

Fasé blinked and I laughed at the shock on her face.

"I'm serious. He told me to talk to you. I would have missed the chance with everything that was going on."

"I suppose I will have to, then, won't I?"

I laughed again. "Try to say it a little less like you just got stuck on barracks bathroom duty."

"There is nothing worse than that." Fasé shuddered with a grin. Then she sobered. "What is bothering you?"

"So many things." I rubbed a hand over my face as I tipped it back. "Do you know what's going on with Mia? She seems distant."

"We have not talked beyond all the negotiations. I know she tangled with Thyra just after you all left, but—"

"What?" I had to wave a hand at Emmory before he started over. "Hao said she wouldn't let Thyra on the ship, not that they fought. Why is this the first I'm hearing of it?"

"Not physically." Fasé shook her head. "But after Thyra dumped you on Adora's ship and came back, Mia tore into her. Demanded that Thyra take her to the ship. Thyra refused." Fasé grinned. "I'm still not a hundred percent sure that Mia didn't tell Gita not to let Thyra come with us to get you purely out of spite."

"Hao said Thyra wanted to come with you."

"Initially yes, and Gita would have refused anyway based on that vision Sybil showed us. She felt it would be safer not to have the Farian Hiervet on board. When Thyra heard the Hiervet were there and shooting at Adora's ship, she scuttled back off to the Pedalion chamber." This time Fasé's smile was sharp, just shy of vicious. "They are really afraid of the Hiervet, Hail."

"It makes me nervous." I shook my head and watched her smile fade. "That would be issue number two. As powerful as they are, how are we supposed to win against something they're afraid of?"

"I have faith in you."

"Let's just hope that faith doesn't get us all killed." I watched her for a moment. "Fasé, I—have you seen me die? Permanently, I mean."

She tipped her head to the side, staring at me curiously. "You have never asked me that. Why now?"

"I don't know." It wasn't entirely true. I wanted to know if Mia's visions were part of a chain or opposing choices, but I couldn't force the words out into the air. I shook my head and shoved a hand into my hair with a sigh. "Morbid curiosity, I guess?"

She studied me for a moment longer, golden eyes on mine until I was sure she was going to call me on my cowshit. "It will be all right, Hail. I am not going to tell you what is coming and for good reason. I think it is better this way. As I have faith in you, have some in me."

"Okay." I exhaled a shaky breath. "I don't want to mess this up."

"Trust yourself, Star of Indrana, you have never gone astray."

"Don't let Hao tell you about the time I got us lost on Yavin-18, then."

Fasé's laughter was bright as sunshine. "You know what I mean and he would, too. I meant what I said about the pair of you, a strange and contented orbit. At the time I may have viewed it with some contempt, but now? He is an anchor point for you and you for him. Hold on to that, you will need it later."

Something told me she was talking about long past what we were currently wrapped up in. I held out my hand. "I have been blessed with many great things in my life, but none so great as my friends."

Fasé reached out and took the hand I offered. "I do have a request. If you feel you could survive without Stasia for a short time I would not complain to have her with me."

"Done." My maid wouldn't go without an order and I was happy enough to issue it.

"Thank you. Go talk to Mia." Fasé squeezed my hand and then left me alone.

Something told me I was going to have to say good-bye to Stasia sooner rather than later. The thought was accompanied by a funny little twist of sadness. She and Fasé deserved a happy ending after everything they'd been through, but I would miss her desperately.

The same was true of all my people, really. As well as Aiz and Mia. The Shen had been at war for too long; they deserved peace.

It was up to me to figure out some way to give it to them for good.

"Astéri." Talos tipped his head at me from the doorway of Aiz and Mia's quarters.

"I'd like to speak with Mia?"

"Ah. She is not here. I believe she's in the gym with your Body-Guard. With Starzin," he clarified.

"Oh." I glanced over my shoulder, surprising myself with the hesitation. "Will they mind if I interrupt?"

"I can't see it being a problem." Talos smiled.

I nodded to him and headed off down the corridor, Kisah trailing along at my side.

The gym wasn't crowded, but a number of people—Indranan, Farian, and Shen alike—were working out, sparring, or even just chatting. I spotted Johar leaning against a wall on the far side watching Mia and Zin spar and made my way over to her.

"Hey," Jo said. "How's the shoulder?"

"Almost healed." I suspected the ache would linger for a while, but I had my range of motion back and Emmory promised a return to sparring before we left to meet with the Istrevitel. "What are you up to?"

"I like watching them spar," she replied, tipping her head toward the mat. Mia threw Zin effortlessly, but he hit and rolled back onto his feet with a grin. "It's like watching dancers."

"Zin mentioned that they've been doing this awhile."

"Since shortly after you came back to us."

I leaned against the wall next to Jo, pressing my shoulder into hers. "Did I tell you thank you?"

"For what?"

"Being you. Looking out for me. Knocking my ass out and carrying me through the jungle. Even if you did fall for me knocking you over and stealing your knife."

"I wondered if that was when you did it. You always were a hell of a pickpocket." Johar snorted a laugh. "I don't need it. You're my friend. I was there to watch over you."

"I owe you for it. I know I wasn't particularly grateful for it at the time, or particularly cooperative."

"I believe the term you're looking for is *massive pain in my ass*." She grinned and waved a hand. "Seriously, though, don't worry about it."

I glared. "Will you let me say thank you?"

"Or you're welcome, Your Majesty. Whichever."

"I should send your ass home."

"You like having me around."

I didn't reply but instead leaned against her again. Johar smiled and slipped her arm around my waist and we settled into a comfortable silence as we watched the pair in front of us.

I knew how good Zin had gotten from our bout the other day, but watching Mia fight was beyond impressive. I'd experienced how fast she was the one time I'd tried attacking her on Sparkos, but I'd been so lost to my rage in the moment I hadn't been able to appreciate her fluid grace.

"Shiva," I murmured as Mia spun out of the way and flipped, her brown braid trailing behind her. She landed, kicked the back of Zin's knee, and followed the strike with a move that put two fingers into the hollow of Zin's throat.

But her control was perfect and a hit that otherwise would have killed him was nothing more than fingertips to skin.

Zin laughed and folded his hands together in acknowledgment. Mia smiled in return and helped him to his feet. They separated, bowed, and started again.

"It's fucking impressive to watch," Johar said. "She's really good, but all the Shen fight at a level so far above what we're used to." She glanced at me. "Well, what I'm used to anyway."

"I don't know that you can group me in with them after only a few months. They've been fighting all their lives."

"Maybe not, but I'd still put a lot of money on you in a fight."

"Aiz probably would have taught you," I murmured.

"Oh no." Johar objected with a laugh. "As fascinating as they were, I wasn't about to try to go toe-to-toe with either of them. Too many things could have gone wrong. I was set on just popping them both as fast and cleanly as we could so we could get you out of there."

I wasn't entirely surprised by the idea that Johar had planned on killing the Cevallas while we were on Sparkos. If I'd been even remotely coherent it probably would have been my plan, too.

"Gita stopped me."

"Gita?" That surprised me. I'd have thought for sure my *Dve* would have supported a plan by Johar to kill Aiz and Mia.

Jo shrugged. "It was a good call. You were attached. In the end we were reasonably certain that killing them would have pushed you completely over the edge."

"She wasn't wrong," I said after a few minutes of watching Zin and Mia spar in silence. "I wasn't myself."

"No, you were." Johar squeezed me against her side with a sad smile. "You were lost to your grief and on the edge of a fury I hope to never see from you again, but you were yourself."

I didn't know quite what to make of that, but I didn't argue. Outside of Hao, Johar had known me the longest. Even if our association had been in bits and pieces over the years, Jo had always been straight with me. It made me more willing to listen to her when she said things like that.

"They're done," Johar announced, removing her arm from around me and stretching. "Who do you need me to distract?"

"What?"

"Did you come to talk to Mia or to Zin?"

"Oh." I huffed a laugh. "Mia."

"I expected as much," Johar said, and headed toward Zin. "Hey, Hail?" She stopped. "I know you're busy, do you mind if Gita and I look into that army problem for you?"

"Did you get more out of Orrin?"

"Not really." Johar wiggled a hand with a frown. "Interesting stuff, let's say. I don't want to talk about it in the open."

Now, that was interesting. Enough so that I almost told her we should gather the others and talk about it now. "I don't have to—"

Jo laughed and shook her head. "I'll keep you updated. Go talk to your girl." She tipped her head in Mia's direction and waved a hand at me.

I tried to ignore the sudden thumping of my heart and wondered if Zin was watching me. It was probably a good thing; at least he'd tell Emmory I was fine. "Do you have a minute?" I asked Mia as she passed.

"I do. I'd like to shower if you can walk with me back to my quarters." She rubbed at the back of her neck with her towel.

I swallowed the offer of my shower and nodded instead. We headed out of the gym and into the corridor with Kisah in front.

The biggest problem with this plan of mine, I realized, was that I had no idea what I needed to say to Mia. I'd managed to talk myself out of the idea that she was mad at me for some unknown transgression, but beyond that I wasn't sure what I should say.

"What is it, Hail?" Mia asked, startling me out of my thoughts.

"I've been worried about you." The words slipped out and I bit my lip with a glance at the ceiling. "Are you okay? How are you feeling?"

"I am feeling fine."

"Good." We continued to her quarters. Talos sent me a sympathetic smile as we came in and joined Kisah in the corridor without comment. I waited for the door to close. "Are you going to tell me what you and Aiz argued about?"

Mia stopped on her way to the bathroom and looked over her shoulder. "I would if I thought it concerned you."

"You want to come with me, I figure that qualifies me to at least know the basics."

Mia smiled, but it was edged with a sharpness I hadn't yet seen directed my way. "Don't use that empress voice on me, Hail."

I raised an eyebrow. "My apologies," I said, switching to Shen. "I am the one in charge."

"It pleases my brother to give up control for a while, especially to someone he trusts."

I didn't want to fight with her. I wanted to know what was wrong. Taking a deep breath, I crossed to her, slipped my hands into the pockets of my pants, and leaned against the wall next to the bathroom door. "What about you? Do you trust me?"

This time Mia's smile was softer and she reached a hand out, trailing it over my lower lip as she passed. The jolt of electricity that shot through me was very real, but I didn't move.

"I have built my whole life on knowing what is coming," Mia said, continuing into the bathroom, and I tipped my head back against the wall with a silent exhale. "It made things more secure, but it also gave me an illusion of control."

The water came on and for a moment it was the only sound in the room.

"I didn't tell you the other day when you apologized, but you weren't entirely wrong, Hail. I suspect of the two of us, you are far better equipped for the idea of not being in control. I am still trying to find my way."

"I can't quite figure out if this means you're going to tell me why Aiz was upset that you want to come with me or not."

Mia's answering laugh was muffled as she stepped into the shower, and I stared at the ceiling for a long moment before closing my eyes. "Would you believe me if I told you it was as mundane as him being worried for my safety?"

"I might." I couldn't see a reason for her to lie to me about it anyway.

"It was, mostly anyway," Mia continued. "I know the risks. The Svatir are friendly enough with the Shen, but it is important we make contact with the Istrevitel at the same time you do." The water stopped. "I do trust you, Hail, with the lives of my people and my brother." She sighed and I stayed where I was, my heart thudding in my ears as Mia wrestled with whatever it was she needed to say.

I hadn't missed that she didn't say she'd trust me with her life. Was she so certain of the future that put her on that cold metal table?

"Will you take it the wrong way if I say I do not want the Shen to get lost in the blaze of the Star of Indrana? You burn so brightly." Her words were accompanied by the touch of her hand on my arm, and only then did I open my eyes to look at her.

I smiled down at her, thankful she'd gotten dressed and wasn't standing there in a towel. Though that thought sent my brain spinning in a whole other direction and I cleared my throat. "I won't. You have your people to think of, it's only right."

It was easy enough to say, even more easy to realize I meant it. Mia's devotion to her people ran deeper than this thing between us. I didn't blame her. I had to put my people first also, and the time we had together was fast ticking away.

Mia stepped closer, sliding her arms around my waist with a smile. "You are an amazing human being, Hail Bristol. It would be all too easy to get pulled into your orbit and never want to leave."

Gita's fears of Mia being swept away by some adoration of me were apparently unfounded, but her fears that this would be the death of me were spot on. Which made the next words difficult but so very necessary.

"Should we step back from this?" I flexed my hands where they rested on her hips and watched the confusion flicker through her gray eyes.

"Is that what you want?"

I wanted forever, but I already knew I wasn't getting that. One of us was going to die, or maybe both of us. I shoved my desire away in the back of my heart along with everything else I'd hidden since waking up on the floor of my ship covered in Portis's blood. I swallowed and leaned in, pressing my forehead to hers and resisting the urge to close my eyes.

"This thing between us is so tangled it's sometimes hard to believe it's real. I can't breathe when I look at you, and the thought of losing you—" I couldn't hold her gaze and pulled away, looking at the ceiling until the tears cleared from my eyes as I wrestled with the need to demand that she tell me how I could save her. "I would survive it, I think, knowing everything I know now."

"That's not really an answer," Mia said. "I have asked myself the same questions, you know, and my thoughts run on the same path as yours. Now you see why it was so important to get it right back on Sparkos? Why you needed that space and this time to see if what you were feeling was real?"

"I do," I whispered. "I knew it at the time, too, I just didn't want to admit it."

"What do you want, Hail?"

"I want whatever you are willing to give." I pressed my forehead to hers again. "But I am also all too aware of the responsibilities both of us have."

She smiled and cupped my face in her hands, pressing her lips to mine. "That's the thing about responsibilities," she murmured against my mouth. "If you have enough of them it also usually means you're in a position to ignore them for a while."

I put everything else aside and sank into the kiss.

26

I stood on the bridge of the *Hailimi* and kept my mouth shut through sheer force of will at the sight of the impressive starship that had greeted us at the rendezvous point.

It was so black that if it hadn't been in front of Ndrog, the bright green planet below, I'd have had trouble picking it out against the backdrop of space. And something told me that the only reason it was showing up on our sensors was that they wanted to be seen.

The Istrevitel, it seemed, took their mission as protectors of the Svatir very seriously. Understandable, given how the Svatir's pacifist ways left them vulnerable to the rest of us.

Humans didn't travel to the Svatir homeworld often, but there were enough conclaves in human space that a curious person could seek them out. I'd done just that on a trip to Binphos when Hao had left me to my own devices while he closed a deal.

The group I'd found had been older, weathered faces and wrinkled hands, but they'd welcomed me into their home—a spacious warren of rooms that were all interconnected, much like the Svatir themselves. They'd cooed over my green hair, their own colored hair mostly dulled with age, and fed me until Hao had shown up with a roll of his eyes and shake of his head to lead me back to the ship.

I'd sought out more Svatir as we traveled; something about their quiet, peaceful nature had drawn me in, despite my gunrunner ways.

But the sight before us was unlike anything of the Svatir. This was a ship built for war.

"Jealous?" Hao murmured from my right side.

"A little," I admitted. "But can you imagine?"

"Oh yeah. Give me half a dozen and we'd run the whole human arm of the galaxy within the month."

"Are you two finished?" Gita asked, and I turned to her with a beaming smile.

"Vessel is hailing us, Your Majesty," Captain Saito said before I could respond to Gita.

"Put it through."

I straightened as the screen at the front of the bridge resolved to show Captain Zov. There were two Istrevitel behind her, both with snow-white hair and a single white dot on their left cheeks.

"Star of Indrana, we thank you for coming."

"Captain Zov. It's a pleasure to be here."

"I wish that were the case." Her smile was humorless. "We have much to discuss. The Svatir representatives are already here. We will meet you on the surface unarmed. You are welcome to bring whatever weapons you feel necessary, though I give you my word we are here to help you with the coming threat."

"My *Ekam* appreciates the gesture, Captain. We'll see you on the ground." I turned to Emmory as the connection was terminated. "Take us down, Captain Saito. *Ekam*, shall we?"

Emmory nodded once, falling into step next to me. Gita and Hao were in front as we headed for the cargo bay where the other BodyGuards along with Johar, Alba, and Dailun were waiting. Mia stood apart, her arms wrapped around her waist and her eyes locked on nothing across the cargo bay.

She'd been silent on the trip, even though she shared my bed without question. The quiet worried me. As did Aiz's words just before we'd left Faria, which were still ringing in my head.

"Keep her safe."

"She's perfectly capable." My smile faded when he didn't echo it. "What, Aiz? What am I missing?"

"I don't know." He looked around for his sister as he dropped his voice and leaned in. "She would kill me for telling you and she won't tell me the details, so I can't share them. I only know that something awful has been stalking my sister's steps for her whole life, and you are the only one who can keep her safe. So I'll beg you, Hail, on the strength of our friendship. Don't let her get hurt."

"I won't. I swear." I put my hands over his, but I didn't tell him that I'd seen some of what was coming. That even if Mia wouldn't share it with him, I knew enough to know I'd do anything to keep that vision of her dead on an autopsy table from coming true.

I was already armed, my Glocks still in place as we came down the ramp. The soil under our boots was blue-black, shimmering in the midday sun like the volcanic deposits of Santa Pirata.

The crowd that waited for us a respectful distance from the ramp was similar to something one would see in Shanghai Port or the massive planetary market of Jemaa Fin. But though the handful of people had hair in a riot of colors, they were not human. They all had those distinctive Svatir black eyes that were shot through with silver.

I spotted Captain Zov and the pair I assumed were her lieutenants standing just a bit apart. They were the only ones with the markings on their faces. The other Svatir had bare cheeks. Zov and her people were dressed in blue-gray uniforms built for movement rather than show, and they were all unarmed as promised.

But they were relaxed, at ease, and smiling at us.

A Svatir with long hair a lighter pink than Dailun's stepped forward with hands extended, palms up. They looked feminine, but Dailun had told me a great many of his people didn't care for the binary explanations of gender and that those who did would introduce themselves as Dirah had done.

"Your Imperial Majesty. I am *Tsia* Santi Brov, of the Svatir. It is a great honor to meet you, circumstances being what they are."

Dailun had already given me a refresher on greetings, so I laid my own hands on top of theirs with a smile. "It is the same for us, *Tsia* Brov. If I could also introduce Mia Cevalla, co-leader of the Shen."

Santi repeated the gesture with Mia. "If you would follow me. I can tell you about this planet as we walk."

Once upon a time the formality of the Svatir had been a comfort to me, but now it just chafed like a too-tight bandage over a healing wound.

At an order from Emmory, no doubt issued via *smati*, Iza, Indula, and Kisah went ahead of us toward the low-slung building a dozen meters away. Santi gestured and a Svatir with deep red hair followed them.

The others would not be introduced to me. They could speak to my people, and if I chose to speak to them, they could introduce themselves, but Santi was apparently the only Svatir allowed the dubious honor of this ceremony.

Captain Zov watched the exchange with hard eyes and an amazingly impassive face I was reasonably sure was hiding her annoyance at the formality.

As tempting as it was to throw a social grenade down and disrupt the proceedings, I allowed Santi to lead us toward the building, Mia between us and Emmory on my other side. The Istrevitel had fallen back with Dailun, a nod of greeting between them but no words.

"This is a remote planet. There are some scientists on the other side, but it is otherwise uninhabited. We would have loved to receive you on our homeworld with the sort of recognition that a person such as yourself is due, but—"

I raised an eyebrow. "But what?"

"We cannot allow the people to see the Istrevitel."

"Ah. That's right, you've kept the information from your people that there's a group who've sworn to protect them." I was apparently going for the grenade option, judging from Santi's shocked look and the indrawn breaths behind me.

"We have chosen the path of peace, Star of Indrana. To allow such knowledge is counter to that path. We do not need our people dreaming of violence and war and death."

"It's been my experience that those things happen even if you don't dream of them."

Santi sighed. "I do not expect you of all humans to understand our choices, Star of Indrana. The path you walk has been coated in blood almost from the day of your birth; it is hard for one to see past all that and into the truth that less violence, not more, is always an option. We are here."

I slid Emmory a sideways glance as Santi pressed their palm to the panel beside the door. His answering eyebrow was a wealth of silent conversation punctuated by a smile.

The distraction allowed Mia to try to slip into the building ahead of us, but I caught her by the arm before she could clear the door.

"Emmory first." I shook my head when she raised an eyebrow at me and continued in Shen. "Don't give me that look, Mia Cevalla. You're not my BodyGuard, and my ability to bring you back to life alone is probably something we shouldn't put to the test. If you go and get killed, Aiz is going to have words for me."

"You are more important than me."

I tightened my grip on her upper arm, watched her mouth thin in response. "Don't ever say that. I am no more important than any other living being."

She opened her mouth to reply, but then we both realized

everyone was staring at us and she snapped it shut, forcing a smile as she slipped out of my grasp and through the doorway. The others followed, leaving me alone with my *Ekam*.

"Everything okay?"

I didn't look at Emmory as the question came over our private com. *"Fine. Strategy discussion."*

"That's what you're calling it?"

"Close enough."

"You know Aiz gave us a database of the Shen language for our sma-tis, *right?"*

I had not known that and I closed my eyes as the embarrassment swamped me. "Any particular reason I didn't get an upload?" I asked out loud as we crossed the threshold into the wide corridor.

Emmory looked embarrassed for just a moment before the expression vanished. "I assumed you wanted to keep working on it. I should have asked."

"It's fine." I patted his arm and glanced ahead. "Don't let her go first again, okay?"

"Of course, Majesty." To his credit Emmory didn't mention that three of my BodyGuards were already inside, a fact I remembered when I spotted Indula standing by a door farther down the corridor. Though this planet was only for research, the building was designed the same as the conclaves I'd visited in my youth, and the comforting, enclosed design was soothing rather than setting off my claustrophobia.

Still, when I followed Emmory into the room, I automatically searched for the exit on the far side.

The first half of the meeting passed with little more than small talk until we took a short break for lunch. I leaned against the far wall, wrestling with my impatience at the performative politics even as I reminded myself that it was all necessary.

Santi and the other Svatir were clustered on one side, with Iza standing between us and them.

Captain Zov and her people were opposite them. They were relaxed, fascinatingly so, and she smiled when I caught her eye.

You're focusing on the wrong thing, Haili. My father's voice was loud in my head.

"Hai Ram." I rubbed a hand over my cheek. He was right. I wasn't here for a state visit with the Svatir. They weren't going to help me with the threat of the Hiervet no matter what we did.

The Istrevitel would, and here I was ignoring the one person who'd come to talk to me in the first place.

I caught Hao's tiny smile of approval when I gestured to Mia and we crossed the room to where Captain Zov stood with her people. "Captain, I hope you'll forgive me. I should have greeted you sooner," I said. "This is Mia Cevalla, the leader of the Shen."

"It is a pleasure." Dirah smiled at Mia. "We understand the demands on your time and the necessities of this performance," Dirah replied, extending her hand palm out to me in a surprisingly Indranan gesture. "And we go where our leadership tells us, so you did no insult speaking with *Tsia* Brov and the others before me."

I touched my palm to hers in greeting. That was a twist I wasn't expecting. I'd thought they were essentially an independent force, but it appeared the Istrevitel were still willing to follow the orders of the Svatir government even as they disagreed with the pacifist majority.

"I'd like to know more about the Istrevitel and it seems you'd be the person to speak with, Captain."

"Ask your questions, Star of Indrana."

"To start, Hail, please." I closed my eyes briefly at Emmory's unsubtle throat-clearing. "Your Majesty, if necessary. That Star of Indrana title is cumbersome. Will you explain to me how this all works? I'll admit my initial assumptions seem to be wrong."

Dirah's smile lit up her face and she gestured at the nearby chairs, waiting as I picked one that put my back to the wall before choosing her own. "Officially, of course, the Istrevitel don't exist. When we join, we are wiped from the collective memory."

"Dailun told me it wasn't possible to alter memories." I glanced across the room where he and Alba were in conversation with Santi.

"He wouldn't know," Dirah replied. "Only the Memory Keepers have this power and it is only used to keep the Istrevitel a secret."

I doubted that. No government in existence would use that kind of power for only one thing.

"I don't understand why the need for such secrecy." I shook my head. "Why not just have a defense force? That is not unusual among our people."

"It is not our way, Your Majesty," Dirah replied, her smile patient. "The Svatir put down their weapons because of our past and the horror of the war with the Hiervet. Some of us make the sacrifice of being forgotten to ensure that tragedy never happens again." She braced a hand on her knee and stared at the floor for a long moment. "I realize this is strange to you, Your Majesty, but our nature does not allow for much subtlety. With our collective memories we remember every transgression, every injury done to us and our loved ones. It pushed us into madness."

It was an echo of Thyra's words—though I doubted Dirah would appreciate the comparison, so I kept the thought to myself. It was so ironically alien to me, this idea that people couldn't change.

Was it truly just a human concept? An ability unique to us that allowed us to change our lives, our natures, our very souls? Except I had seen Aiz and Fasé change, both Farian and Shen willing to walk away from the hurts of the past. And they were as long-lived as the Svatir, so what made them different?

"So you live apart from the rest of your people, but you are space-faring; how do they keep you a secret?"

"We live in a system not far from here on the outer edge of Svatir space. One that is recorded as uninhabitable and dangerous. It is, in fact, quite pleasant. Two of the planets are well suited for our needs.

We use the third for training and have a shipyard on it as well. We get the majority of our supplies from home through a variety of channels. Commandant Fej is in charge of administrative issues; I am in charge of the troops."

"How many troops?"

"Five million or so." Dirah wiggled a hand. "Our newest recruits are only a few months into their training but could be called to fight if necessary."

"What age do your children join? Are there options for those who don't want to fight?"

She laughed and shook her head. "Oh no, Your Majesty. There are no children. We are all sterilized when we join."

27

"Y ou are what?" My exclamation was loud enough to get the attention of the Svatir, and Santi came over to join us. "You sterilize them?" I demanded.

"The Istrevitel do not have children, Your Majesty. That would not be fair to them," Santi said. "We allow the oath-breakers to recruit in secret once a season, but there are no children born to those who walked away from peace."

Dirah snorted. "We had to plead our case on that front. If we did not recruit we'd end up with only the criminals and cast-offs that the government wishes to get rid of, not a great foundation for a fighting force."

"You'd be surprised," I replied. "Some of the best people I've had at my side were technically criminals."

Dirah answered my smile with one of her own. "Not in the least, Your Majesty. I am a criminal myself, given the choice of joining the Istrevitel or death for my part in the murder of a man who killed my little sister." Dirah's smile widened at my raised eyebrow. "He deserved it and I do not regret my choice to join the Istrevitel. It led me here with my comrades. Funny how the universe works, isn't it?"

Funny wasn't the word I'd have chosen. I'd done the same thing—murdered the man who killed my family—even though some would say it was self-defense. I'd gotten a crown out of the deal, not exile from everything I'd ever known.

"You've never actually been in combat, though, right?"

She didn't seem the least bit bothered by my question. "We have not, Your Majesty. There is no one to fight. We train in simulations using models programmed from the memories of the fight with the Hiervet. There are some obvious assumptions given the passing of time, but the simulations try to account for any possible advances in technology and fighting style."

"Interesting. I have some data from our recent interaction with a Hiervet ship that you might find helpful."

"You have done battle with them?" Dirah sat upright, the expression on her face a mixture of surprise and anticipation, and Santi gasped in horror.

"Not directly." I shook my head. "I was otherwise occupied when the Hiervet ships attacked a Farian fleet."

"They are back." Dirah was practically vibrating with excitement. Her companions were grinning. "Santi, you must speak with the government to release us to fight."

"You have no proof the Hiervet are coming." Santi shook their head. "And without that we cannot in good conscience release the Istrevitel."

"She just gave you proof!"

"Hold on." I put my hand up. "*Tsia* Brov, I understand the hesitation by the Svatir, but the fact of the matter is the Hiervet are coming. I saw them with my own eyes. They blew up a Farian ship and nearly took me with it. We suspect they are coming because of the Farian Hiervet, but—"

All the Svatir and Istrevitel stiffened at my words. "Forgive me, Your Majesty, but what did you say?" Captain Zov's voice was filled with poorly restrained astonishment.

I tucked my tongue into my cheek to keep my curse in my mouth.

"Probably should have led with that, *sha zhu*," Hao said from Gita's side.

"I would have had I known." I shot Dailun a stern look. "I thought you passed that information along."

He shook his head. "I'm sorry, *jiejie*. I did not."

I folded my hands and bowed in my seat, first toward Santi and then to Dirah. "My apologies. We apparently forgot to relay a key piece of information to you in the midst of all this excitement. The 'gods' who have been guiding the Farians for all this time are a trio of Hiervet. They are what's left of the ten who found their way to the planet after their ship was damaged in the fight with your people."

"You killed the others?"

"I did not." I lifted a hand. "Aiz Cevalla and some others were responsible—"

"We have heard the story of Aiz Cevalla versus the Farian gods but did not understand the implications." Dirah picked up the thread when I fumbled over how to describe what had happened with Aiz all those years ago. "Now that you tell us they were Hiervet it seems he did the galaxy a great service."

Mia accepted the smile the Istrevitel offered with a nod and a smile of her own. "I'll pass that along to him, Captain."

"I appreciate it."

The jealousy that surged up in my gut was startling in its intensity, and I had to consciously take my hand off the butt of my gun.

Emmory, of course, noticed and raised a curious eyebrow at me. I shook my head. Even if I'd had words to explain what had just gone on in my head, this was so far away from the place to discuss it as to be back on Pashati.

"Why have you not killed these Farian Hiervet, Your Majesty?" Dirah asked.

"I have my reasons." My response was sharper than I'd intended, but something about the question rankled.

"What possible reason would be good enough? We know of the brutality of the Hiervet; every Svatir has those memories."

Chance had me looking across the room when the Istrevitel captain spoke, and I saw the Svatir in the back, who'd been watching us silently, flinch.

That's interesting.

"The Star's reasons were sound at the time, Captain Zov," Mia said, pulling my attention away from the silent Svatir in the corner. "There are politics at work you are not familiar with that required certain concessions. Her decision was supported not only by my brother and me but by the new leadership of the Farians."

Dirah inclined her head. "My apologies, Your Majesty. I should have considered that you have more things to manage than just this."

"Apology accepted," I replied. "I think what I would love, Captain Zov, is a tour of your training facilities. We could do that while *Tsia* Brov goes back to the government and speaks with them about the necessity of allowing you to work with us given the new information they now have."

Santi's mouth tightened briefly, but they knew I'd made a move they couldn't ignore. "Very well, Your Majesty. You have clearance to go with Captain Zov if she agrees. I will head back to speak with the others."

"I will send your ship the coordinates, Your Majesty," the captain said.

I folded my hands together and shook them in her direction. "We look forward to seeing what your people can do."

"You okay?"

Mia turned away from the window with a smile. "Tired." She pulled her knees up to her chest when I sat on the bed next to her.

"May I?" I gestured at her hair and she shifted to give me access. I undid her braid, letting the brown curls wrap around my fingers as I carefully combed her hair out.

Mia sighed, the tension in her shoulders loosening, and she relaxed back against me. "I should message Aiz."

"He can wait." I slid my hands up over her neck, into her hair, and rubbed gently at her scalp. "My sisters and I used to do this when we were little."

"Not quite the same," Mia murmured, and I laughed softly at the desire in her voice as she turned her head toward mine.

"Not quite."

"You were jealous of Captain Zov's flirting today."

I froze, my hands buried in her hair and my mouth almost touching hers.

Mia caught me before I could pull away, the smile on her face brighter than the sun. She kissed me and laughed. "It was cute. You practically snarled at her."

"Is that why you backed me about not killing Thyra and Adaran?"

"No." Mia kissed me again, wrapping her arms around my neck. "I did that because you've been right about everything else and we both know that killing them would destroy this fragile peace we have all worked for," she whispered against my ear, the brush of her lips along my skin sending shocks down my spine.

"For one who has lived so long, you understand so little." Mia was defiant, blood spilling from the cut in her cheek as she got to her feet.

"This fragile peace of yours comes to an end above us. There is nothing you can do. Your Star is not coming for you. We will raise our children to meet our failed siblings in battle and destroy them. Then we will conquer this galaxy the way it should have been so long ago."

Mia smiled. "She will find a way to defeat you. I know this as well as I know my death is yours. I've known that for my whole life and I welcome the cost of keeping everyone I love safe from you."

Thyra hissed and slammed her limb into Mia's chest, piercing her through the heart.

"Hail!"

I scrambled away from Mia, forgetting where I was as the scream of anguish caught itself in my throat, sharp claws of pain digging in. I hit the floor hard as the door slid open and Emmory skidded through with his Hessian in his hand.

"What happened?"

"I don't know," Mia said. She hadn't moved from the bed. Emmory wasn't pointing his gun at her, but Gita was. "We were talking and then she screamed."

"Majesty?" Emmory holstered his gun as Gita came through the door behind him and went to a knee by my head. "Stay down for a moment," he ordered.

"I'm fine." I pushed myself up on an elbow. "Please tell me you didn't call Dr. Vohra?"

A smile pulled at the corner of his mouth. "I might still if you don't stay down."

"I'm all right." I closed my eyes, saw the image of Mia dying again, and opened them with a curse. "I'm all right, Emmory, I promise. I'll explain later."

He helped me up but held on and studied my face for a long minute before he let go and ushered Gita back out of the room.

"Hail, what happened?"

I dragged both hands through my hair, disheveling the still-braided strands until Mia tsked and dragged me back to the bed. She allowed me the silence to collect my thoughts as she carefully undid her morning work and rebraided my hair into a single plait.

The memory of that last piece of the vision I'd seen from Mia rolled through me, clamoring for attention. I was going to have to disrupt our peace; there was no way I could ignore it any longer. "Can I ask you something and get a straight answer?"

"Of course you can."

"Do you know when Thyra is going to kill you?"

"What?" I felt her hands still in my hair. "Hail, how did you—"

"I saw it. Back when you had the vision of Adora escaping and I was...I don't know why I saw it. Because I was touching you? I saw that and I saw you die. Aiz told me you had seen something you wouldn't share with him; I didn't tell him I knew, but I can't—" Suddenly needing to do anything but sit there, I got to my feet and paced the bedroom. "It's lodged in my head like a splinter of glass. I keep seeing it in bits and pieces, Mia, and I can't be quiet about it any longer."

"Hail."

I spun on my heel to look at her. Mia's face was ashen and there were tears in her eyes. "I am sorry," she whispered. "Sorry you had to see that."

"I'm not. You should have told me."

"You don't understand."

"I understand what I saw, Mia. You dead. You split open on a table. Me dead, also because of Thyra." I forced the words out; putting them into the air made them all the more real. "Tell me how we avoid this."

She shook her head slowly and my heart broke into a thousand pieces. "We cannot. You can avoid this death, but not me. This is where every path takes us and it is the only way we win."

"I don't believe you."

"It's the truth. The only way you stay alive is by staying away."

"No."

"It's all right, Hail." Mia slid off the bed and crossed to me, taking my hands. "I made my peace with this a very long time ago. It is what's meant to be. One life for the safety of the galaxy is nothing. One life for my people's future is nothing."

"It's not all right!" Anger overtook the grief. "Is that what you meant on Ndrog about my life being more important?"

"You are the Star of Indrana. Everything hinges on your survival," Mia said, her voice so calm it cut to the bone. "You must be protected at all costs or everything is lost."

"I am no more fucking valuable than anyone else, Mia."

Images crashed into my head even as I said the words. Of Jet grabbing Ramani and running through a crowded square. Of Cas with his head bowed. Of every single one of my people, putting themselves into the line of fire to keep my ass safe. I shook my head so hard it sent my braid flying into the air. "I am not worth this."

"You can't fight it." Mia reached out and touched my cheek. "What you saw are the options. If you live, it's because you made the right choice. The one where you didn't come for me. Where you didn't die. You saw what happens if you try to save me, Hail. You will not save me. You will die and that cannot be allowed to come to pass."

Your Star is not coming for you.

One would think I'd be less sanguine about the idea of my impending death, but the truth of the matter was I was ready to face it if I had to. I hadn't lied to Hao; I didn't have a death wish. Not in the sense he'd meant. I wasn't going to throw my life away without a purpose. I just knew how this story needed to end for everyone else to make it out safe and I'd made my peace with it.

The irony of how alike Mia and I were in this was not lost on me, but I wasn't about to admit that to anyone, let alone her.

I shook my head, dislodging Mia's hand. "You are mad if you think I will walk away from this. If you think I would leave you there alone. I will always come for you."

"You cannot follow where I will go." She gripped my hands. "Please do this for me, make me this one promise. I won't be the cause of your death, Hail. I can't do what needs to be done if I think you're going to die because of me."

"But you want me to do the same." I choked down a bitter laugh. "You know how many people I have let die. I won't do it again. And Aiz? You have to tell your brother."

"He cannot know." Fear flashed into Mia's eyes. "His path is to rule the Shen, Hail. To forge this peace with Fasé and bring our people home. Whatever grand pronouncements he makes about holding to that, he will throw it all away to save me. You know this. I can't let that happen."

"You don't get to make these choices for us. Don't you understand?" I threw my hands up in the air and swore in frustration. "This is the very thing that infuriates me about you, about Fasé, about Sybil. You see these things and then make a choice for the rest of us without the slightest regard for our feelings."

"You're asking me to live forever knowing I caused the death of everything I hold dear!"

"And you're asking me to stand by and let yet another person I care about die! Look, I know there was never going to be a happy ending for me. I'm fine with that. But you want Aiz to live for eternity knowing he could have saved your life? How dare you."

"Hail, I—what?"

"*Hai Ram*, surely you've thought of what this would do to him?" She stared at me, one eyebrow raised in a look I knew all too well now.

"What?"

Mia muttered a curse at the ceiling. "Do I—" Her laugh was bitter. "You don't even know what you just said."

"I do. I said Aiz—"

"I am not talking about Aiz." She leveled me with a look that would have impressed Emmory.

"Fuck me. Look, I'm not going to guess."

"Then play it back."

I gritted my teeth, wondering just when I'd lost control of this conversation, and played the vid back. I knew what it was she'd latched onto the minute I heard the words again and sighed, rubbing my face with both hands.

"'There was never going to be a happy ending for me.'" She hurled my own words at me and they hit like a punch.

"Have you seen my life?" I asked softly, dropping my hands. "Of course you have. You of anyone should know, Mia, how this fucking thing plays out."

"You think you're going to die." She surged to her feet, crossing the room to get in my face. "Worse, you're okay with it! You stand there and lecture me while you're prepared to throw your life away."

"I'm not throwing my life away. I'm going to die, because it's what humans do. Even more likely when you're the target of a Shiva-damned prophecy that's intent on throwing every obstacle in the book at you. I'm a realist, Mia." I took a step forward until we were almost touching. "Besides, we were just in the middle of your 'don't come after me' speech. You're a fine hypocrite to shout at me about this when *you* are all set to die."

"I don't want you coming after me because I know what will happen if you do!" She jabbed a finger off to the side. "I don't want you sacrificing yourself just for me."

"You don't understand. I will never leave you in the dark." The words were hoarse and something of my anguish must have shown on my face because Mia's anger melted away.

"Hail—"

"I won't ever leave any of you alone in the dark," I said in a rush. "You have to understand that. I have done it too many times. Never again. I'm not sorry for the fact that I will throw myself at death a thousand times if it means keeping the people I love safe."

"Will you ever think of yourself first?"

I shook my head, felt the tears start their slide down my cheeks despite my efforts to stop them. "I did that. Remember? I stayed out in the black and my whole family died because of it. Never again, Mia. I won't ever do that again."

"Hail—"

"You tell Aiz or I will," I said, opening the bedroom door and walking out. My ultimatum hung in the air, and the sound of Mia's tears followed me as I left my quarters.

28

leaned against the railing, one booted foot propped up as I watched the movement below with a critical eye. We were on the Istrevitel's training planet of Horst, standing on a platform overlooking an intricate complex where the top-ranked squad from their latest round of war games along with Captain Zov and some other ranking officers were going head-to-head with some pretty tough-looking Hiervet simulations.

"Thoughts?" I murmured to Gita. I'd managed to push the argument with Mia mostly out of my head so I could focus on the forces below, but the pain of it lingered much like the healed wound in my shoulder.

"They're not bad." Her tone of voice suggested that was the kindest thing she could come up with.

Johar's amused snort was little more than a breath of air. "They are children playing games. The five of us could take both of these squads apart in three minutes."

Neither Emmory nor Hao commented, but their carefully blank faces told me all I needed to know. To the unexperienced eye the Istrevitel's training was impressive. The squads moved well together, their tactics were flawless, and they'd won three of the four engagements we'd watched.

What was painfully obvious, though, was that it wasn't real to them. The relaxation I'd spotted in Captain Zov when we'd first met was now clearly a lack of experience; and that along with a dozen other clues I'd missed in our initial meetings was now going to haunt me.

Though if I was being fair it wasn't entirely their fault. They'd had nowhere to test their skills in the real world; all they had were these simulations. Simulations that were clearly nowhere near the fighting capabilities of the Hiervet. I had ignored those signs before this moment in my rush to impress them.

Now the reality of it was coming back to kick my ass.

The five of us had been through combat and we could spot the differences between lived experience and training. Training taught you a lot—how to carry yourself, how to watch exits and recognize other warriors.

There were things about combat that no simulation could prepare you for—the way your heart kicked into high gear, the way you buried your grief for a fallen comrade and kept going, the split-second decisions you couldn't ever take back.

And most importantly, if your training was going to work or if you were just going to freeze up.

That was almost impossible to predict.

The Istrevitel were missing the practical real-world experience and the only way to get it was to send them into a fight, but none of us wanted to be there for the potential chaos that could happen with an untested ally at our side.

Hao turned toward me as the final simulation ended. "They'll get us all killed," he said in a low voice, and headed for the door shaking his head.

The succinct and damning judgment was the final nail. Even if my own thoughts hadn't run parallel, there wasn't a force in the universe that could make me ignore Hao's concerns about something this important. I wanted to give Dirah the benefit of the doubt, but ego or inexperience, Hao was still right. If we took the Istrevitel into battle with us against an opponent built for war like the Hiervet, the odds that we'd end up dead were better than I liked.

Contrary to Mia's belief, I could be prepared to die for this cause while actually not wanting to die at the same time.

"Majesty, I'd advise waiting to break the news on this until we're back at the meeting site," Gita said as we followed Hao out to where Captain Zov waited.

"You think we'll have a problem?" That had been another strike against them. Dirah had chosen to participate in the demonstration rather than staying with us to gauge our reactions. It reminded me of the time I'd wanted to show off for my father and his quiet "Leaders lead, Haili, but they also know when to step back and let their people shine instead. Don't let your ego get in the way of your duty."

"Unlikely that they'll give us any trouble," Emmory answered for Gita as he caught up to us. "It's just safer."

I pasted a smile on my face when Captain Zov joined us. "That was very informative, Captain. Why don't you and your people get cleaned up? I have a com from home I need to take. We can head back to the meeting site and talk with *Tsia* Brov."

"Absolutely, Your Majesty," Dirah replied. She was bouncing on the balls of her feet like a child.

"Bugger me," I muttered after we were out of earshot and rubbed at my face. My entire plan had collapsed like a punctured lung. "What are we going to do?"

"Just because we don't want to fight with them doesn't mean we couldn't use them," Johar said as we hit the ramp of the *Hailimi*. "We could throw them at the Hiervet first, stay out of the way. Maybe they'll surprise us and buy us time to fight that army on the ground?"

"That's mercenary, even for you," Gita replied.

"With this army it might be necessary," I said. The briefing we'd had this morning had only added more tension to my shoulders.

Gita and Johar hadn't gotten any new information from Orrin, but they had been able to piece together enough of a timeline with his testimony and some rumors from Fasé's people. The whole thing had disaster written on it and I was starting to wonder if I should just pull the mercenaries into this fray before things got truly out of hand.

At least with them, I knew what I was getting and knew that they'd be able to work together to fight not only Thyra's army on Faria but the Hiervet also. "I'm not discounting it," Gita continued. "Just pointing out that we have to consider what it might do to Indrana's relationship with the Svatir."

"Fair enough." Johar nodded. "I'll admit I didn't think of that."

"It's not your job," I said as we boarded the *Hailimi* once more. "It's mine." I had thought of it and discarded the idea almost immediately. Not only because of the potential political impact, but because the thought of sacrificing these people made me deeply uneasy.

"True." Johar grinned. "If I'm throwing out suggestions I should keep shit like that in mind, though. I'll do better next time."

"Majesty, a reminder that you're already asking a lot of the Farian and Shen forces. Integrating two previously opposed forces is difficult enough without adding in a completely unknown element like the Istrevitel."

I met Emmory's grim pronouncement with a shake of my head. "*Dhatt.* I know. We can't use them at all." I blew out a frustrated breath. "Let's get back to the meeting site and get this over with. What a fucking waste of time."

I headed for my quarters without waiting for anyone else and Emmory let me go only because we were safely in the ship. I didn't want the placating words I knew they'd offer up. I should have known better.

Mia wasn't in my quarters. I hadn't seen her since our fight the day before. She'd declined to come with us to the planet's surface, but I had no idea if she'd talked to her brother about her visions or if I was going to have to follow through with my threat.

I commed Aiz, frowning when he didn't answer, and instead sent him a quick message that I wanted to talk.

"Majesty." Alba knocked on the door frame. "Do you have a minute?"

"I do. Come in."

"How did it go?"

I shook my head. "Not good. They're trained well, but they've never seen combat and it shows."

"I'll admit it's not entirely unsurprising," she said. "The Svatir's entire lives are so set on peace that it has to be difficult for them to overcome that. Even if they separate themselves and train as the Istrevitel have."

I sighed. "We have no way of knowing how it will go in a real altercation. Anyway, we're headed back to Ndrog and I'll figure out some way to tell them there."

"Would you like some help with that?"

"Always." I laughed. "You are far more diplomatic than I am."

"Hardly, ma'am. You've done an amazing job given the circumstances."

"With a great deal of assistance from you." I held my hand out and she took it, letting me pull her into a hug. "I'm sure this is not what you signed up for when I offered you this job, and I owe you a massive raise, but thank you for sticking around."

"Of course, Majesty." Alba squeezed me tight and then stepped away. "I won't say no to the raise."

I laughed. "I probably owe you hazard pay, too. What did you need?"

"Have you spoken to anyone on Faria since we left?"

"I haven't," I replied, waving Emmory into the room. "I just tried to com Aiz before you came in but I didn't get him." I pulled Fasé up on my *smati* as I spoke with the same results.

"There's no answer, is there, ma'am?"

I shook my head at Alba as the worry in my chest grew. "Emmory, bridge. I want to talk to Inana and Captain Saito, tell them both to meet us there. Alba, walk with me." I sent Mia a message asking her to meet us on the bridge as we headed out into the corridor.

"There was a strange blackout with the news this morning," Alba said. "I didn't think much of it, but everything since then has been odd."

"Define *odd* for me," I said.

"Majesty, I can't get a hold of Sergeant Patil either," Emmory reported, and I cursed. The woman in charge of the contingent of Royal Marines I'd left with Fasé should have been easily accessible.

"Hold that thought, Alba." I gestured at Hao and Gita as they came around the corner. "Have either of you two talked to your contacts on Faria today?"

"No," Hao replied with a frown. "What's up?"

"Do it." I continued past them and took the stairs to the next level two at a time, trusting the others to follow me.

"Majesty." Both Admiral Hassan and Captain Saito greeted me as I came onto the bridge, and the three of us headed for the ready room.

"What do you have?"

"There is a complete blackout of coms around Faria. We can't get a hold of anyone on the planet or in system. The squad of Marines I left with Fasé isn't answering on any channel."

"Is it a jammer or just nothing there?" I hated to even voice the suggestion that Faria was gone.

"We can't tell from here. I've never seen any kind of signal jammer with that range. So if it's that?" Inana shook her head. "We don't know what the situation is, Majesty, and because of that I can't allow you to go back. I think we should go to Ndrog as planned and regroup from there."

"No response, Hail," Hao said.

"We may fucking need the Istrevitel after all." I shared a grim look with Hao. "Alba, send Captain Zov a message that we are leaving ASAP. If she's not ready we'll meet her at Ndrog. If you can also contact *Tsia* Brov and let them know I'd like to speak with them as soon as we get in system, I'd appreciate it."

"Of course, Majesty."

"Ma'am, I'll go see about getting us under way," Isabelle said, and I nodded as she left the room.

"What in the Dark Mother's name happened?" I muttered, then looked around the room. "All right, people, give me ideas. What are we looking at?"

"Thyra and Adaran somehow orchestrated a coup using Adora's people."

"The Farians and the Shen started shooting at each other again."

"The Hiervet attacked Faria."

I winced at Emmory's suggestion. "Oh gods, I hope not."

"Sorry, Majesty. The Farians are the next best target in this area, and we can assume the Hiervet might steer clear of the Svatir given their history."

"One would hope so," I replied. "But at this point it wouldn't surprise me to have a Hiervet ship drop out of warp onto our heads."

I will, one of these days before my death, learn not to say such flippant things. The gods have a sense of humor to rival my own and have very much delighted over the years in making me eat my words.

Mia joined us on the bridge just before we left Horst. Her shoulders were stiff with tension and it took all my self-control not to wrap my arms around her.

"Did someone catch you up on what's happening?" I asked, and she nodded.

"I have not spoken to anyone since last night, neither Aiz nor Talos. I tell myself I would know, Hail, if something had happened to them." She didn't look at me, her storm-gray eyes locked on the bridge screen.

I wanted to promise everything would be fine, but my gut was telling me otherwise. So instead I stood in silence, listening to the buzz of the bridge crew as they prepared for our jump.

This wasn't like the float of an Alcubierre/White Drive. The Farian tech was essentially ripping the ship from one point in space and depositing it in another, but the translation was smooth as a silk sari. One moment we were staring at the dull gray surface of Horst and the next I could see the brilliant green of Ndrog in the viewscreen.

Captain Zov's ship flashed into solidity nearby, the black surface all but invisible against the backdrop of space.

"I am still really jealous of their ships," I murmured.

"If you manage not to piss them off when you tell them they're shit fighters, we could ask to borrow a few," Hao suggested as he stepped up to my side, and I snorted.

"Captain, I've got multiple signatures incoming." Commander Nejem's announcement cut me off before I could respond, and several seconds later all Naraka broke loose in the black.

Mia gasped as four ships appeared right in front of us, one of them vomiting fire into space.

"Evasive maneuvers!" Isabelle shouted, but her crew was already responding.

I grabbed for Mia with one hand and Hao with the other, back-pedaling to the nearest console as the internal systems fought with the sudden shift in direction.

"Got you." I felt Hao lock a hand in my belt. "Also, you had to say it, didn't you?"

"Do not even try to blame this on me." I shook my head. "Those aren't Hiervet ships."

"Majesty, status report." Emmory's voice came over our com.

"We're fine," I replied out loud. "Someone give me a read on whose ships those are!"

"They're Shen." Mia's agonized whisper came just as the ship closest to the *Hailimi* exploded.

29

tightened my grip on Mia as our ship shook from the pressure wave and tried not to think about how much of the debris had made it past our shields.

"Shields are down to eighty-eight percent, Captain."

"I'm reading damage on decks three and fourteen. Casualties reported."

"Tell medical to prepare for possible wounded," Isabelle ordered.

"Captain, I'm getting more ships dropping out of warp on our position."

"Someone get me an actual ID on those ships," she snapped. "I want to know what's going on, preferably before someone takes a shot at us."

"Captain Saito," I called, my voice rising over the din. "They're Shen. Do not fire on them. Relay that to Captain Zov, immediately."

"Yes, Majesty. Helm, get us out of this mess however you can."

"Aye-aye, Captain." Ensign Virat Kohli hit the thrusters on the *Hail-imi* to full and I could do little else but hang on and watch as she piloted us out of the debris field. The young helmswoman had developed nerves of steel somewhere along the line, and I watched in a kind of terrified awe as we shot through the carnage of the broken ships around us.

"Why aren't they saying anything, Hail?" Mia's broken whisper dragged my attention away from the front end of our ship passing well within safety parameters of the starboard side of the Shen ship. "I can't raise anyone on the coms."

She was right and I would have slapped myself in the forehead if

I'd had a free hand. I hadn't even considered trying to contact one of the Shen vessels in the middle of this chaos.

"Hao?"

"Nothing," he said, anticipating my question before I could ask it. "It's dead air out there. I don't know what's going down but they either can't or won't contact us."

The ship leveled out as the space cleared in front of us. I shared a look with Hao before we both stood. Mia was still leaning into me, her eyes unfocused and her mouth moving as she desperately tried to contact her people.

"Majesty, are you all right?"

I pointed at Inana. "Find out why the coms aren't working, Admiral. We need to know if those ships are compromised."

"Captain Zov is on the line, ma'am," Captain Saito called, and I handed Mia off to Hao without a thought as I crossed to her chair with Inana on my heels.

"Put her through."

Dirah appeared on the screen. "Your Majesty. We are unable to contact any of the Shen ships. *Tsia* Brov is on the ground and requesting information."

"Tell them I don't have any at the moment. We're reasonably sure that the Shen ships are not a threat, but whatever is causing this coms blackout might be." There wasn't time to explain our concerns about our inability to contact anyone on Faria, and part of my brain was currently trying to figure out the best way to contact Aiz—if he was with the Shen fleet at all. "I want you all to hold fast and do not do anything without my express order."

"Yes, ma'am." Captain Zov nodded and disconnected the com.

"All right, people, start problem solving," I announced, and the conversations on the bridge stopped. "I care less at the moment about what's causing this blackout and more how to communicate with at least one of those ships without using coms. Ragini." I pointed at the senior tech.

She swallowed. "It's not quite that easy, Your Majesty. We need to know if they can't send and receive messages. Or if our coms are being interrupted somehow. The cause is important in figuring out—"

"Senior Tech." Captain Saito's voice held a note of warning, and Ragini swallowed.

"Yes, ma'am. Sorry. We could use Morse code. Get close enough for them to see our running lights from their bridge and flash a message. Get them to land on the planet. It's messy, but it might—"

"Captain, I've got another ship!" Commander Nejem called from her station.

"Coming out of warp? Where?" Both my and Isabelle's questions tumbled over the top of one another's.

"Not warp, ma'am. It just appeared. Directly in front of us."

I turned to the viewscreen. The ship was close enough to be easily visible, but the computer brought up an enhanced image on an inset screen and my heart lodged itself into my throat.

"Oh Shiva." I recognized the ship. It was the same sleek black thing I'd seen just before Adora's ship exploded. "It's the Hiervet."

"Go to red alert. Shields up," Captain Saito demanded. "Where did they come from?"

The klaxon rang and I braced myself against Isabelle's chair, but the Hiervet ship didn't move.

"Captain, they're hailing us," Ragini said. "But the translators aren't recognizing it."

"Is there only one ship?" I asked.

"Yes, ma'am. They're just sitting there. I'm getting more incoming coms, every single one is different. This is weird. Hang on."

"Captain Saito, you are not authorized to fire until we figure out what is going on, is that understood?"

"Yes, ma'am."

I'd no sooner issued that order than fire streaked over our heads, slamming into the Hiervet ship.

"It's the Istrevitel ship, Captain!" Commander Nejem turned in her seat.

"Ragini, open up a com channel." I gave the order in tandem with Captain Saito and shot her an apologetic look she answered with a quick smile.

"Go ahead, Your Majesty."

The bridge of Captain Zov's ship came into view. "Stand down, Captain, that's an order!"

But my words were lost to the bloodlust of the Istrevitel, and they poured fire into the vessel from their own ship.

The sick feeling in my gut exploded at the same time the Hiervet ship did, and the silence on the bridge was only made worse by the celebration coming from Captain Zov's com link. I didn't say a word as I crossed to the coms and stabbed my finger down onto the button to terminate the connection.

"Ragini?"

She shook her head. "They were cycling through languages, ma'am, trying to figure out who we were. The translation software got confused by the deluge of information. I think the collection of ships threw them off." She stopped and swallowed. "I finally found the one in really old Standard. It said, *We've come to talk, not to fight. Our shields and weapons are inactive.*"

I heard the shocked curses behind me as I pressed my fingertips to my mouth.

"You tried to stop them, Hail," Mia whispered.

"It wasn't enough."

"Your Majesty, permission to flash our running lights at the nearest Shen ship," Captain Saito said. "We'll tell them to send a party to the surface if they're able."

"Do it and then put us on the ground." I looked around the bridge, spotted Emmory standing by the door. "Tell Captain Zov to get her ass on the ground also."

"Yes, ma'am."

* * *

I did not realize how badly I needed Aiz to be the one who came off the Shen shuttle that landed on Ndrog until I saw him and the sob of relief fought its way free of my mouth.

Thankfully Mia calling her brother's name and sprinting across the landing pad covered up my own reaction, though I followed her at a pace just short of a run.

"What happened?" I demanded as I skidded to a stop.

Aiz had his arms wrapped around Mia and lifted his head to meet my gaze. "I don't know, Hail." The admission was as startling as the grief in his voice. "It all happened so fast. I've never seen anything like it. Our coms went down, our *renimi*—"

My blood froze. "Your *smatis* are compromised?"

Aiz nodded. "We cannot communicate. It is a computer virus, not spread by contact but only if your software connects. It spread from ship to ship, person to person before we realized what was happening. The attack was right on the heels of it. If we hadn't had an escape plan in place we would have been slaughtered." The muscles in his jaw flexed. "It was Thyra's army, Hail. They are Farians, but bigger, stronger. It was almost like fighting Hiervet. We had to run or be slaughtered."

I was suddenly, desperately grateful for the paranoia that had led Aiz to split up the Shen fleet.

"We couldn't contact Fasé either."

"I'm sorry. She wasn't with us. Several Farian ships that had been with us were attacked; we tried to get coordinates to them before we jumped but I don't think any of them made it." Aiz shook his head, his face grim. "I can't tell you what happened or where she is now. Your Marines were with her and Sybil. Maybe they got out."

"Where is Talos?" Mia asked.

My heart twisted at the expression that slid across Aiz's face. "He stepped in front of a shot meant for me," he said, shaking his head. "There wasn't time for us to do anything but run."

I pressed a hand to my mouth as the grief wailed in my chest. A hundred moments with Talos flashed through my head. Aiz reached out with a smile and wiped away the tear that slid down my cheek.

"It's all right, Hail. With luck he is back with Jibun and we will see each other again."

I didn't want to ask what would happen if he was unlucky; I already knew the answer. Instead I reached up and gripped Aiz's hand tight. "I have to deal with something," I said, hearing the tears in my voice. "Then we'll sit down and figure out what in Shiva's name is going on and what our next move is."

I headed for the same building where our first meeting with the Svatir had been. Dailun and Hao, along with Zin and Gita, had headed off Captain Zov when she landed and escorted her to where *Tsia* Brov and the other Svatir were waiting.

I could hear Mia whispering to Aiz as they followed, catching him up on the events that had happened aboard the *Hailimi*, but my thoughts were quickly distracted by the memory of the Hiervet ship exploding and Ragini's voice telling me that they'd been broadcasting what was essentially a message of peace.

A message Captain Zov and the Istrevitel had ignored along with my orders.

Gita met us at the outside entrance. "They're inside, Majesty. The Istrevitel are armed."

"I don't care. Your job is to make sure they don't try to shoot anyone—me included. Use whatever force is necessary."

"Yes, ma'am."

We headed down the corridor and I stopped just outside the door, holding my hands up. "Guns," I said, and Emmory leaned in, taking my Glocks away from me without a word.

The Svatir and the Istrevitel turned as I entered the room. Hao took one look at my face and said something to Dailun, and the younger man nodded and backed up a step.

"Did you see it? Wasn't it glorious?" Captain Zov was joyful. It was hard to blame her for misreading the situation or just not noticing how dangerous it was in the split second before I was on her.

I grabbed Dirah by the shirtfront, propelling her across the room so quickly her feet barely touched the floor, and slammed her into the far wall.

"I told you to stand down," I snarled, hearing the sounds of weapons powering up behind me and trusting that Emmory and the others could handle whatever came of my decision. "I gave you a direct fucking order. You murdered those people."

"They weren't people. They were Hiervet." Dirah struggled in my grip but I shook her until her teeth rattled. "We did our duty as soldiers."

"You are not soldiers! You are children with dangerous toys who neither are aware nor seem to care about the damage you can inflict on those around you." I shoved her into the wall again, fighting with the snarling voice that was telling me to put my fist into her face. "They came to talk with us and you killed them!" I ignored the snide voice in my head that reminded me we'd been planning on doing the very same thing. The situation had changed, even I could see that, but Dirah in her obsessive vendetta had not.

"Your Majesty, I must—" *Tsia* Brov's protest died under the weight of Emmory's growled order to stay still.

"We swore an oath to protect our people from those creatures, but you would have us stand there and do nothing when they appeared?"

"I would have you use your Shiva-damned brain, woman! Anyone with a lick of common sense could tell they weren't attacking. They were broadcasting a message of peace—one you ignored in favor of violence." The weight of it all came crashing down on me. I exhaled, forcing myself to unclench my fist from her shirtfront and take a step back. "I shouldn't have come here. I should have left you to rot on that planet with your endless games, not let you out into the universe to rain down death and destruction on innocents."

Silence fell on the room. I took a deep breath. "*Tsia* Brov, my apologies for wasting your time. We will remove ourselves from your space." I nodded to them and turned on my heel.

"Your Majesty."

I stopped at the doorway next to Aiz. Captain Zov hadn't raised her voice, but her call was loud in the stunned silence.

"What?"

"Your people are injured. Your ships damaged. You are right that I don't have the experience of combat, but I know enough to know something bad has happened to your fleet. And that you have nowhere to go."

I shared a look with Aiz and he dipped his head just a fraction in acknowledgment of the truth of Dirah's words. Many of his ships were probably unable to jump, and even the *Hailimi* had suffered minor damage from the debris. Until we figured out what was wrong with their coms systems and repaired our ships, it was dangerous to go anywhere.

"Your point, Captain?"

"The Istrevitel will gladly provide you with safe haven on Ganyin. We have shipyards for repairing the damage and medical facilities if they are needed."

"And what do you expect in exchange?" I asked as I faced her.

"Nothing, Your Majesty. If you have wisdom you wish to share we will gladly listen, but the offer is made out of friendship and a desire to rectify my mistake. Nothing more."

"I see. What do you have to say about this?"

Tsia Brov's answering smile was tight. "There is nothing I can say, Your Majesty. The law is very clear on our duty to offer safe haven to those in distress."

I nodded once. Dirah was right, we were hurting and had nowhere to go. We needed somewhere safe to regroup and despite my harsh words the Istrevitel were our best hope.

"Captain Zov, I accept your offer of safe haven."

30

With little else to do besides fix our ships and figure out what in Naraka was going on with the Shen coms, Emmory took my suggestion that we train together seriously, and our days were spent on Horst in the simulator or back on Ganyin at Captain Zov's headquarters.

Hao joined us more often than not, as did Johar and Dailun. Aiz and Mia were occupied with Ragini, or at least that was what I told myself.

The truth was more complex and more painful than I wanted to admit to, so I buried it in long days composing and refining battle scenarios that found a middle ground between Emmory's need to keep me safe and my need to be useful.

I knew he'd overheard at least part of my fight with Mia, but I hadn't yet admitted that I'd seen my own death. Emmory, in turn, hadn't pressed me about it.

"Your Ragini is very clever," Aiz said, leaning back in his chair one morning with a steaming cup of something the Istrevitel called *yablok*. It was strange, almost apple-like but with a bitterness a number of my people found unpleasant. I on the other hand enjoyed it. A winter storm had descended on the area where Captain Zov's headquarters on Ganyin were located and it kept my hands warm.

The young soldier who'd delivered the drinks had green hair

several shades brighter than mine and a nervous stammer. She wasn't anything like Stasia but made me ache for my maid all the same.

That Fasé would keep her safe was the lie I told myself to assuage the creeping guilt that grew day by day. I had fucked this up. I'd left Thyra alive on Faria while I chased a useless force instead of keeping my focus where it should have been.

"Hail?"

"Sorry." I shook my head. "Virus?"

"She's eighty-seven or eighty-eight percent sure." His teeth flashed white in a quick grin and I could hear Ragini's rambling qualifications in my own head. "No verdict yet on if she'll be able to fix it, but—"

"She will. Have some faith."

"I'm running a bit thin on that at the moment, Hail. I won't lie." Aiz rubbed at his eyes with one hand. "We were so close to everything we wanted. I'm sorry. I fucked this up."

"No, you didn't. I'm the one who fucked up."

Aiz dropped his hand and stared at me. I shrugged.

"You and I both know it. I got overconfident. I shouldn't have left, that much is obvious. I should have dealt with Thyra. We knew she was up to something and I gave her the perfect opportunity to strike while my back was turned. Chasing the Istrevitel was a mistake."

"I don't recall any of us objecting to the plan."

I smiled. "I'm in charge, remember? It was my call and my mistake. Just like with the Hiervet at Ndrog."

"You really think they wanted to just talk?"

"I do." I couldn't articulate how I knew, but Aiz didn't seem to need an explanation.

"So why did the other ship attack Adora's?" Aiz gestured with his mug. "I get wanting to kill my sister. But it doesn't make much sense for anyone else."

"The assumption is that they were after Priam," I said with a shrug. "That would explain the aggression. Even Thyra has admitted they're hiding from the other Hiervet."

"Your *Ekam* spoiled that kill for the Hiervet." He grinned but it faded, and we stared at each other.

"Aiz, they were still shooting even after Priam was dead. We could see it from the shuttle. They kept firing until the ship exploded. Why would they do that if they were only after Priam?"

The answer was a sick rolling in my gut.

"Someone came back for Adora." Aiz set his mug down with a curse and got up to pace the barracks that had become our new home for the last week. "I am an idiot."

"No, you're not. Thyra came back for her. Shiva." I pushed to my feet, my own mug in one hand while I snapped the fingers of the other. "Thyra was on the ship, that's why the Hiervet were still shooting. Thyra rescued Adora and hid her, and then the moment they saw an opening they attacked."

"Bugger me," I cursed. "Do you think it's too much to hope Fasé and the others aren't all dead?"

"Weren't you just saying something about having faith?"

I drained the last of my *yablok* and set the mug down. "We haven't sparred in a while. Help me piece this together," I said with a wave of my hand.

Aiz smiled, but rolled his left shoulder and advanced on me. "Slow," he said. "You know I'd have to call Mia to heal you."

I nodded in acknowledgment. We still weren't sure if the coms virus had only affected the Shen's communication systems or if Aiz trying to heal me would impact my *smati*. So at the moment the safest course of action was to wait and keep everything separated.

"Though," he said after a moment, "maybe getting you two in a room together so you can tell me what's going on between you might be a good thing."

Apparently he had noticed the tension between us.

"So Adora's on the ship and the Hiervet show." I decided to ignore his comment and took a swing at Aiz instead, reversed it into an elbow, and clipped him on the jaw. He moved fast enough that it was only a glancing blow and I watched the pleased smile curve his lips. "She figures she can get out with Priam, but then Emmory puts a crimp in that plan so she calls Thyra instead."

"All right, I'll play along here. You're going to have to tell me eventually, though," Aiz warned. "Thyra jumps in, gets Adora, and is back out before the ship blows." He stepped in, slipping a palm thrust past my guard into my ribs with enough force to knock me back a step. "That's why the Hiervet stopped shooting and left rather than continuing the fight. They did what they were there to do. We assumed Adora was dead and out of the way. I should have followed up on that."

"We all should have." I caught his arm, dragging him with me. My attempt to sweep his leg failed, so I slid my hand up the underside of his arm and jammed my thumb into the soft flesh just below his armpit.

Aiz yelped and laughed as he danced away from me. "Thyra hid Adora from us. While we were finishing the peace negotiations, she was gathering her troops."

"Explains why the riots calmed down so quickly, too. Then the moment I left she moved in on Faria." I snarled several colorful Cheng curses. "I miss being a gunrunner. Everything was so much simpler then."

Aiz grinned and launched an attack. "If it helps, I am glad you are here. We couldn't manage this on our own." He threw a punch. I countered and responded with one of my own, but Aiz was already behind me and his kick to the back of my knee put me on the ground.

I landed harder than either of us had intended and felt the pain shoot up my legs as my knees connected with the concrete floor. I fell forward onto my hands.

"Damn it," Aiz swore. "Hail?"

"Majesty?"

"I'm fine." I held up a hand to Gita. She still moved from her spot at the doorway toward us, but not before Aiz could hook his arms underneath mine and lift me to my feet.

"This whole thing is still supposition," he said, letting me go once I'd patted him. "We don't know for sure if this is Adora. It could be Rotem working with Thyra."

"I know, but it fits." I shook my head. "Honestly we don't have the luxury of spending too much time wondering. We need to figure out what we're going to do."

A shadow flickered in the corner of my vision and I froze. But when I turned my head to stare at the corner of the room there was nothing there. I frowned.

"Majesty? What is it?"

"Nothing. I thought I saw—" I shook my head. "Nothing. Where's Emmory?"

"Working on the *Hailimi*." Gita smiled at my sigh. "You know he won't let anyone but us mess with her, Majesty."

"I'm not judging. It's just more than a little amusing he's willing to leave me unsupervised in favor of the ship."

"It's our only way home. No offense," Gita said to Aiz.

"None taken." He grinned.

"Speaking of home, have you talked to Admiral Amo?" The few Shen ships with us had avoided the strange virus infecting the coms. It was a bonus both in allowing Ragini and her team a control group as they tried to figure out what the problem was, and in that we still had access to the Shen codes necessary to contact the rest of the fleet.

"This morning," Aiz replied. "We've worked out a new system to let ships know when they can accept an incoming com. I still want to know how the fuck they infected us in the first place."

"You and me both. Ragini will figure it out." The unspoken fear the virus had caused was still hanging heavy in the air. My tech thought she'd isolated it and that none of the rest of us were at risk as long as we kept things apart, but the thought of losing all our coms and our *smatis* at a crucial moment was paralyzing.

"Speaking of that, I need to go meet with her. She's going to test out a new solution on me." Aiz gave Gita a nod and left the room.

"I'm proud of you, you didn't put your hand on your gun once," I teased, and Gita shot me a look.

"The enemy of my enemy," she said with a shrug.

"Is not my friend, but worth working with given the right circumstances," I finished with a grin. "Hao used to say that all the time."

"Hao's an ass," Gita said, but there was too much softness in her face for the words to carry much weight. "Majesty, are you all right?"

The abrupt question surprised me. "Yes, why?"

"I have noticed—to be honest, we all have—that you haven't spoken to Mia since we arrived back here. And you seem distracted."

Make that multiple people who've noticed.

"Emmory told me of your fight. I understand if you don't want to talk about it, but I wanted to let you know I'm here for you."

I wrapped an arm around Gita's waist and leaned into her. "You've always been there for me. I am okay. What's going on between me and Mia needs to stay between us until she chooses to deal with it. Well, mostly." I sighed. "I'm going to have to drag Aiz into it to get her to see reason and I'm not looking forward to the fallout from that. But there's nothing you can do for me."

"Of course, Majesty. I didn't mean to pry."

"You weren't." I felt a little sliver of guilt at her quick apology, but I wasn't about to tell my *Dve* all the details of the argument. Just like I hadn't told Emmory anything beyond the basics of what I'd seen with Mia. It shouldn't have surprised me that he told the others about my fight with Mia.

I knew without a doubt if I did that the moment the *Hailimi* was repaired I'd be back on it and safe on Pashati in the blink of an eye.

I squeezed Gita again and felt her arm tighten in response before she let me go.

"What else is bothering you?"

"You mean right now?" I laughed. "There's a whole list."

"What's at the top?" Gita waved, and I turned my head to see Johar and Alba in the doorway.

"Why did the Hiervet want to talk with us?" I asked.

"Exactly what I want to know," Johar said, grabbing a chair and spinning it around to sit in it with her forearms braced on the back. "I've been talking with Captain Zov. It's a bit hard to blame her for reacting the way she did."

"She disobeyed an order, but I'm less mad about it than I was." Dirah had done a lot in the last few days to make up for her mistake, and that wasn't limited to the offer of safe haven for us or the repair of our ships. I'd seen her talking with Johar and Mia, and there seemed to be Shen everywhere now patiently working with Istrevitel troops.

It couldn't replace actual combat experience, but maybe the presence of so many war veterans and the incident with the Hiervet ship would wipe away the impulsiveness that had been clinging to them.

"Majesty, I think what Johar is trying to bring up is that the Istrevitel's attitude is wrapped up in the histories of the Svatir." Alba sat next to me with a smile. "Which is part of the problem, isn't it?"

"How so?" Gita didn't sit with us, but she hadn't moved back to her position with Kisah at the door.

I shared a look with Alba. "Stop me if I'm not having the same thought you are. The problem is we're getting two stories about the Hiervet—or three really, just to confuse things. Thyra started with saying their people were harmless, but she's backtracked on that and her story lines up more with what the Svatir experienced."

Alba nodded in agreement. "And we've seen the Hiervet act out both those lines of thought. They attacked Adora's ship, but left ours alone. They didn't even fire back when Captain Zov's ship attacked them."

"There wasn't really time for them to react."

"There was," Johar replied with a shake of her head. "We've been over the video. It would have been close, but if they were as experienced at war as everyone claims? They could have gotten out of there. Shit, they could have disappeared the same way they just appeared." She spread her hands wide. "Because we still don't know how they got there without setting off any of our radars."

I muttered a curse. "Who's lying?"

"It's not even about lying anymore, Majesty," Gita said. "We've seen the apparently paradoxical behavior with our own eyes. It's a bit like watching someone you know can take a punch flinch when you throw one. Something's changed the narrative."

A flinch.

I held up a hand and Jo dropped back into silence as I got to my feet and paced toward the door, willing my brain to remember why that word seemed to resonate with me.

"The Svatir," I said. "He flinched."

"Need you to tell the rest of us what's going on in your brain, Hail," Johar said.

"In a minute. Gita, where's Dailun?"

"With Hao, I think. Hang on." A moment later, Gita nodded. "They weren't far, they'll be here in a moment."

"Do we have to wait?" Jo asked, and I sat back down in the chair next to her.

"When we met with *Tsia* Brov and the others the first time. Captain Zov was talking about the ferocity of the Hiervet. There was a guy in the back of the room who never introduced himself to me. He flinched when she said it."

"Why?" Alba asked. Johar looked thoughtful.

"That's what I want to know," I said.

31

W ho is this person?" I played back the memory for Dailun. "They never introduced themselves to me."

"His name is Timur, *jiejie*."

"Why was he there?"

Dailun was surprised by my question. "He is a Memory Keeper. They are required to be present for events like this." He sat across from me when I gestured at the chair.

"You mentioned this before," Hao said.

"My people do have access to all our memories, but for obvious reasons no one carries them all."

"A lot, though?"

"Yes." His smile was quick. "Compared to humans, it's overwhelming. But there are those among us, the Memory Keepers, who are responsible for holding the memories of every Svatir who has ever lived."

"He's a walking library of your people." I lifted my eyebrows as I picked up my fresh mug of *yablok* and drank, remembering how Dirah had told me that the Memory Keepers could erase and alter memories. "Interesting. How many are there?"

"I don't know," Dailun replied. "There are some who are public figures—the ones who are part of the *Tsias* and the Librarians, for example. But many are kept secret and sworn to secrecy."

"To keep your people safe?"

"Yes, it's to preserve us should something happen. As long as one of the Memory Keepers survives, so will the Svatir."

"So you want to tell me why he flinched when Captain Zov was talking about how brutal the Hiervet were?"

"I'm sorry, *jiejie*, what?"

Everyone was looking at me now. Emmory had shown up with food at the same time Hao and Dailun had arrived, and I'd ignored my plate in favor of pressing Dailun about the mysterious Svatir. Johar, of course, had dived right into the food, but now she stopped eating and watched me with a half smile playing on her lips.

"You saw it, didn't you?"

"Now that I know what you're talking about, yeah." She nodded. "Didn't know what to make of it."

I pointed my cup at Emmory.

"It didn't move him anywhere on the danger list, Majesty, but it did bump him in the list to watch."

"The danger list?" Aiz asked. He'd returned shortly after Emmory, but his report on the virus progress had been shelved in favor of this more pressing topic.

"Emmory keeps a running tally of people who are a danger to me. Mostly the ones he might have to kill," I murmured. "You and Mia were probably in the top spots there for a while." I resisted the urge to ask where Mia was. I'd expected her to join Aiz for this meeting, but he'd arrived alone.

Emmory tipped his head. "For security reasons, I'm not sharing who's on the list right now."

"Fair enough," Aiz replied with a smile.

"It was guilt."

Everyone's eyes, mine included, slid to Hao. He lifted a shoulder and then reached for his cup. "I just rewatched it. I'm slipping, didn't see it the first time."

"Guilt?"

Hao shrugged at Gita's question. "Watch it yourself. He curls inward, like he's trying to escape something. If he'd been outraged or offended he would have straightened, puffed his chest out. Gotten ready to respond to the allegations. Timur did none of that. Instead he looked like he wanted to disappear through the floor."

"He's right," I murmured, calling up the scene on my *smati* again. "The moment Dirah says 'brutality' it's like he's trying to escape from the word."

"It gets worse, though." Even as Hao spoke I saw the rest of the playback and could immediately pick out the reaction. "Something about not only that memory but the fact that all Svatir have that memory really upset him."

The second flinch, Timur curling even further into himself like he wanted to disappear.

"Dailun, how do I speak with Timur alone?"

"Alone?" He shook his head. "The *Tsias* will not allow it, honored sister. You are not only an outsider, but you are dangerous."

I couldn't stop the grin from spreading over my face and several people laughed.

"I'm reasonably sure that wasn't a compliment, Majesty," Emmory said with a chuckle.

"I'll take them where I can get them. Figure out a way to get me into a room alone with Timur, Emmory. I'll handle the rest."

"Your Majesty, I have an idea." Alba tapped a finger on the table. "What if you don't make it about Timur? Isn't there a Memory Keeper stationed here with the Istrevitel?"

"There's not," Dailun replied with a shake of his head.

"Really?" I didn't know why I found that surprising. From everything we'd seen, it fit in line with how the Svatir treated the Istrevitel as if they were a separate, unspoken race.

Alba wasn't deterred. "Dai, what if she invites *Tsia* Brov here? They will bring a Memory Keeper with them, won't they?"

I grinned when Dailun nodded.

"Yes, I believe so. They don't often travel anywhere without one given their positions, and the empress is enough of a reason to make sure there is a Memory Keeper present for an unfiltered memory. It would most likely be Timur who came with them."

"Well, I guess I should come up with a reason for an invitation, then, shouldn't I?" I rubbed my hands together.

"*Jiejie*, you still won't be able to be alone with Timur."

"Oh, you let me worry about that," I replied.

"Your Majesty, Captain Zov wishes to speak with you."

I looked away from the falling snow and nodded to Zin, who in turn gestured the Istrevitel captain forward. She had a dark knit cap pulled down low and was bundled up in a heavy coat that was the same as my own.

Dirah didn't speak right away. Instead she stood in silence with me, watching the snow fall. It had been snowing steadily for most of the day, the white flakes collecting on the trees clustered around the building turning them into great white rockets pointed at the steadily darkening sky.

"Your *Ekam* came to speak with a group of new recruits today. It was most informative."

"You sat in?"

Dirah dipped her head with a smile. "It seems as though I should set an example for my people and be the first in line to not only admit I don't know what I'm doing but be willing to learn."

I ran my tongue over my teeth. "I was perhaps a tad harsh with my words, Captain."

"You were not, Your Majesty. They were necessary and needed. We had not seen true combat until that moment, and in my arrogance I ignored your order. I did not think it mattered, but I see the way your people carry themselves and now I can recognize the difference. I hope to change that."

"I hope you realize the intent when I say I hope you never go to war."

Dirah's laugh was as bright as her hair. "I understand the sentiment, especially coming from you. You have seen enough war for a lifetime, Your Majesty. Your suggestions for the simulators were interesting."

"You can just say you think I'm nuts," I replied.

Dirah laughed. "You are not at all what I expected."

I shot her a wry grin. "I get that a lot. What did you expect?"

"No disrespect, but I thought you would be colder."

"I'm plenty cold."

She laughed again. "We can go inside."

"I was mostly joking," I replied. "I like this. I haven't seen much snow since I left home." I smiled at the memory. "Though it was snowing the night I came back to Krishan."

"Why did you go home?"

"Honestly? Emmory didn't give me much of a choice." I laughed. "But I stayed because my people needed me. I tried the unfeeling empress, Captain; it didn't feel right. So I decided to be myself instead."

"I have seen the video of your death. That is how I thought you would be, calm and composed. You are far more human, to steal a phrase, than that moment shows."

I almost asked her which death before I realized she meant the only one that had been broadcast throughout the human sectors of the galaxy. But apparently it had made it all the way out here as well.

The rush of water filled my ears and I couldn't stop the shudder.

"I am sorry, Your Majesty, I probably shouldn't have brought that up."

"No, it's fine. Probably not a great example of my personality," I said with a shrug. "I had two choices there—lose my shit, which was exactly what Wilson wanted, or stay composed and beat him at his own game." I looked back at the falling snow, trying to ignore the echoing of running water in my head. "It wasn't anything more than stubbornness, really."

Zin's snort was loud in the stillness and I saw Dirah smile out of the corner of my eye. "I suspect your people would object to that characterization of yourself."

"Maybe," I admitted. "That's what being a leader really is, though, Captain. Doing what needs to be done, be it messy or unpleasant or difficult. I won't lie and say my parents didn't instill some of that in me from the beginning, but the bulk of it I learned from a gunrunner. You do the work. Apologize when you're wrong. Fix your own fuckups. And if you have to go down, do it swinging."

"Captain Hao is far more than just a gunrunner."

"I know, but he likes to pretend otherwise so I play along."

Captain Zov chuckled and we fell back into an easy silence for several minutes before she spoke again. "I understand you have contacted *Tsia* Brov and asked them to come here. May I ask why?"

"I have some questions about a puzzle we're trying to unravel. You should be there. I suspect it is going to be enlightening."

"That's all the context I'm going to get, isn't it?" Dirah asked when I didn't continue.

I patted her arm in sympathy. "I'm being honest with you when I say I only have a suspicion, not any actual proof. If I'm right it's better you hear it from your own people than from an outsider."

This time Dirah's laugh was sharp. "Your Majesty, we are outsiders among our own people. We are Istrevitel—the forgotten ones."

"Still, it's better to wait." I frowned as the flicker that had been plaguing the edge of my vision returned. "Do you miss your family?"

"My father left when we were children. My mother passed from the grief of my sister's death. There was no one left. It was an easy choice for me to do this. Others were not so lucky." She shook her head. "No, I do not regret my choices. Well, most of them anyway. I sometimes wonder what would have happened if I had taken my Traveling the way Dailun did."

"Is there still time for you to do it?"

Dirah pursed her lips. "An interesting question. No?" She exhaled. "It is a missed opportunity. I am here now and here I will stay until my dreaming."

"I know one thing," I said. "We wouldn't have met this way, but maybe another. If I've learned anything, it's that the universe is strange like that."

"True." She laughed. "You know, the Farians said that to our people the first time they met also. They were so young then, not technologically advanced at all, so we thought it best to leave them alone. Though they had an ability even then to manipulate the energy of the universe in such fantastic ways. Perhaps we should have paid closer attention." Dirah paused and then sighed. "It is past, though. Thank you, Your Majesty. I will leave you to your contemplation of the snow."

I nodded and let her go, dragging in a deep breath of cold air and blowing it out, watching it curl through the space in front of me.

The flicker I saw out of the corner of my eye again was almost lost to the shifting snow. I froze, my heart kicking into my throat. Had that been a Hiervet? It was so hard to pick out the gray-skinned alien against the snow and when I turned fully toward it there was nothing there.

"Majesty?" Zin stepped to my side. "What is it?"

I squinted into the snow. Shook my head. Sighed. "Nothing. Sorry, I thought I saw—nothing."

"We should go inside." Zin put his hand on my back, the other still on his Hessian 45, his gray-green eyes scanning the terrain in front of us.

I let him lead me back into the building, but I threw one last look over my shoulder as we went through the door. I wasn't sure what I was expecting, or what I wanted to see, but there was nothing but falling snow.

32

We doing divide and conquer here?" Hao murmured to me as we watched the people moving through the room. *Tsia* Brov and their entourage had arrived a few moments ago. I'd spotted Timur and the way he melted into the opposite corner from us almost immediately. No one approached him; it was almost like they didn't notice him at all.

I stiffened at the movement in the corner of my vision before I realized it was just Iza. I relaxed, but it was too late.

"You're jumpy. What's up?"

I am seeing things again, gege.

I couldn't make the words leave my mouth and I knew Hao wouldn't buy my nonchalant shrug, so I went for the next best thing—a lie wrapped in the truth. "There's a lot riding on this. I don't know how to explain it but my gut is telling me that whatever Timur knows, we need to know, too."

"That all your gut is telling you?"

I should have known he wouldn't let it go. "Later."

"Tell me now, Hail."

Oh, I hadn't heard that tone of voice in what felt like a very long time. Hao and I had settled into our new roles so firmly that the sound of what I used to teasingly call his "captain voice" was enough to make it impossible for me to deny him.

I straightened my spine and kept my eyes on the people in the room rather than looking at my brother. "I keep seeing something out of the corner of my eye. A shadow or a form. Just a flicker. If I look right at it, it's gone."

"Thank you." Hao nodded once. "Any voices?"

"No." I was surprised by the burst of relief that admission carried with it. "All quiet in my brain." I sighed. "It's only happened a few times. I am probably just jumpy."

"Maybe, not like you don't have a reason for it. But let me know if things change."

"What are you? The new keeper of my mental health?"

He snorted and shook his head. "Sort of. What I am is your brother and that covers a whole range of things, *sha zhu*. Up to and including making sure you're okay." He patted me on the arm. "We'll talk about it later in a more private setting."

"Okay. To answer your earlier question it's about two parts divide and conquer and three parts introduce as much chaos as possible so that *Tsia* Brov can't intervene. If they will at all. All I know is I'm really not supposed to be talking with the Memory Keepers." I gestured at Captain Zov and the other Istrevitel in the room. "I want them here because I want some firsthand witnesses to whatever it is Timur tells me."

"You think it's going to be that kind of bomb?"

"Yes. This has been building for a few days now." I tapped my stomach and Hao whistled.

"All right. Just give me the signal, then, and we'll go."

"I was waiting for Dailun." I spotted the pink-haired pilot as he slipped into the room and wove his way through the crowd to where Timur watched from the corner. "And there he is."

"Good luck."

I pushed away from the wall. It is far more challenging to blend into a crowd when you are taller than most of the people in the room, never mind when you are a somewhat notorious green-haired empress. But I'd learned how to blend in from Gy, a man who could walk on stage during an opera and steal the jewels off the neck of the soprano in the middle of their aria.

Aiz and Mia were talking to *Tsia* Brov, expertly maneuvering the Svatir politician so their back was to the corner where Dailun spoke with Timur. I slipped through the crowd, exchanging smiles with Istrevitel and my own people as I passed.

"Dailun," I said, and my little brother turned to smile at me. "Will you introduce me to your friend?"

"Empress Hailimi Bristol, this is Memory Keeper Timur."

Now that I was close enough I realized his hair wasn't black as I'd first assumed, but a very dark blue. "Memory Keeper. It's a great pleasure."

"Your Majesty." His eyes flicked to where *Tsia* Brov stood and then back at me. "You realize this is not entirely appropriate."

"You probably have heard enough about me to know that I don't care about appropriate. I have a question for you, Timur, if you'll indulge me. Would you like to tell me why it bothered you so for Captain Zov to speak of the Hiervet's brutality?"

He could not hide his automatic flinch. "I am not sure what you mean, Your Majesty."

"You don't have much of a poker face." I smiled slowly. "I, however, have played some deadly hands in my day. There is a lot riding on this. I'd advise you not to test me."

"Your Majesty, you are asking me a question I cannot answer. You are not Svatir. You don't understand—"

"Here's what I understand," I said, cutting him off. I don't often use my height to intimidate people. It feels too much like a bully move and one that unnecessarily relies upon my size rather than the strength of my words and reputation to give weight to whatever it is that I want done. But this time I got right up in Timur's face, even though the poor Svatir was a full sixteen centimeters shorter than me. "The safety of the galaxy is at stake and for whatever reason the gods decided I was its best hope. I was practically nose to nose with a Hiervet ship but they didn't shoot at me. In fact, they wanted to talk to me. But before we could make that happen, Captain Zov blew them out of the sky, because she believes they are dangerous."

The grief in Timur's dark eyes was a surprise, but I didn't let up.

"I keep hearing conflicting reports about the Hiervet and now I've seen it with my own eyes. I want you to tell me the truth because we need to know everything before we start a war."

Timur flinched again and swallowed. "The war with the Hiervet was complicated. Far more so than our people realize."

"Define *complicated* for me."

"*Jiejie.*" Dailun's murmured warning arrived just before *Tsia* Brov's voice.

"Your Majesty." That practiced politician smile was the same no matter who was wearing it. "We do not typically speak directly with Memory Keepers while they are working. What was it you called me here for?"

I shot Dailun an apologetic look that he answered with a half smile and a roll of his eyes before I replied. "To be perfectly honest, *Tsia*, I wanted to speak with Timur. Not with you."

"With Timur? Your Majesty, it's not something that I can—"

"We're here," I said cheerfully, cutting their protest short. "May as well get it over with. Timur was just telling me that the war with the Hiervet was more complicated than people realize."

The conversation in the room fell away. I watched the emotions ripple across *Tsia* Brov's face—confusion, frustration, and a healthy dose of annoyance. While Timur looked flat-out terrified.

Interesting. I was now willing to put money down on Timur knowing something that *Tsia* Brov did not.

"What is this?" Captain Zov asked.

"This is a reckoning," I said. "There are truths we all need to hear."

"This is inappropriate." *Tsia* Brov tried once again to gain some control of the situation. "I must formally protest, Your Majesty. We cannot—"

"Santi." Timur raised a hand and the *Tsia* fell silent.

I realized that the Memory Keepers had more power than I'd initially assumed.

Timur shook his head. "This would be better to speak of in private, Your Majesty."

"Maybe," I replied, crossing my arms over my chest. "But I'm awful sick of secrets and something tells me that the Istrevitel deserve to hear this even more than me."

"You cannot force me to tell you." He looked around the room, but there wasn't a single friendly face.

"Oh, Timur, you'd be surprised at what I can do. But I'll let you have your privacy, to a point. I'm bringing Captain Zov and my *Ekam* with me."

"I will come also," *Tsia* Brov said, and the concerned expression that flashed across Timur's face pushed me to nod my agreement.

"Emmory?"

"Room across the hall, Majesty." My *Ekam* gestured, his face expressionless as he fell into step next to me. *"Nicely done,"* he subvocalized over our private com link.

I allowed the tiniest smile to show. We'd known going into this that just asking *Tsia* Brov or Timur for a smaller meeting would have resulted in a definitive no. But people had a way of adjusting their expectations when faced with spilling secrets to a whole roomful of ears. Presented with the choice between the room and just a few of us, they were more than happy to pick the latter.

The room across the hall was half the size of the one we'd just left, but with only the five of us it felt spacious. I boosted myself up onto the desk at the front of the room, Emmory falling into parade rest at my side.

Captain Zov hesitated for a heartbeat before she surprised me and came to stand on my other side with her arms crossed. The gesture did not go unnoticed by Timur or *Tsia* Brov, though of the two, the Svatir governmental representative was the one who looked annoyed.

"Your Majesty, I would like to know what it is you plan to do with the knowledge?"

"I'm afraid I don't have an answer for that until I hear what you have to tell me."

He exhaled a long sigh and I had to bite the inside of my cheek to keep from grinning at him.

Dirah was less amused. "Stop stalling, Memory Keeper, and tell us what is going on."

Santi opened their mouth to protest but Timur held up a hand. "It is a difficult story to tell, Captain Zov, not only for the content but because of the way it must be told."

"Get on with it, then," she replied.

"I will show you." Timur gestured at the desk. "Your Majesty, if I may use that?"

"Sure." I hopped off the polished surface and slipped my hands into the pockets of my pants as Timur pressed his hands flat to the desktop. "That's a neat trick," I murmured as the image spread over the surface.

We watched as the Hiervet landed on Svatir. I couldn't see through their glamour on the recording, but I could tell it was them by the way they looked like the Svatir, only better. Ten Hiervet.

Thyra's squad. This time I recognized her immediately.

"They landed and we welcomed them," Timur said. "The Svatir had been at war with each other for so long that when the Hiervet came with promises of peace, we accepted with grateful hearts. They taught us a different way to live; a better way, they said. It was only later that we realized the cost of their lessons. We were nearly enslaved, would have been ground under their boot heels had the braver among us not risen up to fight."

"I've heard that story before," I said. "Almost word for word, in fact."

Timur lowered his head. "This is true, Your Majesty. It is the memories of our people."

The scene on the desktop shifted to war and I watched Dirah's hands flex on the edge of the picture.

"There is nothing new here," she snarled. "We have all seen this! We won the fight and then you all turned your backs on the very thing that had saved us."

"We turned our backs on violence and slaughter!" *Tsia* Brov protested. "I don't expect such as you to understand, but—"

"Enough. That is not what happened. We were not winning. We were losing."

The shocked noises that came from both Dirah and Santi as the images changed again were indescribable. Timur didn't look at either of them as he continued talking.

"The tech they gave us didn't work on them; we could not fight against the monsters they created. We were dying. Had it not been for the arrival of the other Hiervet, all would have been lost. But in a sense it was anyway. We were beyond madness, unable to think rationally, and we turned on these new Hiervet in our fury. Even though they had saved us.

"The Hiervet retreated and vanished. We discovered the truth as we pieced together our stories. The Hiervet who'd saved us had come hunting their own—our visitors who had subjugated us. By the time we realized what we had done, it was too late. Our leaders knew it was the violence that had kept us from seeing the truth. It was the violence that had led us here in the first place." Timur lifted his hands and the images faded away.

"So you buried it?"

"It was decided unanimously by our leaders to lay down our weapons, wipe the memory from our people, and start again."

"You lied to us." Dirah's eyes were wide with horror, and my heart broke at the tears that she wiped impatiently away. "We thought we were keeping our people safe, but we have given up everything for a lie? There is no reason for the Istrevitel to exist. The Hiervet are not a threat to the Svatir." She turned to me and my heart broke a second time as I saw the realization hit her full force. "I killed them. Oh, erase me from memory, Your Majesty. I murdered—"

"You were operating on shitty intelligence, Captain," I said, putting my hand on her shoulder. "It doesn't change what you did, but don't take on that burden in addition to the one you carry." I knew full well that if we met with the Hiervet, Captain Zov would have to answer for what she'd done, but I'd already decided to do what I could for her.

The flicker in the corner of my vision appeared. This time I was able to keep my breathing even as I turned my head, but the shadow was gone.

"How could you?" *Tsia* Brov's breathless demand dragged my attention back to the desk. They were staring at Timur, their expression a mixture of outrage and despair. "We have sent millions to this place on a lie. Encouraged violence. Everything we claim to oppose we have seeded into the Istrevitel. For what?"

"*Tsia* Brov, I am simply the keeper. I did not make these decisions."

"You have the knowledge and you do not share. We could put a stop to this."

"I do not have the authority to share these memories with others," Timur protested. "I am skirting the bounds of my authority as it is by letting you see it, Santi."

"So why did you?" I asked.

Timur bowed. "I was told to cooperate with the Star."

Dirah was watching at Santi with new eyes. "I am in agreement with *Tsia* Brov. This needs to be shown to the Istrevitel, to the Svatir. We have lived in this lie for long enough." She held out her hand to the Svatir rep. "Will you help me tell our people the truth?"

Santi nodded to Dirah and took her hand. Together the pair left the room. Timur leaned both hands on the desk again and sighed.

"How did you know?" he asked.

I shook my head. "You give me too much credit. I didn't. I merely knew something was wrong."

Timur looked at the door, indecision on his face.

"You know," I said with a soft smile. "Nothing stays buried forever. Better to get this wound out into the air where it can heal."

"I will lose my position for this." Timur headed for the door as he spoke.

"Just blame it on me," I called after him. "I'm used to it."

33

The fallout from my reveal of the Svatir's fabricated history was not as rocky as I had expected. The majority of the Istrevitel were uninterested in returning to Svatir society and took the news of their false past with a surprising amount of aplomb.

As for the Svatir, all I had to go on were the reports filtering back in to Captain Zov from *Tsia* Brov. The pair had struck up an unlikely friendship, Santi's moral objections to the Istrevitel being pressed into service under false pretenses being the driving force behind their campaign to bring the truth to light.

And Timur was proving to be a promising ally on that front. The Memory Keeper seemed to have thrown his lot in with Santi under the auspices of my last words to him.

"I just hope it doesn't result in the Svatir holding Indrana accountable in some fashion," Alice said with a sigh. We were having our weekly com in the quiet of my quarters on board the *Hailimi*. I was curled up in my favorite chair, still dressed in the clothes I'd slept in.

I tried to hold back my grin at Alice's disapproval, unsuccessfully if her look had anything to say about it.

"Hail."

"What?" I lifted my mug of *yablok* to hide my second, wider smile. "I was barely involved."

"You told him to blame you." Alice's eyes flicked past my right shoulder to where I knew Emmory was standing, but my *Ekam* didn't change expression and she sighed. "Are you coming home?"

"No."

"Hail, if the Hiervet aren't an issue, you—"

"The regular Hiervet may not be, we don't know for sure, but the two Farian ones are." I set my mug on the nearby table. "There's that little matter of an army on Faria that's taken over, and if you think I'm leaving Fasé and Stasia, not to mention a squad of Royal Marines, at the mercy of Thyra, you haven't been paying attention, Alice."

"You know I'm not suggesting we leave them, but we could send someone else. An actual military team, which I apparently have to remind you, you are not," she replied. "You belong back here, Hail."

You belong with your people.

Your Star is not coming for you.

I rubbed at my forehead and tried to ignore the persistent flickering in the corner of my vision. I'd stopped looking over the last week; the futility of trying to see what wasn't truly there was exhausting and a distraction I didn't need.

You're losing it. Again. The voice that had been silent for a long while was back in my head with a vicious singsong glee.

"Hail?"

I dropped my hand into my lap. "Give me some time to wrap things up here and talk with Aiz about the next steps as far as Faria goes. Ragini has a working program to clean the virus out of their ships and their *smati*, but I'd like to make sure it's all gone before we leave."

You mean before you run.

Alice nodded and we closed out the com without our usual goodbye. I leaned forward in my chair, resting my head on the edge of the table.

If I leave, Mia dies.

"Leaving feels wrong," I whispered, but I knew Emmory could hear me.

"Then we don't go. You are in charge, Your Majesty. We only go on your word."

"Am I really needed here, though? What if I'm just fooling myself that I could have made any difference in this conflict? I don't know." I blew out a frustrated breath.

"Hail." Emmory's hand settled on the back of my neck.

"I'm fine." I could feel the vibrations of his chuckle through his palm, and I sighed.

"The only time you say that you're fine to me is when you're not. You don't have many tells, Hail, but that's one of them."

I lifted my head and offered up a wan smile. "That's a nice way of saying you know when I'm lying to you."

"I had to come up with something." Emmory squeezed my neck gently before he removed his hand. "You don't lie to us much anymore, which makes when you do all the more evident. You want to tell me about these shadows you're seeing?"

I blinked at him, so surprised by the change of subject I couldn't come up with an appropriate denial. "How did you know?"

"Hao talked to me."

"Of course he did," I muttered. I hadn't intentionally been dodging that conversation with my brother, but it shouldn't have surprised me he'd go to Emmory about it.

"To be fair, Zin mentioned something about it before that, and everyone else has noticed you seem slightly more on edge that normal. Though we assumed it was because of the fight with Mia."

I sighed. "I'm impressed they can parse that out given how often I've been on edge lately."

Emmory gave me the Look.

"It was right there." I pointed into the corner of the room. "The whole time I was talking to Alice there was a shadow, not really a shadow, just a flicker. Like I could see something trying to resolve itself on a screen and failing. It's gone now. Do we think it's something from Priam?" I tapped myself in the now-healed spot where the Farian Hiervet had impaled me. "Or something from my time on Sparkos because let's be honest, Emmy, I wasn't emotionally stable then and I may still not be."

His expression didn't change and he didn't move when I pushed to my feet.

"What?"

"Given everything you've been through I would say you're extremely stable. Which means this is something else."

"But?"

"It's interesting that your first assumption is that you're losing your mind. What happened on Sparkos wasn't your fault, Hail, you know this. So why do you keep trying to blame yourself for a perfectly normal reaction?"

Because I'd buried away how badly it hurt to think of everyone dead. I'd dug a grave and covered it and built a heavy foundation on top because that was easier than coming to terms with the idea of how losing everything could break me.

"I don't want to think about it," I whispered, rubbing the palms of my hands over my arms in an effort to ward off the sudden chill.

"You're going to have to. Maybe not now, but eventually." Emmory reached out and took me by the shoulders. "Everyone dies, Hail, and it's not your responsibility to stop it from happening."

It didn't take any encouragement from my *Ekam* for me to step into his hug. I exhaled, tightening my arms around his waist as the tension went out of my shoulders.

"I have watched you tear yourself into pieces over this time and again," he murmured. "From your family all the way down to a little girl in Garuda Square. You are never thoughtless with the lives of the people around you, and yet you have somehow convinced yourself that you are because you can't stop the inevitable."

"I am the Star of Indrana."

Emmory chuckled. "You are. Star of Indrana, yes. Empress, yes. Legendary gunrunner, yes. Occasional gigantic pain in my ass, yes. You are also human, Hail, and none of us expect miracles from you."

"I don't think I've ever told you how much I appreciate that," I said as I hugged him once more and then stepped back with an exhale. "Have you been taking notes from your husband? That was very Zin-like speech."

Emmory smiled. "I have my moments, Your Majesty. Speaking of Zin, though."

The door chimed once and opened. Zin poked his head into the room. "Aiz and Mia are here, Majesty. Do you have a minute?"

"Yes." I felt my stomach knot back up as the pair came through the door. Aiz's look was grim and Mia wouldn't meet my eyes.

Bugger me.

"Zin, have Gita come in here. You stay on the door. Emmory will just tell you all about this after we're done anyway."

Zin's answering smile was short-lived as he left the room. Gita appeared a moment later and closed the door behind her.

"She told you," I said to Aiz even though his tight jaw told me all I needed to know.

"You want to fill the rest of us in, Your Majesty?"

I looked at Emmory, slipped my hands into my pockets, and told them about Mia's visions. All of it, from her death to mine.

Johar bumped me in the shoulder and settled into the spot next to me, propping her booted foot up next to mine and leaning on the railing of the small alcove in the upper floors of the Istrevitel's head-quarters. "Drink?" She dangled the bottle of whiskey within reach and smiled at my snort.

I took it, pulled out the top, and tipped back the bottle. It was an Earth blend with more smoke than I liked, but our stock was running low and beggars couldn't be choosers. "That bad, huh?"

"The whole facility heard you three. I'll admit, I didn't think Mia could get that sort of volume. She always seemed like the speak-softly type."

"Oh, she is." I rubbed at my chest and took another drink as I watched the Istrevitel moving around below. "Except when she chooses not to. Did you steal this off my ship?"

Johar winked. "I planned on sharing it with you anyway, so I don't think you can technically call it stealing. You want to talk about it?"

"Not really," I admitted after a moment, and handed the bottle back. "But you can go and ask Gita. It's not a secret."

"I may do that." Johar shrugged and took a drink. To my surprise she didn't leave. "You know this thing with Rai has lasted longer than any other relationship."

"You decided not to kill him, huh?"

"About the same as you." She shot me a sideways glance as she passed over the whiskey. "Too many other people in front of him on the list. We hunting down Jamison after this is over?"

"Maybe," I replied, appreciating how she assumed we'd both be around when this was done. "I'll have to tell Alice and everyone I'm just taking a vacation."

"You sound less than thrilled about the idea of going home. You know..." She glanced over her shoulder at where Indula stood just out of earshot. "I know a few people who could make Hail Bristol disappear."

I narrowly avoided choking on my mouthful of whiskey and tears filled my eyes from the burn of the hastily swallowed alcohol. "It would take Emmory and Zin less than a year to find me and you know it."

"Eh, maybe." Johar grinned. "I figured you'd get a few years, because they might cut you a break, but it's a lot more running than a vacation should contain."

"I've had my share of those." I swung the bottle from side to side with a laugh, watching the amber liquid coat the inside of the glass. "Ask Hao to tell you about the time we went to Fiji VI for a vacation."

"Let me guess, he got shot."

"Actually I did." I grinned. "Though at the time I was sure Portis was going to shoot Hao. The fact that I was bleeding all over and Hao was holding me up was probably the only thing that kept him intact."

Johar laughed until she wheezed. "I swear the more stories I hear about your time out in the black, the more I am amazed that Hao didn't kick you both off his ship."

"He threatened a lot, but he loves me."

"He does. I've never seen the like."

We lapsed into silence, passing the bottle back and forth as we stared out over the bustling facility below us.

"Hail." Johar cleared her throat, the bottle dangling between her fingers. "Captain Zov has offered us the use of a ship. I thought I'd take it along with a few Shen and Istrevitel and go see if we can't get a firsthand look at what's happened on Faria."

My heart twisted in protest at the thought of sending yet another person into danger. I dragged in a breath. "Jo, I can't let you do this."

"You should know I'm not really asking for permission." She smiled at me and shook her head. "You don't get to be all noble and set on sacrificing yourself while the rest of us sit back and do nothing. We need to get the intel. There's a good chance that the Farians won't even see the ship, and if they do are they really going to fire on it?"

I felt like there was a very good chance they'd shoot, especially if Thyra was in charge.

"Do you want to risk your life on a maybe?"

"We all do, every single day," Johar replied. "I would be lying if I said anything beyond *I want to get this shit over and done with and go back to room service.* But you and I both know we're at a standstill as long as we have that yawning black void of the unknown over there."

"All right." I bumped my shoulder into hers when she laughed. "I'm giving you permission since you will apparently just do what you want regardless, and you're not wrong."

"Good deal." Johar handed the bottle over. "I'll see you in a couple of days, week at the most." She patted me on the shoulder and pushed away from the railing.

"Jo?"

She turned, one eyebrow raised, and I smiled.

"For the record, I don't plan on dying."

"Good to hear it. I'd hate to have to drag your ass back to the land of the living by force."

"See Ragini and get the protection protocols before you go, and be careful. You won't be able to help Fasé and the others if they're infected, but you'll be able to keep yourself safe."

"Can do. We'll see you."

I leaned back on the railing, bottle still dangling from my hand, mostly forgotten. We'd drunk a good chunk of the bottle and my head was starting to buzz a little. The temptation to drain the rest of the whiskey was there, but I resisted. Things were only partially settled between Mia and Aiz; I knew there was another conversation to be had once the fires from the initial outburst died down.

And I probably owed Mia an apology for forcing her hand the way I had.

"Shiva," I muttered. The memory of the broken look on her face as she pleaded with us not to interfere kicked me in the gut. I brought the bottle up to my mouth and took a long drink.

This time the shadow in the corner of my eye resolved itself into the distinct shape of a Hiervet and I almost dropped the bottle of whiskey on the floor.

34

Whiskey, like all liquids, burns when you inhale it.

"Majesty!"

I folded in half, then went to a knee, coughing and choking on my poorly timed breathing experiment. Indula was at my side, a hand on my back, and if I could have talked I would have ordered him to watch for the Hiervet I'd just seen.

Except I wasn't sure I'd really seen it.

When I lifted my tear-blurred gaze to the spot, that little corner of the alcove was empty of everything but shadows.

I felt the vibrations of the pounding feet on the stairs and then Gita was on my other side. "Majesty?"

I waved a hand, finally regained my breath, and managed a wheezing "I'm fine."

"Drinking problem?"

I laughed, which set me off coughing again, and I heard Indula unsuccessfully smother a snicker. Gita let me wind back down before she helped me to my feet. She didn't release my shoulders and stared at me for a long moment, her expression unreadable.

"You okay?" she asked finally.

"I thought I saw something." It took an enormous effort to get the words out. "A Hiervet in the corner over there."

Indula had his Hessian out before I finished, and was inspecting the corner, but Gita didn't move. "Nothing there now," she said.

I glared at her.

"And the coughing?" she asked.

"I'd taken a drink when I saw it and the whiskey went down the wrong pipe."

"That'll do it." Gita let me go, bending down and picking up the bottle. "You probably should eat something, Majesty."

"All right. Jo's going to Faria with Captain Zov in an Istrevitel ship to do some recon."

"She talked with me already."

"Honestly, what do you need me for?"

Gita laughed and took a hold of my arm as we headed down the stairs. "We need you, Majesty, believe me."

"I'm glad someone does." I cleared my throat; the whiskey was kicking in, and I sank into a chair in the barracks with a sigh.

"Indula's gone to get you some food, do you want anything else?"

"A vacation," I murmured wistfully as I stared at the ceiling. "Somewhere with sand and no one shooting at me."

"I'll talk to Emmory and see what we can do." Gita patted me on the shoulder. "Some water probably wouldn't hurt either."

"I'm not even remotely drunk, Gita. It was barely a third, okay, maybe half a bottle of whiskey."

She laughed and headed for the bathroom. I rubbed a hand over my eyes and found myself wishing she hadn't taken the whiskey with her. I wasn't drunk, but I could be, and right now that sounded like a really good plan.

Metal scraped on metal and I dropped my hand, staring across the table at Aiz.

"Someone told me there was whiskey," he said.

"Gita's got it," I replied, pointing as she came back into the barracks with the whiskey in one hand and water in the other. She passed the bottle to Aiz.

"Really?"

Gita wiggled the water in my direction. "His sobriety isn't my concern."

I took the water with a sigh and then pulled the tray of food closer. "I think my *Dve* is warming up to you."

Gita snorted and went to stand by the door. Aiz grinned and took a drink. "She hasn't threatened to cut me into pieces lately, so I'd agree."

I eyed the whiskey in his hand, but Aiz smiled and shook his head, tipping the bottle at the food in front of me. "Eat, Hail."

"Mia still mad?" I asked, picking up a *piero* and biting into the flaky dough. The sharp spice of something that reminded me of curry filled my senses and I felt an abrupt longing for home.

"She'll be mad for another fifty hours or so," he replied, and took another, longer drink. "But it's fine. I'd rather she's mad and alive. I appreciate what you did, Hail. I know what it cost you. If it helps at all, once she calms down she'll realize it, too."

"I meant what I said." I put the *piero* back down, my appetite suddenly gone, and pushed the tray away. "I'm tired of the choice being taken from me because they think they know better. You don't get to have this both ways, dragging me into this fight and then withholding information from me."

"I'm on your side on this, Hail. Though don't think I missed the part about Mia seeing your death also."

"I guess you'll just have to follow us around, then, and make sure we're okay." I was surprised how easily the joke came to me.

Aiz glanced over his shoulder and then held the bottle out to me with a smile.

"She's kept this from you a lot longer, how are you so calm?" I took a quick drink but Gita didn't move from her spot.

"I trust my sister. Don't get me wrong, I was—am—furious at her for hiding this," Aiz said. "But I've known something was wrong for years, I just didn't have the specifics. It's easier for me to roll with it in a number of ways."

He leaned forward and patted me with one hand, stealing the bottle back with the other and holding it out of my reach when I protested. "Plus, you will find a solution. One that doesn't involve either of you dying." Aiz got to his feet. "Eat your dinner, Hail, you'll feel like shit in the morning if you don't."

I made a face at him, but picked up my discarded *piero* and finished my meal.

It wasn't quite fifty hours, but it was close. I spotted Mia watching us as we ran through what amounted to a full-contact game of capture the flag late one afternoon on Horst. It was me, Emmory, and Zin versus Gita, Iza, and Indula, with Kisah refereeing the hits.

"Hail!" Emmory's shout dragged my attention away from Mia and back to what I was supposed to be focused on.

Namely, Gita.

I managed to turn to the side, deflecting most of Gita's punch, but the impact rocked through my shoulder and I knew it was going to bruise. I used my momentum and hit her in the diaphragm with the flat of my palm, knocking her back into Emmory.

"You're down, Gita," Kisah called, no small amount of glee in her voice. Emmory and I had gotten her with that same move on the last round when we'd defeated her, Hao, and Johar.

"Keep your head in the game," Emmory said, and I nodded once. "Let's go."

With Gita down, Iza was alone at the flag. I would put money on Zin in a head-to-head against Indula any day. Which was less a commentary on Indula's abilities than it was my faith in Zin's.

"How are we going in?"

"You circle around," Emmory said. "I'll come in from the front and distract her."

"She'll expect it, and knowing Indula there's probably some awful trap near their flag."

Emmory chuckled. Yesterday, he, Hao, and Zin had decimated the rest of us until they'd been stopped by Indula somehow electrifying the area around our flag.

"I should have asked him how he did that," I said with a shrug.

"Might have been a good idea. What's your idea?"

"Go back to Zin. I've been wanting to try something but if she sees you it'll blow the whole thing."

Emmory studied me for a moment before melting back into the junglelike terrain we'd picked for this round. I took a deep breath and brought up an image of Indula on my *smati*.

I'd tried Priam's trick of vanishing entirely, but it was surprisingly harder than changing my face. Aiz had explained it as projecting one image—a person, rather than the multiple images a background would require. That made sense, in a strange sort of way, though even he admitted that there was a difference between looking like a person and pretending to be that person.

"The longer you have to keep up the pretense, the more chances you have to fuck it up. Most people have pretty good instincts and the better they know a person, the more those instincts are going to be telling them something is wrong."

I released the breath I'd been holding. There was no mirror to check my work and it never felt any different to me. "Only way is forward," I muttered in Indula's voice.

"What are you doing? I thought you were going after Zin?"

"No good, we need to regroup."

Iza frowned and I was equal parts frustrated and proud of her. Not only for how fast her gut was telling her something was off but for the fact that she listened.

Speed was my friend here, so I moved in quickly. "We've only got a minute before they head this way, so—"

"Iza!" Indula's voice rang through the air.

"Well, that's the risk of it." I laughed and dropped my façade.

"Majesty?" Iza took a step back.

I winked, grabbed the flag, and took off running. Iza's swearing was quickly replaced by the sounds of her pursuit.

"Coming in hot, Emmory," I said over the coms. *"Where's Indula?"*

"No sign of him, Majesty. Keep your eyes out."

The words had no sooner echoed in my ear than Indula emerged from the heavy leaves on my left. I dropped and rolled forward, avoiding his lunge with a breathless laugh, and bounced to my feet to take off running again.

I knew I could outrun Indula, but Emmory was waiting as I rounded a bend and I dropped a second time so he could shoot Indula with the specially designed pistols the Istrevitel used for the courses.

"Her Majesty's team is the winner," Kisah announced.

"That was a good one," I said, holding my hand out to Gita as the scene around us disappeared. She took it with a smile but shot a stern look at my *Ekam*.

"After all the shit you've given me. You are entirely too comfortable using her as bait."

"Maybe, but she's more than capable and we may as well play to our strengths. We all know it's an unusual situation." Emmory's smile was soft. "And I trust her to stay alive."

"I feel like we're in some weird role reversal with you two," I joked, letting Gita go and reaching out for Iza with a smile.

"That was a good idea with the masking program, Majesty," she said.

"Not a program."

"What did you do?" Emmory asked, and I grinned.

"Keeping up with my Shen practice. I looked like Indula." I demonstrated and everyone but Emmory inhaled in shock.

"That is wild," Indula said.

Iza snapped her fingers. "You are too tall, that's what it was!"

"Ouch," Indula joked, putting a hand to his heart. "Her Majesty is not that much taller than me."

"She is," Zin said as I released the illusion. "That's a neat trick."

"We should talk about teaching everyone," I replied, but Emmory shook his head.

"One thing at a time, Majesty."

"Fine."

"You could have just gotten a kill, Majesty," Iza said as we gathered our things and headed out of the simulator toward the shuttle. "Why didn't you?"

I reached out and cupped the back of her head, touching my forehead to hers. "Honestly? That would have been too easy. This way was more fun." I glanced across the shuttle bay where Dailun stood talking with Mia. "Less violence, not more, right?"

35

It didn't escape my attention that everyone had found something interesting to focus on at the front of the shuttle and left Mia and me with a rather large buffer of empty ship around us as we headed back to Ganyin.

"I am sorry." Mia looked down at her hands and then back up at me with a small smile. "You were right, Hail. You are right about me taking your choices from you because I thought I knew best. I didn't ever expect this to be so difficult."

"What changed?"

"You."

"How could that have been a surprise? You saw all of it happen. Didn't you?"

"I didn't." She shook her head and laughed. "I saw you, but I saw the end before you and set myself on that path with the utmost resolution long before we met. I don't see the whole of it play out in front of me; that's not how this works. I see pieces, flashes, and I try to put them in order. Sybil has been doing this longer than any of us; she's better at putting the pieces into order. I am also guilty of letting the things I fear take precedence over the whole."

I held my hand out and told myself that the fluttering in my stomach when she took it was totally normal. "I don't want to die, Mia, but I won't sacrifice you just to save my own life. You should understand me well enough by now to know I can't."

"It was wrong of me to expect anything less from you. Your loyalty to those you care about has always been something I admired about you." She squeezed my fingers. "I saw your shift during the training, it was good."

"Iza figured it out pretty quickly."

"Your people are very good at their jobs." Mia reached out with her other hand, paused, and offered up a smile. "I also saw Gita's punch. You must be sore?"

"I avoided most of it, but be my guest."

This feeling I was familiar with, and I relaxed as the warmth of Mia's energy flooded my arm, soothing away the aching muscle at the impact spot and radiating outward.

"Better?"

"Much," I murmured. "Does this mean you're not mad at me anymore?"

"For the moment." She smiled. "To be honest I wasn't ever really mad at you. I was mad at myself because you were right. But also because I am afraid." Tears gathered in her storm-colored eyes. "I have seen what happens when you follow me, and while I can admit it is wrong of me to expect you to walk away, I still want you to."

"You can't ask me not to follow you. Don't you get it?" I reached out and cupped her face in my hands, pressing my forehead to hers. "I have let so many people go in my life for the noblest of reasons. But I can't—please don't ask that of me."

"I won't survive the loss of you," she whispered.

"Of course you will, but have some faith in me?" I smiled. "That's all I ask. I am very hard to kill and we are nowhere near the end of this. Trust in me rather than the things you've seen. Stay alive for me, and I will come for you. I promise."

Mia closed her eyes and blew out a shuddering breath. Then she opened them again and I could see my whole world reflected back at me. "I trust you, Hail. Completely and forever."

The words were simple, but the feeling wrapped itself around my heart and squeezed to the point of pain.

"How's Aiz?" I asked, clearing my throat and pulling back a fraction before I gave in to the need to kiss her. The illusion of privacy was just that, an illusion, and I didn't much feel like an audience for that part of things.

"Much better." Mia smiled. "Your Ragini has really impressed him. The fleet's coms are back up, all the *renimi* have been fixed, and we have a defense against it if they try to infect us again."

"Good." I'd read the report from the senior tech that morning and was beyond pleased that she and her team had not only fixed the issue but figured out just how the Farians had slipped the virus past the complex security already in place for all *smatis*.

This had been something we'd never seen before, a combination of code and some kind of biological component that allowed the code to bypass the normal safety protocols. I hadn't understood most of the explanation, but Ragini did and more importantly she had assured me it wouldn't happen to the Shen again and that she'd put new safeguards in place for our programs to keep the Indranans and our equipment safe.

"Majesty," Emmory said, and I tore my gaze away from Mia. "Captain Zov is back. Apparently Johar's not with her."

"What?" I got to my feet, Mia following. "What do you mean she's not with her?"

"Exactly what I said, Majesty, or what Hao is telling me. I don't have an answer for the question I know you're about to ask me. We're coming into the bay and will be on the ground in five minutes and you can ask her then."

"Fine." I reached out and patted Emmory on the arm. "Sorry, I shouldn't take that out on you."

"We know Johar can take care of herself, Majesty. She's fine."

I knew that, but knowing wasn't going to make the knot in my gut go away.

A hush fell over the shuttle, some of our lighthearted feelings dimmed by the news and the worry. I caught myself clinging to Mia's hand as we landed, but when I tried to let her go she smiled at me and squeezed my hand gently.

I suspected she kept a hold of me in part to force me to slow down, as striding off the shuttle at a faster speed would have left Mia scrambling to keep up and it would also prove damned difficult to take a swing at Captain Zov if Mia was still holding my hand.

But Dirah was smiling when I came off the ramp, even though a very pissed-off-looking Hao was standing next to her.

"Your Majesty."

"Where's Jo?"

Captain Zov held her hand out. "She decided to stay behind, Your Majesty. She recorded a message for you."

"You could have told me that," Hao protested.

Dirah gave him a sideways look and smiled at me. "Johar said to tell you first, Your Majesty."

"Fair enough." I glanced at Emmory, who nodded, and then I reached out to take the file from Dirah. "Barracks," I said, and tipped my head at Dirah. "Join us, Captain?"

"Of course."

"You weren't spotted?" I asked.

"No, Your Majesty." She smiled. "It may have been they weren't looking for us, but also it appeared that the Farians were a little light on ships in the space above the planet. We are not sure why."

We got to the barracks and I put the file from Johar up on the wall so everyone could see it. Hao leaned against the wall next to me.

"Hail." Johar smiled. "We made it here in one piece and made contact with the rebellion." The camera shifted sideways and my breath caught at the sight of not only Fasé but Stasia as well. "As you can see, everyone's here and in good shape. I decided to stay since I'm the only one here with an uncompromised brain. Ha, how's that for irony. Anyhow, that way we can get some messages going back and forth better than what they're working with right now, which is not much."

"Find Ragini," I said to Gita. "We'll want to figure out if we can transmit the antivirus to them and how best to do that."

"Yes, Majesty."

The flicker in the corner of my vision was back, but I steadfastly ignored it in favor of Johar's message.

"If you had money down on the Adora theory, Hail, you're the winner. Fasé says that shortly after you left, Adora's supporters marched on the Pedalion. The virus started spreading and everything went completely to shit. Sort of like that Pinbree job. Fasé doesn't know if Sybil and the others are alive or not but our current guess is that they are." Johar's easy smile faded at that. "I can tell you that it's messy down here and I am not sure how we're going to do this. We've got a lot of innocent people on the ground who don't support the Farian broadcasting from the Pedalion facility. I've attached a few of those broadcasts from Adora; have fun watching those."

Jo gestured around. "We're holed up on the southwest side of the capital. Adora's got forces out but there's a lot of fighting going on. I hate to say it but you're going to have to move and move fast. We'll see you." She saluted and the image went black.

"Pinbree," Hao murmured, and I whistled.

"It's Jo and she's fine." Relief was sharp in my chest at the knowledge that Fasé and Stasia were safe, and I'd spotted the Royal Marines in the background when Johar had panned the room.

"You know that how, Majesty?" Emmory asked.

"We worked a job at Pinbree with Jo. Delivering medical supplies, legal run into a rather nasty contamination zone. It was exciting."

Zin raised an eyebrow, clearly not getting the reference. While Gita's expression cycled from confused to curious to horrified.

"I read up on the Pinbree outbreak. That was the Reev virus."

"Regular medical corps wouldn't go down to the planet." Hao shrugged. "It was good money."

"Until you end up with your intestines leaking out your ass," she snapped.

"True. Portis was so mad at me we didn't speak for a week. Money was good, though." I ignored Emmory's Look, but my smile faded as the memory played itself out. "It was awful. The Solarians firebombed the planet a month later when a ship of refugees tried to break quarantine. Anyway, it's basic gunrunner code for 'I'm fine.' You mention a job we've all done together. If Johar was in trouble she'd have made up a job or not said anything at all."

What I didn't say out loud was that her choice of Pinbree wasn't random. It told me a lot about the situation we'd be walking into on Faria, but primarily that it was extremely dangerous and potentially deadly.

I rubbed my hands over the tops of my thighs. "So, we were unfortunately right about Adora surviving the Hiervet attack on her fleet, which means we're probably right about Thyra and Adaran and we've already had confirmation about this fucking army of theirs from Aiz. Where do we go from here? Do we have a timetable for ship repairs?"

Mia shook her head. "I'll speak with Aiz and see where we are. I know the virus problem was holding up some of it, but since we've gotten it fixed we're probably much further along."

"Go talk to him." I hated to let her go, but my plans for the evening had taken a turn that looked like it wasn't going to involve finding a quiet corner to kiss her in. "We'll regroup at dinner and start putting together a plan."

Mia nodded and left the room.

"Your Majesty." Captain Zov stepped up. "Istrevitel are still untested in battle but if we can help in any fashion, including a show of force at Faria, we are here for you."

"I have a feeling the *Tsia* may protest that, Captain. Though I would accept, and gladly, if I could."

Dirah smiled slowly. "I suspect that *Tsia* Brov may be persuaded to delay her reports until we are back."

"Well." I smiled back. "I may accept your kind offer to act as observers as we investigate whatever the crisis is that has befallen our Farian allies."

"Let me go see what I can do," Dirah replied, and headed for the door.

I surveyed Hao and my BodyGuards, the only people left in the room, and closed my eyes briefly at the flicker in the corner closest to me. "We will need to get the others. Alba and Admiral Hassan. Emmory, send out a notice that we'll be having a meeting in that conference room off Captain Zov's office at twenty-three hundred hours."

"Yes, Majesty."

"What are you thinking, ma'am?" Gita asked, and I leaned against a table, pressing my fingers to my mouth.

"I don't know," I said, dropping my hand and meeting her brown gaze. "If we do this right we could coordinate a rescue of Fasé and Stasia, our Marines, maybe a few ships with Fasé's people if we're using the Shen and Istrevitel as decoys. Go back to Pashati and regroup?"

It meant leaving Sybil, Yadira, and Delphine and millions of other Farians at the mercy of Thyra's and Adora's madness.

It meant an end to Indrana's alliance with Faria and a war we couldn't possibly win.

It also meant giving up any hope the human-born Shen had of figuring out why their souls didn't come back.

Fasé's voice whispered in my ear, a memory of a conversation on Encubier when I'd seen firsthand a prophet speaking words pulled from the stars themselves.

"You will have to make a choice, Star of Indrana. I can't tell you exactly what the choice is, only that it will not be what you think. You

cannot let this paralyze you with fear of making the wrong choice, because there is no wrong choice. People will die, that is the way of things. You hold the fate of the galaxy in the balance. Do not disrupt it."

Somehow I knew that this was the choice. Still one of many, but if we were talking about balance and the fate of the galaxy, the last thing I could do was leave Faria in the hands of Adora and her so-called gods.

"You all understand why we can't do that? Why I can't in good conscience run from this? Why I need to see it through to the end?"

"We do," Emmory said, and Hao nodded.

"I know I speak for everyone in this room, Your Majesty, when I say if you choose to march into Naraka, we will follow you."

"Shiva, let's hope we don't have to." My laugh felt brittle in my mouth and the flickering in the corner of my eye seemed to solidify for just a moment before it vanished entirely.

"All right. Iza, you and Indula are on the door. Gita, you and Kisah go get me an up-to-date report on ships. I want everything focused on a potential assault of Faria, even if we don't end up having to do it."

"I'm going to go talk with Ragini and see how fast we can get Johar the antivirus," Zin said before Emmory could open his mouth again. "That's what you were going to say, *hridayam*, yes?"

"Get out of here," Emmory replied, but he was smiling when he tipped his head toward the door.

I took a deep breath as the others left and then another, struggling to get air into my lungs past the panic that seemed to be filling them instead.

Hao joined me, a hand resting on my back. "Look at me," he said, and I lifted my head. "What?"

"Everything seems so important," I whispered. "Like I make one wrong move, one bad choice and it will all come crashing down."

"Hail." Emmory didn't say anything more when Hao raised his hand.

My brother smiled. "*Sha zhu*, hasn't it always been this way? Our choices change our lives, sometimes forever. They change the lives of those around us, those depending on us." He reached out and cupped my chin with a hand. "You have always known what choice to make; don't let all this"—he waved his free hand in the air— "distract you."

I couldn't stop the laugh even though it sounded so brittle to my ears. "Don't forget I've been seeing things. Am still seeing things." I pointed at the empty corner without looking. "You make losing my mind sound like nothing more than an inconvenience."

Emmory pulled his gun free at the same time Hao did, and I froze with my hands in the air. The sound of their guns powering up was loud in the sudden silence. Part of me was screaming to grab for my own weapons, but a more rational part kept my hands right where they were.

"You're not losing your mind, Hail," Hao replied, his voice strained.

I turned, my breath catching in my lungs when I saw the pair of Hiervet standing in the corner of the room. "You can see them?" I whispered.

Emmory and Hao closing ranks in front of me before I finished the sentence was all the answer I needed. Hao reached back and I grabbed his hand like a lifeline.

"We do not mean you harm." The Hiervet on the right was speaking in what sounded like a mashup of modern Indranan and the Old Tongue, the accent like nothing I'd ever heard before, and both Hiervet did an impressive replication of a very old greeting I only knew from a few ancient palace rituals of my youth.

They finished by pressing the tips of their limbs to their chests, then their mouths, and then to their foreheads as they bowed in unison. The final gesture was much more familiar, but I didn't echo it.

As they came up I saw the confusion pass over their faces

when Hao and Emmory did not return the gesture. "Are you not Indranan? Have we miscalculated?"

"What are they saying?" Hao whispered in Cheng. "It sounds like Indranan, but not."

"It's the Old Tongue," Emmory murmured back. "Sort of; you're picking up some of the Indranan that's come from it."

"You got a translation for that you can give me?"

"No, the Old Tongue isn't allowed to be in the database," I murmured. "Emmory can translate for you, now hush.

"We are Indranan." I let go of Hao's hand and slipped between the two men to face our visitors. "That is an ancient greeting, though, and your language is not what we are used to. Where did you learn it?"

"It has been a very long time since we looked in on your people. What would be appropriate as a greeting now?"

Emmory cleared his throat before I could step forward with my hand outstretched.

"I'll have to show you a little later. My *Ekam* objects to the idea of me touching you right now." Instead I mimicked the gesture they'd made. "I have seen you watching us, haven't I? Out of the corner of my eye?"

"Yes. You seem to have a talent for it, it is fascinating." I could have sworn that was a smile on the Hiervet's face. "We have not met many who can see past our defenses."

"Lucky me," I muttered. "Emmory, we're not going to have a bunch of armed BodyGuards burst through that door, are we?"

"No, Majesty," he murmured in reply. "I told them to stand down for the moment. But they are outside."

"Why are you here?" I asked.

The Hiervet shared a glance, and then the taller one spoke. "After the incident with our ship it seemed the safest course of action to watch until we could figure out who was in command."

"I'm sorry about that."

"We know it was not your fault." The Hiervet tipped their head to the side and studied me. "This one calls you Majesty, which is a title we recognize. Others call you Star of Indrana; it also seems formal though we don't know it. Your name is Hail? Though that one calls you—"

"Yes, we know what he calls me." I cut off the Hiervet with a smile. I heard Hao choke on his laughter as Emmory continued murmuring a translation.

"May we ask who you are?"

The unexpected question hung in the air for several breaths before I laughed. "Oh, thank Shiva, that's refreshing. Someone who doesn't know me." I cleared my throat at their confused looks. "My apologies. I am Empress Hailimi Bristol of the Indranan Empire."

"You are a long way from home, Empress Hailimi."

I smiled. "Oh, you have no idea."

"You are in charge of all this? Of the Istrevitel?"

"Am I—" I shook my head in denial even as the reality of it sank into my bones. We had just been talking about forming a fleet to deal with the Hiervet, to stop Thyra and Adora, and to liberate Faria. A fleet that would undoubtedly answer to me. "Yes, I'm in charge."

"Good. We would like to surrender with you."

"You would—I'm sorry, what?" It was as much the archaic form of the word as the implications that stunned me.

"I thought they didn't know who you were," Hao muttered.

"We have been trying to hunt criminals, Empress Hailimi, but it does not appear to be something we can do on our own any longer. We blundered into a battle once already and it cost us in equipment. We would like to not make the same mistake twice."

"We are not at war, are we?" I replied carefully. "What reason would you have to surrender to me?"

"It is not about war. It is about the safety of our people. You are in charge; it makes the most sense to surrender with you."

There was something wrong, but I couldn't put my finger on just what it was. "Look, I—do you have names?" I tapped the skin of my cheek under my left eye. "The others have similar designs under their eyes, but they took Farian names."

"The criminals?" The Hiervet shared a look and then the shorter of the pair with a trio of dots and a half a circle in bright blue on their cheek extended a limb. "You have met the criminals."

"We did. We killed one of them. He lived with the Farians and called himself Priam. He had a solid horizontal rectangle on his face bisected vertically by four dots." I don't know why I felt the need to mention that, but my comment had all the effect of dropping a silencer nuke into the middle of the room.

For a moment at least. The Hiervet broke into a conversation in what I could only assume was their language, though it sounded different from what I'd heard from Thyra and Adaran.

Then the pair bowed low.

"I am Biea and this is Tolm." The taller Hiervet had a series of gold marks under their left cheek consisting of a single line with dots on opposite sides and two Vs pointing at each other. "We thank you, Empress Hailimi, for this good news and for your actions. It makes even more sense to surrender with you."

"Why do you want to surr—oh, wait." Realization dawned on me. My brain had been recognizing a word as *surrender* because the Hiervet were lacking the proper ending that would turn it into something more like—working together.

"Sorry." I folded my hands together and shook them in apology. "Two things. I didn't kill Priam." I pointed over my shoulder at Emmory. "He did it. And I don't think you truly mean your entire race wants to surrender to me."

The Hiervet tilted their heads to the side in obvious confusion. "He follows your orders?"

"I suppose so," I admitted, trying not to laugh.

"I will kick you, Majesty," Emmory subvocalized over our private com, and the warning only made me want to laugh all the more.

"Emmory killed Priam because the Farian Hiervet was trying to kill me. Emmory is my BodyGuard."

"Ah. We do not understand your term for the criminals, but you still have our thanks. That means there are only two more to deal with." The Hiervet paused. "You used a word much like the one we used, but not?"

"*Surrender?* It means you submit to my authority. That I have won a victory over you."

"This is not the word we want."

I smiled. "I figured. What you want to say is you would like for us to work together, and I would very much like that. May I bring a few others into this conversation and maybe pass along an updated version of Indranan to you?"

I was reasonably sure Hao was going to tell people the story about the time an entire fleet surrendered to me until the day he died.

36

realized shortly after the appearance of Biea and Tolm that we'd been calling the Hiervet by the Svatir's name for them this whole time. A name that was not at all appropriate, and so a last-minute scramble had happened to figure out what the Selan actually called themselves.

Thankfully, they didn't take offense to the question.

"Is the lack of Istrevitel because of us?" Biea asked, looking around the small room we'd gathered in. Captain Zov was there, as were Aiz and Mia. Admiral Hassan stood against the far wall talking with Gita.

Dirah dipped her head. "I thought it for the best. We have only just learned the truth of what happened between you and our Svatir brethren; it is raw for some and I did not want another incident."

"Another?"

The smile on Dirah's face was heavy with pain. "I was the one who shot at your people when you tried to contact us the first time. Whatever consequence there is for the destruction of your ship, I will face it. The empress ordered us not to fire and I ignored her."

I sucked in a breath. We hadn't discussed how to handle this, and I was regretting that now. Dirah's intentions were noble, but I needed her alive and functioning as the head of the Istrevitel for the coming fight.

I also knew I might need the Selan to help me fight this army of Thyra's.

"Ah." Biea tilted their head to the side. "You are the one responsible?" They gestured at me. "This is the one who you mentioned."

"Yes, but—"

Biea held up a limb. "The ship was empty of crew, Your Majesty, Captain." They nodded to each of us in turn. "It was an older vessel we piloted remotely, though the loss of the parts we could have scavenged from it does hurt us some. We can discuss reparations at a time more suited to such things."

"Of course," I replied, because Captain Zov was just staring with her mouth open at the Selan. "Thank you."

"Your Majesty, if Tolm and I could confer a moment before we start the proceedings?"

"Of course." I hooked a hand under Dirah's elbow and led her away. "Take a breath, Captain."

"I didn't kill anyone?"

"Apparently not. You got lucky. It happens occasionally." I hoped my smile softened the words. "Remember how that felt, Captain, and don't ever be so hasty with people's lives again. The lives of your enemies matter; the lives of your people matter more, understood?"

"Yes, ma'am." She nodded to me and then to Emmory, and I let her cross to the opposite side of the room with her arms wrapped around her waist.

"I like her," I said, blowing out a breath of my own. "We dodged a Shiva-damned rail shot there, Emmory."

He hummed in agreement. "The timing on this worked out well," he replied. "A week earlier and she'd be trying to kill them both."

"Things are going smoothly," I said to Gita and Inana as we joined them.

"Makes you nervous, doesn't it?" Admiral Hassan said.

I slid her a sideways look. "Doesn't matter how smooth any of this is, we're looking at a pitched battle both in the space above Faria and on the ground. Unknown odds. We've got three forces who've never worked together to take on a unified force of unknown

ability. I don't know about you, but those odds make me nervous."
I pointed a finger at the Selan as I leaned against the wall between
the two women. "Besides, whatever Thyra and the others told us,
not all the Selan are fighters."

"You noticed that, too, huh?" Gita asked.

I shifted, my shoulder touching hers; the warmth and solidity
was comforting and eased some of the tension in my neck.

"Thyra said they were created to be soldiers, not just any soldiers
either but the elite. The Svatir told us they had to fight for their lives
against the Selan. For a race that was well versed in the art of war to
lose to such a force? It may have not ended the way we thought, but
that part wasn't a lie.

"Aiz trained me for a fight against an opponent who was far
above my level." I pursed my lips and shook my head. "Priam was
fucking good. I wasn't remotely ready for him. Thyra and Adaran
will be the same, I suspect. Those Selan? Biea might give me a fight,
but I would probably win, and Tolm's not a fighter at all."

"Is it an act?" Gita asked, rubbing at her cheek.

"No." I shook my head. "I have been watching them and if it's an
act, they've been keeping it up without it slipping in the slightest."

"Maybe they've been taught how to hide it," Gita suggested,
though her frown indicated she didn't really believe it.

"Something always shows," Inana replied.

"Maybe they are," I said. "But what would be the point? No one
wants to hear it but if they wanted any of us dead, that would have
happened long before I spotted that first flicker." I smiled at Gita's
grumble. "You know I'm right. They're only here for Thyra and
Adaran, and thank Shiva for it. If even half of what we heard about
them is correct, that was a fight that I didn't want."

"The prophecy, all those visions?"

"Fasé told me that all the visions are filtered through our percep-
tion, our fears," I replied. "What if everything from the start of it
was—"

"Filtered through Thyra and the others' fear that the Hiervet, excuse me, the Selan were coming for them?" Inana finished. "Oddly enough, that makes perfect sense."

Gita pushed away from the wall as Mia turned and waved a hand at us, and Inana and I followed, crossing the room. Emmory stayed just behind me like a shadow.

"Are you all right?" I asked Dirah. The Istrevitel captain was still slightly glassy-eyed with shock, and I reached a hand out to steady her.

"This is a lot to take in, Your Majesty." She smiled sheepishly. "None of you seem the least bit fazed by it."

"To be fair, this has happened to us a lot in the last year." I smiled and squeezed her shoulder, then let her go. "And you are coming off a pretty big worldview shift. You're entitled to feel a little off-balance, Captain." I looked at the Selan, who were watching us closely. "I think some formal introductions are in order; we have chairs but I wasn't sure if they would be comfortable for you."

"We can sit." The taller Selan nodded.

There was a moment of silence, filled only with the shuffling of people and chairs as we took our places around the oval-shaped table in the corner of the room.

"I suspect," I said, resting my forearms on the tabletop, "that given the circumstances Standard is the best language to proceed in; is everyone agreed?"

Heads nodded around the table. The Selan had been provided with an updated download of a number of languages courtesy of my *Ekam* and they, in turn, had given us a download of Selan.

"Your Majesty." Biea began the formal introduction. "I am Biea of the Selan; it is my heart's joy to greet you."

"Your Majesty, I am Tolm of the Selan, it is my heart's joy to greet you."

I touched my folded hands to my heart, lips, and forehead. "I greet you in the name of the Empire of Indrana."

The introductions went around the table. The pair of Selan shared a look and then Biea rested their limbs on the tabletop.

"Empress Hailimi has told me that you each have different versions of the story of our people, and she requested that we tell you the truth." An expression I recognized as amusement crossed their face. "Or our version of the events, as it were."

That was met with chuckles from the table and I relaxed a fraction, leaning back in my chair as Biea launched into the story of the Selan.

"We were created as soldiers. Your languages are agreed that *clones* is the correct translation. We were developed by the Infrastructure as their latest model—a fully integrated force complete with all the tools one would need for intergalactic warfare."

"Not going to lie, the idea that there's a lot more out there willing to start a fight with us doesn't give me the warm fuzzies," Inana said.

"You are in a unique position here, Admiral. This area around your galaxy is mostly vacant and those who do live here don't wish to be disturbed." Biea nodded. "I understand the concern and you are not wrong. The universe outside your galaxy is dangerous, especially for those as young as you."

"Let's focus on the issue at hand," I said.

"We were created for war," Biea repeated. "And we were very good at it. However, our creators had not just made us warriors. As I said, we were a fully integrated force, with no need for outside support. There were technicians and mechanics, and intelligence forces, and those who created things of their own. We had our own cloning facilities so we could make more of us as the situation required. We were taught how to fix and grow ourselves. We were designed to be self-sufficient, with the one exception of the proprietary genetic material used for our clones." They lifted a bony shoulder and looked at their companion. "I do not think our creators understood the ramifications of allowing us that kind of self-determination."

"Some of us liked the violence." Tolm picked up the narrative when Biea fell silent. "They revolted against their owners and laid waste to friend and enemy alike. A decision was made by the Infrastructure to destroy their product—even those of us who had not joined in the rebellion."

"They were going to commit genocide?" Captain Zov's question was filled with a surprising amount of outrage, and I exchanged a quick look with Mia.

"In their minds we were not a race, but property to be disposed of, Captain," Tolm replied. "Property that had some kind of fatal flaw. It was a better investment to dispose of us all and go back to the drawing board to fix the mistake."

"Obviously that's not the end of the story," Aiz said. "What happened?"

"A smaller force of us, a little under half a million, correct?" They looked to Biea for confirmation, and the taller Selan nodded. "Were sold to a mining consortium on the outer rim. They were involved in a property dispute over several planets and an asteroid belt, and we had been working for them for several generations. When the recall notice came, the miners helped us disable our return protocols and the Infrastructure's destruction program and told us to run."

Tolm lapsed into silence and I tapped my fingers against my lip as I watched them. However long ago this had been, it was clear the Selan still had deep feelings about the people who'd helped them escape their deaths.

"We ran," Biea said, laying the end of their limb over Tolm's. "We did not know where we would go or how we would survive. We only knew we didn't want to die."

"So you fled," I said. "By my understanding this all happened very long ago, Biea. How have you survived for all this time?"

"Oh." Biea's large eyelids snapped closed and then open again in surprise. "We are not. We were not the ones who ran, Your Majesty."

"We are their descendants," Tolm said.

37

"You know, every time I say to myself that things can't get stranger around here, someone has to prove me wrong."

I choked back my laugh at Hao's muttered comment. We were taking a short break while Dirah called for food and the Selan composed themselves from their emotional recounting of their escape.

"I have a feeling we're in for a few more before this is over, *gege*, so I wouldn't say anything else just yet."

"My life was really quiet before I met you."

"Liar. Gy told me you got shot twice as much before I came on board."

Hao smirked at the memory. "Maybe." His smile faded. "Do you believe them?"

I glanced across the room where Biea and Tolm stood with their heads pressed together. "I don't know. My gut isn't screaming at me, if that's what you're really asking. But we can't exactly verify this story, can we?"

"Not without going outside the galaxy." Hao shrugged. "Which, I'd be lying if I said I wasn't sort of intrigued by the idea of it, but if it's so bad out there that a whole race of genetically engineered super soldiers went *Fuck this, we're out*, how long do you think we'd last?"

I only just managed to muffle my laugh into something that wouldn't draw attention to us and bumped into Hao's shoulder with my own. "It would be kind of fun, though, wouldn't it?"

He smiled. "It would. Except I might be getting too old for that kind of fun."

"I hope not." I leaned into him, tangling my fingers with his and squeezing for just a moment before I pulled away.

"Your Majesty, do you mind if we stand for a while?" Biea asked as they approached. "Your chairs are more uncomfortable than I imagined." They glanced past me to where several Shen were bringing food into the room. "It may also be less awkward for you to eat without Tolm and me sitting and watching?"

"You don't eat?"

"We were not designed to ingest food the way you all do." They dipped their head. "It was one of the things our ancestors decided to keep due to its efficiency."

"I confess I can't imagine a life without eating."

Biea answered with a laugh. "I cannot imagine the tediousness of having to do it, Your Majesty, so I suppose we are even."

"Fair enough. Would you like to continue?" I leaned against the other side of the table, taking the bowl Emmory handed me with a smile of thanks. The others took their clues from me and found spots around the room to listen.

"The question I am sure you are all asking is who Thyra and her companions are," Biea said, tapping their limbs together as they looked around the room. "I would love to lay that blame on the backs of my fellow Selan who lost themselves to violence, but to the best of our knowledge they were all killed. Thyra and the others were part of our group. They fled with us. But, as we discovered later, they did sympathize with the others.

"The one you call Thyra was a battlefield doctor. She was obsessed with finding a way for the Selan not only to survive, but to continue the work our creators had started, to make a perfect warrior. One that would live forever. We did not realize it at the time but she had been in contact with the leaders of the rebellion to try to find a way to re-create the genetic material necessary to make the clones."

"Hold up a second," Hao said, raising his hand. "Are you saying Thyra *is* one of the original Selan?"

"Yes, she was an original clone. All the criminals are," Tolm replied. "Our ancestors were aware of the Svatir but were trying to avoid them. They were dangerous. You—sorry, Captain, I mean your ancestors—were not to be messed with."

"It's all right," Dirah replied. "I know that part of our history well enough."

"Thyra had been pressing our ancestors for an attack on the Svatir. She was insistent there was something about them that was necessary to our survival and that we could subjugate them easily with our technical advantage. Our leadership refused, so Thyra and her followers left." Tolm rubbed their limbs together in that same embarrassed gesture I'd seen from Thyra back on Faria. "Our ancestors did not realize at the time they would go to the Svatir, and that they would attempt to set themselves up as these gods." They blinked. "I confess I don't quite understand the concept, though I have read much on it."

"The concept of gods?" I smiled. "Don't worry about it. You could spend your whole life on that one and still not understand it."

"A scouting mission told our leaders of Thyra's crimes and the ensuing war. They came to help, but it was almost too late and the Svatir were not able to realize we were not the enemy. So we retreated."

"I saw far more than ten Selan in the recordings of the war, Biea."

"Yes. She had many followers. Most were killed in the war. We hunted down the scattered ones; they could not survive without her support. Thyra and her squad—the ten you speak of—were all that were left. We have been hunting them all these years."

I shared a look with Captain Zov. The story aligned too closely with what we'd learned from Timur to not be the truth, and I thought of the memory from the Istrevitel I'd seen with the captured Selan.

"We apologize for our failure to capture the last of these criminals," Biea said. "It appears that after their attempt to subjugate the Svatir they fled and landed on Faria. We were not able to follow because of the conflict with the Svatir, and by the time we extricated ourselves and started looking again they had managed to hide themselves from our eyes. We would not have even known they were there if not for you."

"That architecture on Faria makes sense now," I murmured. "Biea, forgive me, but it has been thousands of our years, possibly more, since the Svatir war. Where have you been?"

"Hiding," they replied. "Trying to survive. Thyra was our best scientist and doctor. She stole so much from us when she fled. Documents, research, a chunk of the genetic material we had saved. Between that and the war with the Svatir, we nearly did not survive."

"We have reason to believe that Thyra has created an army of Farians. We're not entirely sure what that means or what they could be capable of, but we were hoping you could give us an idea?"

"An army?" Biea shared a worried look with Tolm. "Your Majesty, do you have any confirmation?"

"We saw soldiers," Aiz replied. "Not for a long enough period to give you any detail, only that they didn't move like Farians. They were wrong."

Before I could say that we did have detailed descriptions from Johar, Tolm vanished.

"My apologies, Your Majesty," Biea said when several people jerked in surprise. "Tolm has gone to tell the others. This is beyond worrisome. We must move. Thyra cannot be allowed to do this. They are dedicated to this path of destruction, and if they have an army to command we must destroy them. We will have to destroy the whole planet."

Images of the Farian ships firing on planets filled my head and I was struck with the dreadful certainty that those weapons were Selan tech. Biea was serious about wiping out Faria just to stop Thyra.

"What? Wait, no," I said, putting my hands up. "There are innocent people on Faria. My *people* are on the planet."

"Your Majesty, it is the only way to be sure that they are stopped. That army cannot be allowed to escape."

"The fuck it is!" I slammed both hands onto the table, and this time Biea jumped. "You tell your people right now if they so much as look in the direction of that planet without my approval I will burn what's left of your fleet to the ground."

Biea blinked at me in stunned surprise. "It is my understanding that you have a single ship, Your Majesty."

"No, she doesn't." Aiz and Dirah spoke at the same time, and the Selan's expressions shifted as they realized they were surrounded by impassive faces.

"I don't understand. We have no quarrel with any of you. Our mission is to bring these criminals to justice. We thought you were in agreement."

"I agree with that part," I replied. "Just not your methods."

"Thyra is dangerous. This army she's created will be even more so. This is the safest way."

"You are talking about genocide," I said, all too aware of how the others in the room had shifted, preparing for a fight. "I would think that you of all beings would appreciate how utterly wrong your solution is."

Dark Mother, please let my words get through. I don't want to have to fight them.

Biea stared at me, their face clean of expression. "I will go speak with the others."

"Take me with you." I grabbed for their limb, heard Emmory's shouted protest and then nothing.

"Your Majesty, that was incredibly dangerous."

I blinked up at Biea until my vision resolved. "I do that occasionally."

"We should go back, your people—"

"They're going to yell regardless." I got to my feet; the floor was a strange textured gray substance that was slightly spongy when I moved. "This is important. I need to speak to your leaders directly. Though, can I send a message?"

Biea reached out their other limb and touched my head. "That should allow for your coms to work."

I knew I should message Emmory, but I also knew the reaction I would get, so I went for what I thought was a safer option. "Hao, are you there?"

"Hail, where the fuck are you?"

Okay, maybe not safer. I winced at the volume of his response. "I'm assuming a Selan ship. Tell Emmory I'm fine. I'll be right back. My coms will be off after this."

"Coward."

"I love you, too." I disconnected the com. I knew Emmory would be on it the moment Hao passed the message on.

"He doesn't speak to you the way the others do. Why is that?"

I looked up at Biea with a smile. "It's a very long story and I'm not sure it would make any sense."

"We do understand what love is," they replied, and I imagined that if the Selan had a human face I'd see a raised eyebrow.

"I didn't mean to imply otherwise." A door opened in the wall and the silence of the room was suddenly filled with noise. "Just that Hao and I are complicated." I rubbed a hand over my upper chest. "He is my brother, not of my blood but of my heart."

"I understand better than you may think. Tolm and I are much the same. Stay close, Your Majesty." Biea put a limb around my shoulders as we headed down the corridor. Selan stopped to stare at us as we passed, but the noise that came from Biea encouraged them to move on.

The walls were the same spongy gray as the floor and they were curved into a wide circle. I reached a hand out to touch the surface, surprised by how warm it was.

"We grow the materials for our newer ships, Your Majesty." Biea answered the question before I could ask it. "It's the most efficient way to do repairs."

"It's fascinating, is it alive?"

"No, Your Majesty. It's—"

A high-pitched trilling cut through the air and Biea grabbed for me as a mass of Selan barely taller than my shoulder came down the corridor at a run. The first one to catch sight of me skidded to a halt, resulting in several others crashing into a pile behind them.

Questions, helpfully translated by my *smati*, peppered the air.

"What is that?"

"It's a human."

"Is not."

"It's got plants on its head. Humans don't have plants on their heads."

"Don't touch it, Zel!"

I looked down just in time to see one of the smallest yanking their limb back before it touched my hand. They were children, I realized. Selan children.

"Hello, I'm Hail. I am a human and my hair isn't plants, it's just green," I said in Selan with a smile.

The Selan child's mouth opened in awe and the others laughed.

"You sound funny!"

A larger Selan ran up. "Children! What are you doing?" They gaped at me for a moment before turning those dark eyes to Biea and tapping their limbs to their chest. "Commander-General, I am so sorry."

"It's no worry, Pani. You have quite the handful to deal with. They mean no harm. Though we are in a hurry."

"Of course, Commander-General. Go along, children."

I watched as the Selan herded the group away, winking as the one named Zel threw a last glance over their shoulder at me.

You'll have to kill them if you can't convince the Selan not to attack Faria, Hail.

My amusement left me like the rush of air escaping from a wounded ship.

We made it to our destination without any further interruptions and Biea ushered me into a round room. I spotted Tolm standing with three others.

"This is the Selan leadership," Biea said. "There are four of us, two each from the divisions of defense and livelihood. The fifth is a civilian who is chosen at random to provide perspective."

"Biea, what is this?" The Selan speaking had a gold pattern on their face similar to theirs.

"Her Majesty Empress Hailimi Bristol requested that I bring her to speak with you all. There are concerns about the fate of the Farians."

"They should have thought about that before they dealt with criminals," the Selan replied.

"They didn't know," I replied to the Selan who'd just spoken. "How could the Farians have possibly known what Thyra and the others had done? You're talking about condemning an entire race because of your people's actions."

"Your Majesty," Tolm said. "There is no other solution."

"Cowshit. I'm the solution."

Confused looks spread over their faces. "You are a single human," the tallest of the Selan said with a frown. They had a spiral of neon orange under their eye. "You are no match for Thyra alone, never mind if she has an army of her creations."

I smiled slowly, pleased as the Selan responded with the same nervous shift any rational living being did when presented with a predator. "You have no idea who I am. I am the Star of Indrana. Everything in my life has conspired to put me here so that I can stop this. I will stop Thyra, but I must go to Faria to do it and I need time."

The five Selan started talking too rapidly for my *smati* to keep up, and I watched the discussion rage for several minutes before they finally subsided. Biea seemed satisfied, though annoyed as they turned to me.

"Your Majesty, we can give you no more than a hundred of your standard hours to bring the criminals to us for justice. After that we will be forced to take action to remove them from Faria no matter the cost."

"You know what will happen if you do that," I replied. "I am allied with the Farians. I cannot stand by and let you attack them."

Biea studied me for a moment and sighed. "I have no wish to fight you. In fact, I will offer to join you in this hunt of yours, if you will have me, but this is the decision we have made. You have until the clock runs out, Your Majesty. I hope you are as good as you believe."

38

How are you so calm?"

I turned my attention away from what could be called the organized chaos of the Istrevitel's headquarters and smiled at Captain Zov. "Experience?"

"Temperament," Hao said. "You can learn it, Captain, but Hail's been like that her whole life, don't let her tell you otherwise."

I shrugged and smiled. "I have something of a reputation."

"It's earned." Dirah smiled and held out her hand. "I suppose I will not see you again until this is done, Your Majesty. Thank you, for everything."

"Take care of yourself, Captain." I reached out and clasped her forearm in the traditional Istrevitel greeting.

Hao did the same and then Gita; my *Dve* leaned in and whispered something to the Istrevitel before she released her. The three of us watched as she wove her way through the mass of people.

"I like her, I hope she doesn't die," Hao said.

"If we're lucky they won't see any action at all."

"When are we ever lucky, *sha zhu*?"

"Fair enough." I sighed and returned my gaze to the preparations. "You still mad at me?"

"Yes," he said, but he smiled when he said it and bumped his shoulder into mine. "Stop being so fucking reckless."

"It was kind of necessary," I murmured. "I wasn't about to let them make that decision without listening to me. I know I couldn't convince them, but I at least bought us some time."

In the almost two days since the Selan had revealed themselves to us, we'd managed to put together a battle plan that relied a little too heavily on three separate forces who'd never fought together before.

Beggars, however, could not be choosers. So I'd worked with Admiral Amo and Inana, Captain Zov, and Biea to coordinate the forces of the Shen, the Istrevitel, and the Selan into a plan that would hopefully allow them to all play to their strengths while not stumbling over each other too much.

The bulk of the plans belonged to those involved as I would be otherwise occupied—taking a Selan ship down to Faria to link up with Johar and Fasé.

After that, I wasn't entirely sure what we were going to do, but the clock ticking steadily away in the corner of my vision reminded me that if I failed, a lot of people were going to die.

"You don't have a plan on how to take on Thyra, do you?"

I shot Hao a look and he held his hands up in surrender with a laugh.

"I'm just asking."

"I'm working on it. I don't have a lot of information to go on, you know." We'd finally gotten the antivirus to Johar, but the consensus was that it was safer to wait until we were on the ground to discuss both the situation on Faria and what we planned to do once we got there.

I had the barest minimal report from Jo about the army we were facing, and I'd used it to build a preliminary plan for the ground forces.

None of it changed the fact that I was going to have to face Thyra, and the vision of her impaling me on her limb was as constant as the timer rapidly clicking down in my vision.

"There's Emmory," Hao said, knocking me out of my thoughts. "You can carry your own bag, Your Majesty."

I tripped him, hooking his foot with mine as he tried to walk away. Hao only just regained his balance and didn't look at either Gita or me as he continued across the bay.

"My younger sister was as bad as you growing up, Majesty," she said, laughing.

"It keeps him humble."

"True. Shiva knows he needs it." Her humor faded. "I sent your message to Princess Alice as requested."

"I figured. Even though I told her we'd be out of coms range, I got four messages before I turned off my notifications."

"All the BodyGuards got three, and Emmory and I have gotten two from General Suvish requesting that we check in."

"Whatever they say, they can't fire you."

"I am not concerned about that." Her mouth curved. "Though they could technically bring us all up on charges."

"I'll just refuse to come home until they're dropped." I grabbed my bag and slung it over my shoulder, shifting out of the way before she could take it from me.

Admiral Hassan met us halfway across the bustling room. "Majesty."

"Inana." I set my bag down.

"I am supposed to, and I quote, 'bash her over the head and bring her home if her damn BodyGuards won't. She can't fire me, I'm the Heir.'" Inana smiled. "I told Her Highness that I was unsure of your whereabouts, so I'd appreciate it if you'd get on that alien ship and get out of here so I'm not a complete liar."

"We're headed out now," I replied, and stuck my hand out, clasping her by the arm and pulling her into a hug as the emotion rose up in my throat. I'd respected this woman when we'd met each other again, but now it was too much like sending my own family into battle. "Stay safe. Please."

"You, too, Majesty."

We separated. I reached for my bag, came up empty, and glared at Gita's unrepentant grin.

"Bad enough we're letting you march into a war zone, Majesty, at least let me carry your bag." Her grin softened. "I get it, Hail, and I highly doubt you'll ever become the kind of person who assumes someone else should carry anything for you."

"Well, not if I keep Hao around, that's for sure."

Gita's laughter carried with us to the waiting Selan ship.

Biea had joined us on what I understood was a midsized ship much the same as our Sarama-class destroyers. Tolm had not, but another Selan by the name of Weil seemed to be in charge of the ship.

They had a trio of horizontal lines with a single dot under their left eye in the same gold as Biea's. The other Selan on the bridge also had marks in varying metallic shades.

"Biea," I said, trying to keep my voice low. The bridge had the same familiar background conversation of any that I'd been on, though this was all in Selan. "May I ask a question?"

"Of course, Your Majesty."

"What is the significance of the marks on your faces?" I tapped my cheek. "Thyra has marks but they are all black."

Biea was silent for a moment. Then they tapped their limbs together twice. "The best words in your language seems to be a product code. Though that would be in reference to what Thyra and the others had. And theirs were only black, unchanging. It was an indicator of our purpose and a tracking system for the Infrastructure."

"You know, the more I hear about this group the more I dislike them."

The chitter that echoed from Biea's mouth drew looks from some of the nearby Selan. "I do like you, Your Majesty. As you may suspect, the meaning of our *melak*—" They paused and tapped at the symbol on their cheek with an expression I assumed was a thoughtful frown. "There is not a good word in Indranan for this."

"I would say tattoo, though that probably leaves out some of the significance?"

"Yes," they replied with a nod. "And it does but it works. Now the tattoos signify our place within the whole."

"You can change them?"

"Of course." Biea blinked their wide eyes. "Our people are free to change their jobs, and those who serve in defense of the whole are promoted as their skills progress. You do the same, yes?"

"Yes, in some cases. Our indicators are usually on the uniform." I smiled. "And in my case, I didn't really earn my position."

"That is not what I have heard."

Emmory choked back a laugh behind me and I resisted the urge to elbow him in the stomach. "Well, don't believe everything you hear about me, Biea."

"Of course, Your Majesty." I honestly couldn't tell if they were joking or not; the inflections and tone of the Selan didn't change much and I was sure the translations were imperfect. "Did you have other questions?"

"You don't live on a planet?"

"Correct." Biea dipped their head.

"Why? There have to be habitable planets in this sector or elsewhere."

"It did not feel right while the criminals were still free, Your Majesty, and this has been our life. I suppose we may think of it after this is all over, but it would still be somewhat dangerous. Our creators, or their descendants, may still be looking for us."

"They couldn't possibly think to still try to kill you after all this time?"

"I honestly don't know."

I frowned, the beginning of an idea springing to life in my mind. One I hoped I would be able to follow rather than going to war with the Selan over the fate of Faria. "Biea, I'd like to speak with you about this again. Hopefully after this is over we will still be friends."

"Of course, Your Majesty. Tolm and the rest of the leadership would need to be involved. I am just a defender."

"Just a defender?" I snorted. "That's a bit like Emmory saying he's just a BodyGuard. Technically correct, but the reality is a bit different, yes? I am new to the empress game, Biea, but not how things work. You are part of the Selan's leadership; even if I hadn't seen that, I know your people wouldn't have sent just anyone to meet with us."

"Fair enough, Your Majesty, and you are correct." Biea dipped their head. "I am in command of our defenders."

"That's what I thought." I smiled. "Well, shall we get this show on the road?"

"We are jumping straight to the planet, Your Majesty."

This time I did elbow Emmory when he laughed. "It's an idiom. I'll explain them to you on the way."

"Nice ship." Johar pulled me into a quick hug, letting go and stepping out of the way so that I could wrap my arms around Fasé and Stasia.

"I was so worried for both of you," I whispered, blinking away the tears.

"We are fine, Your Majesty," Stasia replied, her arms tight around my waist. "Sergeant Patil took very good care of us."

I pressed my cheek to the top of her head. My Royal Marines were standing in parade rest behind her. "You have my gratitude, Sergeant."

"We were doing our jobs, Your Majesty." Patil was barely taller than my maid, but her voice was firm and all seven of her Marines came to attention at her words.

"Emmory has instructions and briefing files for you." I looked around. The Farians were watching the small group of Selan who'd disembarked with open distrust. "We should probably all get somewhere safer for the rest of this?"

"This way," Johar said, jerking her head to the side. Sergeant Patil barked an order and the Marines separated, moving out ahead of us.

I let Stasia go but kept my arm around Fasé. She hadn't said a word and her fingers were digging into my hip as though she were afraid I'd vanish if she let go. "You okay?" I murmured.

"I saw you go back to Pashati." Her voice was thick with tears, but her gold eyes were dry. "You left us here and we tried to fight but they were too strong. This army is—"

"It didn't happen. I'm here, and you did a good job keeping everyone alive, Fasé." I tightened my arm around her. "I wouldn't have ever left you." My heart twisted at how close I'd come, though, how I'd nearly let Alice convince me to go home and let someone else do my job for me.

It would have been too little, too late, when help arrived.

"I brought some friends," I said. "Sort of, anyway. We'll do a round of introductions and catch everyone up on what's happened."

"How do we know we can trust them?" Fasé eyed Biea, who was walking alongside Hao and Gita.

"At the moment they're going to blow up the planet if I can't find a way to stop Thyra in sixty-two hours," I admitted, waving a hand at Fasé's startled look. "They already know I won't let that happen, Fasé. But I don't want to have to fight them in the space above the planet and Thyra's army on the ground. At the moment we've got time, and I figure that's as good as on our side as we're going to get." I smiled and hugged her to my side once more as we headed down a flight of stairs toward a long tunnel, pushing aside my sudden knotted anxiety about going underground. "Biea has offered whatever help they can to take Thyra out, and I'm not going to turn anyone down at this point."

"We haven't heard from Sybil or the new leadership since Adora's first attack," Fasé said. "I would like to hope they are alive, but I don't know." She sighed and headed into the building.

I saw Biea hesitate at the door and turned to look at the Selan. "Are you all right?"

Biea tipped their head, shaking it slowly. "These buildings are unpleasant."

"Tell me about it," I said. "Are they hurting you?"

"No," they replied. "But they are too sharp and they will restrict our movement. It causes interference here." They shook their head as they tapped on their chest with a single limb. "We will be limited in our abilities while we are here."

"Interesting that the others didn't have that problem," Hao murmured.

"Funny what several thousand years of living with it will do for you. We knew they'd designed the architecture to hide themselves; now it appears it also will impact the Selan in other ways." I looked back at Biea. "Do you think Thyra will be able to tell that you are here?"

"I do not know. The ship is well concealed, but we were not expecting this. We will move forward and see how we can combat this. I am sending data to our people as we speak."

"Good." I nodded and gestured to the door. "After you." I waited for Biea and their people to go through, and fell into step with Emmory. "Put Iza and Indula on the door; as soon as you have the Marines briefed I want them back outside with a radius far enough out to give us some warning if we have incoming."

"Yes, ma'am."

"Well, let's go plan a party." I walked through the doorway.

39

I rubbed both hands over my eyes as the map lines of the Pedalion facility blurred and muttered a curse. "There is no good way in here."

"There is, Hail," Aiz said. "You've just got to stop thinking like a human."

I glared over my shoulder at him. He was sprawled in a chair, chin resting in his hand. We'd been going rounds about this since Aiz had first suggested it three hours ago. I didn't care that the Farians and Shen could come back from death. The very idea of using them as shields was abhorrent.

"I am not going in through the front door, Aiz. I'm not sacrificing Farian and Shen lives when there has to be another way in."

"We'll come back."

"What if you don't? What if Thyra has done something to these Farians that will allow them to kill you permanently?"

"She's right, we can't risk it," Mia said from the back of the room. "Stop needling her, Aiz, you know she's not going to agree to it. We're better off if they don't know we're coming anyway."

"It would be less of a fight," Aiz conceded with a sigh.

"Haven't I been saying that for the last hour?" I muttered.

"There is a way in," Hao said, rubbing at the back of his neck. "You're not going to like it, though."

"You're probably right; hit me anyway."

Hao crossed to the schematic on the display and tapped a finger against an outside wall. "There's no such thing as a zero-access building, it's just a question of where and when. Air goes in somewhere, comes out somewhere. Same with water. Shit." He grinned when I made a face at him. "Wherever the kitchens are is probably our best bet. We could—"

"Kitchen?" I held up my hand. "Wait. I have a better idea than what you're about to suggest," I said, and pointed at Aiz. "Front door. Or the side door, rather."

"*Sha zhu*, you just said—"

"Let me think." I waved a hand at Hao, trying to chase the idea that hovered just out of reach in my head. "Kitchen. I need to speak with Vada."

Everyone stared at me, but Emmory thankfully seemed to realize where I was going. "You want to speak with the restaurant owner who fed you?"

"Yes. Her granddaughter Prosa worked for Delphine. Vada can put us in contact with Prosa, hopefully, who in turn can tell us what's going on inside the Pedalion buildings and maybe even get us inside."

"There's a lot of hope and maybe in that plan."

I smiled at Aiz. "I'd think you'd be used to it by now."

The streets of Sicenae were sparsely populated even though by the clock on my *smati* it was still early in the evening and Farians should have been out in droves.

"People are afraid," Fasé murmured.

She, Hao, Emmory, and Gita were all using Hao's masking programs. Aiz, Mia, and I were using the Shen ability to change our faces, though of the three of us I was the only one with a backup program on my *smati*.

And Biea was with us, but all I could see was that flickering in the corner of my eye to indicate their presence.

My *Ekam* was slightly ahead of the group with Fasé, and I was following him. Aiz and Mia trailed behind us with Hao and Gita bringing up the rear. To the casual observer we looked like separate groups.

At least that was what I hoped.

"Emmory knows where he's going?" Aiz said over the coms.

"Yes, he put the location into his map. It's just around the corner."

Shouting filled the air and a Farian came sprinting around the corner. She avoided Emmory but crashed right into me, sending us both sprawling to the ground.

"I'm sorry! I—Star of Indrana?"

"Hail, your mask." Mia choked out the words and I activated the program on my *smati* as a group of guards rounded the corner on us.

Three of them grabbed the Farian, dragging her to her feet, but her wide silver eyes remained locked on me and for a terrifying moment I wasn't sure what she was going to do.

She straightened in the guards' grip, back straight and chin jutting up. "Death to the false gods. Long live the *Mardis* and the Star of Indrana." Her voice was loud, ringing in the sudden silence of the street.

One of the guards hit her and blood sprayed across the sidewalk. The Farian went limp and I felt my hands tighten into fists.

"If you intervene they will take you also."

I realized there was a guard next to me with his hand outstretched. He seemed young, and there was a kindness in his golden eyes. He wiggled his hand and I took it, letting him help me to my feet. He offered up a sad smile as he let my hand go and followed the others who were dragging the Farian away.

"Let's go." Emmory grabbed me by the arm and hustled me down the sidewalk. We rushed around the corner and spotted Vada standing at the door of her café, talking to another Farian woman in low tones. They froze when they saw us but relaxed just as quickly.

Presumably because we weren't wearing guard uniforms.

Emmory gave Vada a curt nod as he ushered me through the doorway.

"Sit," he ordered, going to a knee. There was a tear in my sleeve and blood on my hands. Only when Emmory took them did I feel the sting of the scrapes I'd gotten when the Farian had crashed into me.

"I couldn't—Emmory, we have to help her."

"We're in the middle of a hostile city, Majesty," he murmured. "There's nothing we can do."

"Is she hurt?" Vada asked. "Let me get a towel."

"Hao, door," Aiz said, unslinging the pack on his back and pulling the guns free. Hao caught them, handing one over to Gita.

"I'm going to check the back. Hopefully, there's another way out of here if we need it," he said.

"It was those awful guards, wasn't it? They've been—" Vada broke off, staring at us with a towel in her hands. "Are you rebellion troops?"

I dropped my masking program and Vada gasped. "Star of Indrana."

"Where is Prosa?" I started to get up, but Emmory stopped me, his hands still around my wrists.

"Emmory, let me." Mia reached out and laid her hands over mine. The stinging abated and I closed my eyes, still fighting the sick feeling in my gut.

Vada crossed to us, holding out the damp towel. Mia took it with a smile, cleaning my hands and then her own.

"You are Shen?"

"Yes. I am Mia."

Vada swallowed. "You are Mia Cevalla. I have seen your face. On the news they say you attacked the Pedalion, replaced them. Then the Pedalion guards started grabbing people in the street." She folded her hands together and shook her head. "It is not true, is it?"

"Do you want it to be true?" I asked.

"No," Vada replied. "Star of Indrana, I want my world back. My granddaughter is—she has not been herself since this all happened. She won't say the words out loud. None of us will. We are terrified. We rejoiced over the idea of peace with the Shen and though the news of our gods was a shock, it was a comfort to know it had been foretold."

"Vada." Fasé stepped forward with her hands held out, and she smiled when the older Farian took them. "You know who I am?"

"I do, *Mardis.*"

"All will be well. I promise. Now, where is Prosa?"

"At the Pedalion building. She still visits in the late day, but there will be a guard with her."

"We can deal with the guard," I said, after a look at Mia and her confirming nod. "In such a way that doesn't—"

The sudden appearance of Biea in the middle of the café with the Farian woman resulted in startled shouts and the whine of weaponry.

"Everyone settle down." Emmory's sharp command cut through the din like a laser.

Fasé had released Vada and rushed forward, catching the Farian woman as she sagged to the floor and I slipped out of Mia's grasp, awkwardly grabbing Biea when the Selan staggered back a few steps.

"I am all right, Your Majesty," they managed. "It was more disorienting than I expected to attempt such a thing in this place."

"What did you do?"

"You seemed distressed over the idea that those guards would take that one, so I retrieved her."

"We're going to have guards swarming this place in two minutes," Aiz said.

Biea shook their head. "No, they do not remember her or anything about the last few moments. We will be safe from them."

"Mia." I gestured her over and the Shen helped Biea to a table. Fasé was on the ground with the Farian, her hands in her hair. Aiz had gone to a knee at her side, one hand resting on Fasé's back.

"Vada, are you all right?" I put my arm around the Farian's shoulders.

"This is a lot of excitement for an old Farian, Star of Indrana."

"It's a lot of excitement for a young human, believe me," I replied, and she laughed.

"What is that?" she whispered, pointing at Biea.

"They are Selan, Vada, by the name of Biea. They came hunting your false gods. Thyra and the others are criminals of their people. We are helping them."

"Will it bring peace?"

"Yes."

"How can I help?"

I looked around the café. We'd been lucky so far that no customers had come in. "Do you have a back room we could move to? It will be safer for you if we are not here when you get customers."

"Of course; my living quarters are upstairs, back toward the kitchen."

I shared a look with Emmory and switched on the com. "Gita, there's an upstairs, will you check it out?"

"Already done, Your Majesty, are you moving there?"

I smiled. "Yes. We've had a bit of excitement. Have Emmory catch you up."

"He's got me on his vid-feed, ma'am. I saw."

"Aren't you efficient," I murmured to Emmory, and he grinned.

"We aren't going to want to stay much longer."

"I have to speak with Prosa."

"I know, but we've gotten lucky twice now and that's way over our normal limits."

I laughed. "You're not wrong there. Vada, we're going to want to clean up here before we go upstairs."

"I've got it, Star of Indrana, don't worry." She waved a hand and went into the back.

I turned back to Fasé as the Farian on the floor stirred. She stiffened and then her silver eyes went wide. She looked around the room quickly before settling on Fasé. *"Mardis?"*

"What's your name?"

"Tesha, holy one."

I spotted the flinch Fasé tried to hide, and Aiz must have felt it because his hand flexed on her back.

He rose to his feet. "I'm going to take a look around outside."

"Be careful."

He tapped me on the shoulder with a fist before heading for the door. After a quick conversation with Hao, who'd returned from the back, Aiz opened the door and slipped through.

"Star of Indrana, it was you," Tesha whispered as I crouched at Fasé's side. "You saved me."

"Not me, Tesha, but Biea there."

She turned and gasped at the sight of the Selan. "They look like the false gods."

"They do." I explained the situation as I helped her to her feet.

"Tesha, what cell are you part of?"

"I am not, *Mardis*. The cells have had to go dark here in the capital. I volunteered to help spread the word, but Adora has begun to suspect everyone. She has spies everywhere. Both in the flesh and in the walls."

"In the walls?" I stiffened. "Emmory, surveillance?"

"Not here, Majesty," Emmory said. "We checked. Let's move this upstairs. Hao?"

"Right behind you."

Biea was walking under their own power for the stairs, but Mia walked close to the Selan and the worried look she shot me as they passed spoke volumes. We were going to have to get Biea out of the capital before whatever it was about this fucking architecture caused permanent damage.

I herded Fasé and Tesha toward the stairs, looking back over my shoulder at the blood smeared on the white tiled floor. Dread settled itself into my gut, staying even as Vada passed us and started mopping up the mess.

"The Pedalion is alive?"

Tesha nodded. "When last I saw, yes. Prosa may be able to give you more updated information as I haven't been in the building for several days. They are not themselves, though. I don't know what Adora and the false gods did to them, but they act as though they are sleepwalking."

"What about Sybil?" Fasé asked. "The Council of Eyes?"

"I do not know, *Mardis*." Tesha shook her head. "I haven't seen them. No one has."

"Hail, see your girl coming up the street," Aiz said over the coms. *"One guard with her."*

"You can't kill them," I subvocalized.

"I don't need to."

"Prosa's on her way," I announced to the room. "Mia, will you take Fasé, Tesha, and Biea back? We'll follow as soon as we're done here."

"Be careful," Mia replied, reaching for my hand.

I squeezed her fingers and headed downstairs, Emmory on my heels. Gita and Hao were in quiet conversation at the foot of the stairs, and they stopped when we reached them.

"Mia's taking Fasé and the others back," I said. "Once I talk to Prosa, we'll head out, too."

"Probably a good idea, Majesty," Gita said. "Things are getting quiet out there; too many of us in a group would attract attention."

"You okay?" I asked Hao.

"Itchy." He tapped the side of his gun and shook his head.

"I feel you there. We got most of our questions answered by Tesha. I just want to see if Prosa can tell me where Sybil and the other future-seers are and if there's a way to get us into the Pedalion compound. Then we can go."

"Grandmother!" Prosa's call was strained with forced cheerfulness as she opened the door and stepped into the café. I heard her cry out and the brief sound of a scuffle and when I peeked around the corner Aiz was lowering the guard down into the booth by the door.

"Prosa," I said. "Are you all right?"

"Your Majesty. Where is my grandmother?"

"I am here, Prosa, I am fine."

"You must go," Prosa said, extending her arms to me. "They'll know something happened to my guard."

Emmory and the others stiffened and my *Ekam* muttered a curse. "How?"

"I don't know, but they always do."

"Prosa, is the Council alive? Do you know where they are?"

"They are, Majesty. They're being held in the cells. The Pedalion members are free, but Thyra is controlling them. And there are creatures all over, Your Majesty. Things that look like Farians but are not. They speak like new clones. The ones who are woken before they get a soul." She shook her head, tears in her eyes. "It is awful."

"Can you get us inside?"

"Inside the Pedalion?" Prosa shook her head, frowning in thought. "I don't know, maybe? I would need to think on it and see where—"

"There's no time, Prosa. It has to happen today."

She bit her lower lip at my urgent tone. "Do you remember the spot where I showed you the city?"

I thought of the tower and the wraparound balcony that had looked out over all of Sicenae. "Yes."

"It is open to the street; there are no guards to that stairwell. Come at the thirtieth hour; it is quiet and there is a guard change. I can slip away and open the door for you."

"We will be there," I replied, and leaned in to hug her. "Be careful, Prosa."

"May the universe watch over you, Star of Indrana."

There was shouting in the street. Emmory grabbed me by the arm and pulled me toward the back where Gita and Hao were waiting.

"Lay him on the floor," Vada said to Aiz, and the Shen frowned but pulled the guard from the booth. "Prosa, act as though you are trying to wake him. All of you go, we will be fine."

"Thank you, Grandmother," I replied, and Vada smiled.

"Go now." She gave Aiz a little push in my direction. He nodded to her and we slipped out the back door.

We made it several streets away before I spotted the first sign of Thyra's army. Or, rather, they spotted us.

"Stop!" The voice was tinny and metallic and put chills down my spine. The creature resembled a Farian, but taller and more gaunt, the skin stretched across its face, and the eyes were black and empty.

Aiz shot the Farian in the head and it crumpled to the ground as the five of us continued to run.

The sounds of pursuit filled the air mixing with Emmory's cool orders over the coms as we dodged down a street.

"I'll take whatever support you can give us. We're currently headed toward sector eight-five on the map. Pursuit by unknown number of hostiles."

"Emmory!"

He managed to avoid the Farians who'd emerged from the growing shadows, shooting one before it tackled him. I brought my Glocks up and shot a second in the back.

Gita grabbed me. "Down, Majesty." She pulled me behind the sharp-edged cover of a building. "Hail," she said at my level look. "Let them do this."

Aiz and Hao had rushed forward and along with Emmory dispatched the other three Farians with ruthless efficiency before I could argue.

"Majesty?"

"I'm fine," I replied to Emmory's call as I stood.

The laser blast streaked in from above us, slamming into a nearby building and filling the air with debris.

More Farian soldiers poured into the street around us.

40

Gita, take Hail and go!" Emmory's order echoed both in the air and over the coms, but before my *Dve* could respond a Farian crashed into her, taking them both to the ground.

I brought my Glocks up. Too late. Gita shot the creature in the chest and shoved them to the side.

Another blast rocked the area and I spat curses into the air at the small Farian crafts raining fire down on us from above.

"Less shouting, Majesty, more running." Gita grabbed me by the arm and dragged me down a side street, away from the others. "I don't like it either," she said before I could protest. "But Emmory will shoot us both if we don't do what he says."

We ran and though the foot soldiers didn't follow us, the fighters did. I could hear the constant stream of updates on the coms. Emmory and the others had fought their way free of the mass of soldiers and were trying to circle around to us.

"Negative, Emmory. We've got the air support on our tail. Make for the rendezvous point and we'll meet you there."

"Majesty—"

"I am too busy being shot at to argue with you, *Ekam*, do it. Gita, go left!" I shouted as we raced across a platform. She sprinted ahead of me and slid over the low wall. I followed and blasts from the fighter singed the air around me as I braced a hand on the wall and leapt over. I fired a useless shot at the fighter with my Glock after I landed, pleased when the pilot reflexively swerved.

"Come on, Majesty." Gita gestured to the stairs and I followed her. We sprinted down the stairs and around a corner.

Straight into a pair of Farian soldiers.

"Don't shoot!" They both dropped their guns and put up their hands. "We're with the rebellion, Star of Indrana."

"That's a good way to get killed," I replied, not lowering my guns. "Who are you?"

"I am Pelagia," she said and pointed at her companion. "This is Dimi. We've been undercover in the traitor's guard and were sent out to find you when word came in that you were on the planet. The *Mardis* put out a call for any available fighters to lead you out of the city."

I shared a look with Gita. *"Already on it,"* she subvocalized. *"I've sent their photos to Fasé."*

"We can't wait around here for long. Those fighters are going to find us again."

Gita nodded, then said out loud. "Fasé confirms they're with the resistance. We're good."

I lowered my gun and the Farians relaxed. "Get your weapons, we need to keep moving."

Gita put the pair of Farians in the front while she watched my back, and the four of us made our way through the now eerily silent streets.

We'd lost the fighters who'd been chasing us, a fact for which I was extremely grateful, but the sudden stillness made me nervous. I hesitated a moment, skin prickling on my arms.

"Majesty?"

The creature dropped from above us, landing on Dimi, and the sharp crack of the rebel's neck snapping was loud in the air. Pelagia froze in shock and I fired my Glock just past her left ear as the Farian soldier turned on her with a snarl.

"Go-go-go!" I jumped forward, pushing Pelagia ahead of me as several other Farian soldiers landed in the street around us. Gita shot one before it even hit the ground and it fell dead in our path.

Pelagia recovered from her shock and vaulted the corpse, shooting at the pair of soldiers ahead of us. Warnings went off on my *smati*, and I realized they were for Gita, not me.

Spinning, I saw that she'd taken down one of the soldiers behind us but the other had her pinned to the wall with an arm across her throat. I took aim, snarling when I realized my Glocks were empty, and launched myself at the pair.

I dropped my guns and pulled Johar's knife from its sheath, jamming it into the Farian soldier's exposed neck and wrenching it back and forth until they collapsed.

Gita folded over and the horrible sounds she made drove straight into my heart. My *smati* screamed at me.

"Let me see." I dropped the knife and went to a knee, putting both hands on her throat. The soldier had crushed her trachea and I fought past my own panic, dragging in the energy around me.

"Star of Indrana?"

"I've got it," I gritted out between clenched teeth. "Keep watch. There will be more."

Rebuilding someone's throat was a lot different than closing a cut, and I found myself eternally grateful for the fact that all my BodyGuards' medical scans were at my fingertips. In the blink of an eye I had an image of Gita's throat in my vision and the energy went to work.

"Easy," I murmured when she gasped for air. "Stay down." I grabbed for her gun at the sound of pounding feet, but lowered it just as quickly when Emmory and the others came around the corner. "Pelagia, they're friendlies."

She stared at me, the awe in her face hard to hide. "You healed her."

"It's a very long story."

"Gita!"

"She's all right," I said as Hao dropped to my side. "Give her a minute." I got to my feet and hugged Emmory. "I am really glad to see you."

"Likewise, Majesty. We're not out of this yet, though. Can she walk?"

"She's fine. A little shaky," Aiz said, getting up from Gita's other side and helping Hao lift my *Dve* onto her feet. "You did good, Hail."

I returned his nod and went to retrieve my Glocks. "Let's get moving."

"Zin's incoming with a shuttle, Majesty. We're not far from the landing zone." Emmory put a hand on my back and pointed. "We're going that way."

I lifted Gita's gun and the six of us took off down the street.

"Are you all right?"

Biea looked away from the city. The white buildings glowed in the rising sun and I suppressed a shudder at the ominous reddish hue coating them. By the time we'd made it back to base it had been too late to make the meeting with Prosa. Now I was back to square one because of Thyra's fucking creatures and rapidly running out of time.

"This entire planet is unpleasant, Your Majesty, but it is not as bad here." They sighed. "I had hoped we could be of more help but until we figure out how to combat this"—they waved a limb in the direction of the spikes jutting up into the sky—"we must be cautious about our forays into the city."

"You have helped. You saved Tesha's life. You argued for more time for us."

"Would that I had been as successful on that last piece," they said. "I have read the words of my ancestors. Learning to value life was difficult for them, perhaps the most difficult thing they learned once they were free."

"Being treated as something disposable would do that to you, I suspect," I murmured. "That is the biggest reason humans made cloning sentient beings illegal."

"It has been interesting watching you humans grown up. In some ways I am grateful you are so isolated," Biea said with a tiny smile. "Though I confess it would be fascinating to see the rest of the universe react to what you have become."

"I confess I'm curious as to what's out there," I replied. "But as Hao said it would probably end badly for us were we to go."

"Possibly." Biea dipped their head in acknowledgment. "Or maybe it would be a much-needed surprise. We cannot leave this galaxy for fear that the Infrastructure may still exist and be looking for us. I have considered sending probes, but it is a risk."

We fell into silence, watching the light wash over the buildings until the cloak of night was pulled back from the landscape and the lights of Sicenae winked out one by one.

"I had my people dig in the archives for information on Thyra as you requested, Majesty. I have passed the files on to your *Ekam*. May I ask what you're looking for?"

"I don't know, maybe nothing," I admitted. "I'm trying to understand my opponent better before I face her."

Biea blinked. "You would not survive a fight against them, Your Majesty."

"You'd be surprised what I've survived," I replied.

"Your people seem unbothered by that fact that you are planning to go to your death."

I glanced back at Emmory. "Oh, they're bothered. They're also used to it and I'm very hard to kill. If your people won't give us more time, the only way to do this is for me to sneak into the Pedalion and kill Thyra on my own."

"Is that the outcome you seek, Your Majesty?"

"I want to go home," I whispered. "I want the Farians safe from these criminals. I want peace between them and the Shen. I want the Shen, all of them, to be able to come back to this place they started from. I don't want to fight your people. I would rather we be friends." I thought of the children I'd seen on the ship.

Biea was silent for a long moment, then spoke. "I don't want to fight you either, Your Majesty. You are a good leader. You care about not only your people but the lives of others. This is uncommon."

I shifted uncomfortably at the praise. "I'm nothing special."

"Watching your people tells me otherwise." They smiled. "They would follow you into this fight without hesitation."

"Which is why I don't want them to, but I will let them." I glanced at Emmory again. "My empire is secure in the hands of good people. The Shen require their leaders to help them rebuild. And Faria needs Fasé. I am the expendable one. Less violence is a great concept, but I know the world well enough to know that sometimes violence up front can prevent even more down the road. It's not pretty and when you're the one who makes the call you get to live with the weight of the lives you've taken.

"I already know who I'm dealing with. They won't listen to reason even if your people gave us the time. They won't stop. I don't negotiate with people like that because you can't; they will happily drown us all in blood to get what they want." I rubbed at the back of my neck. "I'm sure that must sound bloodthirsty, Biea, and I understand if you want no part of it. I have been through a fight like this once before and it nearly killed me. But I took down the man who murdered my family. Thyra's creatures or your people, it makes no difference, I will not stand by and let it happen again."

"It does not sound like anything beyond the duty of a leader, Your Majesty. You wear that burden well."

"I'm glad someone thinks so, as I often doubt it myself."

Biea shook their head. "That is the way of it, Your Majesty. We who are at the front try to see every angle, guess every battle plan of our enemies, all the while wondering if we have made the right choice." They tapped their limbs together twice in a decisive gesture. "I am going to my ship and we are going off-planet to see what help we can be with the battle that will surely happen up in the sky. I wish you luck, Your Majesty, and here." They held out a limb, a small black square balanced on the end. "Call me if you have need and I will try to come."

"I appreciate it." I took the square and slipped it into my pocket. Biea nodded once more and vanished.

"I don't want to fight them," Emmory said as he stepped up to my side. "Even this far out from their original design, they've got advantages we could never match."

"I don't want to fight them because they're decent beings and there's a lack of that in the universe." I hooked my fingers together at the back of my head and stretched. "I wish we had more time, Emmory."

"I started in on those files Biea sent me. There's a lot of information there. Almost too much. If you don't know what you're looking for, it's going to be a struggle to find anything."

"Anything I can use against her. We already know she was after the Farians' ability to control the energy, but I want specifics on how it applies to her. Put Ragini on it," I said. "Tell her to look for anything that ties back into that idea. We can cross-reference from there and get with Biea to—"

Thyra appeared in front of us with a handful of creatures and the rest of my words were lost to Emmory's shout. She threw my *Ekam* out of the way with one long limb and kicked me in the chest with another, knocking me back against the outside wall.

I scrambled to my feet, adrenaline crowding out the pain, but Thyra moved fast, wrapping a limb around my throat and jerking me into the air. "You are infuriating in your persistence," she snarled, tightening her grip until spots appeared in my vision. I could hear the faint sounds of fighting in the background and I hoped that Emmory was still alive as Thyra ripped me away from him.

41

The only thing worse than getting choked out is when you wake up afterward by hitting a wall. I slid awkwardly to the cold floor, my brain trying to make sense of the chaos that had just happened and my *smati* screaming enough warnings at me to be worrisome.

My instincts were also screaming, and the training from Aiz had me back on my feet despite my injuries. I slapped away the hand that reached for me with a snarl.

"We mean you no harm."

I blinked several times before I could get my vision to focus on Sybil. The future-seer was standing out of arm's reach, her hands held out to me. The rest of the Council of Eyes was behind her, though at the moment I was hard pressed to remember names and my *smati* was otherwise occupied detailing what was wrong.

"Give me a second," I mumbled, and sat back down, burying my head in my hands.

"We have the time," she replied, crouching down but not moving any closer.

"We don't have time. The Selan." I cursed in Cheng. "How the fuck did Thyra know where I was?"

"What happened?" Sybil asked.

"Just now? I was fighting Thyra a moment ago." I lifted my head, squinting in the dim light. "I was getting my ass kicked, rather. Where am I?"

I tried my coms but only static filled my head.

"The penitent cells in the basement of the Pedalion compound. You will not be able to reach any of your people. They are shielded against communication and prevent us from using any energy."

I blew out a careful breath. The air felt strange. It was heavy and pressed down on me, but I could feel my own energy rolling around in my gut and drew on a little of it until my ears stopped ringing.

"I may be exempt from that," I murmured, smiling at Sybil's tiny gasp and holding out my hand. She stood and took it, pulling me to my feet and into a surprising embrace.

"We are very relieved you are still alive, Star of Indrana."

I chuckled and hugged her back. "Well, this is a bit shit as rescues go, but it's good to see you, too. Are any of you hurt?"

"No," Sybil said, stepping back with a shake of her head. "The guards have been deferential, either by order or their own reverence, it is hard to tell. We are thankful for it all the same."

"Thyra created an army."

Sybil nodded. "They look like Farians but have no souls. Adora knew about it. She does Thyra's bidding and has all these years. Once upon a time I thought she could be turned from this path, but she is committed. It will be her final death."

"We met the Selan. Thyra's people," I clarified. "They have been hunting for Thyra and her squad. All this"—I gestured at the sharp edges around us—"is designed to keep them out. Thyra and the others are criminals. She's trying to turn you all into her army so she can take over the galaxy."

There were gasps from the others of the council, and I couldn't blame them. It sounded pretty strange to my ears as well. Sybil seemed unsurprised and I studied her with narrowed eyes. "You knew."

"Yes. I'm sorry." She nodded. "There is so much I have not told you. So much I did not tell them. I knew. I knew who the gods were when they first landed. Quiet." She lifted a hand, cutting off the exclamations from the others. "I knew why they were there, Star of Indrana. I saw everything in an instant—including the knowledge that we could not fight them off in the beginning. That any attempt would result in our complete subjugation and a loss of any chance to save my people. And then I saw you.

"So instead I told them what they wanted to hear. Let their fears filter the visions when I showed them and kept the true interpretation from them. I showed them the fate that would bring all of this about."

"Why?"

"For my people. For your people. For everyone. There are such things out there, Hail. Worse than Thyra. Humanity will not survive without people like you. Faria needs people like Fasé. And the Shen without Mia would be lost. That part of it was real—there is no true shelter for sides that will collapse without each other to lean on."

I recognized the words of the prophecy she'd spoken what seemed like a very long time ago on Pashati. We'd guessed as much—that we needed the stability of me, Mia, and Fasé—but to hear it again now?

Something about it was like the sound of the bells of the mountaintop monastery of Oni-Bistr and I felt an answering vibration deep in my own chest.

Sybil looked over her shoulder at the sound outside our cell. "We don't have much time left. You need to listen to what I have to say." She reached out, wrapping cold fingers around my bare wrist.

My heart skipped a beat, but I stayed silent.

"You must follow," she said. "You will want to stay. For the first you will want to stay but know that you cannot. For the second it will be your choice and everything will hinge on it."

I realized there were tears in her eyes. "Sybil—"

"Remember this, Hail Bristol: Hope is a living thing. You must feed it with faith to keep it alive."

I had time to nod and then the door to the cell slid open. Two guards stood on the other side. Actual Farians with their guns pointed at us.

"On the ground, facedown," one barked. "You so much as breathe wrong and I'll put a shot in your skull."

"At least we're all taking this seriously," I replied, dropping into a crouch and crawling forward. The second guard pulled my arms behind my back and cuffed them. They hauled me to my feet and marched me out of the cell.

"Where are we going, fellas?"

"Shut up and walk." One of them shoved their gun into my side and pushed me toward the stairs.

I tried the coms again the second we hit the stairs but still only got static, so I sent a flash message to Hao that simply read: *Alive, rescue my ass.*

I recognized the guard at the door of the Pedalion chamber as the one who'd been on the street when Tesha had crashed into me. Now his face was blank, an impassive mask designed to hide anything and everything going on behind it. But his eyes gave him away and I smiled, hoping it would get through to him.

He didn't react.

The blank faces of the Pedalion were of an altogether different sort. Delphine and Yadira, Rotem and Sou, all sat at their spots on the dais with wooden expressions and unblinking eyes. Guarded by the creatures who looked like poor replicas of Farians and had almost the same blank looks on their faces.

Adora and Thyra were in discussion on one end and didn't look up as I was marched into the center of the room to stand on top of the sixteen-pointed star.

"If you're trying to impress me, Adora, it's going to take a bit more than just ignoring me."

The guard on my left hit me in the back. I kicked without looking, and the sharp crack of his knee snapping echoed in the room.

The second guard was smarter and the shot to my back felt like a sledgehammer. I went down, my *smati* screaming alarms at me, but despite the noise and pain nothing vital had been damaged.

"Energy weapon?" I asked, my laugh turning to a groan as I rolled over. "I'd thought so. That's got a punch to it."

"I can have him shoot you again, Hail," Adora said, crossing the room to us. "In the mouth, perhaps?"

"Such violence." I tutted at her. "You know, once I'd have thought the Farians were above such things, but you've thrown that theory into the wind. Attacking embassies, murdering my people, consorting with mercenaries, and now this."

Adora held up a hand before the guard could shoot me again. "That was the Shen."

"You don't need to keep lying to me, Adora. I know how to follow a money trail. Pro tip for you, when choosing front names for your companies don't use obvious shit like Star Optics. When I get done here I'm going to hunt Jamison down and skin him. You two will be examples for what happens when people dare to fuck with me."

"Are you going to skin me, too, Hail?"

"I might." I smiled. "I'm feeling generous enough, though, that if you let me go and turn Thyra and Adaran over I'll give you a head start. It probably won't do much for you since I'm sure Aiz, not to mention the Pedalion, would like a word with you." I tipped my head toward the dais.

"The Pedalion has almost outlived its usefulness," Adora replied with a smile. "As have you."

"Adora." Thyra's quiet reprimand filled the sudden silence. "I told you both of them were not to be harmed before I figure out what happened. I will take her down to the lab."

I grinned. "Figured you weren't in charge here."

Adora snapped her fingers and the guard kicked me. I folded in on his leg, rolling into the strike rather than trying to avoid it, and the satisfying snap of his knee breaking filled the air. I kept rolling over the top of him, making it to my feet before anyone else reacted.

The explosion was close enough to shake the floor and pieces of the ceiling on the far side crashed down. I bolted for the still-open door, shoulder-checking the guard standing there hard enough to knock his head into the wall, and scrambled around the corner before Adora's shouts reached my ears.

"Emmory!" I yelled over the coms. "Can anyone read me?"

Static fuzzed in my ears.

I skidded around the corner and went down hard as the sounds of howling echoed through the air. "Fuck." I straightened my back, slipping my cuffed hands below my ass and pulling my legs in until I could maneuver my hands in front.

I made it to my feet as the first guard came around the corner. Only a Farian, thankfully.

Hands cuffed in front was still a disadvantage, but all those days with the Shen meant the guard had almost no chance and once I eliminated the threat of his gun, his chance dropped to zero.

It also meant I could scoop up his gun and shoot the next three guards I ran into in quick succession. The building shook again as I pulled up the maps we'd gotten from Tesha on my *smati*. I still couldn't raise anyone on the coms, but I assumed this bombardment had something to do with my people.

I wouldn't put it past my *Ekam* to level a building just to get to me.

The penitent cells were on the other side of the complex, but I put the route onto the map. I wasn't leaving Sybil and the others here.

"Whoa!"

I pulled my shot to the left, narrowly missing Hao. Gita skidded to a stop behind him. "Sorry."

"Majesty, are you okay?"

"Well enough." I winced when she patted my ribs. "Little sore there, Gita, gently. You got anything that will get these off?"

"Possibly, let me see." She took my gun and shouldered it along with her own.

"'Alive, rescue my ass'?"

I grinned at Hao. "I didn't know how long a message I could send and figured that way you'd know it was me."

He laughed and shook his head. "You weren't wrong."

"Where's everyone else?"

"We split up, figured we had a better chance of finding you that way. Coms aren't responding for shit," Hao replied. "Though we've got Ragini working on the problem from above."

"Was that our ship blowing holes in the building?"

"Ground ordnance, courtesy of the Shen, if you can believe it."

I thought of all those long hours on Sparkos listening to Aiz and Mia discuss the war. "I can, actually."

"Mia had a theory about the Selan being affected by the architecture that evolved into the best solution being destroying the architecture." Hao grinned. "Which seemed like a good plan no matter what."

The cuffs clicked open and clattered to the floor. I kicked them out of the way and held my hand out to Gita for my gun. "Sybil and the rest of the Council of Eyes are in the penitent cells. We need to get them out."

Gita grabbed me at the sound of feet pounding down the hallway but relaxed when Aiz, Mia, and a squad of Shen appeared. The building shook again.

"Hail," Mia said, stepping forward. I took her hand.

"I'm fine." I smiled when she linked her fingers through mine and arched an eyebrow at me. The wash of energy flooded me a moment later and my injuries healed. "Thank you."

"Where's Adora?"

I tipped my head behind me. "Pedalion chambers, maybe. I don't know what Thyra's done to the other members; they were nonresponsive, but still alive as far as I could tell. Sybil and the council are in the basement. We were just about to go rescue them."

"We'll go to the chamber," Aiz said.

"Be careful. Thyra's there."

He barked an order to the Shen and they took off the way I'd come. Mia released my hand and smiled, then followed.

The sudden sick feeling at the sight of her back retreating from me almost made me call out to her, but I swallowed her name and headed in the opposite direction.

We stared at the empty cells.

"Someone else let them out?" Hao asked with a frown.

"I just hope it was one of our people and not Adora's," I muttered, and glanced ceilingward. "I haven't asked you for much, Father, but it would be nice if we could have the coms back up."

"This is Senior Tech Ragini Triskan with the Vajrayana, Hailimi Bristol, *does anyone read me?"*

I laughed and shared a look with Gita. "Remind me to make an appearance at Ganesh's temple when we get home."

"Dve Desai, do you copy?" It was Indula's voice, not Emmory's, on the com, and my heart stuttered with panic.

"Yes, we copy. The empress is with us. Has anyone heard from Emmory and Zin?"

"We're upper level, southwest side," Emmory said. *"Copy on the empress's location. Where are you?"*

"Just below you, Emmory," I replied. "Does anyone have eyes on Sybil or the other members of the council?"

"We've got them, Majesty," Emmory replied. *"Or almost all of them, Sybil wasn't with them."*

"Where's Fasé?"

"I just met up with Aiz and Mia," she replied. *"We're headed into the Pedalion chamber now—"* The coms cut out again and I muttered a curse.

"Aiz, do you copy?"

"We're meeting resistance here—"

I was running before his response was finished. Gita's protest faded as I took the stairs two at a time. I crashed into a pair of Adora's guards, clocking one in the jaw with the butt of my gun.

"Gita, two hostiles right in front of you," I said over the com.

Her reply was garbled as the coms cut out again and I swore, vaulting over a pile of rubble in the hallway and turning the corner to the narrow stretch that led to the Pedalion chamber.

There were bodies strewn across the floor—Shen and Farian both—and I gasped a second, breathless prayer to the Dark Mother when I saw Aiz.

"Aiz!" I dropped to my knees next to him and rolled him over.

"Thyra took Mia." There was blood everywhere and I realized in horror there was a gaping hole in the middle of his chest.

"Where's Adora?"

"Still in the chamber. She'd have finished me off if Sybil hadn't shown up."

"Stay still." I put my hands over the wound in the front and dragged in a breath and felt my skin cool as I started pushing energy into him.

"Stop, Hail. You can't heal this. You have to go after Mia."

"I'm currently occupied trying to save your life."

He shook his head and smiled weakly. "I'll come back from this. She won't."

"But it won't be you." The protest slid out, choked with tears.

"Humans." He laughed, coughed, and spat the blood to the side. "It'll always be me, Hail. Please go."

It was the hardest thing in the universe to stop healing him and pull my hands away. I wiped at the tears, smearing Aiz's blood across my cheeks, and sprinted down the hallway toward the Pedalion chamber.

"Don't come after me." Mia's words were loud in my head, and I realized what she meant as I ran through the open door. *"You'll die if you follow, Hail, and I won't survive the loss of you."*

Adora, Fasé, and Sybil stood inside, all three Farians bloody and

347

their hands interlaced, the other members of the Pedalion watching like a row of dolls.

I snagged a knife off the corpse of a Shen, crossed the room, and plunged it into Adora's back in a spot I knew wouldn't kill her but would put her on the floor. The Farian gasped in pain. Fasé and Sybil pushed her to her knees with a triumphant cry.

"You stay right where you are," I ordered, putting my gun to the back of Adora's head. "I don't need a reason to pull this trigger."

"Release them," Sybil ordered as she let Adora go and stepped back, her hands folded at her waist.

Adora's mouth was tight, but she waved a hand and all four members of the Pedalion blinked.

"What is going on? Adora—" Rotem's demand died in his throat as he registered the death and destruction in the chamber.

"Majesty!" Gita sprinted into the chamber.

"Gun on her," I ordered, my own still pointed at Adora, and only when Gita complied did I pull mine away.

Sybil touched her bloody fingers to her lips three times and smiled. "Star of Indrana. We have reached the end of this. Your final choice on this path. The last fork in the road."

"There's no choice. Not for me. You know this already. Open that," I said, pointing at the star on the floor. "Now."

"Hail—" Gita's protest was choked and I sent her an apologetic smile.

"You have to stay here." I knew that all our plans were useless. I had to face Thyra alone.

"Follow the water." Sybil touched her hand to the table on the dais. The floor rumbled and slid open, revealing the shimmering pool in the center. Fasé didn't hesitate, jumping through before I could stop her, and I swore.

"Are you sure about this, Hail? You could die." Another strange smile.

"Everyone dies," I replied, and jumped after Fasé.

42

I hit the water hard but managed to hold my breath until I surfaced and crawled up onto the bank, lying there for a moment before I pushed to my feet and went to find Fasé.

The cavern seemed the same as it had the first time we came through. The smooth black walls curving and spiraling, shimmers winking in and out of existence like the stars in the night sky on any atmospheric planet in the galaxy.

By some miracle the little black box Biea had given me was in my pocket and seemed to be unharmed. "I don't know if you'll work down here, but it's worth a try," I murmured, pressing my thumb to a side. A blue light glowed within and I shoved it back into my pocket.

Fasé stood, staring at the water, and looked up at me when I approached with a smile on her face. "Are you injured?"

"No," I said with a shake of my head. "Mia healed me just before they went for the Pedalion. Fasé, why did you jump?" The words caught in my throat, hot with pain.

"Because I need to be here with you." Fasé reached for me, linking her fingers through mine. "We should get moving, though."

"Sybil said, *Follow the water*," I murmured, looking around. We hadn't explored much the first time we'd been here, instead moving quickly forward for the *ilios porthmeios*. This time I walked the perimeter of the cave until I heard the sound of rushing water.

"You are fucking kidding me." I gave my brain exactly five seconds to freak out over the waterfall at my feet, swore a second time, and jumped, knowing that Fasé would follow.

The roaring filled my head as the water wrapped around me, and it was just high enough that I went into free fall for a heartbeat before I slammed into the water below.

I'd opened my eyes and to my surprise was not met with pitch-blackness but a thousand stars and galaxies spinning in the water in front of me. They danced and shone, mesmerizing me until my lungs reminded me of their rather urgent need to expel the air inside. I kicked until the water separated above my head. Fasé had already surfaced. She tipped her head to the side in a silent question and we swam away from the waterfall, the turbulent water calming into a river that grew narrower the farther we went on.

Follow the river, but how far?

The answer came around a bend, when up ahead I spotted a pair of large turbines. We made a beeline for the shore and I hauled myself, then Fasé, dripping, up onto the bank.

This wasn't a natural cavern, but a large smooth area that had been hollowed out and filled with machinery. I squeezed the water from my hair and unslung the weapon from my back, pleased with the blinking lights and slight vibration that greeted my touch. I was going to take that as a sign that Farian guns were waterproof. Fasé was wringing water from her shirt. We exchanged a silent nod and slipped between the softly humming machines.

They were taller than I was, stretching up toward the black ceiling, but gave no hint what purpose hid behind their white exteriors. Cables stretched across the ground and from the ceiling. Some led out of the room and I traced the others back to the turbines.

"Generators," I said to Fasé. "Pulling from the water?" Even as I said it I felt a strange sensation on the surface of my skin and I glanced down at my hands. The stars were under my skin, spinning just below the surface. "Fasé?"

She held up her own hands, as star-filled as mine. "It's not water, Hail, it's us. Farians. You were right. Our energy, our prayers. They've stolen it all." She angrily wiped a tear away and I pulled her into a hug.

"I'm sorry. We're going to fix this." My own fury at everything Thyra and the others had stolen from the Farians had reached a boiling point. They had to be stopped, not only for Mia's sake, but for all of the Farians and Shen.

"Over there."

I spotted the door Fasé was pointing at on the other side and headed for it. As far as I could tell this place was deserted—with the exception of Thyra and Mia.

Or possibly Adaran.

Bugger me, I hope not. Bad enough I'll have to fight one of them.

I blew out a breath and continued on. A door was open at the far end and light streamed from it into the dim corridor. I slowed, pushing Fasé behind me and making my steps as light as possible. We were dry now and the energy hummed under my skin.

A shadow moved across the light in the doorway and my *smati* started to translate the Selan it picked up in fits and starts, and after a moment I realized why.

Thyra was speaking what was probably the original form of Selan, while Biea and the others spoke a language that had evolved with them.

"What...that is wrong. And this, too. All the...are wrong. Why?"

I gestured to Fasé to stay put and crept closer to the door, crouching down and peeking in. Thyra stood with her back to me and my heart lurched when I spotted Mia's boots on the floor.

The alien moved, still talking to herself, the words coming too fast now for me to even decipher my *smati*'s translation attempts.

Not that I cared; my eyes were glued to the table she'd just moved away from as I sent a third desperate prayer to the gods of my homeland, any of them who would listen.

Please let Mia be alive.

I pressed my fingers to my lips to hold in the gasp that tried to break free when I saw her—unconscious but still breathing, not broken open and violated like in her vision. Tears clouded my eyes for a long moment until I blinked, sending them scattering and falling down through the air.

"Fasé, no matter what happens, I want you to stay out of sight and if she kills me, you run," I subvocalized over our com channel, which seemed to be working just fine now that we were out of the range of whatever had been interfering on the surface.

"She will not kill you. She needs you alive. She wants you willing. You must not be."

I knew she was right, I just wasn't sure if I could withstand that honeyed voice. Either way it didn't make a whole lot of difference; I had to move. I carefully got to my feet.

Hao had taught me a long time ago that honorable fights were for dead men and if you had the choice between shooting someone in the back and tangling with them in a fair fight, you should always pick the win.

I didn't know if this gun would even hurt Thyra, given that the Koros 101 didn't, but it was all I had. I lifted the gun and sighted it on Thyra's back, pulling the trigger without hesitation or remorse.

The shot hit her in the back, shimmered for a moment, and then dissipated.

"Hail." Thyra looked over her shoulder at me. "Do you really think I would teach the Farians how to make a weapon that would hurt me?" she asked in Indranan.

"It was worth a shot." I tensed, keeping the curse I wanted to let fly behind my teeth, and waited for that first twitch from Thyra to indicate she was coming at me.

But she didn't; instead she turned back to Mia.

"You may keep it if it makes you feel better, but it won't do you any good."

352

I looped the strap over my head and shoulder as I stepped into the room. "This is over, Thyra."

"Do you think this is one of those vid-dramas? You the righteous hero here to save the girl?" She made a popping sound and waved a limb when I tried to shift toward Mia. "Stay right there or I will pin you to the wall and we will finish this conversation with you dangling like a piece of meat on a butcher's hook."

"You know my people are mostly vegetarian, right?"

Thyra stared at me and I lifted my hands as I bared my teeth at her in a vicious smile.

"You probably know by now that my people don't eat at all," Thyra replied, turning back to the counter and taking a sheet that shimmered like rainbows. "Priam loved your people. And your vid-dramas. Do you know how excited he was the day we heard of your appearance, Star of Indrana? How long we'd waited for the vision Sybil saw to come to fruition?" She moved closer to Mia, reaching out and brushing a curl off her forehead with the end of her limb. "It almost made all the years of putting up with the Shen and their little rebellion worth it. You crushed his hopes, you disappointing thing. And then your *Ekam* killed him."

Oh, I knew that calm fury. It filled the air, crackling with an energy all its own. It was the same hate I'd carried on Sparkos for months. The grief of failure. The grief of losing those you love. The bone-deep desire for vengeance.

"If I had time," Thyra said, peeling the rainbow film apart and draping it over Mia's face, "I would hunt down your Emmory and his husband. Make you watch as I hurt them. Make him watch as I take the two most precious things in his life from him and then leave him to his painful death." The glee in her voice chilled me as much as her words, but it also lit a fire in my chest that burned away the last remnants of my frozen fear.

"You won't touch my Trackers," I replied calmly.

Thyra gave the same little trill I'd heard from the children on the

Selan ship, but this one was cold and absent of joy. "Have you seen Trackers die, Your Majesty?"

I wanted to ask what she was doing, but instead I thought of Zin's scream in the cargo bay of Hao's ship. That awful, lonely sound that ripped the heart out of me. I thought of Fasé in the hallway and everything she had sacrificed for us. "I have."

"Not really. Fasé stopped it. I think that is what twisted the path. Had you lost their influence you would have been more inclined to listen to Adora when she came to see you. I saw how your *Ekam*"— she spat the word—"stopped you from listening to me. I nearly killed him right then, but it would have done no good." She sighed a surprisingly human noise. "I have studied your Trackers, Your Majesty; they are incredible things. I have seen them broken and begging for death when the other half of their soul dies, and whatever that pain is, mine was a million times worse when Priam died. How I wish I had the time to repay your *Ekam* for what he took from me."

It was my turn to put fury into my words, both at the implication that Thyra had taken Indranan Trackers and experimented on them and at her threat. "You should remember how things ended for Priam when he went up against me and Emmory and speak with more caution. I'm done with you. You're going to let her go. We're going to walk out of here and your people will mete out justice on you like the criminal you are."

The film had disappeared beneath Mia's skin, the tan surface now shimmering with a faint rainbow sheen that vanished entirely a moment later.

"You're not in a position to bargain just yet." Thyra smiled. "Your bombardment would have destroyed our protection from my self-righteous descendants, but we have time before they get here and I would have answers before you let me go."

"You think I'm going to let you go?"

"To save this one's life? I do. She should not exist. It's another puzzle. Another twisting of the way things should be." Thyra poked a limb into Mia's shoulder, abruptly changing the topic of the conversation. "I made sure the Farians could not reproduce without our assistance—not with each other and certainly not with humans. And yet, the damn Shen spread like a disease. They should not be here, she should not be able to see and do the things she does, and I want to know why."

"Because you can't control life, no one can."

"I am a god. I can do whatever I please!"

I wished I had even an early-model Grendel in my hands. From this range it would at least do some damage on Thyra and give me enough of a chance to rush her. Or a knife. I cast around as subtly as I could, searching for a weapon. "Look, there's no way out of this for you. Your people are here, they're going to take you into custody, and you're going to pay for your crimes. But if you let Mia go—"

"You'll do what, Star of Indrana? Put in a good word for me?" The sound that came out of Thyra's mouth was supposed to be laughter, but it ripped down my spine like a knife.

Bugger me.

I spotted the scalpel jutting out from the tray just past Thyra's right side.

"You shouldn't be here either," Thyra said. "Not as you are, anyway. It wasn't just your *Ekam*. The Shen corrupted you. Fasé corrupted you. You were supposed to save us."

"I was never here to save you," I replied, Sybil's words echoing in my head. "I am here to save everyone from you."

"Liar! I saw it. That's how it was supposed to be!" The metal of the cabinet top bent when she slammed her limb down. "Sybil was right about everything else. I still can't figure out why she was wrong about you." She turned back toward the table and Mia's still form. "Except, once again the Shen corrupt everything they come into contact with." She grabbed the scalpel and spun toward Mia, fury burning in her wide, dark eyes.

I launched myself at her, plan forgotten, and we crashed into the cabinets. Pain spiked through my shoulder when it slammed into the floor and I nearly got the scalpel through my eye for the distraction.

I caught the limb that was holding it with my left hand, and instead of taking an eye it sliced a hot line of pain across my cheek as I wrenched her to the side. I punched Thyra twice in the head with my free hand until she yelped and rolled away.

I followed, pulling the gun over my shoulder and swinging it with as much force as I could muster. The butt of the gun caught her in the face and I knew it hurt. I could feel the energy from the river surging in my veins. Making me stronger and faster. I kicked Thyra, dodging her answering punch. I missed the follow-up, and her strike flung me into the cabinets. I grabbed for the instrument tray as I fell and flung it at Thyra with all my newfound strength.

Thyra staggered back. I rolled toward Mia and the doorway, bouncing to my feet, gun still in my hand.

"Star of Indrana, we do not have to fight." Thyra put her limbs up in an oddly placating gesture. Grayish blood streamed from a cut at her temple.

"Oh, I think we do. You've threatened my Trackers, killed my people. Betrayed my allies. Hurt those I care about. You started this fight and I am going to finish it." I was breathing heavily and took advantage of the pause to pull the energy in from the air around me. The temperature cooled, but my aching injuries eased and the blood welling from the cut on my cheek slowed.

Thyra noticed, and something very much like hatred crossed her face before she could control it. "You should not be able to do that."

"If humans are good at anything it's our constant ability to adapt." I gave a little bow before realization hit me through my sarcasm. "You can't? Is that it? You can't heal yourself. You can steal the energy from the Farians but you can't use it yourself for anything more than keeping you alive. Is that what this has all been about? So you could heal yourself?"

"Healing?" Thyra scoffed. "I already heal faster than you ever could. I don't need something so trivial. I was *designed* to heal quickly. There's very little value in a weapon that's easily broken. You don't understand a thing. We were created as property for a specific purpose, and then meant to be disposed of when we were no longer of use. When we were freed I swore I would find a way to undo all that and give us the lives we deserved. No longer temporary, but eternal."

"Your people did just that without bloodshed," I said. "They survived, and they're free."

"They die." Thyra spat the words at me, fear and hatred clinging like the mud of Xeros B. "The Farians can live forever but they are fragile, imperfect things. Even after all these years the bodies break down. It did us no good. Until I found a way around it."

I'd already seen the proof of that with my own eyes, but still the confirmation that Thyra had experimented on Farians made my stomach twist unpleasantly and I tightened my grip on the gun, praying that Fasé would follow my orders and stay put.

"Star of Indrana, I can give you what you want."

I didn't blink at the subject change. "Which is what?"

Thyra glanced past me at Mia's still form and bared her teeth. "You want to live forever so you can stay with her. I can make that happen."

"No, you can't."

"I can. I swear." Thyra kept one limb raised while she lowered the other, sticking the scalpel into the top of the nearby chair. "I have finally figured it out and I can make it happen. You just have to promise me something if I do."

"Which is what?" I repeated, even though I already had a suspicion just what she was going to ask.

"Let me go. Tell the others I overpowered you and escaped. They can look for me if they want but I'll be long gone."

I didn't think it was a good idea to joke that she obviously hadn't been paying attention and that I was fairly sure no matter what kind of head start she had it wouldn't take Emmory and Zin long to track her down.

I allowed myself for just a second to entertain the notion of immortality and then discarded it with an internal sigh. I didn't need a future-seer to tell me that would end very badly.

Beyond that, I wasn't about to let her get close enough to do anything to me, let alone willingly hold still for some science experiment.

"You know that's not going to happen."

"It was worth a try." Thyra flashed that awful smile again. "I am perfectly fine with killing you and escaping here on my own with Mia. I am good at starting over."

"Good luck with that." I let go of the gun and made a come-here gesture with one hand. "You're not touching her again. All I have to do is hold you off until the others show up."

Whatever Thyra's reply had been, it was lost to my rush. I threw the gun at her and then hit her square on when she flinched, knocking her through the doorway of the lab into the adjoining room. We hit the ground hard, my teeth snapping down from the force of the impact and narrowly missing my tongue.

It was worth it, because it got her away from Mia and away from the scalpel, and judging by the noise she made it hurt her just as much as it hurt me. I swung for Thyra's throat, but she blocked it and the snarled curse was in Selan and untranslatable by my *smati*.

I got my own left hand up before her second shot hit me in the head and rolled with the blow, landing on my side. I kicked out as I fell, and my boot impacted with something.

Then Thyra vanished. Just like Priam had.

43

I froze in shock and the hesitation cost me. The metal tray flew through the air at me and I barely blocked it, flipping it up and over my head with my forearm.

She didn't follow with an attack and I thanked my luck for her lack of practice. Thyra might have been a warrior once, but the long years had betrayed her. She was too used to being in charge, being the stronger, faster one, and it had dulled her instincts.

Whereas I was coming straight from what was essentially "Fight the Gods 101."

But I couldn't fight what I couldn't fucking see. I didn't dare close my eyes like I had with Priam; that had ended in a disaster that only Emmory had saved me from.

And this time I was on my own.

Think, Hail. You can see through all their other tricks, why not this one?

It's just light. Aiz's voice was in my head. *Just energy. We can shape it however we choose.*

I dove to the wall, hoping for my luck to hold out. It did and the panel on the wall controlled the lights—plunging us into darkness when I hit it.

The room went black, except for the light streaming in from the other room. It sliced through the open door and left a wide rectangle on the floor. The downside was that light made it impossible to use my night vision setting on my *smati*, but I was hoping it meant the same for Thyra as I felt along the edge of the cabinet behind me in search of something else to use as a weapon.

I'd just closed my hand around a metal dish when I saw the shadow shifting at the edge of the light. Whatever ability Thyra had, it wasn't enough to keep her from casting a shadow.

I flung the dish not at Thyra but farther into the room, praying she'd take the bait and follow. The shadow shifted, crossing at the bottom edge of the light and melting into the dark.

Holding my breath, I slipped around the edge of the door back into the room with Mia, grabbing the gun on my way by.

The table was empty.

I scrambled for the hallway and found Fasé cradling Mia on the floor. Mia's head lolled sickeningly and I had to stomp hard on the surge of anger that screamed at me to go back into that darkness and finish what I'd started.

"We have to move," I said, gathering Mia into my arms and standing so she was leaning against me. Fasé followed, taking the gun from me. "It won't do any good."

"I heard," she replied with a tiny smile. "Still, better to take it than to leave it here for her to use on us, right?"

"Hail?" Mia's whisper was weak, barely more than a breath of air against my throat.

"It's me. I need you to stay quiet," I murmured against her ear. "And to run if you can."

There was a crash from the room behind us and I picked up my pace, Mia stumbling along beside me. The first door Fasé tried slid open and I hoped that didn't mean our luck was going to run out when we needed it most. We slipped in, tapped the panel, and lowered Mia to the floor as the door slid shut.

I heard Thyra yelling and then the strange offbeat pattern of her footsteps as she ran down the hallway.

The room was almost black, with a dim light shining at floor level on the far side. Fasé touched Mia's face, winced, and shook her head. "You try. I don't know what Thyra's done to her."

I put a hand on the exposed skin of Mia's upper chest, whispered a prayer, and gathered in the energy around me.

When I tried to heal her, it was like crashing headfirst into a wall. The energy I tried to send to her bounced back at me with enough force to put me on my ass and make my ears ring, adding to the buzz of what was still left in me from the river. I shook my head at Fasé as the pain subsided. "I can't heal her either. Thyra put some sort of film across her face. Did you see it?"

Fasé shook her head, her golden eyes wide and haunted.

Bugger me.

"Mia, look at me." I cupped her face in my hands, my heart skipping in relief when her eyes fluttered open. "Hey." I brushed a thumb over her lower lip.

"Hail? Is it really you?"

"I promised, didn't I?"

"Where are we?" She looked around with a frown. "What happened?"

"Etrelia. Thyra grabbed you and ran. I don't know what she did to you, but I can't heal you. Do you remember anything?"

"No, I—" I watched her eyes fog and tightened my fingers on her cheeks until she blinked. "I remember we rushed into the Pedalion chamber; Fasé had just joined up with us. There was shouting and then nothing. I'm sorry."

"It's all right." I touched the injury at her temple gently. "Neither Fasé nor I can seem to get through to you. Do you want to try to heal yourself? We have to get out of here. I need you mobile."

Mia closed her eyes and I watched as the wound closed with agonizing slowness. But her color paled at the same time and she gasped for air.

"What is it?"

"I can't feel anything outside myself. It's like—" She fumbled for the words, but I had them.

"Being behind a wall of glass?"

"Yes. How did you know?"

"Been there." I leaned in and kissed her, smiling gently as I pulled away. "We're going to have to get out of here first, then we'll figure out what's going on with you."

"I feel a little better," she said. "But it's exhausting to only tap into my own energy."

"Rest for a minute. I want to see if there's another way out of this room." I also didn't know if Thyra had some sort of monitoring system in place, but judging from the silence outside I doubted it.

The room we were in was larger than the others and my breath caught as I realized why.

The light on the far side came from a wide doorway, and behind it were thousands of beings who were a mix of Farian and Selan. The upright tubes stretched out—row upon row—all of them glowing a faint greenish-blue in the dim light.

The batch isn't ready.

The realization slammed down on me—Priam's words about ruining thousands of years of work, Thyra's relentless search for a way to stop the Selan from dying, the Farians' ability to manipulate energy. How dismissive Thyra had been about their healing abilities and the deaths of her followers. Her focus on their inability to come back from death like the Farians could.

Ice froze in my chest—Trackers, she'd been trying to figure out how their connection worked.

This wasn't just about her trying to find a way not to die or making an army of soulless Farians, it was something far more horrific.

She had created an army of Hiervet. Not the Selan as they were now, but the warriors they'd come from. An army capable of taking down anything in its path.

"Oh Shiva, protect us," I murmured. I sprinted back to Mia and helped her to her feet.

"She can lean on me," Fasé said, looking up at me with a shake of her head. "Your hands should be free."

She was right and I took point as we made our way farther into the room, past the rows of still and silent beings.

"What is this?"

"Thyra's been making a fucking hybrid army," I muttered. "Bugger me. That's what I missed. The ones we saw above were part of a failed batch. She's been trying to re-create herself. Using all of us. She's spent thousands of years pulling the best pieces out of all of us in a mad attempt to breed a new version of herself, and she's done it." The knowledge had settled into my gut with a heavy thud. Because what else would a slightly mad alien scientist be doing? My mind spun as I tried to figure out what to do next.

"Why does she need Mia?" Fasé asked.

"Because her brother stole something from us and I want it back."

I pushed Mia and Fasé behind me as I turned to face Thyra. "Well, that's not happening." I gestured at the tubes. "Who are your friends?"

"The next evolution." Thyra's smile was a thing of horror. "The ones you saw above were the previous attempt. Failed, as you said. These are my triumph. I've collected samples for years and perfected it into this." She spread her limbs wide. "Not just for an army, though, it was meant to be liberation for us from this planet."

"You're trapped here," Fasé whispered, but her words echoed.

Thyra smiled, baring her teeth. "We couldn't risk leaving Faria. Not only because our descendants might have found us, but because to be that far away from Faria was to risk going to sleep and never waking up."

"This is not going to end the way you think it is," I said.

"I could say the same of you, Star of Indrana. Since you refused my generous offer. I have no further use for you beyond a final test of my creation." She tapped a limb to the panel on the tube, and the fluid inside started to drain out. "If it works, we'll wake up all of them. They can take care of this problem and I can get back to work on the final piece of the puzzle." She pointed a limb at Mia.

"Figuring out what it is about the Shen that's interfering in my immortality. What they stole from us when the Cevallas revolted and murdered my people."

"Dark Mother." I already knew the gun in my hand wouldn't hurt Thyra, but it was worth it to fire a shot at the creature. Just to even the odds I shot at the tube and it shattered, glass flying through the air.

A scream filled the air as the top collapsed and the creature was crushed between the heavy metal and a jagged piece of glass. It thrashed a moment, grayish blood spraying outward, and then went still.

There was a moment of stunned silence.

I pushed Fasé and Mia. "Run."

Thyra's scream ripped at our ears as we sprinted for the doorway. I herded the pair through it and slapped the panel on the side, breathing a slight sigh of relief as it slid closed.

Thyra hit it full force, putting a dent in the metal, and I cursed, backpedaling away from the door. "Move, we need to move."

We dodged through the smaller room, running past unknown canisters and cargo boxes as Thyra continued to hammer at the door, lost to her rage. There was an exit at the back of the room and I whispered a thank-you when I discovered it led to another hallway.

We slipped through and I shut it behind us, firing the Farian weapon into the panel. It sparked and fizzled and I prayed it was enough to jam the door permanently closed.

I was doing a lot of praying lately; either it was going to help or the gods would take notice and strike me down for my hypocrisy.

"I'm sorry, I have to rest a moment," Mia gasped, doubling over. I reached a hand out and touched her neck; the same wall greeted me when I attempted to give her energy. But it felt weaker, less stable.

"Fasé, do you know how to get us out of here?"

"I don't, Majesty. But there has to be an exit."

Unless there wasn't. A chill ran up my spine at the thought. Thyra and the others could teleport. They wouldn't have any reason to tunnel to the surface.

"I want you both to go," I said, touching their faces. "Find a way to the surface."

"Hail, no."

"I can't fight these things and keep you safe." Not only the creatures, but Thyra as well. She would release more of them once her rage settled, and the silence from behind us was telling me she'd calmed down enough to think. My brain was spinning, trying to come up with a solution.

I needed a fucking minute to think and I didn't have it. I looked around the hallway, opened the closest door, and gestured them inside. "You hide, I'll lead them off. You can double back to the river."

"No." Fasé's refusal was calm and Mia shook her head. "We won't leave you. We're stronger together."

"Please—"

"Hail." Mia reached out and touched her fingers to my lips, silencing me. "We'll do anything you ask, except leave. Now think."

"Okay." I dragged in a breath, and then another, some of my panic receding, and continued down the hallway at a jog. "I don't know anything about these creatures. We can assume the gun won't work on them."

"But it will work on other things. Like the door panel," Fasé said.

"Yes."

"You could shoot something out of the ceiling on it. That seems extremely effective."

I gave Mia a flat look. She grinned and Fasé unsuccessfully hid her own smile behind her free hand. The laugh that bubbled free from my chest was surprising and I pulled both of them into a quick hug.

"I can't go back to that room and just shoot them all as they're emerging," I said as I let them go, and then paused. "Wait. You might have something."

"I was teasing, Hail."

"I know, but listen." I snapped my fingers. "Basics. The gun won't hurt Thyra and likely won't hurt them, but regular electricity might."

"The generators," Fasé said.

"What do you want to bet the generators power the incubators?" I said with a sharp grin that the women echoed. "How do we get back to the river without running headlong into Thyra?"

"I don't think we need to double back, this hallway is curving." Fasé pointed. "Let's keep moving and see where it dumps us."

I exhaled. "I want you two to keep going, I'm going to cover our retreat." I smiled at the identical looks from the two women. "I promise I'll follow. All right?"

"You'd better," Mia said, and though she was smiling I could see the worry in her eyes.

I sprinted back down the corridor. The silence at the jammed door was both reassuring and nerve racking as I waited for Thyra or her creatures to burst through. I wondered briefly why she hadn't just teleported in and tried to kill us when I realized it was because she couldn't tell where we were.

I filed the information away, ducking into the first room on the right and pulling open the cabinets to search.

Wire. Buckets. A bottle of chemicals my *smati* took an agonizing minute to decipher.

Iza's voice was in my ear as I pushed myself into the far corner of the room and lined up a shot on the window facing the corridor. I covered my eyes with my other forearm and fired.

"Hail!" Fasé's voice was clear on the coms despite my ringing ears.

"I'm all right. Just leaving a few presents." My shot had taken out one window in its entirety and damaged the one on the other side of the hallway. I used the butt of the gun to knock the glass from that into the bucket and then stretched two lines of wire from one window to the other.

It had been funny when Iza had done it to Indula. The wires had been harmless rubber tubes that did little more than land my Body-Guard on his ass when he came sliding into their quarters. These probably wouldn't kill anything following us unless we got lucky, but it would hurt and it would slow them down.

I slung the weapon over my shoulder, grabbed the bottle in one hand and the bucket in the other, and headed for the next bend in the hallway.

"It's dangerous, Majesty." Kisah's voice had echoed up in my memory when I'd seen the chemical name. *"It'll burn through skin, clothing, concrete if given enough time. If you can dump it on an enemy, you can do serious damage, but even just pouring it out for them to walk through will slow them down. All the better if they slip and fall in it."*

I opened the bottle with a sleeve-covered hand and laid it carefully on its side, watching as the clear, slightly viscous liquid chugged out and spread across the white tiled floor.

I caught up with Mia and Fasé. It was hard to tell if Mia was improving or if she was just as determined as I was to stay ahead of the things chasing us. "Rest a moment," I said, and set the bucket off to one side. "I want to look at something. Fasé, do you have a knife?"

She pulled one out of her pocket with a smile. "I asked Johar for one before we left. I thought you might need it."

I took it and flipped it open, prying away the casing on the Farian weapon. "You know what I like about energy weapons?" I asked. "No one gets fancy with them. These innards look the same as any of the human models and as any of the Shen ones. We got it from you, or vice versa, it doesn't even matter."

"What are you doing?"

"I'm going to overload the power. Kaboom." Grinning, I tipped my head at the bucket. "Even better with it jammed into that bucket. The energy from this gun can hurt Thyra and her creations with a little help from the glass."

My com fuzzed in my ear as if someone were trying to get a hold of me, and I looked at Fasé. "Did you hear that?"

"Yes."

"Emmory, this is Hail, do you copy?"

There was only silence. Then a crash and the sound of metal screaming in protest echoed down the hallway.

"Go," I said to Fasé. "I have to guess at the timing on this and I want you two as far away as possible. Get to the generators. I'll meet you there."

"Hail—" Mia broke off at the screams that rent the air.

"That was one," I said. "Go."

They ran. I waited, listening for the sound of the second set of screams as Thyra's creatures hit the chemical spill, and when that came I turned back to the gun. Three wires, pulled free and twisted together. A minute, maybe less.

I remembered Portis's terrified look the first time I'd shown him this and smiled as I jammed the nose of the gun down into the glass shards.

I was sprinting down the corridor when the gun went off, the explosion shaking the hallway around me, and I allowed myself to hope that at least one if not more of the super soldiers had been injured in my impromptu explosion as I slid through the open doorway in front of me.

I was on the opposite side of the river. Fasé and Mia were nowhere in sight, a fact I was grateful for when the blow hit me from behind and sent me flying.

I hit the ground, rolled, and came up on my feet, the knife still in my hand. Thyra rushed me, furious and bleeding.

"You killed them!"

"Oh, thank Shiva." I had the chance to breathe out the words just a split second before she hit me again. I felt the knife strike something and thrust my arm forward; her yelp of pain and sudden backpedaling gave me just enough room to scramble free.

Straight into one of the creatures.

Fuck, she'd been smart enough to wake up more than one to send after me.

The extra energy from the river was still humming under my skin, but I didn't want to be distracted in a fight with this creature. I dodged, but not fast enough to avoid Thyra's super soldier, who grabbed me by the arm and flung me into the air. I flew across the river and crashed into one of the generators, hitting it hard enough to leave a dent before I slid to the floor.

"Only two left?" I spat the blood out of my mouth as I staggered to my feet, staring at Thyra and her creatures on the other side of the river. "You should have woken them all up."

"I am going to take you apart myself," she snarled. "Find the Shen. Bring her back to me."

The soldiers jumped over the river in a single leap. I knew better than to watch them and dragged my eyes away just in time to see Thyra take her own leap and land in front of me.

Jo's never going to let you live this down if you lose this fight.

The irrational thought made me laugh and I could see the confusion flash across Thyra's face before she lunged at me.

Everything fell away. All the pain. My worry over Fasé and Mia and the two creatures now hunting them through the rows of generators. My fear that this was it, the final moments of my life if I couldn't avoid her second strike.

I discarded it all to fight the way Aiz had taught me.

Ducking under Thyra's swing, I brought my right hand around with the knife and plunged it into her side just below the first wound.

A wound that was already closing.

I remembered Thyra's scoffing reply about healing and knew I couldn't afford to let this fight go on for any length of time. I jerked my hand up and Thyra screamed. Her limb hit me right in the face and I staggered backward.

She was faster than me and a searing pain cut through my chest.

Thyra yanked her limb free with a wicked smile and for a second I thought she'd killed me with her first hit. But then my heart beat a painful tattoo against the inside of my ribs and I coughed, blood flying into the air, spattering over Thyra's grinning face.

"Don't get so focused on the weapons in your hands, Hail, that you forget you are the weapon." The memory of Aiz's advice was barely a whisper over the pounding of my heart, followed immediately by Mia's words. *"This can save your life, don't hesitate to use it. Especially where the Farian Hiervet are involved. It may be the only thing you have left to fight with when the time comes."*

I dropped the knife and caught Thyra's limb with both hands before she could impale me a second time. The pain was rolling through me—collapsed and punctured lung, hole front to back, broken nose, wrenched shoulder, too many other things to catalog. The energy from the river surged through me, mixing with my pain, and I pulled on it all, focusing it out of my hands into her skin.

The noise she made was indescribable, nearly drowned out by the sudden, booming explosion deep within the incubator room, and I held on as she tried to get free.

"I need you to remember," I said as she dragged us both to the ground. "You chose this. I tried to save you. I offered you a better way and you chose this."

My *smati* was screaming a hundred warnings at me and I ignored them all.

"You are an abomination," Thyra gasped. "A thing that should not exist."

"Sybil knew I was your death from the beginning." I could taste the hot copper of my own blood on my tongue and could feel the flickering of her life like a candle in the darkness. "I am the Star of Indrana."

It took no more than a thought to extinguish her, and her wide eyes closed as she went limp beneath me.

Oh Dark Mother, what have I done? I staggered away from her, dragging a breath into one lung as the other was useless. The pain spiked through me and I went down on a knee.

Two more. There are still two more. Get up, Hail.

The voice in my head. My father's voice. Or my mother's. Emmory's. Aiz's. Hao's. Gita's. Johar's. I wasn't sure who it was. All I knew was I wanted to obey, but I couldn't.

I tried, sobbing, for another breath that wouldn't come. Heard my own *smati* flatline and the strange buzz of my com before I collapsed, facedown on the ground next to the river.

44

Hail, wake up."

The voice cut through my nausea and the bitter tang of blood filled my mouth and nose when I inhaled, rusted iron and the awful smell of death. For a moment I floundered, lost in a memory that seemed so far away.

"Easy there, Hail. We've got you."

I blinked up at Johar and Gita in confusion.

"That was exciting. I think I just saved your life," Jo said with a smile. "Don't move, I just patched the worst of it. Someone who's better at this needs to do the heavy lifting and they're still a minute out."

"Those creatures, Fasé, Mia—"

"They're fine. It's taken care of. Seriously, Hail, keep your ass down." Johar pushed on my chest with a little more force and the pain made me see stars. "You did some damage in here when you all blew things the hell up. Sybil's got the place locked down from above. We've got Captain Zov's people and some Selan doing a sweep. I want you to hold still."

"Not me, Fasé and Mia blew it up. Where are they?"

More pressure. More pain. I coughed and Johar lifted an eyebrow.

"Mia and Fasé are fine," Gita replied. "They're on the other side of the river. It's all right, Majesty. We've got it under control."

Her reassurance finally sank in and I let my head fall back against the stone floor. The alarms were still screaming in my head and I turned them off with a thought.

It was done. I could scarcely believe those words. The weight of the prophecy and everything it carried lifted off me and I blinked back the tears of relief welling up in my eyes.

"Majesty?"

"I'm all right." I felt about for Gita's hand, laughing as the absurdity of that statement hit and then cursing as the pain followed. "*Hai Ram*, she got some good shots in."

"She stabbed you, Majesty."

"Oh yeah, that was her fucking limb. That's twice." I reached up and rubbed a hand over my forehead. "I don't want to ever do that again, Gita. Next time tell me fighting genetically engineered super soldiers is a bad idea."

"I believe I told you this time."

I was alternating between laughing and wincing from the pain when Aiz appeared, Biea at his side.

Relief was hotter than the blood oozing out of my chest. "Look at you, Aiz Cevalla, not dead after all."

"Sybil found me. I'm starting to agree with your *Ekam*, Hail," he said, kneeling at my side and putting a hand over the gaping wound still throbbing in my chest. "You end up covered in blood far more than a human should."

I reached a hand up to his face, surprised not only by my shaking fingers but the fresh tears in my eyes. "You're really not dead."

"I am really not dead. Neither is Mia and neither are you. I knew you could do it." He smiled and then the familiar jolt of energy streaked through my system like lightning. I gasped, letting go of Gita to grab his wrist as my vision whited out for a moment. "Breathe," Aiz murmured, leaning down and touching his lips to my forehead.

"I killed her," I whispered. "I snuffed her out with a thought." I heard Gita gasp and I was gripped by a sudden and desperate fear. "Take this away, Aiz, please. I shouldn't have this much power."

"It's all right, Hail." Aiz smiled gently, though I could see the worry in his eyes. "If I trust anyone in this universe to handle such a thing with great care, it's you." He helped me to my feet as Emmory and Zin ran up.

There were no words for the sheer relief on their faces, and I choked on another sob as I staggered forward the two steps and threw myself into their waiting arms.

"You're alive," I whispered.

"That's supposed to be our line, Majesty," Emmory said, pressing his cheek into my hair. "When your vitals went down I thought—"

"I'm okay. It's done." I felt the tears start and this time didn't try to hold them back, sobbing my relief into my Tracker's shoulders.

"You okay?" Hao's question was soft as he sat down next to me and took my hands in his, rubbing the warmth back into them.

I dragged my attention away from where Aiz and Biea examined Mia. We were aboveground again, a fact that brought me more relief than I wanted to admit, though the rubble was still scattered about the floor of the Pedalion chamber and the sounds outside suggested there was still some fighting going on.

I cycled through several answers before settling on the truth. "I'm worried. Thyra did something to Mia, blocked her off from being able to access the energy around her. What if they can't fix it?"

"People live their whole lives without having to be healed by a Farian."

"She's not human, Hao. She's Shen."

I have to say good-bye to her.

"Ah." Hao smiled and his hands tightened around mine. "That's what this is about?"

"I just told you what this was about." I tried to pull free but he didn't let me go.

"You were this painfully obtuse about Portis, too." Now he did let me go but cupped my face in both hands and turned my head until I had to look him in the eyes. "Life is too short, little sister. Duty is one thing, love is more important. Don't let one get in the way of the other." He smiled and touched his forehead to mine. "I did and it nearly cost me everything. Listen to me for once in your life and don't make my mistakes."

My heart thumped hard at his words.

"I love you, *gege*." I threw my arms around his neck and hugged him tight.

"I love you, too," he whispered, hugging me back. "Killing a genetically engineered super soldier with a pocketknife is going to be a hell of a story to add to your legend, little sister."

As we separated, I saw the truth of it in his eyes and was grateful to Hao for doing what he always had—looking out for me. I also heard the unspoken warning.

Better to not let anyone else know what had truly happened here today. Better to let it be buried with the wreckage and the corpses.

"Hao, find Emmory," I whispered as Thyra's words about the Trackers came back to me. "There were—Trackers. Thyra said she'd taken Trackers and we have to see if there's—" The words stuck in my throat but Hao patted my hand and stood.

"I'll find him."

He passed Aiz headed my way as I sank down on the ledge with my hands in my lap.

"They've gone to Biea's ship," he said, offering up a smile that didn't hide the worry in his eyes as he sat next to me. "They think Mia will be all right but want their doctors to check her out."

"You didn't go with her?"

"She said I should stay here and help. We need to have a presence. There are files down there that will have survived the fire. Thyra's records of what she was doing."

"Aiz, about what I did—"

"I meant what I said, Hail. Of any human, you are best suited to handle this." He smiled and though it was fleeting, it was also genuine. "Don't think I'll let you flounder. I am here for you. I will help you navigate how to handle it and so will Mia."

We sat in silence for a long moment before I spoke up. "What's next?"

"I don't know," he replied. "Biea thinks they may be able to figure out what Thyra did to not only us but the Farians also. It will take some time. The peace treaty is still intact despite my sister's best efforts."

I'd forgotten all about Adora. "Where is she?"

"In holding with a Selan guard. I'm told there is some discussion about turning her over to them for her complicity in Thyra's crimes. Since Adaran is also dead there is no way to truly kill her." He rolled the thought around in his mouth for a moment. "As strange as it sounds I am uncomfortable with the idea of leaving my sister in a jar for all eternity."

"It's not strange at all. This is far more complicated than any of us could have dreamed."

"You did good, Hail. We couldn't have done this without you and I won't ever be able to repay you for it."

"I'm sure I'll need a favor at some point." I bumped my shoulder into his. "I'll even be nice and not make it totally outrageous."

It was the better part of a Farian day before I saw Biea again. Alba and I were wrapping up a late-afternoon meeting when Indula stuck his head in the doorway of my quarters on the *Hailimi Bristol*.

"Your Majesty, Biea is here if you have a moment to speak with them?"

"Of course." I got to my feet as they came in the room. "It is good to see you."

"Yourself as well, Your Majesty," they said. "You have fully recovered."

"Yes, thank you." I resisted the urge to pepper them with questions on how Mia was doing.

"I understand the Istrevitel will be leaving in the morning."

"Yes, I was planning on having dinner with Captain Zov tonight if you'd like to join us."

"Thank you, no, we have said our good-byes."

I rubbed a hand over the back of my neck as I asked the question I knew could change everything. "Biea, may I ask you what you plan to do now?"

"I don't know, Your Majesty." Biea dipped their head briefly. "We have offered our help to the Farians and Shen, but for obvious reasons it would be best if we only leave a few scientists here and take the rest of our people elsewhere. The wounds are fresh and deep and we don't wish to cause further harm."

"You're done with your hunt," I said with a smile. "Is it time to settle down?"

"Perhaps," they replied. "If we can find a suitable place. Again, it is probably best not to stay in this area and court disaster."

"Do you have specific requirements for a suitable planet?" I asked. "I am assuming they would be somewhat different from humans'."

"Not all that different, Your Majesty, but yes. I can give them to you." Biea extended their limb and Alba reached out to touch her hand to it with a smile.

"I can think of four off the top of my head, Majesty," she said after a moment. "More with some time."

Biea looked between us, confusion plain on their face. "I am not understanding."

I folded my hands together. "Biea, I realize you are not the sole decision maker for your people, so you are welcome to pass this along and discuss it. I would like to offer the Selan membership into my empire—as allies, a protectorate, or merely guests for a time. Whatever works best for your people."

"Your Majesty? You truly mean this?"

"Of course. I meant what I said about wanting to be friends and disagreements aside, we could not have done this without you. You have no reason to keep wandering alone through the stars unless you wish to do so."

"No, it is—" They fumbled over the words, tapping their limbs together. "It is so very appreciated. I will go speak to my people right away." They vanished.

Alba and I exchanged a look and I laughed. "Well—"

Biea reappeared and we both jumped. Indula cursed from the doorway.

"I am sorry, Your Majesty. I forgot to tell you, Mia is much better. She will soon be back to full health. My people will have a full report on what Thyra did to her." Biea dipped their head and left us again.

Alba and I shared a look. "Well, that went better than I expected," I said with a laugh.

"You still have to tell the councils, Majesty."

"True, but that's the nice thing about being empress." I winked at her and waved to Admiral Hassan, who'd come to the doorway with Emmory.

"I thought Biea was here," he asked.

"They left the easy way," I said, smiling at his worried look. "All the more reason to make them part of the empire. Inana." I reached a hand out and took her by the forearm, pulling her into a hug. "It's good to see you safe."

"You also, Majesty. Are we ready to head home?"

"In the morning."

I wanted to stay, but I couldn't think of a good reason to. The Farians could handle the reconstruction on their own and it wasn't my place to interfere in the judgments and subsequent punishments of the people involved in Adora's reign of terror.

The Shen would find their own way, with Mia and Aiz to guide them.

"We know you prefer being out here," Emmory said.

"Maybe once," I admitted with a sigh and a shake of my head. "Now I don't know that I do. I don't belong out here any more than I do in a palace, but I'm supposed to be in the palace. And that's what matters."

Inana smiled. "You know your parents would be proud of you. I'm proud of you."

"Thank you." I blinked away the tears as her words warmed my heart. "We should com Alice before she starts to worry. Alba?"

"Already have it cued up, ma'am."

I brushed at an invisible piece of lint on my black uniform as the screen on the wall of my front room resolved to show Alice, Caspel, and Caterina.

"Your Majesty, we're relieved to see you well." Alice pinned me with a stern look. "In light of your success I suppose we'll just not talk about the fact that you ignored all of us here telling you not to do it."

"Probably a good idea." I nodded at the others without so much as a hint of a smile. "I trust you read our reports?" We'd left some things out after a long discussion. I'd tell Alice in person about my abilities once we were home, but it seemed unwise to put something like that into the official record.

Hao was right, it was better to let people think I killed an alien super soldier with a pocketknife.

"We did, and I saw that you're planning on being home soon?"

I leaned against the desk, Alba and Inana on either side. "We have a few things to wrap up here and good-byes to say."

"It will be good to have you back."

"I have a matter to discuss before we get into this morning's business." I paused, knowing full well the next words out of my mouth were going to cause an uproar, but I'd weighed the choices available to me and hadn't come to this decision with anything less than the full knowledge of what it would bring to Indrana—both the good and the bad.

"I've offered the Selan entry into the empire under whatever terms suit them best and am waiting for their answer. Here is a list of possible worlds for them to settle on. I expect documents to be drawn up within the day if they agree."

"Your Majesty."

"You cannot just—"

"What were you thinking?"

I waited for the protests to stop and studied the faces on the screen for several moments before I spoke. "I was thinking they need a place to live. I was thinking they can bring a lot to the empire in the way of tech. I was thinking it would be better to have a race of genetically engineered soldiers as allies than let them roam out in the black, or worse let the Solarians take them in. I was also thinking I'm the empress and you're all welcome to fuss about this, but I've made my decision and if the Selan agree it will be done." I made eye contact with each of them in turn until they nodded. "I'll send you word of their decision as soon as I have it. I expect things to be ready when we arrive. Now, Alice, moving on to the next item."

45

I am going to miss you." I whispered the words against Stasia's golden hair.

"We'll come visit, Majesty, I promise." She hugged me back.

"Thank you, for everything." I was suddenly grateful we'd decided to say these good-byes in my quarters on the ship rather than out in public where everyone could see me crying.

I smiled through my tears as I let Stasia go. Giving her a little push toward Emmory, I turned to Fasé.

"Yadira and Delphine have asked me to help them forge a new path forward," she said, stepping into my open arms and wrapping her arms around my waist. "I don't know what shape the new Farian government will take, but I promise you we will remain Indrana's ally."

"You will be amazing. I am just a com away if you need help." I pressed my cheek to the top of her head.

"I am the same," Fasé replied. "Our people are alive because of you. Thank you, Majesty, for bringing this peace."

"Thank you for helping me." I let her go and moved out of the way as my BodyGuards and the others said their good-byes.

Sybil took my offered hands with the same gentle smile she'd given me the first time we met. "It is done. Thank you, Your Majesty."

"To say *you're welcome* seems very arrogant of me."

Her smile widened. "Perhaps, but also very you. I wish you all the joy in the universe."

I resisted the urge to ask if that was just a formality or if what the future-seer saw coming for me was truly just joy from here on out. "I wish the same for you and your people, Sybil." I leaned down and pressed my cheek to hers.

I straightened and saw Mia and Aiz standing in the doorway.

My heart twisted.

You need to do the right thing here, Hail, no matter what Hao says about love being more important than duty. You know it doesn't work like that when you have an empire to consider. This is the end of it. No more running off to save the galaxy.

I felt the mask slip into place and forced a smile. "Well, that's it, then, isn't it?"

Sybil passed them, touching Aiz on the arm as she did. The confused frown flickered so quickly across his face I was sure I'd imagined it, especially when he extended his hands and crossed the room to me, pulling me into a hug.

"Thank you, Hail. For everything. I dislike good-byes. I will see you both soon," he murmured against my ear, then kissed my cheek and left my quarters with a nod only to Emmory.

"How are you?" I reached for Mia, stopped, and shoved my hands awkwardly into the pockets of my pants instead. If I grabbed her now I'd never let her go.

"I am better." She watched me, emotions hidden carefully behind those storm-gray eyes. "I thought you would come to visit me."

"The cleanup was taking most of my time. Aiz and Biea kept me updated. I am glad you've recovered. It will be good for you going forward." The next words hurt like being spaced, but I forced them out anyway. "I will miss you."

"Miss me?"

I was suddenly aware of how quiet it was in the room and looked away from Mia to find it empty. As though my *Ekam* had quietly ushered everyone out and now stood in the hallway with his back to the open door.

"Hail, I—"

"Shiva, I can't do this," I whispered, pulling a hand free from my pocket and pressing it to my mouth for a moment as I turned away. The sob escaped around my fingers. "I have to let you go. This is not a fairy tale with a happily-ever-after. It's real life and we both have—"

Mia circled me, reaching up and grabbing my face. "Hail, be quiet." She tipped her head, studied me for a moment, and then smiled. "Who said I was going anywhere?"

"You have your people to lead."

Her smile carried a hope I hadn't dared to feel. "I do, but I also have my brother and an amazingly fast ship and the ability to communicate long distance. I assumed—" She stopped as a blush crept over her cheeks. "I probably should have asked if it was all right if I came home with you."

"Home?"

"To Indrana. To Pashati. I would like the chance to see more of your empire."

"I—yes?"

Mia pulled me down into a kiss that was all too brief. "I have watched you, Hail Bristol. Your duty to your empire and to your people is something you have never put aside. You will throw your life into danger to spare the people you love. You are kind and intelligent and I would very much like to spend time with you that doesn't involve mortal peril." She grinned and it was like the sun breaking through the clouds.

"I would also like that." I put my hands on her hips and tugged her closer and touched my forehead to hers. "Mia, I—"

"I know." This time she sank into the kiss.

I pulled away and rested my forehead against hers. "Emmory?"

"Yes, Majesty?"

"It's time to go."

*   *   *

The massive blue-green planet of Pashati hung in the blackness of space, growing larger on the screen of the *Hailimi*'s bridge. I kept one arm wrapped around Mia's waist as we dove through the atmosphere and the *Vajrayana* came to a gentle stop in the late-morning sunlight on the newly constructed hangar just off the palace.

"Your Majesty, we should head for the cargo bay," Emmory said as he came up behind us. He was resplendent in a matte-black uniform with the familiar crimson piping along the cuffs and worked into the detail of the intricate star pattern on the left breast. A final gift from Stasia, as was my sari—a gorgeous slubbed Farian silk in a pale shimmering gray with the imperial star stitched on it in brilliant green.

"Of course." I turned and reached for his hand and for Zin's, squeezing them both for just a moment before I let them go. There weren't any words and judging from the looks on their faces we didn't need any. "Captain Saito, thank you for the ride home."

"Our pleasure, Your Majesty."

I followed Emmory and Zin down the corridor and out of the cargo bay, disembarking into the warm sunshine with Mia's hand in mine.

Hao, Johar, Alba, and Dailun stood off to the side and I caught my brother's eyes with a smile. He folded his hands together and bowed his head in response.

The other BodyGuards were waiting on the landing pad. They all snapped to attention at Emmory's silent command and Gita stepped forward.

"Your Imperial Majesty, welcome home."

ACKNOWLEDGMENTS

Writing a book in the midst of burnout was a new experience for me, made even more challenging by doing edits in the midst of a pandemic and then more edits as a series of necessary protests rocked my country. The sense of loss as I say good-bye to these characters and this story that has dominated a decade of my life is nothing compared to the sense of loss felt by Black people in a system that relentlessly grinds them down and treats their lives with such callous disregard.

Black Lives Matter. Black Trans Lives Matter.

I have been lucky enough to be a white person telling the story of a woman with Indian ancestry in a world filled with as diverse a cast of characters as I could manage. A world that has some hope for a future better than what we have now. Any mistakes and short-sighted bias in this or other books are solely my responsibility and not on the endless list of people who've helped me along the way with numerous representation questions.

This is a long list of thanks, buckle in, kiddos.

I would be remiss to not mention the people who kept me alive through this—my partner, Don, for their unfailing ability to make me laugh at precisely the right moment. My friends and family who checked in, who listened when I cried about not being able to write, who sent me messages and showed up to give their love and support. Everything I do here, I do because of you. Thank you especially to Lisa, Rob, Beena, Mike, Jenny, Rook, Hannah, Jenn, Lion, Katrina, Jo, Kallyn, and CJ. I love you all.

A special shout out to Cass Morris for talking with me about language for a ridiculous amount of time purely so I could make a joke work. You are an amazing human being and friend. I love you lots.

To my agent, Andy Zack, for your unfailing support and tireless effort. Thank you for taking a chance on Hail and on me and for all the work you do.

Thanks to the amazing people at Orbit, starting with my previous editor, Sarah Guan, and my current editor, Nivia Evans, who took up the difficult task of finishing out this trilogy with a great deal of grace and insight. Creating a book isn't a solo endeavor and my thanks go out to Paola Crespo and Laura Fitzgerald in Marketing, Angela Man and Ellen Wright in Publicity, Rachel Goldstein in Managing Editorial, Lauren Panepinto and her amazing team in the Art Department, Stephan Martiniere for his stunning covers that brought the world of the Farian War to life, and anyone else I may have forgotten to name specifically.

To the Crew on Patreon: Allyson Burns, Amy Ottinger, Ana Ramsey, Andrew Marshall, Anna Sierra, Annie Muirhead, Beena, Blair MacGregor, Brandi Blackburn, Brenda, Brendon Towle, Caroline Morris, Cass Morris, Christine Hanolsy, Christine Mendoza, Christy Stevens, CleverByHalfProductions, Crini, Crystal Bollinger, CynnieZee, Cynthia Porter, Dan Cole, Danica Redfern, Danielle Billing, Dee, Donnie J., E. W., Emory Noakes, Evaine Devereaux, Florence, Freaktiful, Girl In Space, Glori Medina, Greg Sideyr, Heather Ruth, Heather W., Ian Stewart, Jean Hontz, Jennifer Miller-Smith, Jenny Hanniver, Jeremy Barber, Jessie L. Kwak, Jo O'Brien, Jo Van, Jon Grilz, Josh McGraw, K. Doore, Katherine Moehrke, Kathryn Jonell, Keith Frampton, Kellie Hultgren, Kelly, Kelly Bradford, kerry leehan, Kristen Blount, Kristi Chadwick, Kristyn Merbeth, Larisa LaBrant, Lisa Baxter, Marissa Priest, Matias W., Matt Doyle, Megan Cross, Melissa Shumake, Michael Mock, Natalie J. Case, Paul Holmes, Paul Moss, Paul Weimer, Rae, Rae Grimm, Sandra Clifford Teeple, Sara Piorr, Steve Radabaugh,

ACKNOWLEDGMENTS

Tamra Von Strodt, Tara Salinas, The Gayest Jess, Tony James, Tormented Artifacts, Tracey Abla, Uffe Stegmann, Veryl Ann Grace, Vicki Pech, Vivek P., Wendy Perez, and Winx & Ink—I love you all, thanks for going the extra kilometer to support the work I do.

Lastly, and from the bottom of my heart, thank you dear readers. Thank you for your love of Hail and company. Thank you for coming on this journey with me. Thank you for your reviews and your art and your endless support. It means the universe to me and I'm looking forward to our next adventure together.

meet the author

Photo Credit: Donald S. Branum

K. B. Wagers is the author of the Indranan War and Farian War trilogies with Orbit and the new NeoG novels from Harper Voyager. They hold a bachelor's degree in Russian studies and a second-degree black belt in Shaolin Kung Fu. A native of Colorado, K. B. lives at the base of the Rocky Mountains with their partner and a crew of recalcitrant cats. In between books, they can be found attempting to learn Spanish, dying in video games, dancing to music, and scribbling new ideas in their bullet journal. They are represented by Andrew Zack of The Zack Company.

Find out more about K. B. Wagers and other Orbit authors by registering for the free monthly newsletter at orbitbooks.net.